THE LAND OF STORIES

THE WISHING SPELL

THE LAND OF STORIES
THE WISHING SPELL

CHRIS COLFER

ILLUSTRATED BY BRANDON DORMAN

LB

LITTLE, BROWN AND COMPANY
NEW YORK   BOSTON

Copyright © 2012 by Christopher Colfer
Jacket and interior art copyright © 2012 by Brandon Dorman

Little, Brown and Company

Hachette Book Group
237 Park Avenue, New York, NY 10017

Visit our website at www.lb-kids.com

Little, Brown and Company is a division of Hachette Book Group, Inc.
The Little, Brown name and logo are trademarks of Hachette Book Group, Inc.
The publisher is not responsible for websites (or their content) that
are not owned by the publisher.

First Edition: July 2012

Library of Congress Cataloging-in-Publication Data

Colfer, Chris, 1990–
The land of stories : the wishing spell / by Chris Colfer. — 1st ed.
p. cm.
Summary: "Through the mysterious powers of a cherished book of stories, twins
Alex and Conner leave their world behind and find themselves in a foreign land full of
wonder and magic where they come face-to-face with the fairy tale characters they grew up
reading about." — Provided by publisher.
ISBN 978-0-316-20157-5 (hardcover)
[1. Fairy tales—Fiction. 2. Characters in literature—Fiction. 3. Magic—Fiction.
4. Brothers and sisters—Fiction. 5. Twins—Fiction. 6. Youths' writings.]
I. Title. II. Title: Wishing spell.
PZ7.C677474Lan 2012
[Fic]—dc23

2012007258

10 9 8 7 6 5 4 3 2 1

RRD-C

Printed in the United States of America

To Grandma,
for being my first editor
and giving me the best writing advice
I've ever received: "Christopher,
I think you should wait until you're done
with elementary school before worrying
about being a failed writer."

———◆◆◆◆◆———

"SOME DAY YOU WILL BE OLD ENOUGH
TO START READING FAIRY TALES AGAIN."

—C. S. LEWIS

THE QUEENS' VISIT

The dungeon was a miserable place. Light was scarce and flickered from the torches bolted to the stone walls. Foul-smelling water dripped inside from the moat circling the palace above. Large rats chased each other across the floor searching for food. This was no place for a queen.

It was just past midnight, and all was quiet except for the occasional rustle of a chain. Through the heavy silence a single set of footsteps echoed throughout the halls as someone climbed down the spiral steps into the dungeon.

A young woman emerged down the steps dressed head-to-toe in a long emerald cloak. She cautiously made her way past the row of cells, sparking the interest of the prisoners inside. With every step she took, her pace became slower and slower, and her heart beat faster and faster.

The prisoners were arranged according to crime. The deeper she walked into the dungeon, the crueler and more dangerous the criminals became. Her sights were set on the cell at the very end of the hall, where a prisoner of special interest was being watched by a large private guard.

The woman had come to ask a question. It was a simple question, but it consumed her thoughts every day, kept her lying awake most nights, and was the only thing she dreamed about with the little sleep she managed.

Only one person could give her the answer she needed, and that person was on the other side of the prison bars ahead.

"I wish to see her," the cloaked woman said to the guard.

"No one is allowed to see her," the guard said, almost amused by the request. "I'm on strict orders from the royal family."

The woman lowered her hood and revealed her face. Her skin was as pale as snow, her hair was as dark as coal, and her eyes were as green as a forest. Her beauty was known throughout the land, and her story was known even beyond that.

"Your Majesty, please forgive me!" the stunned guard

apologized. He quickly bent into an overly pronounced bow. "I wasn't expecting anyone from the palace."

"No apology necessary," she said. "But please do not speak of my presence here tonight."

"Of course," the guard said, nodding.

The woman faced the bars, waiting for them to be raised, but the guard hesitated.

"Are you sure you want to go in there, Your Highness?" the guard said. "There's no telling what she's capable of."

"I must see her," the woman said. "At any cost."

The guard began turning a large, circular lever, and the bars of the cell rose. The woman took a deep breath and continued past them.

She journeyed through a longer, darker hallway where a series of bars and barriers were raised and then lowered after she walked past them. Finally, she reached the end of the hall, the last set of bars was raised, and she stepped into the cell.

The prisoner was a woman. She sat on a stool in the center of the cell and stared up at a small window.

The prisoner waited a few moments before acknowledging the visitor behind her. It was the first visitor she had ever had, and she knew who it was without looking; there was only one person it could be.

"Hello, Snow White," the prisoner said softly.

"Hello, Stepmother," Snow White replied with a nervous quiver. "I hope you are well."

Although Snow White had rehearsed exactly what she

wanted to say, she was now finding it nearly impossible to speak.

"I heard that you are the queen now," her stepmother said.

"It's true," said Snow White. "I've inherited the throne as my father intended."

"So, to what do I owe this honor? Have you come to watch me wither away?" her stepmother said. There was such authority and power to her voice; it was known to make the strongest of men melt like ice.

"On the contrary," Snow White said. "I've come to understand."

"To understand *what*?" her stepmother asked harshly.

"Why..." Snow White hesitated. "Why you did what you did."

And with this finally said, Snow White felt a weight lift off of her shoulders. She had finally asked the question that had been so strongly on her mind. Half of the challenge was over.

"There are many things about this world that you don't understand," the stepmother said, and turned to look at her stepdaughter.

It was the first time in a long time that Snow White had seen her stepmother's face. It was the face of a woman who had once possessed beauty without flaw, and the face of a woman who had once been queen. Now, the woman sitting before her was just a prisoner whose looks had faded into a permanent, sorrowful scowl.

"That may be," Snow White said. "But can you blame me for trying to find some sort of reason behind your actions?"

The recent years of Snow White's life had become the most scandalous of the kingdom's royal history. Everyone knew the story of the fair princess who'd taken refuge with the Seven Dwarfs while hiding from her jealous stepmother. Everyone knew of the infamous poisoned apple and the dashing prince who had saved Snow White from a false death.

The story was simple, but the aftermath was not. Even with a new marriage and a monarchy to occupy her time, Snow White found herself constantly wondering if the theories of her stepmother's vanity were true. Something inside the new queen refused to believe that someone could be so malicious.

"Do you know what they're calling you out there?" Snow White asked. "Outside these prison walls the world refers to you as the *Evil Queen.*"

"If that is what the world has labeled me, then that is the name I shall learn to live with," the Evil Queen said. "Once the world has made a decision, there is little anyone can do to change its mind."

Snow White was astonished by how little her stepmother cared, but Snow White needed her to care. She needed to know there was some humanity left in her.

"They wanted to execute you after they discovered your crimes against me! The whole kingdom wanted you dead!"

Snow White's voice faded to a faint whisper as she fought off the emotions building up inside her. "But I wouldn't allow it. I couldn't..."

"Am I supposed to thank you for sparing me?" the Evil Queen asked. "If you expect someone to fall at your feet and express gratitude, you've come to the wrong cell."

"I didn't do it for you. I did it for myself," Snow White said. "Like it or not, you are the only mother I have ever known. I refuse to believe that you are the soulless monster the rest of the world claims you to be. Whether it's true or not, I believe there is a heart deep down inside of you."

Tears rolled down Snow White's pale face. She had promised herself she would stay strong, but she had lost control of her emotions once she was in her stepmother's presence.

"Then I'm afraid you're wrong," the Evil Queen said. "The only soul I've ever had died a long time ago, and the only heart you'll find in my possession is a heart of stone."

The Evil Queen did indeed have a heart of stone, but not inside her. A rock in the shape and size of a human heart was on a small table in the corner of the cell. It was the only item the Evil Queen had been permitted to keep when she was arrested.

Snow White recognized the stone from her childhood. It had always been very precious to her stepmother, and the Evil Queen had never let it out of her sight. Snow White had never been allowed to touch it or hold it, but nothing was stopping her now.

She walked across the cell, picked it up, and curiously stared down at it. It brought back so many memories. All the neglect and sadness her stepmother had caused her as a child rushed through her.

"All my life I only wanted one thing," Snow White said. "Your love. When I was a girl, I used to spend hours hiding in the palace just hoping you would notice I was missing, but you never did. You spent your days in your chambers with your mirrors and your skin creams and this stone. You spent more time with strangers with anti-aging methods than you did with your own daughter. But why?"

The Evil Queen did not answer.

"You tried to kill me four times, three of which you attempted yourself," Snow White said, shaking her head in disbelief. "When you dressed as an old woman and came to me at the dwarfs' cottage, I knew it was you. I knew you were dangerous, but I kept letting you in. I kept hoping that you would change. I let you harm me."

Snow White had never confessed this to anyone, and she couldn't help but bury her face in the palms of her hands and cry after saying it.

"You think *you* know heartbreak?" the Evil Queen said so sharply that it startled her stepdaughter. "You know *nothing* of pain. You never received affection from me, but from the moment you were born you were loved by the whole kingdom. *Others*, however, are not so fortunate. *Others*, Snow White, sometimes have the only loves they've ever known taken from them."

Snow White didn't know what to say. What love was she referring to?

"Are you speaking of my father?" Snow White asked.

The Evil Queen closed her eyes and shook her head. "Naïveté is such a privileged trait," she said. "Believe it or not, Snow White, I had my own life before I came into yours."

Snow White grew quiet and slightly ashamed. Of course she knew her stepmother had had a life prior to marrying her father, but she had never considered what it had consisted of. Her stepmother had always been such a private person, Snow White never had reason to.

"Where is my mirror?" the Evil Queen demanded.

"It's to be destroyed," Snow White told her.

Suddenly, the Evil Queen's stone became much heavier in Snow White's hand. Snow White didn't know if this was really happening, or if she was just imagining it. Her arm became tired from holding the stone heart, and she had to put it aside.

"There's so much you're not telling me," Snow White said. "There are so many things you've kept from me all these years."

The Evil Queen lowered her head and stared at the ground. She remained silent.

"I may be the only person in the world with any compassion for you. Please tell me it isn't going to waste," Snow White pleaded. "If there were events in your past that influenced your recent decisions, please explain them to me."

Still, there was no response.

"I'm not leaving here until you tell me!" Snow White yelled, raising her voice for the first time in her life.

"Fine," the Evil Queen said.

Snow White took a seat on another stool in the cell. The Evil Queen waited a moment before beginning, and Snow White's anticipation grew.

"Your story will forever be romanticized," she told Snow White. "No one will ever think twice about mine. I will continue to be degraded into nothing but a grotesque villain until the end of time. But what the world fails to realize is that a *villain* is just a *victim* whose story hasn't been told. Everything I have done, my life's work and my crimes against you, has all been for *him*."

Snow White felt her own heart grow heavy. Her head was spinning, and curiosity had taken over her entire body.

"Who?" she asked so quickly that she forgot to hold back the desperation in her voice.

The Evil Queen closed her eyes and let her memories surface. Images of places and people from her past flew out from the back of her mind like fireflies in a cave. There was so much she had seen in her younger years, so many things she wished she remembered, and so many things she wished to forget.

"I will tell you about my past, or at least the past of someone I once was," the Evil Queen said. "But consider yourself warned. My story is not one that ends with a happily-ever-after."

CHAPTER ONE

ONCE UPON A TIME

*O*nce upon a time..." Mrs. Peters said to her sixth-grade class. "These are the most magical words our world has ever known and the gateway into the greatest stories ever told. They're an immediate calling to anyone who hears them—a calling into a world where everyone is welcome and anything can happen. Mice can become men, maids can become princesses, and they can teach valuable lessons in the process."

Alex Bailey eagerly sat straight up in her seat. She

usually enjoyed her teacher's lessons, but *this* was something especially close to her heart.

"Fairy tales are much more than silly bedtime stories," the teacher continued. "The solution to almost every problem imaginable can be found in the outcome of a fairy tale. Fairy tales are life lessons disguised with colorful characters and situations.

"'The Boy Who Cried Wolf' teaches us the value of a good reputation and the power of honesty. 'Cinderella' shows us the rewards of having a good heart. 'The Ugly Duckling' teaches us the meaning of inner beauty."

Alex's eyes were wide, and she nodded in agreement. She was a pretty girl with bright blue eyes and short strawberry-blonde hair that was always kept neatly out of her face with a headband.

The way the other students stared at their teacher, as if the lesson being taught were in another language, was something Mrs. Peters had never grown accustomed to. So, Mrs. Peters would often direct entire lessons to the front row, where Alex sat.

Mrs. Peters was a tall, thin woman who always wore dresses that resembled old, patterned sofas. Her hair was dark and curly and sat perfectly on the top of her head like a hat (and her students often thought it was). Through a pair of thick glasses, her eyes were permanently squinted from all the judgmental looks she had given her classes over the years.

"Sadly, these timeless tales are no longer relevant in our society," Mrs. Peters said. "We have traded their brilliant teachings for small-minded entertainment like television and video games. Parents now let obnoxious cartoons and violent movies influence their children.

"The only exposure to the tales some children acquire are versions bastardized by film companies. Fairy tale 'adaptations' are usually stripped of every moral and lesson the stories were originally intended to teach, and replaced with singing and dancing forest animals. I recently read that films are being created depicting Cinderella as a struggling hip-hop singer and Sleeping Beauty as a warrior princess battling zombies!"

"Awesome," a student behind Alex whispered to himself.

Alex shook her head. Hearing this made her soul hurt. She tried to share her disapproval with her fellow classmates but, sadly, her concern was not reciprocated.

"I wonder if the world would be a different place if everyone knew these tales in the way the Brothers Grimm and Hans Christian Andersen intended them to be known," Mrs. Peters said. "I wonder if people would learn from the Little Mermaid's heartbreak when she dies at the end of her real story. I wonder if there would be so many kidnappings if children were shown the true dangers that Little Red Riding Hood faced. I wonder if delinquents would be so inclined to misbehave if they knew about the consequences Goldilocks caused for herself with the Three Bears.

"There is so much to learn and prevent for our futures if we just open our eyes to past teachings. Perhaps if we embraced fairy tales as much as we could, it would be much easier to find our own happily-ever-afters."

If Alex had her way, Mrs. Peters would be rewarded with thunderous applause after each lesson she gave. Unfortunately, all that followed her classes was a mutual sigh of relief among the students, thankful that they were over. "Let's see how well you all know your fairy tales," the teacher said with a smile, and began pacing the room. "In 'Rumpelstiltskin,' what did the young maiden's father tell the king that his daughter could spin hay into? Does anyone know?"

Mrs. Peters scanned the classroom like a shark looking for wounded fish. Only one student raised her hand.

"Yes, Miss Bailey?" Mrs. Peters called.

"He claimed she could spin hay into gold," Alex said.

"Very good, Miss Bailey," Mrs. Peters said. If she had a favorite student—not that she would ever admit to having one—Alex would have been it.

Alex was always eager to please. She was the definition of a bookworm. It didn't matter what time of day it was— before school, during school, after school, before bed—she was always reading. She had a thirst for knowledge and, because of it, Alex was usually the first person to answer Mrs. Peters's questions.

She tried her best to impress her classmates with every chance she got, putting extra effort into each book report and class presentation she was assigned. However, this usually annoyed the other students, and Alex was often teased for it.

She constantly heard other girls making fun of her behind her back. She usually spent lunch alone under a tree somewhere with an open library book. Although she would never tell anyone, Alex was so lonely that sometimes it hurt.

"Now, can anyone tell me what the compromise was that the maiden made with Rumpelstiltskin?"

Alex waited a moment before putting her hand up. She didn't want to seem like a *total* teacher's pet.

"Yes, Miss Bailey?"

"In exchange for turning the hay into gold, the maiden promised to give Rumpelstiltskin her first-born child when she became queen," Alex explained.

"That's a pretty steep deal," said a boy behind Alex.

"What's a creepy old short man want with a baby anyway?" a girl next to him asked.

"Obviously, he couldn't adopt with a name like Rumpelstiltskin," another student added.

"Did he eat the baby?" someone else asked nervously.

Alex turned around to face her clueless peers.

"You're all missing the point of the story," Alex said. "Rumpelstiltskin took advantage of the maiden because she was in need. The story is about the price of a bad negotiation. What are we willing to give up long-term in the future for something short-term in the present? Get it?"

If Mrs. Peters could change her facial expression, she

would have looked very proud. "Nicely put, Miss Bailey," she said. "I must say, in all my years of teaching, I've rarely come across a pupil with as much in-depth knowledge as—"

A loud snore suddenly came from the back of the classroom. A boy in the back row was slouched over his desk and drooling from the corner of his mouth, very much asleep.

Alex had a twin brother, and it was moments like these that made her wish she didn't.

Mrs. Peters diverted her attention to him like a paper clip to a magnet.

"Mr. Bailey?" Mrs. Peters asked.

He continued to snore.

"Mr. Bailey?" Mrs. Peters asked again, kneeling down closer to him.

He let out another enormous snore. A few of the students wondered how it was possible for such a loud noise to come out of him.

"Mr. Bailey!" Mrs. Peters shouted in his ear.

As if someone had lit a firework under his seat, Conner Bailey jumped back to life, almost knocking his desk over.

"Where am I? What happened?" Conner asked in a panicked state of confusion. His eyes darted around the room while his brain tried to remember where he was.

Like his sister, he also had bright blue eyes and strawberry-blond hair. His face was round and freckled and, at the moment, slightly smushed to one side like a basset hound when it first wakes up from a nap.

Alex couldn't have been more embarrassed by her brother. Besides sharing looks and a birth date, she and her brother couldn't have been more different. Conner may have had a lot of friends, but unlike his sister, he had trouble in school... mostly trouble staying awake.

"I'm so glad you could rejoin us, Mr. Bailey," Mrs. Peters said sternly. "Did you have a nice nap?"

Conner turned bright red.

"I'm so sorry, Mrs. Peters," he apologized, trying to be as genuine as possible. "Sometimes when you talk for long periods of time, I doze off. No offense. I can't help it."

"You fall asleep in my class at least twice a week," Mrs. Peters reminded him.

"Well, you *do* talk a lot." Before he could stop himself from saying it, Conner knew it was the wrong thing to say. A few of the students had to bite their hands to stop from laughing.

"I recommend you stay awake while I teach, Mr. Bailey," Mrs. Peters threatened. Conner had never seen anyone squint their eyes so tight without shutting them before. "Unless you know enough about fairy tales to teach this lesson yourself," she added.

"I probably do," Conner said. Once again, he spoke without thinking. "I mean, I know a lot about this stuff, that's all."

"Oh, really?" Mrs. Peters never backed down from a challenge, and every student's worst nightmare was that they'd be her challenger. "All right, Mr. Bailey, if you're so knowledgeable, answer this question."

Conner gulped.

"In the original tale of Sleeping Beauty, how many years does the princess sleep before she is awoken by true love's first kiss?" Mrs. Peters asked, studying his face.

All eyes were on him, impatiently waiting for the slightest indication that he didn't know the answer. But fortunately for Conner, he did.

"One hundred," Conner answered. "Sleeping Beauty slept for one hundred years. That's why the castle grounds were covered in vines and stuff, because the curse affected everyone in the kingdom, and there was no one to garden."

Mrs. Peters didn't know what to say or do. She frowned down at him, immensely surprised. This was the first time he had ever been correct when she'd put him on the spot, and she certainly hadn't expected it.

"Try to stay conscious, Mr. Bailey. Lucky for you, I used my last detention slip this morning, but I can always request more," Mrs. Peters said, and promptly walked to the front of the classroom to continue her lesson.

Conner sighed with relief, and the red drained from his face. His eyes met his sister's; even she was surprised he had gotten the answer right. Alex hadn't expected Conner to remember any fairy tales. . . .

"Now, class, I want you all to get out your literature books, turn to page one hundred and seventy, and read 'Little Red Riding Hood' quietly to yourselves," Mrs. Peters instructed.

The students did as they were told. Conner made

himself as comfortable as possible at his desk and began reading. The story, the pictures, and the characters were all so familiar to him.

One of the things Alex and Conner looked forward to the most when they were very young had been the trips to see their grandmother. She lived up in the mountains in the heart of the woods in a tiny house that could best be described as a cottage, if such a thing still existed.

It was a long journey, a few hours by car, but the twins loved every minute of it. Their anticipation would grow as they traveled up the windy roads and through the endless trees, and when they crossed a yellow bridge, the twins would excitedly exclaim, "We're almost there! We're almost there!"

Once they arrived, their grandmother would greet them at the door with open arms and hugs so tight they would almost pop.

"Look at you two! You've both grown a foot since the last time I saw you!" Grandma would say, even if they hadn't, and then would lead them inside, where a freshly baked batch of cookies waited for them.

Their father had grown up in the woods and would spend hours each day telling the twins his adventures as a kid: all the trees he'd climbed, all the streams he'd swum, and all the ferocious animals he'd barely escaped from. Most of his retellings were highly exaggerated, but they loved this time with him more than anything else in the world.

"Someday, when you're older, I'll take you to all the secret places where I used to play," their father would tease them. He was a tall man with kind eyes that would wrinkle whenever he smiled, and he smiled quite a bit, especially when he was teasing the twins.

At night the twins' mother would help their grand-mother cook dinner and, after they had eaten, as soon as the dishes were done, the family would sit around the fire-place. Their grandmother would open her big storybook, and she and their father would take turns reading the twins fairy tales until they fell asleep. Sometimes the Bailey fam-ily would be up until sunrise.

They told the stories with such detail and passion that it didn't matter how many times the twins heard the same story. They were the best memories any child could ask for.

Unfortunately, the twins hadn't been back to their grandmother's cottage in a very long time. . . .

"MR. BAILEY!" Mrs. Peters shouted. Conner had dozed off again.

"Sorry, Mrs. Peters!" he bellowed back, sitting straight up in his seat like a soldier on guard. If looks could kill, Conner would have been dead from the scowl she was sending him.

"What did we think of the *real* Little Red Riding Hood?" the teacher asked her class.

A girl with frizzy hair and thick braces raised her hand.

"Mrs. Peters?" the frizzy-haired girl asked. "I'm confused."

"And *why* is that?" Mrs. Peters said, as if asking, "What on earth could you possibly be confused about, idiot?"

"Because, it says the Big Bad Wolf is killed by the Hunter," the frizzy-haired girl explained. "I always thought the wolf was just upset because the other wolves in his pack made fun of his snout, and he and Little Red Riding Hood became friends in the end. At least, that's what happened in the cartoon I used to watch when I was little."

Mrs. Peters rolled her eyes so far into the back of her head, she could have seen what was behind her.

"That," she said with a clenched jaw, "is exactly why we're having this lesson."

The frizzy-haired girl became wide-eyed and sad. How could something so dear to her have been so wrong?

"For homework," Mrs. Peters said, and the room unanimously slumped in their seats, "you are to pick your favorite fairy tale and write a paper, due tomorrow, on the real lesson the tale is trying to teach us."

Mrs. Peters went to her desk, and the students began working on their assignment with the little class time remaining.

"Mr. Bailey?" Mrs. Peters summoned Conner to her desk. "A word."

Conner was in deep trouble, and he knew it. He cautiously stood up and walked to Mrs. Peters's desk. The other students gave him sorrowful looks as he walked by, as if he were walking to his executioner.

"Yes, Mrs. Peters?" Conner asked.

"Conner, I'm trying to be very sensitive about your *family situation*," Mrs. Peters said, glaring at him over the frames of her glasses.

Family situation. Two words Conner had heard too many times in the last year.

"However," Mrs. Peters continued, "there is certain behavior I just will not tolerate in my classroom. You're constantly falling asleep in class, you don't pay attention, not to mention you quiz and test very poorly. Your sister seems to be functioning just fine. Perhaps you could follow her example?"

It was a comparison that felt like a kick in the stomach every time someone made it. Indeed, Conner was not his sister by any means, and he was always punished because of it.

"If this continues, I will be forced to have a meeting with your mother, do you understand?" Mrs. Peters warned him.

"Yes, sir—*I mean ma'am! I meant ma'am!* Sorry." It just hadn't been his best day.

"Okay, then. You may have a seat."

Conner slowly walked back to his seat, his head hanging

slightly lower than it had all day. More than anything, he hated feeling like a failure.

Alex had watched the entire conversation between her brother and their teacher. As much as her brother embarrassed her, she did feel for him as only a sister could.

Alex flipped through her literature book, deciding on which story to write about. The pictures weren't as colorful and exciting as they had been in her grandmother's book, but seeing all the characters she had grown up reading about made her feel at home, a feeling that had recently become a rarity.

If only fairy tales were real, she thought. *Somebody could wave a wand and magically make things how they used to be.*

CHAPTER TWO

THE LONGER WALK HOME

I'm so excited about this lesson," Alex told Conner as they walked home from school. This was something Conner was used to hearing his sister declare, and it was usually his cue to stop listening.

"Mrs. Peters made a very good point, you know," Alex continued excitedly, speaking a mile a minute. "Think about everything children miss out on when they're deprived of fairy tales! Oh, how terrible for them! Don't you just feel awful for them? Conner, are you listening to me?"

"Yup," Conner lied. His attention was focused on an abandoned snail shell he was kicking along the sidewalk.

"Can you imagine a childhood without knowing all those characters and places?" Alex continued. "We're so fortunate that Dad and Grandma made such a point of reading them to us when we were little."

"Very lucky..." Conner nodded, although he wasn't exactly sure what he was agreeing with.

Every day after school, the Bailey twins would walk home together. They lived in a charming neighborhood that was surrounded by more charming neighborhoods that were surrounded by another series of charming neighborhoods. It was a sea of suburbia, where each house was similar to the next but uniquely different at the same time.

To pass the time as they walked, Alex would tell her brother everything on her mind: all her current thoughts and concerns, a summary of everything she had learned that day, and what she planned to do as soon as they got home. As much as this daily routine annoyed Conner, he knew he was the only person in the world Alex had to talk to, so he tried his best to listen. But listening had never been Conner's forte.

"How am I ever going to decide which story to write about? It's too difficult to choose!" Alex said, clapping her hands with excitement. "Which one are you going to write your paper on?"

"Um..." Conner said, whipping his head up from

looking at the ground. He had to mentally rewind the conversation to remember what the question was.

"'The Boy Who Cried Wolf,'" he said, choosing the first fairy tale that came to mind.

"You can't choose that one," Alex said, shaking her head. "That's the most obvious one! You have to select something more challenging to impress Mrs. Peters. You should pick something with a message hidden deeper inside it, one that isn't so on-the-surface."

Conner sighed. It was always easier to just go along with Alex instead of arguing with her, but sometimes it was unavoidable.

"Fine, I'll pick 'Sleeping Beauty,'" he decided.

"Interesting selection," Alex said, intrigued. "What do *you* suppose the moral of that story is?"

"Don't piss off your neighbors, I guess," Conner said.

Alex grunted disapprovingly.

"Be serious, Conner! That is *not* the moral of 'Sleeping Beauty,'" she reprimanded.

"Sure it is," Conner explained. "If the king and queen had just invited that crazy enchantress to their daughter's party in the first place, none of that stuff ever would have happened."

"They couldn't have stopped it from happening," said Alex. "That enchantress was evil and probably would have cursed the baby princess anyway. 'Sleeping Beauty' is about trying to prevent the unpreventable. Her parents tried protecting her and had all the spinning wheels in the kingdom destroyed. She was so sheltered, she didn't even know what the danger was, and she still pricked her finger on the first spindle she ever saw."

Conner thought about this possibility and shook his head. He liked his version much better.

"I disagree," Conner told her. "I've seen how upset you get when people don't invite you places, and you usually look like you would curse a baby, too."

Alex gave Conner a dirty look Mrs. Peters would have been proud of.

"While there's no such thing as a wrong *interpretation*, I have to say *that* is definitely a misread," Alex said.

"I'm just saying to be careful who you ignore," Conner clarified. "I always thought Sleeping Beauty's parents had it coming."

"Oh?" Alex questioned him. "And I suppose you thought Hansel and Gretel had it coming, too?"

"Yes," Conner said, feeling clever. "And so did the witch!"

"How so?" Alex asked.

"Because," Conner explained with a smirk on his face, "if you're going to live in a house made of candy, don't move next door to a couple of obese kids. A lot of these fairy-tale characters are missing common sense."

Alex let out another disapproving grunt. Conner figured he could get at least fifty more out of her before they got home.

"The witch didn't live next door! She lived deep in the forest! They had to leave a trail of bread crumbs behind so they could find their way back, remember. And the whole point of the house was to lure the kids in. They were starving!" Alex reminded him. "At least have all the facts straight before you criticize."

"If they were *starving*, what were they doing wasting bread crumbs?" Conner asked. "Sounds like a couple of troublemakers to me."

Alex grunted again.

"And in your deranged mind, what do you think the lesson of 'Goldilocks and the Three Bears' is?" Alex challenged him.

"Easy," Conner said. "Lock your doors! Robbers come in all shapes and sizes. Even curly-haired little girls can't be trusted."

Alex grunted again and crossed her arms. She tried her best not to giggle; she didn't want to validate her brother's opinion.

"'Goldilocks' is about consequences! Mrs. Peters said so herself," Alex said. Although Alex would never admit it, sometimes arguing with her brother was amusing. "What do you suppose 'Jack and the Beanstalk' is about?" she asked.

Conner contemplated a moment and slyly grinned. "Bad beans can cause more than indigestion," he answered, laughing hysterically to himself.

Alex pursed her lips to hide a smile.

"What do you think the lesson of 'Little Red Riding Hood' is?" she asked him. "Do you think she should have just *mailed* her grandmother the gift basket?"

"Now you're thinking!" he said. "Although, I've always

felt sorry for Little Red Riding Hood. It's obvious her parents didn't like her very much."

"Why do you say that?" Alex asked, wondering how he could have possibly construed that from the story.

"Who sends their young daughter into a dark and wolf-occupied forest carrying freshly baked food and wearing a bright jacket?" Conner asked. "They were practically asking for a wolf to eat her! She must have annoyed the heck out of them!"

Alex held back laughter with all her might but, to Conner's delight, she let a quiet chuckle slip.

"I know you secretly agree with me," Conner said, bumping her shoulder with his.

"Conner, it's people like you who ruin fairy tales for the rest of the world," Alex said, forcing the smile on her face to fade. "People make jokes about them, and suddenly the whole message is...is...*lost*—"

Alex suddenly stopped walking. All the color in her face slowly drained away. Something across the street had caught her eye, something very disappointing.

"What's the matter?" Conner asked, turning back to her.

Alex was staring at a large house. It was a lovely home, painted blue with white trim, and had several windows. The front yard was landscaped to perfection; it had just the right amount of grass, patches of colorful flowers, and a large oak tree ideal for climbing.

If a house could smile, this house would be grinning from ear to ear.

"Look," Alex said, and pointed to a For Sale sign next to the oak tree. A bright red stripe with the word *Sold* had recently been added to it.

"It sold," Alex said, slowly shaking her head from side to side in disbelief. "It sold," she repeated, not wanting it to be true.

The little color in Conner's round face drained, too. The twins stared at the house for a moment in silence, each not knowing what to say to the other.

"We both knew it would happen *eventually*," Conner said.

"Then why do I feel so surprised?" Alex asked softly. "I guess it had been for sale for so long, I figured it was just . . . you know . . . *waiting for us*."

Conner saw tears begin to form in his sister's eyes through the tears forming in his own.

"Come on, Alex," Conner said and kept walking. "Let's go home."

She looked at the house for a second more and then followed him. This house was only one thing the Bailey family had recently lost. . . .

A year ago, just a few days before their eleventh birthday, Alex and Conner's father died in a car accident on his way home from work. Mr. Bailey had owned a bookstore a few streets away named Bailey's Books, but all it had taken was a few small streets for a big accident to happen.

The twins and their mother had been anxiously waiting for him at the dinner table when they got the phone call telling them their father wouldn't be joining them that night, or any night after that. He had never been late to dinner before, so as soon as the telephone rang, they all had known something was wrong.

Alex and Conner could never forget the look on their mother's face when she answered the phone—a look that told them, without saying a word, that their lives would never be the same. They had never seen their mother cry like she did that night.

Everything had happened so fast after that. It was hard for the twins to remember what order it all had happened in.

They remembered their mother making tons of phone calls and having to deal with a lot of paperwork. They remembered that their grandmother came to take care of them while their mother made all the funeral arrangements.

They remembered holding their mother's hands as they walked down the church aisle at the funeral. They remembered the white flowers and candles and all the sad expressions on everyone's faces as they passed. They remembered all the food people sent. They remembered how sorry people told them they were.

They didn't remember their eleventh birthday, because no one did.

The twins remembered how strong Grandma and Mom had stayed for them in the following months. They remembered their mother explaining to them why they had to sell the bookstore. They remembered that, eventually, their mother couldn't afford their beautiful blue house anymore, and they'd had to move into a rental house a little way down the street.

They remembered Grandma leaving them once they were settled into their new, smaller house. They remembered returning to school and how falsely normal everything appeared to be. But most of all, the twins remembered not understanding why any of it had to happen.

A full year had passed, and the twins still didn't understand it. People had told them it would get easier with time, but how much time were they talking about? The loss seemed to grow deeper each day without their dad. They missed him so much sometimes that they expected their sadness to swell out of their bodies.

They missed his smile, they missed his laugh, and they missed his stories. . . .

Whenever Alex had had a particularly bad day at school, the first thing she would do when she got home was jump on her bike and pedal to her dad's store. She would run through the front doors, find her dad, and say, "Daddy, I need to talk to you."

It didn't matter if he was helping a customer or putting brand-new books on the shelves, Mr. Bailey would always stop what he was doing, take his daughter to the storage room in the back, and listen to what had happened.

"What's the matter, sweetheart?" he would ask with big, concerned eyes.

"I had a really bad day today, Daddy," Alex said on one occasion.

"Are the other kids still teasing you?" he asked. "I can call the school and ask your teacher to have a talk with them."

"That wouldn't solve anything," Alex said through sniffles. "By publicly persecuting me, they're filling an insecure void caused by social and domestic neglect."

Mr. Bailey scratched his head. "So, what you're saying, sweetheart, is that they're just *jealous?*" he asked her.

"Exactly," Alex said. "I read a psychology book in the library today at lunch that explained it."

Mr. Bailey let out a proud laugh. His daughter's intelligence constantly amazed him. "I think you're just too bright for your own good, Alex," he said.

"Sometimes I wish I was like everyone else," Alex confessed. "I'm tired of being lonely, Daddy. If being smart and being a good student means that I'll never have friends, then I wish I was more like *Conner.*"

"Alex, have I ever told you the story about the Curvy Tree?" Mr. Bailey asked.

"No," Alex answered.

Mr. Bailey's eyes lit up. They always did when he was about to tell a story.

"Well," he started, "one day when I was very young, I was walking around the woods and saw something very peculiar. It was an evergreen tree, but it was different from any other evergreen tree I had ever seen. Instead of growing straight out of the ground, its trunk curved and wound in circles like a large vine."

"How?" Alex asked, utterly entranced. "That isn't possible. Evergreens don't grow like that."

"Perhaps someone forgot to tell that to the tree," Mr. Bailey said. "Anyway, one day the loggers came and cut down every single tree in the area except for the Curvy Tree."

"Why?" Alex asked.

"Because they figured it was unusable," Mr. Bailey answered. "You could never make a table or a chair or a cabinet out of it. You see, the Curvy Tree may have felt different from the other trees, but its uniqueness is what saved it."

"What ever happened to the Curvy Tree?" Alex asked.

"It's still there today," Mr. Bailey said with a smile. "It's growing taller and taller and curvier and curvier every day."

A tiny smile grew on Alex's face. "I think I get what you're trying to tell me, Daddy," she said.

"I'm glad," said Mr. Bailey. "Now all you have to do is wait for the loggers to come and chop down all your peers."

Alex laughed for the first time all day. Mr. Bailey always knew how to cheer her up.

It took the twins twice as long to walk home since they'd moved into the rental house. It was a boring home with brown walls and a flat roof. Windows were few, and the front yard consisted only of a plain grass lawn that was barely alive because the sprinklers didn't work.

The Baileys' home was cozy but cluttered. They had more furniture than they had room for, and none of it matched the house because it was never intended to. Even though they had lived here for more than half a year, unpacked boxes were still lined up against the walls.

None of them wanted to unpack them; none of them wanted to admit they were staying as long as they actually were.

The twins immediately went up the stairs and into their separate bedrooms. Alex sat at her desk and started her homework. Conner laid on his bed and started a nap.

Alex's bedroom could have been mistaken for a library if it weren't for the bright yellow bed tucked away in the corner. Bookshelves of all heights and widths lined the room, holding everything from chapter books to encyclopedias.

Conner's bedroom was more like a cave, in which he appropriately hibernated whenever he could. It was dark and messy; patches of carpet could be seen in between piles of dirty clothes. A half-eaten grilled cheese sandwich rested on the floor and had been there far too long for anyone's peace of mind.

An hour or so later, the twins heard sounds that meant their mother was visiting from work, and they went downstairs to join her in the kitchen. She was sitting at the table while on the phone, flipping through a stack of envelopes she had just collected from the mailbox.

Charlotte Bailey was a very pretty woman with red hair and freckled skin that the twins undoubtedly had inherited from her. She had a huge, caring heart and loved her kids more than anything else in the world. Unfortunately, they hardly ever saw their mother anymore.

She was a nurse at the local children's hospital and was forced to work constant double shifts to support the family since her husband passed away. Mrs. Bailey was already gone before the twins woke up every morning and would get home after the twins had gone to sleep. The only time she had with the twins anymore was on the brief lunch and dinner breaks she spent at home.

Mrs. Bailey loved her job and loved taking care of children at the hospital, but hated that it took time away from her own. In a way, the twins felt they had lost both their parents after their dad's death.

"Hi, guys," Mrs. Bailey said to the twins, covering the receiving end of the phone. "Did you have a good day at school?"

Alex nodded positively. Conner gave her an overly enthusiastic thumbs-up.

"Yes, I can work a double this Monday," she said into the phone, speaking with someone from the hospital. "No problem," she lied.

Most of the envelopes she was looking through had bright red warning stickers saying FINAL NOTICE or PAYMENT DUE.

Even working the hours she worked, Mrs. Bailey had to get creative with money sometimes. She put the envelopes face-down on the table, hiding them from the twins.

"Thank you," Mrs. Bailey said into the phone, and clicked it off. She turned to her children. "How are you guys?"

"Good," they both said passively.

Mrs. Bailey's "mom-tuition" turned on. She knew something was troubling them.

"What's the matter?" she asked, studying their faces. "You seem a little down."

Alex and Conner looked to each other, unsure of what to say. Did their mother know about their old house? Should they tell her?

"Come on," their mother said. "What is it? You can tell me anything."

"We aren't upset," Conner said. "We knew it was going to happen eventually."

"What?" Mrs. Bailey asked.

"The house sold," Alex said. "We saw it today on our way home from school."

There was a moment before anyone said anything. This wasn't news to Mrs. Bailey, but the twins could tell she was just as disappointed about it as they were and had hoped they wouldn't notice it.

"Oh, *that*," Mrs. Bailey said, brushing it off. "Yes, I know. You shouldn't be sad about it, though. We'll find a bigger and better house as soon as we catch up on things here."

And that was that. Mrs. Bailey wasn't a good liar, and

neither were the twins. Still, Alex and Conner always smiled and nodded along with her.

"What did you learn in school today?" their mother asked.

"So much," Alex proclaimed with a huge smile.

"Not much," Conner mumbled with a scowl.

"That's because you fell asleep in class again!" Alex tattled.

Conner gave Alex a dirty look.

"Oh, Conner, not again," Mrs. Bailey said, shaking her head. "What are we going to do with you?"

"It's not my fault!" Conner said. "Mrs. Peters's lessons put me to sleep. It just happens! It's like my brain switches off or something. Sometimes even my old rubber-band trick doesn't work."

"Rubber-band trick?" Mrs. Bailey asked.

"I wear a rubber band around my wrist and snap it every time I get sleepy," Conner explained. "And I was positive it was foolproof!"

Mrs. Bailey shook her head, more amused than anything.

"Well, don't forget how lucky you are to be in that classroom," Mrs. Bailey said with a guilt-inducing "mom look." "All the kids at the hospital would like nothing more than to trade places with you and go to school every day."

"They'd change their minds if they met Mrs. Peters," Conner said under his breath.

The phone rang just as Mrs. Bailey was about to continue scolding her son.

"Hello?" Mrs. Bailey said, answering the phone. The worry lines on her forehead became very prominent. "Tomorrow? No, there must be a mistake. I told them I couldn't work at all tomorrow; it's the twins' twelfth birthday and I was planning on spending the evening with them."

Alex and Conner looked at each other with the same surprised expression. They had almost forgotten they were turning twelve the next day. Almost . . .

"Are you positive there's no one else who can cover it?" Mrs. Bailey asked, her voice more desperate than she wanted it to sound. "No, I understand. . . . Yes, of course . . . I'm aware of the staff cuts. . . . See you tomorrow."

Mrs. Bailey hung up the phone, closed her eyes, and let out a deep, disappointed sigh.

"I've got some bad news, guys," she told them. "It looks like I have to work tomorrow night, so I won't be here for your birthday. But I'll make it up to you! We'll celebrate when I get home from work the next night, all right?"

"That's fine, Mom," Alex said cheerfully, trying to make her feel better. "We understand."

"It's okay," Conner added. "We weren't really expecting anything special anyway."

The situation made Mrs. Bailey feel like the worst mother in the world, and their understanding made her feel even worse. She would have much rather watched them throw a fit or get angry or show any emotion appropriate for their age. They were too young to be *used* to disappointment.

"Oh . . ." Mrs. Bailey said, fighting back the sadness inside her. "Great. Then we'll have dinner . . . and get a cake . . . and have a nice night. . . . Now, I'm just going to go upstairs for a minute before I head back to work."

She left the kitchen and hurried up the stairs and into her bedroom.

The twins waited a beat before climbing up the stairs to check on her.

They peered into their mother's bedroom. She was sitting on her bed crying, with rolled-up balls of tissue in both her hands, talking to a framed photo of her late husband.

"Oh, John," Mrs. Bailey said. "I try to stay strong and keep our family going, but it's really hard to do without you. They're such good kids. They don't deserve this."

She quickly dried her tears once she felt the twins watching her. Alex and Conner slowly walked into her room and sat on either side of her.

"I'm so sorry, for everything," Mrs. Bailey said to them. "It just isn't fair that you've had to go through all of this at such a young age."

"It's going to be okay, Mom," Alex said. "We don't need anything special for our birthday."

"Birthdays are overrated anyway," Conner added. "We know things are tight right now."

Mrs. Bailey put her arms around them. "When did you two become so grown-up?" she asked them with watery eyes. "I am the luckiest mom in the world!"

All their eyes fell on the photo of Mr. Bailey.

"You know what your dad would say if he were here?" Mrs. Bailey asked the twins. "He'd say, 'Right now, we're living in an ugly chapter of our lives, but books always get better!'"

The twins smiled at her, hoping this was true.

CHAPTER THREE

A BIRTHDAY SURPRISE

P encils down," Mrs. Peters ordered from the front of
the classroom. Her students were taking a math test,
and she had been watching them like a prison guard
the entire time. "Pass your tests to the front."

Conner looked down at the test as if it were written in
ancient hieroglyphics. Most of his answers were blank, and
he had just scribbled around the others to make it look like
he had tried. He said a little prayer to himself and passed
the test forward with the others.

The tests were all passed to Alex, who stacked them in a

neat pile for Mrs. Peters. She always felt so refreshed after taking a test, especially one as simple as that one had been for her.

Her brother's test caught her eye since it was the one with the least amount of writing on it. Alex knew Conner always tried his best at school, but his best never seemed to be good enough. She looked back at him, wishing she could help him... and then it occurred to her: Maybe she *could*.

Alex looked up at Mrs. Peters and saw that she was busy looking at the notes in her lesson plan. Would her teacher notice if Alex quickly filled in a couple of answers for her brother? Was Alex even capable of doing something so blatantly wrong?

Was it considered cheating if you were doing it on someone else's test? Would the gracious gesture cancel out the offense in the grand scheme of things?

Alex was prone to over-thinking everything, so she just did it; she quickly filled in some of her brother's answers, making her handwriting slightly sloppier than it usually was, and handed the stack of tests to Mrs. Peters.

It was the most spontaneous thing she had ever done.

"Thank you, Miss Bailey," Mrs. Peters said, making eye contact with her. Alex felt like the pit of her stomach had fallen out of her body. The excitement she had felt from her impulse was now overshadowed by guilt.

Mrs. Peters had always trusted her; how could she do something so juvenile? Should she confess what she had done? What was the punishment for her crime? Would she feel this guilty for the rest of her life?

She looked back at her brother. Conner let out a long but quiet sigh, and Alex sensed her brother's sadness and embarrassment; she could feel his hopelessness as if it were her own.

The critical wheels in Alex's head stopped turning. She knew she'd done the right thing—not as a student, but as a sister.

"I want you all to get out your homework from last night," Mrs. Peters commanded, "and I would like you to briefly present your work in front of the class."

The teacher regularly surprised the class with impromptu presentations to keep them on their toes. She took a seat on a stool in the back of the room uncomfortably close to Conner's seat so she could keep an eye on his consciousness.

One by one, the students presented their assignments to the class. Besides a boy who thought "Jack and the Beanstalk" was about an alien abduction and a girl who claimed "Puss in Boots" was an early example of animal cruelty, all the students seemed to have interpreted the tales correctly.

"It was so hard to choose just one fairy tale to write about," Alex said as she animatedly presented her seven-page paper to the class. "So, I selected the story the theme of which is present in virtually every fairy tale and every story ever written, 'Cinderella'!"

Her excitement was not shared by her peers.

"Many people have had issues with 'Cinderella,' saying

it has anti-feminist elements," Alex continued. "But I think that's completely ridiculous! 'Cinderella' is not about a man saving a woman, it's about *karma*!"

Most of the class began daydreaming about other things. Mrs. Peters was the only person in the room who seemed even slightly interested in what Alex had to say.

"Think about it," Alex went on. "Even after years of constant abuse from her stepmother and her stepsisters, Cinderella remained a good person with high hopes. She never stopped believing in herself and in the good of the world. And although she married the prince in the end, Cinderella always had *inner happiness*. Her story shows that even in the worst of situations—*even when it seems no one in the world appreciates you*—as long as you have hope, everything can get better...."

Alex let her mind linger on what she had said. She questioned the last point she had made in her presentation. Was that really what "Cinderella" was about, or was it what she *needed* "Cinderella" to be about?

"Thank you, Miss Bailey! Very well said," Mrs. Peters said with the closest thing to a smile her face was capable of making.

"Thank you for your time," Alex said, and nodded to the class.

"It's your turn, Mr. Bailey," the teacher announced. She was sitting so close to him that he could feel the warm breath from her nostrils on the back of his neck.

Conner went to the front of the classroom, dragging his

feet as if they were encased in concrete. He had never had trouble talking in front of the class, but he'd rather be anywhere in the world than presenting something in front of a teacher. Alex gave him an encouraging nod.

"I chose 'The Boy Who Cried Wolf,'" Conner said, going against his sister's advice from the day before.

Alex slumped in her seat, and Mrs. Peters rolled her eyes. This was very disappointing.

"I know you're all thinking I went with the easiest one," Conner said. "Except, reading it again, I don't think the story is about the importance of honesty. I think it's about *high expectations*."

Alex and Mrs. Peters both raised an eyebrow. Where was he going with this?

"Sure, the boy was a brat. I can't deny that," Conner continued, gesturing to the half-page paper he had written. "But can you blame him for having a little fun? Clearly his village was having a bit of a wolf problem, and everyone was stressed out about it. He was just a kid; did they really expect him to be perfect all the time?"

His presentation may have not been the best, but it certainly was catching the class's attention.

"And it makes me wonder, why was no one watching this kid?" Conner added. "Maybe if his parents had kept an eye on him, he wouldn't have been eaten. I think the story is trying to tell us to keep an eye on our kids, especially if they're pathological liars. Thank you."

Conner never tried to be funny. He was just painfully

honest about his thoughts and opinions. This honesty always amused his classmates, but never his teacher.

"Thank you, Mr. Bailey," Mrs. Peters said sharply. "You may sit down now."

Conner knew he'd blown it. He took his seat, resuming his position under his teacher's cold stare and warm breath. Why did he even bother trying anymore?

It wasn't the end of a school day unless Conner left feeling completely worthless. There was only one person who was capable of making him feel better when he felt this way. Conner only wished he were still around. . . .

Mr. Bailey always knew when his son needed to talk to him. It didn't have anything to do with observation or intuition, but with location. Occasionally, Mr. Bailey would get home from work and find his son sitting up in the oak tree in the front yard with a contemplative look on his face.

"Conner?" Mr. Bailey would ask, approaching the tree. "Is everything okay, bud?"

"Uh-huh," Conner would mumble.

"Are you sure?" Mr. Bailey would ask.

"Yup," Conner would say unconvincingly. He wasn't as vocal about his troubles as his sister was, but you could see it in his face. Mr. Bailey would climb up the tree and have a seat on the branch next to his son and coax out what was troubling him.

"Are you sure you don't want to talk about it?" Mr. Bailey would continue. "Did something happen at school today?"

Conner would nod his head.

"I got a bad grade on a test," he admitted on one occasion.

"Did you study for it?" his father asked.

"Yes," Conner said. "I studied really hard, Dad. But it's just no use. I'll never be as smart as Alex." His cheeks turned bright red with embarrassment.

"Conner, let me fill you in on something that took me a long time to learn," Mr. Bailey said. "The women in your life are always going to seem smarter; it's just the way it is. I've been married to your mother for thirteen years, and I still have trouble keeping up with her. You can't compare yourself to others."

"But I'm stupid, Dad," Conner said, his eyes filling with tears.

"I find that hard to believe," Mr. Bailey said. "It takes intelligence to be funny and tell a good joke, and you're the funniest kid I know!"

"Humor doesn't help with history or math," Conner said. "It doesn't matter how hard I try in school. I'm always going to be the dumb kid in class. . . ."

Conner's face went white and expressionless; he stared off into nothing, so ashamed of himself that it hurt. Luckily for him, Mr. Bailey had an encouraging story for every situation.

"Conner, have I ever told you the legend about the Walking Fish?" Mr. Bailey asked him.

He looked up at his father. "The Walking Fish?" Conner asked. "Dad, no offense, but I don't think one of your stories is going to make me feel better this time."

"All right, suit yourself," Mr. Bailey said.

A few moments passed, and Conner's curiosity got the best of him.

"Okay, you can tell me about the Walking Fish," Conner said.

Mr. Bailey's eyes lit up as they always did just before he was about to tell a story. Conner could tell this was going to be a good one.

"Once upon a time, there was a large fish who lived in a lake by himself," Mr. Bailey told him. "Every day, the fish would watch longingly as a boy from the village nearby would play with all the horses and dogs and squirrels on land—"

"Is a dog going to die in this story, Dad?" Conner interrupted. "You know I hate stories when dogs die—"

"Let me finish," Mr. Bailey went on. "One day, a fairy came to the lake and granted the fish a wish—"

"That's random," Conner said. "Why do fairies always just show up and do nice things for people they don't know?"

"Employment obligation?" Mr. Bailey shrugged. "But for argument's sake, let's say she dropped her wand in the lake and the fish retrieved it, so she offered him a wish as a thank-you. Happy?"

"That's better," Conner said. "Go on."

"The fish, predictably, wished for legs, so he could play with the boy from the village," Mr. Bailey said. "So the fairy turned his fins into legs and he became the Walking Fish."

"That's weird," Conner said. "Let me guess, the fish was so freaky-looking, the boy never wanted to play with him?"

"Nope, they became great friends and played together with the other land animals," Mr. Bailey told him. "But, one day, the boy fell into the lake and couldn't swim! The Walking Fish tried to save him, but it was no use; he didn't have fins anymore! Sadly, the boy drowned."

Conner's mouth hung open like a broken glove compartment.

"You see, if the fish had just stayed in the lake and not wished to be something else, he could have saved the boy's life," Mr. Bailey finished.

"Dad, that's a horrible story," he said. "How does a boy live by a lake and not know how to swim? Dogs can swim! Couldn't one of them have saved him? Where was that fairy when the boy was drowning?"

"I think you're missing the point of the story," Mr. Bailey said. "Sometimes we forget about our own advantages because we focus on what we don't have. Just because you have to work a little harder at something that seems easier to others doesn't mean you're without your own talents."

Conner thought about this for a moment. "I think I get it, Dad," he said.

Mr. Bailey smiled at him. "Now, why don't we get down from this tree, and I'll help you study for your next test?"

"I told you, studying doesn't help," Conner said. "I've tried and tried and tried. It never helps."

"Then we'll come up with our own way of studying," Mr. Bailey told him. "We'll look at pictures of people in your history book and make up jokes about them so you'll remember their names. And we'll create funny scenarios to help you with all of those math formulas."

Conner slowly but surely nodded and agreed to it.

"Fine," he said with a half smile. "But for future reference, I liked your story about the Curvy Tree much better."

The walk home that day was very quiet. Alex could sense that her brother's presentation had left him a little tense. She tried breaking the silence every few steps with supportive comments—or at least she thought they were supportive.

"I thought you made a good point," she said sweetly. "Granted, it's not a point I ever would have made."

"Thanks," Conner replied. She wasn't helping.

"You may have overanalyzed it, though," Alex said. "I do it all the time. Sometimes I read a story and interpret it the way I want to, rather than the way the author wanted me to. It just takes practice."

He didn't respond. She still wasn't helping.

"Well, it's our birthday today," Alex reminded him. "Are you excited to be twelve?"

"Not really," Conner admitted. "It feels just like eleven. But aren't we supposed to be getting a new set of molars soon?"

"Come on, let's be positive," Alex insisted. "Even though we aren't doing anything exciting for our birthday, we should stay optimistic. There are plenty of things to look forward to! One more year until we'll be teenagers!"

"I suppose," Conner said. "Only four more years left until we can drive!"

"And six years left until we can vote and go to college!" Alex added.

That was all they could come up with. Their cheerfulness was hollow, and they both knew it, so they just stayed silent for the remainder of the walk. Even if they had the most extravagant party in the world waiting for them at home, birthdays were always going to be hard for them.

School had been predictable. The walk home had been typical. The whole day had seemed normal. There wasn't anything out of the ordinary to make their birthday feel special at all... until they got home and saw a bright blue car pull into their driveway.

"Grandma?" the twins said in perfect unison.

"Surprise!" yelled their grandmother, getting out of her car. She was so loud, the entire neighborhood could hear her.

The twins ran up to her with huge smiles on their faces.

They only saw their grandmother a couple times a year and were stunned to see her in their driveway with no prior warning.

Their grandmother hugged both of them so tight they thought they'd pop. "Look at you two!" she said. "You both look like you've grown a foot since the last time I saw you!"

Their grandmother was a petite woman with long, graying brown hair that was pulled back in a tight braid. She had the warmest smile and the kindest eyes in the world, which wrinkled pleasantly when she smiled, just like the twins' dad's eyes had. She was cheerful and energetic, and exactly what the twins needed.

She always wore bright dresses and her signature shoes with white laces and brown heels. She was never more than a few feet away from her large, green travel bag and blue purse. And although their grandfather had died many years before, she always wore her wedding ring.

"We had no idea you were coming!" Conner said.

"It wouldn't be a surprise if you knew I was coming," Grandma said.

"What are you doing here, Grandma?" Alex asked.

"Your mom called and asked me to stay with you while she went to work," Grandma told them. "I couldn't let you spend your birthday alone, could I? Thank goodness I was in the country!"

Their grandmother was retired and spent most of the

year traveling around the world with other retired friends. They traveled to mostly third-world countries and read to sick children in hospitals and taught other children of the communities to read and write.

"Come help me with the groceries," Grandma told the twins. She opened her trunk, and the twins began unloading bags and bags filled with food into the house. It was enough food to last them for weeks.

Mrs. Bailey was sitting at the kitchen table going through another stack of mail with bright red warning labels on them. She quickly pushed them to the side when the twins and their grandmother paraded into the kitchen with the groceries.

"What's all this?" Mrs. Bailey asked.

"Hello, dear!" Grandma said to her. "I'm planning on cooking the twins a huge birthday dinner and wasn't sure what you had in the house, so I went to the store and picked up a couple things."

Their grandmother always had a talent for sugarcoating the truth.

"You didn't have to go to all this trouble," Mrs. Bailey said, shaking her head, unprepared for the kind gesture.

"It wasn't any trouble at all," Grandma said with a small but reassuring smile. "Alex, Conner, how about you go get your birthday presents from the front seat of my car, and I'll catch up with your mom for a second? But don't open them until tonight!"

They happily did as she asked. *Presents* was a word that had been absent from their vocabulary for a long time.

"See, I told you!" Alex said to Conner on their way to their grandmother's car. "Optimism always pays off!"

"Yeah, yeah, yeah..." Conner said.

Half a dozen wrapped presents with bright bows, each marked to one of them, were waiting in the front seat of the car.

The twins returned inside with their gifts. Their grandmother and mother were still having a conversation that they most likely weren't supposed to hear.

"Things are still tough," Mrs. Bailey said. "Even after selling the bookstore, the house foreclosed, and we still have some debt and things unpaid from the funeral. But we're making it somehow. In a few more months we'll be back on our feet."

Grandma took Mrs. Bailey's hands into her own.

"If you need anything, dear, and I mean anything, you know where to find me," she said.

"You've already helped so much," Mrs. Bailey told her. "I don't know where we'd be now if it weren't for you. I could never ask you for anything else."

"You're not asking, I'm offering," Grandma assured.

The twins knew if they eavesdropped any longer, they'd be caught, so they walked back into the kitchen with their presents.

"Well, I have to go back to work," Mrs. Bailey said, and kissed both of the twins on the tops of their heads. "Have a great night, you guys! I'll see you tomorrow. Save some cel-ebration for me!" She gathered her things and mouthed a meaningful *thank you* to their grandmother on her way out.

Grandma put her things away in the guest bedroom and returned to the kitchen, where she found the stack of bills Mrs. Bailey had put aside. She plopped the mail into her own purse with a smile. And that was that. Grandma loved helping people, especially if it was against their will.

"Let's get started on dinner, shall we?" Grandma said, clapping her hands.

Alex and Conner sat at the table and visited with their grandmother while she cooked up a storm. She told them all about her recent trips, the difficulties she and her friends experienced getting into and out of places, and all the inter-esting people she had met along the way.

"I've never met a person I didn't learn something from!" Grandma said. "Even the most monotonous people will surprise you. Remember that."

She was cooking so many different things, it was impos-sible to tell which ingredient was going where. Everything she did was so fast, and she used almost every pan and dish they had. With every second that passed, the twins' stom-achs growled louder and louder, and their mouths salivated more and more.

Finally, after a few hours of aroma-teasing torture, they ate. Alex and Conner had become so accustomed to frozen dinners and takeout, they had forgotten how good food could taste.

There were plates of mashed potatoes and macaroni and cheese, oven-roasted chicken with carrots and peas, and freshly baked rolls. Their kitchen table looked like the cover of a cookbook.

Just when they thought they couldn't possibly eat any more, their grandmother pulled a huge birthday cake out of the oven. The twins were amazed; they hadn't even realized she had been baking one. She sang "Happy Birthday," and the twins blew out the candles.

"Now, open your presents!" Grandma said. "I've been collecting for you all year!"

They opened their boxes and were flooded with knickknacks from all the countries their grandmother had been to.

Alex was given copies of her favorite books in other languages: *Alice's Adventures in Wonderland* in French, *The Wonderful Wizard of Oz* in German, and *Little Women* in Dutch. Conner got a pile of candies and tacky T-shirts that said things like "My crazy Grandma traveled to India and all I got was this lousy T-shirt."

They both received several figurines of famous structures, like the Eiffel Tower and the Leaning Tower of Pisa and the Taj Mahal.

"It's crazy to think that places like this actually exist in the world," Alex said, holding an Eiffel Tower in her hand.

"You would be amazed to know what's out there just waiting to be discovered," their grandma said with a smile and a twinkle in her eye.

A day with very low expectations had turned into one of the best birthdays they'd ever had.

As the night grew later, the visit with their grandmother began to come to a bittersweet end. Since their dad had died, they never saw their grandmother for more than a day at a time, and there were always a few months between each visit. She was always so busy with her travels.

"When do you leave?" Alex asked her grandmother.

"Tomorrow," she said. "As soon as I take you to school."

The twins' postures sank a bit.

"What's the matter?" asked their grandmother, sensing their spirits sink.

"We just wish you could stay longer, Grandma. That's all," Conner said.

"We really miss you when you're gone," Alex added. "Things are so gloomy here without Dad, but you make everything seem like it's going to be okay."

Their grandmother's constant smile faded slightly, and her gaze drifted off toward the window. She stared blankly into the night sky and took a deep breath.

"Oh, kiddos, if I could spend every day with you, I would," Grandma said longingly, perhaps more disheartened than she intended to show. "But sometimes life hands us certain responsibilities—not because we want them, but because we were meant to have them—and it's our duty to see to them. All I can ever think about is how much I miss you two and your dad when I'm away."

It was hard for Alex and Conner to understand. Did she not want to travel as much as she did?

Their grandmother looked back at them; her eyes were bright with a new idea.

"I almost forgot. I have one more gift for you!" Grandma said, and jumped up and skipped into the next room.

She returned carrying a large, old book with a dark emerald cover titled *The Land of Stories* in gold writing. Alex and Conner knew what the book was as soon as they saw it. If their childhood could be symbolized by an object, it was this book.

"It's your old storybook!" Alex proclaimed. "I haven't seen that in years!"

Their grandmother nodded. "It's very old and has been with our family for a long time," Grandma told them. "I take it with me everywhere I go and read it to the children in other countries. But now I want you two to have it."

The twins were shocked by the gesture.

"What?" Conner asked. "We can't take your book, Grandma. That's *The Land of Stories*. It's *your* book. It's always been so important to you."

Their grandmother opened the book and flipped through the pages. The entire room filled with its musty-paper aroma.

"That's very true," said Grandma. "This book and I have spent a lot of time together over the years, but the best times were when I read it to you. So I'd like to pass it down to you now. I don't need it anymore; I have all the stories memorized anyway."

She handed it to them. Alex hesitated but finally accepted the book from her grandmother. It didn't feel right to take it. It was like receiving an heirloom from a relative who was still alive.

"Whenever you're feeling down, on the days you miss your dad the most or when you just wish I were here, all you have to do is open it up and we'll all be together in spirit, reading along," Grandma told them. "Now, it's getting late, and you have school tomorrow. Let's get ready for bed."

They did as she asked. Even though they were too old for it, their grandmother insisted on tucking them into their beds like old times.

Alex took *The Land of Stories* with her to bed that night. She gently flipped through the old pages, being careful not to tear them.

Seeing all the colorful illustrations of the places and characters again made her feel like she was reading an old scrapbook of sorts. She loved spending time reading about fairy-tale characters more than anything. They had always felt so real and accessible to her. They were the best friends she had ever had.

"I wish we got to choose which world we lived in," Alex said, running her fingers over the illustrations. They were so inviting.

In her hands was a world unlike the one she lived in. It

was a world unaltered by political corruption or technology, a world where good things came to good people, and a world she wanted to be a part of with all her being.

Alex imagined what it would be like to be a character in her own fairy tale: the forests she'd run through, the castles she'd live in, and the creatures she'd befriend.

Eventually, Alex's eyelids began to feel heavy. She closed *The Land of Stories*, placed it on her nightstand, clicked off her lamp, and began to drift off to sleep. She was just about to fade into unconsciousness when she heard a funny noise.

A low humming sound filled her room.

"What in the world?" Alex said to herself, and opened her eyes to see what it was. She saw nothing. "That's strange," she said.

She closed her eyes once more and began to drift back to sleep. The humming noise began to buzz through the room again.

Alex sat up and looked around her room and finally found what was making the noise. It was coming from inside *The Land of Stories* on her nightstand and, to her amazement, the pages were unmistakably glowing.

CHAPTER FOUR

THE LAND OF STORIES

Alex had been acting strange all week. Conner had noticed right away, because she wasn't as talkative and upbeat as she usually was. Instead, she was very quiet and looked like she was in a deep state of confusion.

When they ate breakfast, she barely acknowledged it when her brother said, "Good morning." During school, she stopped raising her hand as much. After school, she barely said a word to Conner while they walked home. And as soon as they got home, Alex would run up the stairs and lock herself in her bedroom for the rest of the day.

"Are you feeling okay?" Conner eventually asked her. "You seem different."

"Yes, I'm just tired," Alex said.

Conner knew she must be tired, because she didn't seem to sleep anymore. Every time he had gotten up in the middle of the night to get a glass of water or use the bathroom that week, the lights in his sister's bedroom were still on, and he could hear her rustling about inside, working on something.

He didn't have to be a genius to know that his sister was dealing with more than just insomnia. He had seen enough health videos at school to know that girls his sister's age were expected to start going through mood swings and changes, but Alex had become another person entirely. Something very serious was bothering her, and she was keeping it to herself.

"Can I borrow some of your pencils?" a wide-eyed and wide-awake Alex asked him late one night.

It was like a peacock asking to borrow some feathers. He wasn't certain how to handle the request. Surely she wasn't still doing homework at this hour?

"Don't you have, like, hundreds?" Conner asked her.

"Yes . . . but I've lost them all," she said.

He shared the few that he had with her. Alex took them and quickly disappeared into her room again; she didn't even seem to mind that they were chewed on or were missing the erasers.

The next night, Conner kept waking up to a peculiar

humming sound coming from Alex's room. It was quiet but had a strong vibration that he could feel as much as he could hear.

"Alex?" Conner said, knocking on his sister's door. "What is that sound? I'm trying to sleep, and it's driving me crazy!"

"It's just a bee. I shooed him out the window!" a frantic Alex responded from behind the door.

"A bee?" a puzzled Conner asked.

"Yes, a very big bee. It's mating season, you know, so they're quite aggressive this time of year," Alex called out.

"Err...all right..." Conner said, and went to bed.

But these happenings were nothing compared to the events during the next day at school.

"Can anyone tell me the names of the rivers that ran through ancient Mesopotamia?" Mrs. Peters asked the class during a history lesson. As usual, she had no volunteers.

"Anyone?" Mrs. Peters asked. Everyone was looking at Alex and expecting her hand to shoot into the air any second, but Alex was just staring at the floor. She wasn't paying any attention to anything.

"The Tigris and Euphrates," Mrs. Peters informed the class. "Can anyone tell me what the area between these two rivers is believed to be?" She asked the question in Alex's direction, but it was no use: Alex was lost in her own thoughts.

"Miss Bailey, perhaps you know the answer?" Mrs. Peters pleaded.

"To what?" asked Alex, snapping out of her trance.

"The question," Mrs. Peters said.

"Oh..." Alex said. "No, I don't." She rested her head on her hand and continued staring at the floor.

Mrs. Peters and the rest of the class didn't understand what was happening. Alex *always* knew the answers. How was the class going to function without her?

"The cradle of civilization..." Mrs. Peters told the class, answering the question. "Many believe that mankind started there—*Miss Bailey!*"

Alex sat up quickly in her seat. The most shocking thing that had ever happened in the classroom had occurred: *Alex Bailey had dozed off in the middle of class!*

"I—I—I am so sorry, Mrs. Peters!" Alex pleaded. "I don't know what came over me! I haven't been sleeping very well lately!"

Mrs. Peters was staring at her as if she had just witnessed a gruesome rural animal give birth. "That's...that's all right," the teacher said. "Do you need to see the nurse?"

"No, I'm fine. I'm just a little sleepy," Alex said. "I promise that'll never happen again!"

Conner had been watching the whole thing like it was a train wreck. All he could do was shake his head. What had happened to Alex? Where was his real sister? She was turning into *him*!

The strange humming sound Conner had heard the night before suddenly filled the classroom. Alex sat straight up in her seat, anxious; her eyes grew larger than they had ever been before. A few of the other students looked around, trying to figure out where the sound was coming from.

"Can anyone tell me the technologies Mesopotamia brought into the Bronze Age?" Mrs. Peters asked, oblivious to the humming. "Anyone?" she asked again.

Alex's hand shot straight into the air.

"Yes, Miss Bailey?" Mrs. Peters happily called on her.

"May I use the restroom?" Alex peeped.

Mrs. Peters sighed with disappointment. "Yes, you may," she replied.

Before she had finished granting Alex permission to leave the classroom, Alex had already jumped out of her seat, grabbed her school bag, and headed out the door.

Conner watched his sister leave. His eyes were bulging with suspicion. Why had she taken her backpack with her to the bathroom?

He had to know what was going on. He was going to confront his sister here and now at school, where she had no place to run and no bedroom to lock herself into.

"Mrs. Peters?" Conner called out.

"Yes, Mr. Bailey?" Mrs. Peters asked.

"Can I see the nurse?" he asked.

"What for?" she asked.

He hadn't thought this far into his plan. "Um... my elbow hurts," Conner said.

Mrs. Peters stared at him blankly. She may have believed him more if he had told her he was a dinosaur. "Your elbow hurts?" she asked.

"Yes, really bad. I banged it on my desk, and now it's just killing me," Conner said, clutching his perfectly fine elbow.

Mrs. Peters squinted and rolled her eyes, two of her trademark indications of annoyance in one expression. "Fine," the teacher said. "But I'm going to have to write you a pass—"

Conner was out the door before she could finish her sentence.

Meanwhile, Alex burst into the girls' restroom. She quickly looked underneath all the stalls to make sure she was alone. She zipped open her school bag, pulled out *The Land of Stories*, and set it on top of a sink; it was glowing and humming more than ever.

"Please turn off! Please turn off!" Alex said to the book. "I'm at school! I can't get caught with you here!"

The sound and shine slowly faded, and *The Land of Stories* returned to being just a normal book. Alex sighed with relief but panicked once more when someone else suddenly charged inside the restroom. It was her brother.

"Bees don't have mating seasons, Alex," Conner said with a tightened brow and his hands on his hips. "I looked it up. They come from colonies just like ants, even the big ones. They don't have schedules."

"Conner, what are you doing in here? You can't be in the girls' bathroom!" Alex shouted.

"I'm not leaving until you tell me what's going on!" Conner demanded. "You've been lying to me all week. I know something's up; I have 'twin-tuition.'"

"'Twin-tuition'?" Alex asked sarcastically.

"I made it up," Conner said. "It means I know when something's bothering you, even if you tell me nothing is. At first I thought you were just having *girl issues*—"

"Oh, Conner, please!" Alex interjected.

"Then, after all the strange buzzing noises and late nights, I figured Mom must have gotten you a cell phone and didn't want me to know about it. But then I remembered you have no friends, so who would be calling and texting you?"

Alex grunted. Now he was being accusative *and* rude.

"But I know you well enough to know that it would take something much worse to make you act this way," Conner said. "You're quiet, you don't know any of Mrs. Peters's answers, and you're falling asleep in class! You're acting like *me*! So just tell me, what's your problem?"

Alex didn't say a word; she just stared at her feet. She was so ashamed at how she had been acting, but she knew no one would believe her if she told them why she had been that way, except maybe her brother.

Conner looked around the girls' bathroom. "Gosh, it's so nice in here. The boys' bathroom looks like the bottom of a hazardous waste barrel.... Wait, why do you have Grandma's book with you?"

"I don't know what's going on!" Alex burst into the loud and awkward tears one cries when exhausted and overly stressed.

Conner took a step back for his own protection. He had never seen his sister so hysterical.

"At first I thought I was hallucinating!" Alex said. "I thought maybe I was having a reaction to something Grandma made us for dinner. That was the first night it happened! But then it kept happening, so I knew it wasn't a reaction!"

"Alex, what are you talking about?" Conner asked.

"*The* Land of Stories *book!*" Alex yelled. "*It glows! It hums! Every day it gets louder and brighter!* I've lost so much sleep trying to figure out how and why it does it! It breaks all the laws of science!"

"Ah..." Conner said with raised eyebrows. "Alex, I think we should go see the nurse—"

"You must think I'm insane!" Alex told him. "Anyone would come to that conclusion unless they saw it themselves. But I promise I'm telling the truth!"

"I don't think you're insane," Conner lied, starting to think his sister was *definitely* going insane.

"It happens once or twice a day," Alex said. "I was afraid Mom would find it, so I brought it to school; the last thing she needs to worry about is a possessed book lying around her house."

Conner didn't know what to say. He briefly imagined the future trips he and his mother would take to see his sister in the local asylum and the wisecracks he would make about the *cool white jacket* she got to wear.

Clearly, his sister had lost her mind, but after all they'd been through, he couldn't blame her. He kept thinking about how his dad would have handled this situation. What story would he have used to comfort Alex?

"Alex," Conner said with understanding eyes. "We've been through a lot in the last year. It's perfectly normal to feel overwhelmed and—"

The humming started again. They looked back at *The Land of Stories* on the sink; to Alex's relief and Conner's horror, it was glowing.

Conner jumped back against the wall as if he were in the presence of an explosive.

"The Land of Stories *book!"* Conner yelled. *"It glows! It hums!"*

"I told you!" Alex said.

Conner's mouth was opened so wide, it was almost touching his chest. "Is it radioactive?" he asked.

"I doubt it," Alex told him. She reached for the book.

"Don't touch it, Alex!" Conner shouted.

"Relax, Conner," Alex reassured him. "I've been dealing with it all week."

Using one finger, she flicked the book open, and the entire restroom was illuminated. All the illustrations and writing had disappeared, and the pages seemed to be made out of pure light.

Alex leaned closer to the book.

"Listen. Do you hear that?" she asked. "I can hear birds and leaves. I've never heard sounds come out of it before!"

Conner edged away from the wall and leaned down with his sister. The sound of birds chirping and trees blowing in the wind echoed off the tile and porcelain in the bathroom.

"How is this possible?" Conner asked. "Are you sure it doesn't have batteries or something?"

"My most educated analysis, with all means of science and technology in mind, is that it's magic," Alex said. "There's no other possible explanation!"

"Do you think Grandma knows about this?" Conner asked. "She had the book for years before she gave it to us. Do you think this has happened before?"

"I don't think Grandma would have given it to us if she knew what it was capable of," Alex said.

"You're right," Conner said. "She still cuts up my meat when she comes for dinner, because doesn't trust me with knives."

"There's more," Alex said. She reached into her school bag and pulled out a pencil. Carefully, she placed the pencil on the open book. It quickly sank into the glowing page and disappeared.

"W-w-where did it go?" Conner sputtered in utter astonishment.

"I don't know!" Alex said. "I've been dropping things into it all week! Pencils, books, dirty socks, and anything else I could find that I knew I wouldn't miss. I think it may be some kind of portal."

"A portal to *what*?" Conner asked.

Alex didn't have an answer. Of course, there was one location that she had hoped it might lead to.

The twins leaned down even closer to the book, their

noses almost touching it. They had to squint because it was so bright.

Suddenly, a bright red bird flew out of the book. The twins screamed and ran around the room in panic. They bumped into each other, into the walls, and into the sinks as the bird zoomed above them; it was just as panicked as they were. Finally, Conner opened the bathroom door and the bird flew out of the room and into the world.

"You didn't say things came out of it, too!" Conner yelled.

"I didn't know! That's the first time that's happened!" Alex yelled back at him.

The book slowly dimmed and returned to normal. Conner's head was spinning. He couldn't believe all the things he had just witnessed. No wonder Alex was having such a rough week. He now felt his own sanity might be slipping, too.

"We have to get rid of this book!" Conner exclaimed. "After school we should ride our bikes down to the creek and toss it in so no one ever finds it."

"We can't get rid of it!" Alex said. "It's Grandma's book! It's been in our family forever!"

"Birds are flying out of it, Alex! I'm sure she'll understand!" he said. "What if a lion or a shark comes out of it next? I know it drives you crazy when you don't know about stuff, but this is one matter you need to let go. It could be more dangerous than we think! Who knows what could happen?"

She knew her brother was right, but there was something about the whole situation that intrigued her past the point of reason.

"I think you're overreacting," Alex said. "I don't want to get rid of it until I know more about it." She closed the book, put it back in her school bag, and walked out of the restroom.

"Alex! Don't walk away! Alex!" Conner called out after her.

The twins returned to class. All the students were silently reading their history books.

"Alex, we need to talk!" Conner whispered.

"Mr. and Miss Bailey, please have a seat and read the chapter on Mesopotamia," Mrs. Peters ordered from her desk.

"Yes, Mrs. Peters," Alex said, and then turned back to her brother and whispered, "We'll talk about it later, Conner!"

Conner let out a sound similar to something a bear would make.

"Mr. Bailey, how was the nurse?" Mrs. Peters asked.

"There was no need; my elbow started feeling much better before I got there," Conner said, holding the other elbow than the one he had previously claimed was hurting.

Mrs. Peters raised an eyebrow so high, it was almost above her.

The twins sat at their desks and opened their history books, but neither of them could actually read. Their thoughts were so loud, it was impossible to focus on anything.

Conner kept looking up at his sister, hoping she'd turn around so he could make some sort of gesture to make her understand how serious the situation was. Alex could feel her brother's eyes on the back of her head, so she remained facing forward, set on ignoring him.

And then, the worst possible thing that could have happened *happened*. *The Land of Stories* began humming in the quiet classroom from the inside of Alex's bag.

She looked back at her brother, finally making eye contact. What were they going to do? Mrs. Peters had been so caught up in her lesson plan that she hadn't heard it earlier. Was it possible for her to miss it again?

"What is that noise?" Mrs. Peters demanded.

All of the students were looking around the room, wondering the same thing. Alex and Conner were terrified; they felt like their stomachs had fallen out of their bodies.

Mrs. Peters got up from her desk and started searching around the room, like a coyote sniffing out its prey. She walked up and down the aisles of desks, getting closer and closer to Alex.

"If anyone knows what that is, they'd better tell me before I find it," the teacher warned.

Alex could feel her heartbeat in her throat. There was no telling what could happen if her teacher found the book. She could only imagine what a fuss the school would make of the discovery.... Perhaps they'd call the local news stations.... Perhaps government officials would take the book away for experimental testing. . . . Perhaps her family would be taken away because they had been in such close contact with it. . . .

Mrs. Peters arrived at Alex's desk.

"Miss Bailey, is there something in your bag?" she asked her.

All the color in Alex's face drained away. She needed a miracle!

Suddenly, a large history book flew from the back of the classroom and hit Mrs. Peters on the head, leaving a large dent in her curly hair. The entire class turned to the back of the room and saw Conner's extended hand. *He had just thrown a book at their teacher!*

Mrs. Peters's face turned bright red. A charging bull would have seemed harmless compared to the way she was looking at Conner.

"Mr. Bailey! What on earth has gotten into you?" she screamed. The whole school must have heard her.

For a brief moment, Conner saw his entire life flash before his eyes. He honestly thought he was about to die. His face was so white, he was almost transparent.

"I'm sorry, Mrs. Peters!" Conner whimpered. "There was a bee! I didn't mean to hit you!" he lied.

Steam was practically coming out of the teacher's ears and nostrils.

"Detention, Mr. Bailey! For the rest of this week, next week, and the week after that!" Mrs. Peters said. She

returned to her desk and immediately began filling out every detention slip she had in her possession.

Thankfully, the room had become so tense that everyone had forgotten about the humming sound and, even more thankfully, they hadn't noticed it slowly fade away. Conner's mission was accomplished. He knew he'd done the right thing—not as a student, but as a brother.

Soon, the bell rang, and all the students left their desks and filed out of the classroom—except for Conner, who remained seated. Alex walked up to him.

"Thanks for that," she said.

"You owe me one," Conner told her.

She nodded and then left the classroom to walk home alone. Conner remained seated until Mrs. Peters finished filling out the detention slips.

"Come here, Mr. Bailey," she said.

Conner approached her desk as if it were on fire.

"Throwing things in my classroom will never be tolerated; do you understand me, Mr. Bailey?" she said, heavily pronouncing each syllable of each word. "One more incident like that, and I'll have you expelled!"

He gulped and nodded. She handed him a large stack of detention slips.

"Your mother will need to sign all of these," Mrs. Peters told him.

He nodded again. "I'm really sorry," Conner said. "I hope I didn't hurt you." He was so genuine that even Mrs. Peters could sense his regret. She knew that, deep down, Conner had always been a good kid—a horrible student, but a good kid nonetheless.

"It's all right, Mr. Bailey," she said. "I believe I may have underestimated the effect your family situation has had on you and your sister. I'm going to contact your mother with a list of different after-school programs I think you and your sister should take part in, as well as a list of self-help books that may be beneficial."

Conner nodded in agreement.

"I think if you had someplace to escape to once in a while, it'd help you deal with whatever you're going through," she said.

Conner continued nodding. If there was ever a time in his life when he needed an escape from reality, it was now, and he was sure his sister would agree.

And then, like lightning, the thought hit him.

Oh my God, Alex! Conner thought. *She's gonna travel into the book herself! That's why she's been holding on to it! That's why she refused to get rid of it!*

Conner dropped all the detention slips and bolted toward the door.

"I'm sorry, Mrs. Peters, I can't go to detention today! Something has just come up!"

"Mr. Bailey! Get back here right now!" she yelled after him, but it was too late. He was already gone.

Conner was running as fast as he could down the street. Alex had gotten so much of a head start, would he make it home in time to stop her? What if she was already gone by the time he got there? What if he never saw her again? His feet began to ache, a horrible pain grew in his side, and his heart felt like it was beating out of his chest, but he continued running. He just prayed he wasn't too late. . . .

It hadn't been more than five minutes since Alex had gotten home when *The Land of Stories* began acting up again. She ran up the stairs to her bedroom and promptly shut the door behind her.

Alex took *The Land of Stories* out of her school bag and placed it on her bedroom floor. She opened the cover, and her room lit up from its golden glow. She smiled to herself. Alex had always hoped something magical would happen to her, and now something finally was.

She pulled out a pencil from her school bag and placed it on top of the book and watched it disappear. Alex looked around the room for other disposable things she could drop into the book. She was out of pencils, and the books left in her bookshelves were ones she wanted to keep. She looked down at her school bag; she did have plenty of *school bags*.

She placed her whole bag on top of the book and watched as it, too, slowly sank into the storybook. Where were all these things going? Was it transporting them to another part of the world? Would she find a pile of her school supplies in India or China?

Or did the book send the items someplace else entirely? Was it possible they were going to another world? Was it the world that Alex secretly hoped for?

There was only one way to find out.

It was an idea she had managed to suppress all week. What if she went into the book? No, she couldn't possibly do such a stupid thing. What if she never came out?

But what if she stuck her hand into the book? What would happen? Would it hurt? Would her whole arm disappear? Alex's curiosity overruled her caution. She sat on her knees and bent over the book very carefully.

Alex started with just her fingertips. So far, so good. There was no pain; she only felt a warm, tingly sensation. Alex reached farther. She was wrist deep now, and still nothing had happened that worried her. She went farther; the book was up to her elbow. If the book hadn't been there, her hand would surely be sticking through the ceiling downstairs.

Alex leaned forward even farther, almost shoulder deep into the book. She moved her arm around, seeing if there was anything to grab on to inside it.

Suddenly, her bedroom door burst open, and Conner ran inside, sweating and out of breath. "Alex! Don't do it!"

He completely startled her. Alex lost her balance and fell—headfirst into the book!

"AAALLLEEEXXX!" Conner cried out to his sister. He jumped to the ground, trying to grab her foot before she disappeared entirely, but it was too late. Alex had fallen into *The Land of Stories*.

CHAPTER FIVE

FROM THE MOUTH OF A FROG

Alex was no longer in her bedroom. She was falling into a world of light.

She fell farther and farther, faster and faster. She was dizzy and scared. She screamed out for help but couldn't hear her own voice. Would she ever stop falling? Was she going to die? Was she dead? She wondered if she would ever see her family again.

She could hear birds chirping and trees blowing in the wind. The noise seemed to get closer and closer, but she just kept falling and falling, not knowing where she was falling to. . . .

"Ouch!" Alex said, hitting the ground. Her impact was hard enough to hurt but not hard enough to seriously injure her. Had it not been for the rough landing, she would have thought she was dreaming for sure.

Alex quickly got to her feet. She felt her pulse to make sure her heart was still working; she was still alive, from what she could tell. She was so thankful to have finally stopped falling . . . but where exactly had she fallen to?

She was standing on a dirt path in the middle of a thick forest. The trees were tall and dark with bright green moss covering their trunks. The sun's rays shined through a light mist. Birds squawked from high in the trees and, if she listened closely enough, she could hear a tiny stream in the distance.

Alex spun around, looking in all directions. Her breathing increased as she took in her new surroundings. Was she overreacting or not reacting enough to what had just happened? And what exactly *had* just happened?

She looked up to see if there was an opening she had fallen through, hoping to see some sort of window into her bedroom, but all she saw were tree branches and the sky above her.

"Where am I?" she asked herself.

"AAAAAAAAAAHHHHHHHH!" As if he had fallen right out of thin air, Conner landed hard on the ground beside his sister. He was pale and screaming, and his limbs were stretched out in all directions. "Am I alive? Am I dying? Am I dead?" he asked from the ground with his eyes tightly closed.

"You're alive!" Alex told him. She had never been so happy to see him.

"Alex, is that you?" Conner asked. He slowly opened his eyes one at a time and looked around. "Where are we?" he asked as she helped him to his feet.

"It looks like some kind of... forest," she said.

It was unlike any forest they had ever seen—in real life, at least. The colors were so vivid and the air was so crisp. It was as if they had fallen into a painting, a painting Alex was positive she had seen before.

"Look," Conner said, pointing at the ground. "All of our pencils!"

The path was littered with the pencils Alex had been dropping into the book all week. She also found her school bag and a few of her dirty socks in the middle of the mess. But where were all the books she had dropped into *The Land of Stories*?

"So this is where they all went!" Alex said.

"But where is *here*?" Conner asked. "How far away from home are we?"

Alex couldn't answer him. She was starting to become just as worried as he was. They were worse than lost.

"This is all your fault, Alex!" he said.

"My fault?" Alex yelled. "We wouldn't be here if you

had just knocked on my door instead of barging in like the house was on fire!"

"I knew you were planning this," Conner said. "I had to stop you!"

"I wasn't planning on going into the book. I was just testing it out!" Alex explained. "You didn't have to follow me here."

"Oh, sure! Was I just supposed to leave you in the book by yourself?" he exclaimed. "What was I supposed tell Mom when she got home? 'Hi, Mom, hope you had a good day at work. Alex fell through a book. By the way, what's for dinner?' Give me a break!"

Conner began jumping upward as high as he could.

"What are you doing?" Alex asked.

"We fell. From. Somewhere. Up here. There's. Got. To. be. A way. Back," he said, but all his jumping was pointless. Conner eventually tired himself out, and he took a seat on the ground against a tree trunk.

"What if we were transported to another country or something?" Conner asked; his forehead became more wrinkled the further he thought about it. "What if it took us to Canada or Mongolia or somewhere? How long is it gonna take for Mom or someone to find us?"

Suddenly, the ground started shaking. A powerful rumbling had consumed the forest. The branches of the trees shook, and the small rocks on the ground began jumping as something massive moved closer toward them.

"What's happening now?" Conner yelled.

"Let's take cover!" Alex said.

She grabbed her bag, and the twins ran off the path and into the forest a little way and took refuge behind a particularly wide tree.

They couldn't believe what they were seeing. A huge cavalcade of soldiers on white horses rode past them. Their armor was clean and shiny. They carried green-and-silver shields with large red apples painted on them and waved flags with the same design.

"Alex, did we go back in time?" Conner anxiously asked his sister. "That looks like something straight out of medieval times!"

The pencils were all obliterated under the horses' hooves. The soldiers were moving at such a fast and forceful pace that none of them noticed the awestruck twins peeking out from behind the tree.

Alex was fixated on their shields. A red apple was such an odd thing to be displayed on a shield, but there was something so familiar about it. She couldn't put her finger on it.

The rumbling slowly faded away as the soldiers disappeared down the dirt path. The twins both stayed behind the tree for a few moments, making sure the coast was clear.

"I don't know about you, but I've had about as much excitement as I can handle for one day," Conner told Alex.

A poster pinned to a nearby tree caught Alex's eye. She walked over to it and pulled it off the tree for further inspection. It was old, with faded writing, and a picture of a disgruntled-looking little girl with curly blonde hair was centered on it. The poster read:

WANTED
DEAD OR ALIVE
GOLDILOCKS
FOR BURGLARY, THIEVERY, AND
RUNNING FROM THE LAW

Alex's face went white, and she stopped breathing for a moment; she had realized where they were. No wonder the trees had been so recognizable. She had seen pictures of them so many times growing up. The book had taken them to the exact place she had hoped.

"Is it possible?" she asked herself. The wheels in her head had never spun as fast as they were now.

"Is what possible?" Conner asked. "Do you know where we are?"

"I think so," Alex told him.

"Where?" Conner asked, fearing the answer.

"Conner, we went *into* the book," she explained, but he wasn't following her. "I think we're actually *in* the Land of Stories."

She handed him the Wanted poster, and he read it. His eyes grew as wide as a lemur's.

"No no no! This cannot be happening! This is crazy!" he said, shaking his head. He handed the poster back to his sister as if it were infected with rabies. He couldn't believe what she was saying; he didn't want to believe what she was saying. "Are you telling me we're in the fairy-tale world?"

"I'd recognize this forest anywhere! It's straight out of Grandma's book," Alex said with an unplanned smile. "But it makes perfect sense! Where else would it have taken us?"

"We just fell through a book! *Nothing* makes sense!" Conner said. "So, are we stuck here or what? How do we get home?"

"I don't have all of your answers, Conner," Alex said. "Don't forget, all of this just happened to me, too!"

Conner began pacing around the trees with his hands on his hips. "I can't believe I ditched detention and wound up in another dimension," he said.

Alex was rather grateful her brother had come after her. They had lived together all their lives and had been in the same classrooms since kindergarten. She didn't know if she could handle being in a different dimension by herself.

"I hope you're happy, Alex," Conner said. "I told you we should have thrown the book into the creek!"

"Enough with the blaming," Alex said. "It doesn't matter how we got here, the point is we're here now. What matters is finding someone who can help us get home!"

"Excuse me, may I help you?" said a proper voice behind the twins. They jolted at the sound of another voice besides their own. They turned around to see who it had come from, and once they saw, they both wished they hadn't.

Standing behind Alex and Conner was what could best be described as a frog man. He was tall, with a wide face, big, glossy eyes, and shiny green skin. He wore a dapper three-piece suit and carried a large glass jar of lily pads.

"Forgive me for eavesdropping, but I'm rather good with directions if you need some," he said with a very wide smile.

Alex and Conner were so petrified that they were paralyzed. If they needed any more evidence that they were in the fairy-tale world, this was their proof.

"You look awfully young to be in the forest by yourselves," the frog man said. "Are you lost?"

Conner let out a high-pitched squeal that lasted much longer than it should have. "Please don't eat us!" he said, and dropped to the ground in a fetal position.

The frog man looked down at him with a frown. "Young man, I have no intention of eating you," he said. "Is he always like this?" the frog man asked Alex.

Alex responded with a squeal almost identical to the one her brother had made.

"I know, I know. Don't worry; I'm used to people screaming at me," the frog man told them. "Get it out of your systems. The shock will only last a minute."

"We're sorry!" Alex finally managed to say. "It's just that, where we're from there aren't many...um...frog people? Sorry if that isn't the politically correct term for what you are!"

Conner let out another high-pitched noise. It wasn't a scream this time, but it was embarrassing nonetheless.

The frog man studied their faces and paid special attention to their clothes. "Where exactly are you from?"

"Pretty far from here," Alex said.

A piercing set of wolf howls echoed through the forest. All three of them jumped at the sound. The frog man looked around the trees with fear in his big, glossy eyes.

"It's getting dark," the frog man said. "We'd better get inside. Please, follow me home. It's just a few minutes' walk from here."

"Nice try!" Conner said.

The wolf howls echoed again. This time they were much louder than the first. Wherever the wolves were, they were getting closer.

"I know I look scary now," said the frog man to the twins, "but I'm nothing compared to some of the creatures that lurk around these woods at night. I promise I will not harm you."

There was such concern in his eyes, it was hard not to trust him. The frog man took off at a brisk walk deeper into the forest.

Alex nudged Conner. "We'd better follow him."

"Are you crazy? I'm not going home with the giant frog!" Conner whispered to her.

"What do we have to lose?" Alex asked.

"Besides our lives?" Conner said, but, despite his protests, he was dragged up by his sister and pulled in the direction the frog man was leading them.

The twins hurried behind the frog man for a good while. They zigzagged between trees and jumped over boulders and tree roots that stuck up from the ground. The deeper they went into the forest, the thicker the trees became. It got dark very quickly and was almost pitch-black by the time they reached the frog man's home.

Alex and Conner stayed close together. With every step they second-guessed if they had made a smart choice going with this strange creature.

"This way," he said.

The frog man brushed aside some dead vines growing over a large wooden door that was camouflaged into the side of a small hill. He pulled the door open and led the hesitant twins underground. He looked back into the forest, making sure they hadn't been followed, before shutting the door behind him.

It was very dark underground. Alex and Conner were so close together, they could have been mistaken for Siamese twins.

"Forgive the mess. I wasn't expecting company," the frog man apologized, and lit a lamp with a match.

Alex and Conner didn't know what to expect of the frog man's home, but what they were seeing definitely wasn't it.

They were in a large room with dirt walls and a low, dirt ceiling. Roots from a tree growing above them grew down like a chandelier. A cluster of big, cushy chairs and sofas—many of the cushions had the stuffing sticking out of them—sat in the center of the room and were angled to face a small fireplace. Nearby, teacups and pots hung from hooks over a tiny kitchenette.

To Alex's delight, there were books everywhere. Shelves of books lined the dirt walls; piles of books were stacked on every available surface and on the ground; it was as if the room were infested with literature.

"Conner," Alex whispered close to him. "Look around at this place! It's like we're having our own Lucy and Mr. Tumnus moment!"

Conner looked around and saw what she meant. "If he offers us Turkish delight, I don't care what you say: We're getting out of here!" he whispered back.

"It's a little dirty, but it's cozy," the frog man said. "It's hard to find a landlord who will house a frog, so I did the best I could with what I had."

He placed his jar of lily pads on the mantel and immediately started a fire in the fireplace. He filled a teakettle with water from a pitcher, placed it over the fire, and took a seat in a big, white chair closest to it. He crossed his legs and folded his hands neatly in his lap. He was one proper frog.

"Please have a seat," the frog man said, gesturing to the

sofa in front of him. The twins reluctantly did as he asked. The sofa was rather lumpy, so they had to shift around in their seats to get comfortable.

"What are you?" Conner asked the frog.

"Conner, don't be rude!" said his sister, elbowing him in the side.

"It's quite all right," the frog man said with a complicated smile. "I understand my appearance takes some time to get used to. Even I haven't fully adapted to it yet."

"You mean, you weren't always a...um...frog person?" Alex asked as politely as she could.

"Heavens, no," the frog man said. "I was cursed years ago by a very aggressive witch."

"Why?" Alex asked. She was fascinated by how casually he had said it.

"To teach me a lesson, I suppose," the frog man told her. "I used to be a very vain young man. The witch transformed my appearance so I would lose all of the things I took for granted."

His wide smile softly faded. It had obviously been a very long and painful experience for him, and he still had a sad sense of loss and longing about him. The twins had never seen a frog look so sad.

"I can't even imagine what that must have been like," said Alex, beaming with sympathy.

"Can we call you Froggy?" Conner asked with a small smirk.

"Conner!" Alex reprimanded.

"It's quite all right." The frog man nodded, and his smile returned. "I've learned that the more people embrace their disadvantages, the less disadvantaged they become! Please, call me Froggy. I'd prefer it."

Conner shrugged and smiled.

"May I get you some lily pad tea?" Froggy asked the twins.

Both the twins nodded; they didn't want to be rude. Froggy retrieved the teakettle from the fire and hopped—literally—to the kitchenette and poured water into three teacups. He opened the jar on the mantel and dropped a lily pad into each teacup and stirred.

"Do either of you take flies with your tea?" he asked, reaching for another jar on his mantel, this one filled with dead flies.

"No thanks," Conner said. "Trying to quit."

"Suit yourself," Froggy said, and dropped a few flies into his tea. He handed them each a teacup and reseated himself across from them. They stared down at it for a few moments before deciding they'd at least pretend to drink it.

"What are your names?" Froggy asked the twins.

"I'm Alex and this is my brother, Conner."

A large and happy smile came to Froggy's face.

"Are you by any chance Alex Bailey?" Froggy asked, grinning from ear equivalent to ear equivalent.

"Um...yes." Alex was shocked. How did this amphibian know who she was?

"As in 'This book belongs to Alex Bailey'?" Froggy

asked. He leaned over the side of his chair and pulled up a stack of books, opening one to show where the phrase was written inside it.

"Those are my books!" Alex said excitedly, recognizing the books she had dropped into *The Land of Stories.* "I was wondering what had happened to them."

"It was so peculiar," Froggy explained. "I was out collecting flies and was walking down the path to the swamp when one just fell from the sky and landed on my head. I returned the next day and found several more in the same spot. It was the oddest thing that's ever happened to me!"

"You mean, besides being turned into a frog, right?" Conner asked. "Because if I were you, that would be on the top of my list—*ouch*!" Alex elbowed her brother.

Froggy ignored Conner and went on with his explanation.

"As you can see from my shelves, I love to collect books, especially when I'm not expecting to," he said. "And these books were unlike any I had ever read! They described people and places I had never seen or heard of, and I thought I had seen it all! The authors wrote about such interesting places. Could you imagine a world without witches or trolls or giants? What imaginations!"

Froggy chuckled at the thought of this. The twins laughed along with the best fake laughs they could muster.

"Please keep them. I have duplicate copies at home," Alex told him.

Froggy was delighted to hear this.

"Uh-huh." Conner cleared his throat. "Speaking of home, I don't mean to interrupt this little book club, but we're very lost and would like to know where we are."

Froggy's glossy eyes went back and forth between the twins, watching them closely.

"Oh, children, you wouldn't be here if you knew where you were," Froggy said. "You're in the Dwarf Forests."

He had expected to get some sort of worried reaction from the twins, but Alex and Conner just stared up at him with very little expression.

"The Dwarf Forests?" Alex asked. "What are the Dwarf Forests?"

"You've never heard of them?" Froggy asked, completely appalled. The twins both shook their heads.

"It's a very dangerous place," Froggy told them. "It's the only designated area of land without a ruler or a government; it's a kingdom where everyone is their own king. It used to be populated by dwarfs who worked in the mines, but now it's full of criminals and fugitives mostly. It's a place where people go when they don't want to be found."

Knowing they had not only traveled into another world but were in a dangerous part of that world did nothing to help the twins' anxiety level.

"Are there other kingdoms?" Alex asked.

Froggy was stunned. It was as if she had asked him what color the sky was. However, he seemed to be enjoying their unfamiliarity.

"Of course," he said. "There's the Northern Kingdom,

the Sleeping Kingdom, the Charming Kingdom, the Corner Kingdom, the Fairy Kingdom, the Red Riding Hood Kingdom, the Elf Empire, the Dwarf Forests, and the Troll and Goblin Territory. How can you possibly not know this?"

This was difficult for the twins to wrap their heads around. How big was the fairy-tale world?

Their puzzled faces inspired Froggy to hop out of his seat and cross to one of the bookshelves and return with a large, rolled-up scroll. He handed it to the twins, and they unrolled it.

It was a large, detailed map of the new world they were in. The fairy-tale world was a wide continent bordered by mountain ranges and covered in forests with castles and palaces and villages scattered all around.

The Northern Kingdom was the largest of the kingdoms and took up most of the top of the map. The second largest was the Charming Kingdom, spread across to the south, and the third largest was the Sleeping Kingdom, which stretched along the east. The Dwarf Forests covered the majority of the west.

The tiny Corner Kingdom was tucked away in the southwest corner of the continent, and in the northwest corner was the Elf Empire. In between the Charming Kingdom and the Sleeping Kingdom was the Fairy Kingdom, and just above that was the Troll and Goblin Territory.

The Fairy Kingdom looked beautiful, as it was very colorful and seemed to sparkle on the map. The Troll and

Goblin Territory looked frightening and appeared to be surrounded by large boulders and rocks, preventing anything from going in or coming out.

In the very center of it all was the Red Riding Hood Kingdom, circled by an unmistakable brick wall of gigantic proportions.

Alex and Conner couldn't believe it. The world they had grown up hearing about was real. It was *all* real, and it was bigger and better than they ever could have imagined.

Alex couldn't help but get emotional. Tears began to flood her eyes.

"Together, all the kingdoms create the Happily Ever After Assembly," Froggy explained.

"The Happily Ever After Assembly?" Conner asked with a slight touch of sarcasm in his voice.

"It's the organization formed to uphold the treaty all the rulers signed so that all the kingdoms could live in peace and prosperity," Froggy told them.

"Sounds like our United Nations," Alex whispered to Conner.

"All the kingdoms have their own traditions and celebrated histories," Froggy went on.

"And there are kings and queens, I'm assuming?" Conner asked.

"Oh, yes," Froggy said. "The Northern Kingdom is ruled by Queen Snow White. The Corner Kingdom is watched over by Queen Rapunzel. The Sleeping Kingdom—formerly known as the Eastern Kingdom, but renamed after the dreadful curse under which it was placed—is governed by Queen Sleeping Beauty. And of course, the Charming Kingdom is ruled by King Charming and his wife, Queen Cinderella."

"Wait, are these the current monarchs?" Alex asked, with a spark of excitement in her eyes. "You mean Cinderella, Snow White, Sleeping Beauty...they're all still alive?"

"Of course they are!" Froggy said.

"Oh my goodness, that's wonderful!" Alex said excitedly. "Isn't that wonderful, Conner?"

"Whatever," Conner mumbled.

"How old do you think they are?" Froggy asked. "Queen Snow White and King Charming have only been married a few years. Queen Cinderella and King Charming are expecting their first child soon. Queen Sleeping Beauty and King Charming are sadly still trying to restore their kingdom to consciousness after that horrible sleeping spell it was placed under."

"Wait," Conner said. "Are you saying all these queens are married to the same guy?"

"Certainly not," Froggy said. "There are three King Charmings. They're brothers."

"Of course!" Alex said. "Snow White, Cinderella, and Sleeping Beauty all married *Prince Charming*! There's more than one! How come I never thought about that?"

Conner's eyes were fixated on the map. He kept searching for some kind of road or bridge that would lead them back home, but he found nothing.

"Why are there a bunch of rocks around the Troll and Goblin Territory?" Conner asked.

"As punishment," Froggy said. "Trolls and goblins are nasty creatures and have a habit of kidnapping people and turning them into slaves. The Fairy Council forced the trolls and goblins into one territory, and none of them are allowed to leave without permission."

"Fairy Council?" Alex asked. This world was almost too good to be true.

"Yes, they're a group of the most powerful fairies of the kingdoms," Froggy explained. "Cinderella's Fairy God-mother is one of them, and so is Mother Goose, and all the fairies that blessed Sleeping Beauty when she was a baby are on it, too. They rule the Fairy Kingdom and are the leaders of the Happily Ever After Assembly."

"Is the Red Riding Hood Kingdom under some sort of punishment, too?" Conner asked. "Why is there a huge wall built around it?"

Alex looked down at the map and back up at Froggy, equally curious.

"That was a result of the C.R.A.W.L. Revolution," Froggy said.

"What was the crawl revolution?" Alex asked.

"The Citizen Riots Against Wolf Liberty," Froggy explained. "The Red Riding Hood Kingdom used to be a group of villages in the Northern Kingdom that were constantly under attack by wolves. They begged the Evil Queen—Snow White's stepmother, who was on the throne at the time—to help them. But the Evil Queen was too occupied with her vanity, so they revolted and started their own kingdom. They built a huge wall around it so no wolves could get in."

"And now Red Riding Hood is the queen?" Alex asked.

"Yes, she's the only elected queen in history," Froggy said. "The villagers figured her story was the most symbolic of their struggle, so they chose her to lead them."

"But isn't she just a little girl?" Alex asked.

"No, she's a young woman now. A very self-obsessed young woman, from what I hear. After all, she named the kingdom after herself! Her grandmother does most of the decision-making while she takes all the credit," Froggy said. "Unfortunately the C.R.A.W.L. Revolution only led to the rise of the Big Bad Wolf Pack."

"The Big Bad Wolf Pack?" Conner asked.

"Yes, they're the descendants of the original Big Bad Wolf. They travel around terrorizing villages and attacking unsuspecting travelers," Froggy said.

"Oh joy!" Conner said sarcastically. "I'm sorry I asked."

"But besides that, things are very peaceful throughout the kingdoms," Froggy said. His voice drifted off, and uncertainty grew on his face. "That was, until a week ago."

The twins leaned forward.

"What happened a week ago?" Alex asked.

"The Evil Queen escaped from the dungeons of Snow White's palace," Froggy told them. "I thought everyone had heard."

"It's news to us," Conner said.

"That can't be good," Alex said. "How'd she escape?"

"No one knows," Froggy said. "She just vanished, along with her Magic Mirror. Snow White's army has been searching throughout all of the kingdoms for her. They pass through these woods at least twice a day. So far they've found nothing, not even a footprint, to lead them in her direction."

"Do you think they're going to find her?" Conner asked.

"I hope so," Froggy said. "She's a very dangerous woman. She's the only queen in history to lose her throne; I couldn't imagine the revenge she must be seeking. Who knows what she's planning to do next?"

Alex suddenly became very tense. It had just occurred to her that, along with all the characters she had grown up loving, all the ones she hated and feared actually existed, too. It made her feel very uneasy and very unsafe.

The fire in the fireplace began to fade, and Froggy got up to add another log. The twins' eyes and mouths were wide open, and their heads were spinning from all of this new information.

"Exactly how far away do you live from here?" Froggy asked as he sat back down across from them.

The twins looked to each other, back at Froggy, and then back at each other. They didn't know what to tell him. Would he believe them if they told him the truth?

"It's practically a different world," Conner said. Alex

shot him a dirty look and then nervously laughed, trying to make light of what her brother just said.

Froggy wasn't laughing. He sat straight up in his seat and his face grew very still with an intensity in his eyes, as if he had found the solution to a mystery.

"Interesting," Froggy said, eyeing the twins back and forth. "Because, if I didn't know better, just from the way you dress and the way you speak—and the way you were so surprised at basic history—I would say that there was a very good chance you are indeed from a different world."

They didn't understand what he was trying to say. Did he know something that they didn't?

"Just out of curiosity, have you ever heard of another world?" Alex asked him.

"Or, preferably, how to get back to it?" Conner added.

Froggy studied their faces even more intently for a moment. He got up again and went to a bookshelf on the far side of the room. He rustled through the books, looking for something of special interest. Finally, he found it: a small leather-bound journal with a red band around it.

"Have either of you ever heard of the Wishing Spell?" Froggy asked the twins.

Alex and Conner shook their heads. Froggy flipped through the pages of the journal.

"I assumed not," he said. "It's a legendary spell comprised of a list of items, and, apparently, when you put the items together, you are granted one wish. It doesn't matter how extravagant the wish is, the Wishing Spell will grant it. Many people believe that it's only a myth, and I did, too, until I found this journal."

"What does that journal have to do with anything?" Conner asked.

"It was written by a man from the Charming Kingdom," Froggy said. "He managed to discover what these items were, and he recorded his journey to find them. His one wish was to reunite with the woman he loved, and in the journal he claimed she lived in 'another world.'"

Alex and Conner sat straight up. They were sitting on the edges of their seats without realizing it.

"I thought the man writing the journal was crazy. I didn't believe another world could exist, until I began finding your books, Alex. And then when I saw you bickering in the forest, I knew you two were different," Froggy said. "I knew you had to be from the place that the man had written about."

The twins were happy the truth was out. Froggy seemed genuinely excited about the whole thing.

"Did he make it?" Alex asked. "Did the man cross over into the other world?"

"He must have," Froggy said. "The journal ends when he found the last item." Froggy handed the twins the journal and took a seat in his chair. "Wherever you're from, if it's home that you wish to go back to, I think your best chance is by following this journal."

The twins went silent for a moment. They stared down at the journal in his hands with immense hope.

"What items does the spell require?" Alex asked.

"All sorts, from all over," Froggy told her. "But the journal gives great instructions on where and how to find them. Some of them are very dangerous to get to."

"Of course they are," Conner said. "Typical."

"If the spell will grant whatever wish you want, why didn't you search for the items and wish to be human again?" Alex asked Froggy.

Froggy thought about this for a moment. It was a question he had asked himself many times, and he was ashamed of the answer.

"I've kept the journal all these years in case I ever decided to," Froggy explained with difficulty. "But searching for the items would mean I'd have to face the world looking like this and, frankly, children, that's something I'm not ready to do. It's something I don't think I'll ever be able to do."

He spoke from a place of deep sadness. Clearly he wasn't finished learning the witch's lesson yet.

"It's getting late," Froggy said. "Why don't you sleep on it and decide what you want to do in the morning. You're welcome to stay here as long as you'd like."

"Thank you," Alex said. "I hope we aren't a bother."

"No bother at all." Froggy smiled earnestly.

Froggy got them a large blanket to share. He blew out all the lamps and put out the fire in the fireplace.

Alex and Conner tossed and turned with thoughts of the Wishing Spell all night, but there was no decision to make. If the journal offered a possible way home, they would have to do anything and everything it instructed them to. They had no choice.

They were about to embark on the greatest scavenger hunt of their lives.

CHAPTER SIX

THE DWARF FORESTS

I packed you some food, a couple of blankets, and a few gold coins I've been saving," Froggy told the twins, and handed Conner a sheepskin satchel.

"Thank you so much," Alex said. "It's so kind of you!"

"Now, when you say *food*, what exactly are you referring to?" Conner asked, holding the satchel a safe distance away from him.

"Some rolls and apples," Froggy told him.

"Oh, good," Conner said, relieved.

Froggy handed Alex the map and journal they had been looking at the previous night.

"Are you sure you're ready for this?" Froggy asked them. "You're both awfully young to be going on a quest like this."

Alex and Conner looked to each other, each thinking the same thing. It was hard enough to navigate around their own world at their age; could they really travel around a different world altogether without the help of an adult? But the twins found reassurance in each other's eyes; they knew that, through it all, they'd at least have each other.

"We really don't have any other choice," Alex said. "Thank you so much for all your help, Froggy. We would still be lost in the woods without you."

Froggy smiled widely and nodded.

"Of course," he said. "I should be thanking you. I rarely have an opportunity to feel so useful."

"Are you sure you don't want to come with us?" Alex asked. "A map is great and all, but a tour guide would be better."

At first, Froggy's smile grew with excitement as he was tempted by the idea. The thought of traveling out into the world and leaving his hole-in-the-ground home was so alluring, it was clear he could feel the temptation throughout his entire body. However, his fears and insecurities about the outside world seeing him and what he had become erased the opportunity from his mind.

"I can't, children," Froggy said with a heavy heart. "But I wish you the best."

The twins were disappointed, but they understood. It

was difficult for them even to go to school with just a small blemish on their faces; they couldn't imagine the stress of facing the world as an enormous amphibian.

"It's very important that you get out of the Dwarf Forests by sundown," Froggy instructed. "Go to the path and travel south into the Corner Kingdom. It's a few hours' walk, but you'll be safer there. Travel as quickly and quietly as you can. Promise me."

The twins promised. Alex gave Froggy a big hug and kissed his cheek. Conner shook his hand and then wiped it on his pants.

"I hope we see each other again," Alex told him.

"That would be lovely, but for your sakes, I hope we don't," Froggy said, and winked.

Conner clapped his hands. "All right, those items for the Wishing Spell aren't gonna find themselves," he said. "Let's go."

The twins pushed open the door and climbed up from inside the underground home. As they headed into the forest, Froggy waved good-bye until he was out of their sight. Soon, they were back on the dirt path they had landed on the previous day, and they headed south as they had been instructed.

It was very unnerving for the twins to be alone on the path now that they understood the dangers of the forest. They regretted not trying harder to persuade Froggy into coming with them. They jumped at every tiny sound the trees made.

Alex and Conner remained silent for the first hour or so as they walked, afraid that their voices would attract unwanted attention from some of the creatures Froggy had warned them about.

"We're very brave," Alex finally said to her brother, breaking the silence.

"Or very stupid," Conner said.

The path curved through the forest, revealing new trees and bushes every few feet. After some time had passed, the twins could feel their nerves and tension calm. Their pace became slower and slower the more they walked, as they become more comfortable with being in the forest.

Conner let out a long sigh.

"What's that for?" Alex asked him.

"I was just thinking," Conner said. "Alice went to Wonderland after she fell into a rabbit hole. Dorothy's whole house was scooped up by a tornado that dropped her off in Oz. The Narnia kids traveled through an old wardrobe... and we ended up in the fairy-tale world by *falling through a book*."

"Where are you going with this, Conner?" Alex said.

"I'm just saying, it's kind of lame compared to the others," Conner said with another sigh. "I wonder if there's a support group for people like us? You know, people who accidentally travel into other dimensions and whatnot."

Alex was appalled.

"Do you not get how lucky we are?" she said. "Think about all the things we're going to see! Think about all the people we're going to meet! We're going to be experiencing things *no one* else in our world ever has!"

Conner rolled his eyes. "I'll feel lucky as soon as we get back home."

Alex reached into her bag and pulled out their map. Her eyes became fixated on it, and she only looked up every minute or so to make sure she wasn't about to walk into a tree. Every few seconds she'd snicker or smile when she discovered something new. She looked like a *tourist*.

"Shouldn't we be reading the journal?" Conner asked. "We need to make a list of the Wishing Spell items and find out where we can find them."

"We will," Alex said passively. "There'll be plenty of time for that."

Conner was getting frustrated with her. Did she not realize how serious the situation was?

"We need to go home," Conner said. "What are we waiting for?"

"There are just a couple things I would like to see before we go home," Alex told him.

"What are you talking about?" Conner said, his volume and temper rising.

"We're in the fairy-tale world, Conner. We should make the most of it while we're here!" Alex said. "Who else gets the chance to see Cinderella's palace or Jack's beanstalk or Rapunzel's tower in person?"

Conner's mouth and eyes were wide open. He couldn't believe what his sister was saying.

"We're stuck in another world, and you want to go *sightseeing*?" he said. "Are you hearing yourself right now? Do you know how crazy you sound?"

She stopped walking and turned to face her brother. There was seriousness and desperation in her eyes.

"Conner, the last year of our lives has been horrible. We've lost everything but Mom and each other," Alex said. "Every night, I've wished for a fairy godmother to magically appear and make everything better, and now we're in a place where that is a possibility! I don't have friends to go home to like you do. The only friends I've ever known live here, and I'm not going home until I meet them!"

Alex continued walking down the path. Conner was absolutely dumbstruck.

"Why am I being the logical one?" Conner questioned. "You're always over-thinking everything! How are you not out of your mind with worry?"

"What's there to be worried about?" Alex asked with a laugh.

"For starters, what's Mom gonna do when she finds out we're missing?" Conner pointed out. "She'll think we were kidnapped! And she has enough to worry about already!"

Alex knew he was right, but her desire to see the fairy-tale world was so strong that she was able to ignore him.

"All I need is a day or two," Alex said. "That'll give us plenty of time."

"How are you so sure these worlds run on the same time schedule?" Conner panicked. "Think about it, the stories of Cinderella and Red Riding Hood have been around for hundreds of years in our world, but it only seems like a decade or less has gone by here since! A couple days here and Mom may be in her eighties when we get home!"

Conner rubbed his head; it hurt from thinking so hard. Alex was listening more than she wanted to. He was practically repeating word for word what the logical voices in her head were saying.

"What if something happens while we're gone?" Conner asked. "What if we get back and apes or aliens have taken over our planet? If I miss *that*, I will never forgive you!"

Alex stopped walking and looked up from the map. A very odd expression appeared on her face.

"Didn't think of that, did you?" Conner asked her, but Alex wasn't listening to him. Something else entirely had caught her attention.

"Do you smell that?" Alex asked.

"What?" Conner said. "All I smell are trees and dirt."

Alex took a couple steps further. "No, it's something else. It's sweet, like something's baking."

Conner sniffed. Sure enough, a scrumptious smell was drifting through the air.

"It smells like . . . *gingerbread*!" Alex said. She looked at her brother with large, excited eyes.

"Oh no," Conner said.

Before he could stop her, Alex took off running into the trees, away from the path, toward the direction the aroma was coming from.

"Alex, wait!" Conner ordered. "Come back! You don't know where you're going!"

Alex bolted through the trees, jumping over boulders and bushes as she passed them. The scent became stronger and stronger the farther she strayed from the path. Conner was right behind her, urging her to turn around. Finally, Alex came to a halt, and Conner bumped into her. She had found exactly what she was hoping to see.

A small gingerbread house sat in between two large trees. White frosting covered its pointed roof, gumdrops were clumped around like shrubbery, and candy canes lined the path to the front door like a picket fence.

"Look, Conner!" Alex said, catching her breath. "It's a gingerbread house, a *real* gingerbread house! Look how cute it is!"

"Whoa," Conner said. "I feel like I may get diabetes from just looking at that place."

"Let's go inside!" Alex said, and stepped toward the house.

Conner grabbed her arm. "Have you lost your mind? Do the words *Hansel and Gretel cannibalism incident* mean anything to you?"

"I just want to peek inside for a second, only one second—"

The door of the gingerbread house slowly opened. Alex and Conner froze. A large, hooded figure squeezed out of the door and then raised its head to stare at the twins.

It was, undoubtedly, a witch, and although they had

never seen a real witch to make a comparison to, she was more grotesque than they could have imagined. Her skin was wrinkled and pale with a yellowish tint. Her eyes were bloodshot and bulged out of her head. She was hunched over and had an enormous hump on her back.

"Hello, children," the witch said. Her voice was high-pitched and crackly. "Would you care to join me for a bite to eat?"

It was impossible for the twins to hide their fear; they both stood still staring at her as if she were a rabid Tyrannosaurus rex about to pounce on them at any moment.

"No, thank you," Alex said. "We're just passing by. *You have a lovely home.*"

They slowly backed up, one foot at a time.

"Wouldn't you like to see the inside?" the witch asked.

"The inside of whom?" Conner said, and Alex elbowed him.

"Don't be silly, kiddies, *come inside*," said the witch, losing her patience. She extended an inviting, shaking hand toward them. They noticed it was covered in burn marks, perhaps from the last time she'd had visitors.

"I thought the witch died at the end of 'Hansel and Gretel,'" Alex whispered to Conner.

"Maybe she got hold of a fire extinguisher after they left," Conner whispered back.

They continued backing slowly away from her.

"Thank you so much for the invitation, but we really need to get going," Alex said.

"We're on a really tight schedule," Conner added. "We're meeting a couple of dwarfs for coffee in a half hour, so we better get a move on!"

They quickly took off in the direction they'd come, but came to a jarring stop when the witch suddenly appeared in front of them with a *pop!* They tried running back the other way, but the witch just appeared in front of them again with a *snap!* They were trapped.

"You aren't going anywhere," the witch said. She seemed to grow taller, and her eyes bulged bigger as her patience ran out. "Now, be nice little chickies and follow me *inside*."

"Alex, this is like one of those bad videos about strangers from the first grade," Conner whispered to her. "Do you still have your kidnapping whistle?"

"You don't want to eat us!" Alex told the witch. "We've been walking for a while, so we're really dehydrated! We're practically just skin and bone."

The witch was definitely growing. Her hump shrank as her body rose higher.

"Your friend seems to be rather plump," the witch said, looking at Conner like a praying mantis about to strike. "He has more than enough to spare!" She was practically salivating.

"I beg your pardon?" Conner was so offended, he forgot how terrifying she was. "I'll have you know I'm on the edge of another growth spurt, and I always get a little pudgy before one!"

"Conner, please don't—" Alex tried, but was too late.

"Why do you want your victims chubby, anyway? Wouldn't it be healthier if they were muscular and fit?" Conner said.

The witch looked to the side and raised an eyebrow. She had never considered this. Her consideration must have distracted her from attacking the twins, because she began to shrink back to her normal, humped shape.

"If you ask me," Conner continued, "you should turn your gingerbread house into a gingerbread gym and health club!"

Alex often couldn't believe the crazy things that her brother said, but this one took the cake.

"What a *delicious* idea," the witch cackled. "I'll rebuild as soon as I'm finished with *you*."

The witch began to grow again. This time her mouth opened wide and a set of jagged teeth grew out of it. She was going in for the attack.

Alex screamed, *"Wait!"* With her hands covering her face, she said, *"You owe him!"*

The witch recoiled into her smaller form. "I owe him?" she asked.

"Yes! Isn't that how it works?" Alex said. "He presented you with an idea, and now you owe him a *wish*!"

"A wish?" the witch asked.

"A wish?" Conner asked.

Alex nodded convincingly. The witch grunted.

"Yes, the Happily Ever After Assembly just enacted a new law," Alex said, thinking on the tips of her toes. "Any witch presented with a good idea must return the favor by granting a wish."

"Um...yeah," said Conner, going along with it. "Don't make Mother Goose fly down here. She'll let her geese loose on you, and some of them lay golden eggs, and that can't feel good. Who knows how aggressive they'll be?"

"Fine," the witch said. "I shall grant you *one* wish. But only because I don't want to deal with those fluttering freaks...*again*."

Conner leaned close to his sister. "What should I wish for? Should I wish to go home?" he whispered.

"No, she'll try to trick us with whatever we wish for! It has to be really specific!" Alex said.

"Hurry, child! I'm hungry!" the witch demanded.

"Okay..." said Conner, thinking as fast as he could. It had to be a good one; it had to help them get out of the situation. "I wish you would become a *vegetarian*!" he said to the witch.

Alex turned her head sharply toward her brother. "That's what you picked?"

"Very well," the witch shrieked. The twins weren't sure if she knew what a vegetarian was. She reached her hands toward the sky and clapped, making a sound as loud as thunder.

The twins ducked, but the wish appeared to have done the trick. The witch's hump faded away, the yellowish tint of her skin disappeared, and her bloodshot eyes calmed.

"I've lost my appetite," the witch said. She shrugged her

shoulders, turned away from Alex and Conner, and walked into the gingerbread house, slamming the door behind her.

Alex and Conner took a deep breath. Their bodies had never been so tense.

"That was a close one!" Alex said.

"You're welcome!" Conner said.

"How did you think of wishing for her to become a vegetarian?" Alex asked.

Conner scratched his head. "It was the only sure way I knew she wouldn't eat us."

Alex smiled at him. She wasn't given too many moments to be proud of her brother, so when the chance came, she soaked it up for all it was worth.

"Nice job, but let's get out of here in case your wish wears off."

The twins hurried back through the forest until they returned to the path. They continued heading south, this time keeping to a faster pace. They had had their first dangerous encounter in the fairy-tale world, and they weren't in any hurry for the next.

Alex and Conner had been hurrying along the path for a while, when Conner said, "Alex, I've got to sit down! I feel like my legs are going to fall off!"

"Conner, we have to keep moving! It's already after noon, and Froggy said we need to cross into the Corner Kingdom before nightfall!" Alex warned.

"Easy for him to say—he has frog legs!" Conner said

through heavy breathing. "Just for a couple of minutes, and then we'll keep going, I promise!"

"All right, but let's find someplace safe," Alex said.

They continued walking a little farther and found a pleasant opening between some trees. Conner found a fallen tree to sit on and catch his breath.

Alex looked around at the trees of the forest, noticing that they were all different shapes and sizes and shades of green. She was still bewildered by everything that had happened.

"It's amazing, isn't it?" Alex said. "All of this has been at our fingertips the whole time, and we never knew."

She took a seat next to her brother, grinning from ear to ear.

"What do you think Dad and Grandma would make of all this?" Alex asked him. "What do you think they would say if they knew all of it was actually real?"

"From the way they always talked about fairy tales, you'd think they did," Conner said, and couldn't help but smile at the thought.

"I have a thousand reasons why I wish Dad was still alive," Alex said. "But now I wish it more than ever, just so we could bring him back and show all of this to him and Grandma."

"We have to get back first," Conner reminded her. "And while we're on the subject, I think we should take a look at that journal. The sooner we read it, the sooner we can get back home."

"I know," she told him. "But we should at least see a castle or palace first! Dad and Grandma would have wanted us to!"

Conner grunted. "Alex, we just barely escaped being lunch for a witch. We can't waste any more time—"

The sounds of a few twigs snapping came from across the clearing, as something approached. Alex and Conner ducked down behind the fallen tree, hidden from view.

A cream-colored horse slowly traveled into the clearing. It picked up its hooves in a peculiar manner, as if it had been trained to tiptoe. A woman was riding the horse, and she looked cautiously around the clearing as they entered it.

She was young and beautiful. Her eyes were big and blue, and her hair was half up and flowed into long, golden curls. She wore a long, maroon knit coat with black leggings and very tall boots.

The woman and her horse moved covertly into the center of the clearing.

"Easy, Porridge," said the woman, stroking the horse. "That's a good girl, nice and slow." She hopped down from the horse and made her way to a tree. Alex could see that some sort of paper was pinned to it and, after taking a closer look, saw it was the Wanted poster for Goldilocks that she had seen the day before.

The woman shook her head after reading it. She ripped it off the tree and crumpled it up.

"Who is that? What is she doing?" Conner whispered to his sister.

"Do I look psychic to you?" Alex whispered back at him.

Suddenly, the woman's head jerked in their direction. Whoever she was, she had a remarkable sense of hearing. She drew a large sword from inside her coat and raised it high in the air.

Her gaze was stern and determined; she was obviously someone to be reckoned with. She stepped closer to where Alex and Conner were hiding.

A piercing wolf howl boomed through the forest. It was so loud that Alex and Conner covered their ears. The woman spun around and pointed her sword in the opposite direction of the twins.

"Porridge, get ready! We're about to have company," she said.

"Who?" Alex and Conner mouthed to each other.

Creeping through the trees toward them were half a dozen wolves. However, these wolves were unlike any the twins had ever seen before. They were four times the size of any normal wolf of their world. Their fur was jet-black and matted. Their eyes were red, and their snouts were wide. These wolves were ready to kill at any minute. Without a doubt, the twins had come face-to-face with the Big Bad Wolf Pack.

Alex and Conner held on to each other, shaking with fear. The woman in the maroon coat never showed a hint of panic; she pointed her sword at the largest of the wolves, standing in the middle of the pack. The wolves growled and gritted their teeth toward her.

"Hello, *Malumclaw*," the woman said.

"Hello, *Goldilocks*," Malumclaw growled.

The twins were both in silent hysterics.

"Goldilocks! That's Goldilocks!" Alex mouthed to Conner.

"The wolf talks! It talks!" he mouthed back to her.

"I'm surprised you're not chained down in some Red Riding Hood Kingdom jail cell yet," Malumclaw said to Goldilocks.

"I'm surprised you haven't been turned into a rug for a child's nursery yet," Goldilocks said. "What brings you to this part of the forest? There isn't an innocent village for your pack to torment for miles."

Goldilocks never lowered her sword. The other wolves in Malumclaw's pack slowly surrounded her and Porridge.

"My pack is hungry. We've stopped for an afternoon snack," the wolf said.

"Have you really come to eat me?" Goldilocks said. "I thought you'd have learned your lesson by now. I bite back." She gripped her sword even tighter.

Malumclaw laughed.

"The wolf can laugh! It can laugh!" Conner mouthed to Alex.

"You are far too small a portion," Malumclaw told her with an evil, wolfish grin. "Your horse, however, has plenty to go around!"

Alex and Conner had never seen a horse look as

frightened as Porridge did. Had she not been so light-colored, they would have sworn she had gone pale.

"If you so much as scratch her, I will wear you as a coat, do you understand me?" Goldilocks warned him.

"All people do in this world is eat one another!" Conner whispered to Alex and, as soon as he did, he knew he shouldn't have.

A wolf turned in the twins' direction. "Malumclaw, I think I just heard something," it growled.

Alex covered her mouth so as not to scream.

The wolf began sniffing vigorously in the air. "I smell two children! One boy and one girl."

Goldilocks seemed as surprised as the rest of the wolves to learn this. So *that* was who she had heard behind her moments before.

The twins could hear their own heartbeats. What was going to happen next? Was Goldilocks going to rat them out to save her horse? Had they just narrowly escaped being devoured by a witch only to be eaten by a pack of overgrown wolves?

"I'm afraid you just missed them!" Goldilocks said. "I frightened them away just like I frightened you the last time our paths crossed."

"Then horse it is!" Malumclaw declared.

All the wolves howled together; it was deafening. They began circling Goldilocks and Porridge, getting closer and closer. The wolves snapped at them with their enormous jaws, and Goldilocks swung her sword at them.

One wolf tried to pounce on Porridge, but the horse kicked him away with her hind legs. Another wolf tried to bite Goldilocks, but she struck him with her sword, drawing blood, and he whimpered away.

Goldilocks was the best swords*woman* the twins had ever seen. Anytime one of the wolves got so much as a claw close to her or her horse, she was quick to shield them. Porridge wasn't so bad herself; she wasn't shy about kicking away any wolf that was too close for comfort.

A wolf leaped and sank his claws into Porridge's back. The horse bucked to free herself. In one quick slice, Goldilocks chopped one of the wolf's paws off. He limped into the forest, howling in pain.

Two wolves teamed up on Goldilocks. One leaped toward her, and she tripped over the other one. Her sword flew into the air and landed close to where the twins were hiding. Goldilocks was on the ground, unarmed.

The wolves were closing in on her and the horse, going in for the kill.

"Catch!" Conner yelled, and tossed the sword straight to her. Goldilocks swung it hard at the wolves closing in on her, leaving large gashes in their muzzles.

"Retreat!" Malumclaw ordered his pack. "No snack is worth all of this trouble!"

The wolves stampeded into the forest, growling and howling in anger, letting the rest of the forest know they were on their way.

"Until we meet again, Goldilocks!" Malumclaw called

out, as he disappeared into the trees with the rest of the wolves.

Goldilocks got to her feet and put her sword away. She was out of breath and, now that the enemy had left, much more vulnerable than she had shown in combat. She petted Porridge's nose and dabbed the horse's wounds with the fabric of her coat.

"Good girl, Porridge," Goldilocks said.

She turned and faced the fallen tree Alex and Conner were hiding behind.

"You can come out now," Goldilocks said.

The twins were hesitant at first. Then Conner popped up and exclaimed, *"That was awesome!"*

"Conner!" Alex said, popping up beside him.

"That was one heck of a fight!" Conner continued. "You know, at first I really thought they had you! I never expected a girl and her horse could be any match for six hungry wolves, but you impressed me! Where did you learn to fight like that?"

Goldilocks was not amused by his enthusiasm. "When you've been on the run as long as I have, you pick up a few tricks here and there." She turned around and remounted her horse with a jump.

"So, is it really you?" Alex asked. "Are you really Goldilocks? The woman wanted dead or alive for all her crimes?"

"Don't believe everything you read," she said sternly, and then pulled on Porridge's reins and galloped away. But she only traveled a few feet before she steered Porridge back to the twins.

"Thank you for your assistance," Goldilocks said.

Conner nodded.

"Here, take this. In case you need it." Goldilocks reached into the side of her boot and pulled out a silver dagger. She tossed it on the ground.

"Now get as far away from here as possible; those wolves will be back sooner than you expect." And with that said, Goldilocks and Porridge galloped off into the forest.

Alex and Conner stood motionless watching her ride off out of sight.

"That was amazing!" Conner said. He retrieved the dagger from the ground and put it inside their satchel. "As terrifying as that was, it was kind of nice to see another human for a change."

"We'd better get out of here," Alex said. "And this time we aren't stopping until we know we're out of the Dwarf Forests!"

Conner couldn't agree more. The twins continued down the dirt path, running this time.

They had experienced more danger today than they had ever experienced in their entire lives. Unfortunately for them, it wouldn't be their last encounter with Goldilocks, the Big Bad Wolf Pack, or the Dwarf Forests....

CHAPTER SEVEN

RAPUNZEL'S TOWER

The twins had been running for almost an hour straight, and they were starting to feel it. Their adrenaline was slowly running out, and the pains in their sides were increasing with every step they took. But since something dangerous seemed to happen every time they stopped moving, they were motivated to keep going.

"After all this running, P.E. testing should be a breeze," Conner said through heavy wheezes.

"We're almost there," Alex said unconvincingly. "Just a little farther!"

The forest had changed as they ran through it. The trees weren't so thick, and there was more space and grass between them. More sunlight fell through the branches, so nothing was in the dark. The path became wider, too, and much more visible.

The twins didn't feel as threatened by their surroundings; the forest almost grew *friendlier* the closer they traveled to the Corner Kingdom.

Conner collapsed to the ground. He was breathing harder than a fish out of water.

"I can't run anymore! I can't take another step!" he said with his limbs spread out as if he were making a snow angel in the dirt.

"We can't stop moving until we get into the Corner Kingdom," Alex reminded him through her own heavy breathing.

"I think we're there," Conner said.

"How do you know?" Alex asked.

"That's how," Conner said, and pointed upward.

In the distance, a tall tower was visible above the treetops. It was circular and made of square stones. There was a single window near the top, just below the pointed roof made of hay. It was partially covered in thick vines of ivy.

Alex gasped and clutched her hands together.

"It's Rapunzel's tower!" Alex said, and her eyes became a little misty at the sight of it.

"Are you seriously crying?" said Conner, who was still on the ground.

"It's just how I imagined it!" Alex said. "Get up! We're getting a closer look!"

Alex yanked on her brother's arm until he climbed to his feet, and the twins walked through the trees until they came to the base of the tower.

It was even taller than it looked, a few hundred feet tall at least. The twins' necks began to ache after looking up at the tower for a while. A large golden plaque was displayed in the ground in front of it that said:

QUEEN RAPUNZEL'S TOWER

"It must have been so hard for her," Alex said. "Seeing people and places so far away and never being able to visit them."

"At least she never had to worry about burglars," Conner said.

"I've got to go up there," Alex said.

"Do you have a jet pack or a grappling hook that I'm unaware of?" Conner asked her.

"No, I'll have to climb it," Alex said, surprising herself with the declaration.

"You have officially lost your mind!" Conner said. "We've almost been killed twice, and we haven't even been here a full day yet! *We need to stop fooling around and find a way home, Alex!* What part of that don't you understand?"

"Look," Alex said. "I'm going to climb up there for just a few minutes, and then as soon as I climb back down, we'll read the journal and find out what all the Wishing Spell items are, okay?"

"*Alex . . .*" Conner began. His face was turning pink.

"Please, Conner," Alex said. "I need to do this, or I'll regret it forever!"

Conner shook his head with the frustration that only a sibling could cause. He wanted to lecture her about how childish she was acting. But the way she was looking at him, with her big, wanting eyes, prevented him. It was so rare that Alex ever *needed* something, he supposed one last stop couldn't hurt.

"Don't kill yourself," Conner said. "But while you're up there, I'm going to start reading the journal and make a list of the Wishing Spell items we need to find."

Alex happily nodded and put her bag on the ground. She stretched for the climb she was about to make.

Conner sat on the ground and began flipping through the pages of the journal.

Climbing the tower was easier said than done. After searching around the base of the tower for a place to put her first step, Alex could tell why a long train of golden hair might be needed to get to the top of it. Eventually, she found a stone block with a chip large enough to put her foot in and take her first step.

"Here I go," Alex said. "Gosh, I wish I had a camera!"

"Trust me," Conner said. "The *real* Alex I know isn't going to want proof of this."

It was like climbing the world's most difficult rock-climbing wall. She relied on cracks and chips and uneven bricks sticking out just enough to put her hands and feet on. She moved slowly but carefully. If she were any larger, it wouldn't have worked.

"You're still at the bottom?" Conner said, looking up from the journal after a few minutes.

"Shut up, Conner!" Alex yelled back at him.

"I'm just saying, at the rate you're going Mom's gonna be eighty by the time we get home whether there's a time difference or not," he said.

After some time had gone by and she had gotten the hang of it, Alex moved more quickly, carefully pulling herself up using the ivy. The higher she climbed, the less she looked down at the ground, fearing it would tamper with her effort to reach the top.

She was so determined to see the top of the tower, to be in the room where Rapunzel had lived and to see what Rapunzel had seen through her window every day. She wanted to be where somebody else had been during the loneliest times of *their* life.

Rapunzel's story had always been easy for Alex to identify with. Alex felt she was in a tower of her own, looking at the world from an unreachable location.

She was almost halfway up the tower by now, and she was above all the trees in the forest. Any tiny misstep would no longer result in potential injury, it would mean death.

"There's a reason the witch put Rapunzel up there, you know!" Conner called up to her. "So no one could reach her!"

"I'm not listening to you!" Alex said, and then, stupidly, looked down.

Beads of sweat appeared on Alex's forehead. She felt like her heart had fallen out of her body. What was she doing? There was no way she could climb back down. Was she really risking her life just to see the inside of a tower? If she ever reached the top, would she be able get back down? Would she have to wait until her hair grew long enough to climb before she saw anyone again?

What would Conner do if she got stuck up there? Would he try to find the fairy-tale world equivalent of a fire department with a ladder long enough to get her down? Or would he find the Wishing Spell items on his own and go home without her?

The more Alex worried, the more she climbed. She knew it wouldn't be productive to worry and stay still, so she just kept going. It felt like hours had gone by.

She looked up. *She was only a few feet away from the window!* Just a few more feet and she'd be there! Finally, she felt the windowsill with her hands and slowly pulled herself up to it . . . then through it . . . she was almost through the window . . .

Alex swung her legs over the window and into the tower.

"Thank God," she said to herself. She might be stuck in the tower, but at least she was safe.

Alex looked around the tower; it wasn't at all what she had expected. It was a large, circular room with no furniture or decoration of any kind. In fact, it was completely empty except for some hay and bird droppings littered around the floor.

"Hi, Alex!" said a voice inside the tower.

Alex jumped and screamed. She was completely shocked to see Conner sitting up against the tower wall just a few feet away from her.

"It took you long enough to get up here!" he said with a laugh. He was eating an apple, and he had the journal open in his lap.

"How in the world did you get up here?" Alex demanded. She was still out of breath from her climb.

"I took the stairs," Conner said with a mocking grin. "I was reading the journal. It says that after Rapunzel became queen, she installed a staircase in her tower so she could come back and visit whenever she wanted. The door to the staircase was on the other side of the tower. We just didn't see it."

"Oh," Alex said sheepishly. "That would make sense."

"Apparently, since Rapunzel was the only known ward of the witch, when the witch died, Rapunzel inherited all the land from her. That's how she became a queen," Conner informed her. "But you would have known that if you had read the journal. It's full of fun facts and helpful hints on how to get inside difficult places."

"I suppose," Alex said, and straightened her headband. She wasn't going to let this ruin the accomplishment she had felt after climbing the tower. She turned to look out Rapunzel's window.

The tower was surrounded by a sea of trees. Far off into the distance, Alex could barely see the rooftops of a tiny village; beyond the village was a large mountain range that rolled across the horizon. Now *this* was exactly what Alex had expected.

"It's quite a view, isn't it?" Conner asked.

"Yes," Alex said, almost in a whisper. "It's breathtaking. I just wish we could see it all, everything in the Land of Stories. But I did a lot of thinking on my way up here, and I know we have to get home. That's what we need to focus on."

"About that," Conner said. "You really need to read this, Alex. I've only skipped through a little bit of it—most of it's hard to read, because it's written by hand—but the situation is much more serious than we thought."

He handed her the journal. Alex sat next to him and opened it to the very first page and began reading.

Dear friends,

 I don't know how, why, or where you found this journal, but since it has found its way into your possession, I hope that it will be of use to you.

 What I am about to tell you is going to sound ludicrous, but I ask that you allow me to explain. Had I not seen it with my own eyes, I would have never believed it myself.

 I am but a simple man from a simple village in the Charming Kingdom, but I have been to another world. It's a world with people and technologies that our world has only dreamed of and places we can only imagine. I know it seems absurd, but I promise you that an extraordinary place exists out there. We just can't see it.

During my visit, among the many things I experienced, I fell in love. I fell into a love so deep it was unlike anything I've ever known.

I never thought this kind of love was real. It's as if I am no longer living for myself anymore, but for her. So, I must find a way back. I must find a way to see her again.

The first time I traveled into the other world was simple. A fairy that knew of its existence allowed me to travel with her. She warned me not to get attached to anything or anyone, but while my brain was obedient to her request, my heart betrayed it.

The fairy has hence banned me from traveling with her. So, this time, I must find my way into the other world on my own.

Naturally, I didn't know where to start. How does one go about traveling into another world? Who was I even to ask? How would I even be able to ask without appearing like a lunatic? Cinderellian society is very judgmental, and I surely would have been ridiculed if my mission were discovered.

I came to the conclusion that I'd have to ask someone who was crazy in their own right, so no one would believe them if they spoke of what I had inquired. I needed someone I could trust, but who would never be trusted by the world.

I figured such a person didn't exist, and I lost hope, until I remembered the Traveling Tradesman. He was infamous for finding naïve children in the woods and trading their items of value for items he claimed to be magical. He was rumored to have given Jack the beans that grew his beanstalk.

Surely if anyone had heard of another world, it would be him. He was on the move at all times, since warrants for his arrest had been issued in all the kingdoms. He would be nearly impossible to find, but then again, my entire quest was virtually impossible.

Late one night, I traveled to a tavern up the stream from my home. There I befriended two farmers, and I proceeded to buy them round after round of drinks. After we had had a few laughs about childhood adventures and adolescent mistakes, I asked them if they had ever heard of the Traveling Tradesmen.

They both grew very quiet and were almost offended by the question. I assured them it was purely out of curiosity, and I wasn't accusing them of anything. I purchased another round of drinks, and after they were consumed the farmers confessed they had done business with him in earlier years.

"I traded two goats for a watering can that was supposed to magically water all my crops by itself," one of the farmers said. "The damn thing never worked, and it had a leak! It was the biggest mistake of my life."

"I traded two cows for a goose he told me would lay golden eggs!" the other claimed. "The goose was male! He gave me a gander!"

They tried convincing me to call off my search for him, but after one final round of drinks, they told me of the routes he covertly took through the woods.

I must have searched every patch of trees in the Charming Kingdom. Finally, in the woods just south of the Red Riding Hood Kingdom border, I found him.

The Traveling Tradesman was an odd, elderly, disheveled man. He wore several layers of raggedy clothing, and he had a long, gray beard. There were dark circles under his eyes, and one of the eyes wandered to the left, so it was difficult to tell what or whom he was looking at.

He traveled with a large cart that was pulled by a single mule. He was making a deal with a small boy holding a chicken when I first saw him.

"Wear this bear claw and you'll grow up to be the strongest boy in the village," the Tradesman told the boy, and then placed a necklace with a large bear claw around his neck and took the chicken from him.

The boy smiled and ran off. The Tradesman placed the chicken in the back of his cart. He must have made other trades that day, because he had already collected two geese and a pig.

"Are you a friend or a foe?" the Tradesman asked me.

"A friend, I believe," I said.

"Oh, good," he said with a jolly clap. "Then what may I do for you, friend? Would you like a bag of magic pebbles that grow into boulders? It'll only cost you a duck! Or perhaps you'd like to trade a swine for a loaf of bread that'll make you never be hungry again?"

"No, thank you," I said cautiously. "I've come to ask you for advice."

"Advice?" the Tradesman said. The eyebrow above his wandering eye rose. "That, my friend, is something no one has ever asked me for. What do you wish to know?"

"I am wondering…" I started, but wasn't sure how to put it into words. "What is the farthest distance you've traveled?"

The Tradesman scratched his beard and thought about it.

"Well, I'd honestly say there isn't a place in this world I haven't been," he told me. "I've traveled from the Southwest to the Northeast and from the Southeast to the Northwest. I've been from the bottom of the Corner Kingdom to the top of the Sleeping Kingdom and from the tip of the Elf Empire to the coast of the Fairy Kingdom—"

"What about farther than that?" I interrupted him, fearing he might continue listing every journey he had ever taken.

"Farther than that?" Both of the Tradesman's eyebrows were raised now. "What's farther than that? Only ocean is beyond that, and that's it."

"What about a different world? Have you ever heard of one or how to travel to one?" I finally asked.

The Tradesman got a funny look in his eyes—or should I say eye.

"Young man, I've been all over the world, and I have never seen any suggestion of there being another," he said.

This topic upset him somehow, and he hopped aboard his cart and took the reins of his mule.

"Wait! Please don't go!" I pleaded.

"You youngsters always take pleasure in harassing an old man. Well, I won't allow it," he said.

He began to travel up the path. I was so desperate, I stood in front of his mule and was nearly trampled.

"I mean you no harm, old man!" I assured him. "You don't understand! I've been to another world, another place and time, and have seen extraordinary things! I need to go back! It may be the greatest wish I will ever have."

My arms were spread out, and I fell to my knees. I felt like an imbecile, confessing a preposterous need to a preposterous man.

The Tradesman sat still with his good eye fixed on me.

"Is it truly the most desired wish in your heart?" he asked.

"Yes!" I pleaded. "I've never wanted anything more in my life."

"If it's a wish you desire, then there's only one thing you need," he said.

"What is that?" I asked him.

"The Wishing Spell," the Tradesman said.

At first I thought he was joking.

"The Wishing Spell?" I asked him. "You mean the childish legend?"

"It's as real as the nose on my face," the Tradesman said. "Many men have spent their lives trying to obtain it. Legend has it that if you collect a series of objects and place them in close proximity, the collector's one true wish will be granted."

I didn't know whether or not to believe him. Perhaps he was harassing *me* now. My brain was critical, but my heart chose to learn more.

"And how do I find these items?" I asked.

"I don't have the slightest idea," he said.

Now I was frustrated with him. All of that explanation for nothing! I turned my back on him and began heading back home.

"But I know someone who does!" the Tradesman called after me.

"Who?" I demanded.

"I never trade for free," the Tradesman said, and extended an open palm toward me.

I placed a few gold coins in his hand. He kept his hand extended, and I placed a few more coins into it until he was satisfied.

"Her name is Hagatha," the Tradesman said.

"Where can I find her?"

"Take this path west into the Dwarf Forests, past the three boulders, and then follow the smoke," the Tradesman said, and that was all the direction he gave. He took the reins of his mule and traveled away from me.

Had I been thinking clearly, I would have chased after him and asked for more instructions, but instead I took off running toward the Dwarf Forests.

I had never been inside the Dwarf Forests before. I had been told of their dangers since I was a child, and once I was there I knew why I had been warned. The trees grew so thick and close that someone could be standing three feet away from you and you would never know they were there.

It took two days to find the three boulders the Tradesman had spoken of.

They were three large rocks that stuck straight out of the ground and were tilted in a peculiar position. I thought perhaps they might have been pointing at something, so I lowered my head to look in the direction they pointed.

The boulders pointed directly between two trees separated just enough that you could see a wide patch of the sky, and in this patch I could see *smoke!*

I ran toward the source of the smoke. Wherever it was coming from was completely off the path, and I almost seriously injured myself jumping over bushes and tree roots as I went.

Occasionally, I could see the sky through the tree branches and could tell if I was off track. I must have traveled in circles for hours. Every time I thought I was just about to find the place from which the smoke came, the wind would shift it in another direction.

I was lost. Every way I turned looked exactly the same. I felt as if the forest had swallowed me.

The sun was setting, and the smoke became harder to see. I started to panic; there was no shelter in sight. I thought for sure a treacherous beast would find me during the night and make a feast out of me.

I started running again. I could barely see where I was going at this point. I could hear howling in the distance. I tripped and fell straight through a large thornbush.

I landed hard in the grass on other side of the thornbush. I was scraped, scratched, and bleeding.

I got to my feet and looked around; I was standing in a large, circular clearing in the forest surrounded by a large wall of thornbush. In the center of this clearing was a small hut with a hay roof and a brick chimney. And rising out of this chimney was the smoke I had been following.

No wonder it had been so hard to find! I must have been wandering in circles around it, not knowing it was hidden behind the thornbush.

I approached the hut slowly. It had one door and two windows, and that was all. I went to knock on the door, but it burst open before I had a chance.

"Who are you?" said the woman who emerged from the hut.

I knew from the second I saw her that it was Hagatha. She looked like a human tree stump. She was short and wore a brown hooded cloak. Deep wrinkles circled her face, and one of her eyes was squinted. Her nose was one of the smallest I had ever seen and was neighbored by a gigantic mole.

"Are you Hagatha?" I asked her.

"How did you find me?" she snapped.

"I tripped through the thornbush," I said.

"But how did you know I was here?" she asked. Her squinted eye squinted even more.

"The Traveling Tradesman," I told her. "He said you knew of the Wishing Spell."

Hagatha grunted and sighed at the same time. Her lips wrinkled and looked me up and down. Reluctantly, she gestured me to follow her inside.

"Come in, come in!" Hagatha said.

The inside of the hut was an utter mess. There were vials of strange liquids everywhere; some bubbled, some glistened, some steamed. There were dozens of glass jars containing the strangest things: dead and alive reptiles, insects of every species, even a glass jar of various eyeballs. Even though they had been plucked out from their owner's lids, I swear one of them blinked at me.

I was surprised to see how many animals were inside the hut as well; everything from geese and chickens to hummingbirds and monkeys all resided in cages. They were all restless, prisoners no doubt.

"Have a seat," Hagatha instructed. She pointed to a chair at the end of a table so large that it almost took up the entire hut.

"I see you are a collector of sorts," I said.

She didn't welcome the conversation. She ignored me and collected a few items around the room, a bowl here, a vial there.

"The thornbush surrounding your home is very clever," I said. "It must keep out most unwanted visitors."

"Most," she said, and glared at me. "That thornbush is from the Sleeping Kingdom. I planted it here and it grew around my home in a perfect circle, just as it grew around the castle while the queen was in her one-hundred-year slumber. You are the first to break through it."

"I do apologize—"

"This will cost you fifteen gold coins," Hagatha said, and took a seat across from me.

"For what?" I asked.

"You want to know what the Wishing Spell items are, don't you?" she asked. "That is why you're here, is it not?"

I reached into my pocket and laid all the coins I had left on the table. Unfortunately, doing business with the Tradesman had left me short.

"I only have fourteen coins," I told her.

Hagatha did not look pleased. "You stupid youth and your wishes. Very well," she said, and scooped up all the coins with one swipe.

She placed a bowl in front of her and emptied the contents of two vials into it: one red liquid, the other blue.

"One eye of an eagle, the wings of a pixie, and the heart of a newt," Hagatha said, and added these items into the bowl. "Plus three drops of giant blood, the big toe of an ogre, and a straw of gold hay. That completes the potion."

With all the ingredients added, the liquid in the bowl started to smoke and glow. Hagatha leaned over it and breathed it in. She closed her eyes and lost herself in a moment of deep thought.

"Does this potion tell you what the Wishing Spell items are?" I asked her.

"No, but it helps me remember," Hagatha said. "You aren't the first, and you won't be the last person to request the list. Consider yourself warned: Many people have lost their lives trying to acquire these items. They are impossible to collect."

"I'd rather die trying than live the rest of life wondering if I could have done it," I said.

"Then listen carefully to what I'm about to say, because I'll only say it once," Hagatha said.

I leaned as close to her as I possibly could. The anticipation made every second feel like an hour. This is what I had come all this way for....

"There are eight," Hagatha said. She took a deep breath and then listed the items:

"Glass that housed a lonely soul up 'til midnight's
　　final toll.
A saber from the deepest sea, meant for a groom's
　　mortality.
The bark of a basket held in fright while running from a
　　bark with bite.
A stony crown that's made to share, found deep within a
　　savage lair.
A needle that pierced the lovely skin of a princess with
　　beauty found within.

A wavy lock of golden rope that once was freedom's
   only hope.
Glittering jewels whose value increased after preserving
   the false deceased.
Teardrops of a maiden fairy feeling neither magical
   nor merry.

I repeated the list to myself the entire way home
and wrote the Wishing Spell list and my journey thus
far into this journal. I don't know how I'm going to
gather these items, but my goal is to find them and
then record how I managed it, in case I ever need to
do it again.

If you're reading this, I hope it means I succeeded,
and if you're reading this and are about to start a
journey of your own, I wish you luck.

"Wow," Alex said, looking up from the journal.

"You can say that again," Conner said. "You read that much faster than I did."

"Did you read any farther?" Alex asked. "Did he find all the items? Did he make it back?"

"I don't know. There are a lot of pages missing," Conner said.

Alex scanned through the list of the Wishing Spell items. She hadn't expected them to be hidden within riddles.

"Most of these are pretty easy to figure out," she said. "Like 'A needle that pierced the lovely skin of a princess with beauty found within.' That's obviously the spindle on Sleeping Beauty's spinning wheel."

"And 'A wavy lock of golden rope that once was freedom's only hope,'" Conner said. "That's totally a lock of Rapunzel's hair!"

Conner looked around the space where he was sitting. From between two floorboards he pulled out a lock of long, golden hair.

"Found one!" Conner said. "One of the first things I noticed when I got up here was how much that Rapunzel girl shed! Now we're one-eighth of the way home!"

Alex carefully wrapped the lock of golden hair in a tissue from her school bag.

"What do you suppose 'Glass that housed a lonely soul up 'til midnight's final toll' means?" she asked. "Whose soul was covered in glass?"

"I know!" Conner said. "Cinderella's glass slipper! That covered the sole of her foot!"

"Of course!" Alex said. "This list was spoken. Maybe Hagatha meant *sole*, like on a foot, but the man heard it as *soul*, like a person's spirit! Conner, you're a genius!"

"There's an alternative spelling?" Conner asked, but Alex went on.

"I wonder what 'The bark of a basket held in fright while running from a bark with bite' means," said Alex, thinking hard. "Basket, basket, basket...bite, bite, bite...*Little Red Riding Hood*! Her basket must have been made out of tree bark! And the bark with bite is talking about the Big Bad Wolf!"

"Okay," Conner said. "That would make sense."

Alex stood up and started pacing around the tower.

"'Glittering jewels whose value increased after preserving the false deceased.' That's a tough one," she said. "Who was *falsely deceased*?"

"Didn't people think Snow White was dead after she bit into the poisoned apple?" Conner asked.

"Yes, that's right!" said Alex, jumping up and down. "She had a coffin made of glass and jewels from the dwarf mines! That must be what it means!"

"I'm so glad Dad and Grandma read to us so much growing up!" Conner said. "Who ever would have thought it would be this useful?"

"'Teardrops of a maiden fairy feeling neither magical nor merry.' I guess we'll just have to find a fairy who has recently broken up with her boyfriend or something," Alex surmised.

"You don't think we could just kick her and make her cry?" Conner asked. "That just seems easier to me."

Alex ignored him and vigorously flipped through the journal again.

"Glass slipper? Check! Spindle? Check! Coffin? Check!" Alex said. "According to the notes scribbled in the margins, the author of the journal seems to agree with our guesses. I still don't know what some of these things are, though, like 'A saber from the deepest sea, meant for a groom's mortality' or 'A stony crown that's made to share, found deep within a savage lair.'"

"Like I said, there are a lot of pages missing," Conner said.

Alex was disheartened by this. The items they knew of seemed virtually impossible to collect, let alone the items they didn't know of. She walked over to the window and looked out at the view. The sun was just about to set, and, one by one, the fireplaces in the village nearby were lit and sent trails of smoke into the darkening sky.

"What if we get some of these riddles wrong?" she asked. "What if we guess the wrong thing? What if the author guessed wrong? What if he never made it back? What if he died trying?"

"We'll just have to do our best," Conner said, joining Alex at the window. "Some annoying little girl told me once that optimism always pays off, and she's usually right about things."

Alex smirked warmly at her brother.

"Okay, then," she said. "So far, we have a lock of Rapunzel's hair. We still need to collect Cinderella's slipper, Sleeping Beauty's spindle, jewels from Snow White's coffin, bark from Red Riding Hood's basket, tears from a fairy, plus two other items we have no idea about."

Conner gulped at hearing the list. They both looked out over the horizon and at the sea of trees that surrounded the tower. Somewhere out there, all of these things were waiting to be found.

"It looks like we're going to see more of the Land of Stories than we thought," Conner said.

CHAPTER EIGHT

A HIDDEN PLACE

The northern tip of the Sleeping Kingdom was an ugly and vacant place. It was known for its bare trees, bumpy paths, and dangerously high cliffs. Small stones were scattered on the earth, making it nearly impossible to travel to by carriage. Even though it rained every so often, nothing ever grew, making it impossible for any animals to live there.

In the middle of this dry and deserted place was a small castle surrounded by a deep and empty moat. It was ancient and made of dark bricks, wooden doors, and had been through years of decay. No one knew who had built the castle or why it had been built but, then again, very few people even knew of its existence.

The inside of the castle was covered in a thick layer of dust. Cobwebs almost as old as the castle were on every windowsill, even though there were no spiders to be found. All the rooms and corridors were empty except for the occasional decrepit chair or table placed in a corner.

A great hall completed the eastern wing of the castle. Floor-length windows bordered the hall, letting in a lot of light, but they were so old that the glass distorted the outside world.

The castle couldn't have been a less desirable place to be. But, for one woman, it was the perfect place to hide.

Somehow, the Evil Queen had escaped the dungeons of Snow White's palace. She managed to get ahold of her Magic Mirror and traveled to a place where she knew she would never be found. The castle acted as the perfect sanctuary where she could finish the work she had started so long ago.

The Evil Queen was not a stranger to this place. Over the last century or so, many people had come to the castle, but only she and a few others were fortunate enough to have left it, including someone the former queen had not seen in a great while.

She had recently sent word to this old friend, asking him to come and aid her. And so she waited for him to arrive, knowing that he would any day now, for he owed her his life.

The Evil Queen stood facing her Magic Mirror with open palms and closed eyes. She was quite calm for being the most wanted woman alive. To her right, resting on a short stool, was the heart of stone she had always kept close.

Although it was one of the most infamous objects in all of the kingdoms, very few people had ever seen the Evil Queen's Magic Mirror. Many believed it was made of glamorous materials, like gold and diamonds and glass so pure one would swear they could walk through it.

In reality, the mirror was tall and wide with a black frame that peaked at the top. Tangled vines made of cast iron wove through the frame. The reflection was cloudy, as if it were a glass doorway into a very cold and foggy place. Although there was very little moisture in the air, perspiration dripped down the glass.

The Evil Queen opened her eyes and gazed deep into the mirror.

"Mirror, Mirror, on the wall, how long 'til the Huntsman answers my call?" she asked it.

The ghostly silhouette of a man appeared in the reflection. It spoke slowly and softly with a low and hoarse voice.

"While my queen awaits an old friend, once dear,
The Huntsman travels very near."

The man in the mirror slowly faded away. Within moments, three loud knocks came from the other side of the great hall doors.

"You may enter," the Evil Queen said.

The doors opened, creaking terribly, and a man entered the hall. He was tall, broad, and just on the verge of old age. He wore a variety of animal skins and had a limp in his right leg. His beard was light brown and graying. A cross-bow was attached to his back, and a large hunting knife hung from his waist.

"My Huntsman has returned," the Evil Queen said.

The Huntsman walked across the hall to where the Evil Queen was standing.

"It's been a long time since I last saw your face," she said, "and I still find it hard to stomach looking at you."

The Huntsman fell to his knees and wept at her feet.

"Your Majesty," the Huntsman cried. "Please forgive me, for I have never forgiven myself after failing you!"

The Evil Queen looked down at him coldly. She had no sympathy left inside her for anyone.

"After all you had done for me and after all the mercy you had shown me, I could not kill the princess in the for-est," the Huntsman said. "And just look at all the pain it has caused you. Had I just done as you asked, you would still be queen."

The Evil Queen let his pathetic sobs continue for a while longer. She showed no sign of forgiveness. He deserved to feel this way.

She stepped away from the Huntsman and peered through a window at the lifeless land that surrounded them.

"You and I were both prisoners in this castle once," the Evil Queen said. "I never imagined that one day it would act as my only refuge."

"You saved me," the Huntsman said. "I surely would have died here, had it not been for you. That is why I swore to you then that I would do anything to assist you with your mission. But I failed you—"

"And after all this time, I am still on the same mission as I was back then. So, do not cry, old friend. I have called you here for a chance at redemption."

She walked back to him and gently placed a hand on his cheek. The Huntsman stopped crying and looked up at the queen with huge, sad eyes.

"Redemption?" the Huntsman asked. "You mean, Your Majesty, you're still giving me a chance to serve you after what I've done?" The Huntsman's tears quadrupled in size, and he continued sobbing. "Curse this world for claiming you to be anything less than the saint that you are! I'd kill every person who's tarnished your name if I could!"

"That won't be necessary," the Evil Queen said. "I have another task for you. It requires a great deal of traveling, and since being the most wanted fugitive alive prevents me from doing it myself, I've called you here."

The Huntsman grew quiet and lowered his head shamefully.

"Your Greatness," he said. "I have grown too old to travel. I can barely walk as it is."

The Evil Queen looked down at him with an angry brow.

"You imbecile," she said, raising her voice. "You mean to tell me you traveled all the way here to tell me you are useless?"

The Huntsman rose to his feet with difficulty.

"Not at all, My Queen," he said. "Please let me explain. I am far too old to serve you, but my *daughter* is able and willing to help you complete what I cannot."

"Daughter?" the Evil Queen asked.

The doors at the end of the hall opened again. This time, a woman entered dragging a large wagon behind her. She was tall and thin with hair so dark red, it seemed to have a violet tint. Her eyes were bright green and her clothing was made entirely of plants and leaves and other greenery.

The wagon she pulled contained a large square object. It was large and flat and was covered in a silk cloth for safety.

After seeing her, the Evil Queen could recall a time many years ago when she had known the Huntsman's daughter. She had always been a shy little girl and had lived with her father in the palace when the Evil Queen was on the throne.

"You've grown up," the Evil Queen said.

The Huntsman's daughter nodded in her direction.

"You will speak when I address you!" the Evil Queen demanded.

"My daughter is mute, Your Majesty," the Huntsman said. "She's never said a word in her life. However silent she may be, it does not make her any less capable of doing what you ask of her. She's brought you a gift to prove herself."

The Huntsman's daughter carefully removed the object from her wagon and gently placed it beside the queen's Magic Mirror. Once it was positioned correctly, she removed the silk cloth. It was a mirror, smaller than the Magic Mirror; it was circular, with flowers engraved into a square, golden frame.

The Evil Queen knew exactly what it was the second it was revealed.

"The Mirror of Truth," she said. The former queen had acquired it during her reign. It was another magic mirror that showed one's true self when one stood before it.

"How did you get this?" the Evil Queen asked.

"She broke into the palace to retrieve it for you," the Huntsman said.

The Evil Queen touched the Mirror of Truth's frame; she had forgotten the detail in the carvings. She turned and faced the Huntsman's daughter.

"You shall be my *Huntress*," the Evil Queen declared.

The Huntress bowed and kissed the queen's hand.

"What is the task at hand, Your Majesty?" the Huntsman asked.

"Have either of you ever heard of the Wishing Spell?" the Evil Queen asked.

The Huntsman and the Huntress curiously looked to each other.

"No, My Queen," the Huntsman said. "Unless you are speaking of the old, foolish fable?"

"The very one," she said. "I never took it seriously until I recently heard a prisoner in the dungeon mumbling about it moments before his execution. According to the 'foolish fable,' after a group of select objects are collected and placed together, the collector is granted one wish. It doesn't matter how great or small, the wish is guaranteed to be granted. And, as you know, I have a wish to be granted."

"You want my daughter to collect these items for you, then?" the Huntsman asked.

"Precisely," the Evil Queen said. "From what I've learned, the task is very dangerous and may take some time, but if she succeeds, I will consider whatever debt you owe diminished."

The Huntsman looked to his daughter, and the Huntress nodded.

"Very well," he said. "She will do it. What are the items you seek, My Queen?"

The Evil Queen took her place before her Magic Mirror, extended her open palms, and gazed deep inside it.

"Mirror, Mirror, on the wall, what must we seek for the Wishing Spell that grants all?" she asked.

The ghostly silhouette appeared again.

"Glass that housed a lonely soul up 'til midnight's final toll.
A saber from the deepest sea, meant for a groom's mortality.
The bark of a basket held in fright while running from a bark with bite.

A stony crown that's made to share, found deep
    within a savage lair.
A needle that pierced the lovely skin of a princess
    with beauty found within.
A wavy lock of golden rope that once was freedom's
    only hope.
Glittering jewels whose value increased after
    preserving the false deceased.
Teardrops of a maiden fairy feeling neither magical
    nor merry."

"There you have it," the Evil Queen said to the Huntsman and the Huntress. But the Magic Mirror was not finished.

"But listen to this, my fair queen, for I offer you a
    fair warning.
For one wish you are willing to pay any price,
    unaware that the Wishing Spell can only hap-
    pen twice,
And the spell can only happen once more, for it was
    already used once before.
In this castle, as we stand, a duo move throughout
    the land.
A young brother and sister collect at a quick pace, and
    may defeat my queen in the Wishing Spell race."

The man in the mirror faded away, leaving the queen with the worst possible news. Not only was someone else after the objects she needed, but if they were used before she could collect them, the spell could never be used again.

She closed her eyes and thought about what her next move would be; she couldn't afford to have any more odds stacked against her. After a lifetime of work, she wasn't about to let two children stand in her way.

"I want you to start retrieving the items," the Evil Queen said to the Huntress. "I will handle the brother and sister. Now, leave me."

The Huntsman and the Huntress bowed and left the queen alone in the great hall.

The Evil Queen stood before the Mirror of Truth. Years of being a prisoner had taken its toll on her appearance. It was painful for her to see the aging woman who her reflection had become.

She picked up her heart of stone and examined it closely, lightly stroking its sides. The Evil Queen looked back up at the Mirror of Truth. This time there was no reflection of the disheveled woman she had grown into; this time the face staring back at her was a youthful one.

It belonged to a beautiful young maiden with pale skin and long, dark hair. She wore a long, white dress with a matching ribbon tied around the waist and was also holding the heart of stone.

The girl smiled, but the Evil Queen did not smile back. She knew the girl in the mirror very well, and she was not Snow White. . . .

CHAPTER NINE

THE CHARMING KINGDOM

Alex and Conner woke up on the floor of Rapunzel's tower just after sunrise. They were snuggled under the blankets Froggy had given them and they'd used their bags as pillows.

"How did you sleep?" Alex asked her brother.

"Like I slept on the floor of a tower," Conner said, thinking he'd never take his bed at home for granted again. He stretched his back, and his joints made sounds like firecrackers.

They put away their blankets and decided to get an

early start on their day. Alex insisted on tidying up the tower, leaving it in better condition than they had found it in.

"I'd hate for anyone to think we made this mess," Alex said. Conner rolled his eyes at her and made sure she saw it.

"What's our next stop?" Conner asked Alex. She looked back and forth from the map in one hand and the journal in the other.

"Well, the Charming Kingdom is just east of here," Alex said. "I figure it would be wisest to go there and see if we can get ahold of Cinderella's slipper."

"And how exactly are we going to do that?" Conner asked.

Alex had to think about it. "We'll just ask if we can borrow it," she decided.

"Fat chance," Conner said. "That's like walking into the White House and asking for the Declaration of Independence."

Although Conner was wrong about the whereabouts of the Declaration of Independence, Alex knew he was right to be concerned. How were they going to get their hands on one of Cinderella's slippers? Surely they must be the most prized possessions of the kingdom.

"We'll have to try our best," Alex said. "What other option do we have?"

The twins traveled down the spiral staircase in the core of Rapunzel's tower and returned to the path. They eventually came to a fork, where a new path splintered off in an eastern direction. The sign above the fork said CHARMING KINGDOM and pointed in the direction the new path was headed.

"Conner, look at the sign!" said Alex, pressing her hands against her cheeks. "Now I really wish I had a camera!"

They traveled down the new path for quite a while without discovering anything new but the same dirt path and evergreen trees they had seen for the last two days. Conner became more anxious the farther he walked, letting out large extended sighs every minute or so.

"Are you sure we aren't lost? I swear I've seen that boulder and that tree about twenty times already," he said, pointing.

"I'm positive we're traveling in the right direction. I've been watching the map since we left," Alex said. "We should be approaching a stream very soon, and once we cross it we'll be in the Charming Kingdom!"

Conner sighed again. It would be his last one for a while, so he made sure it lasted extra long.

A couple of hours later, there was no stream in sight. Conner was starting to lose faith in his sister's navigational abilities.

"This place must be bigger than we thought," Alex said. "Or this map is completely off scale."

Eventually, the twins found the stream Alex had seen on the map. The path went across a small bridge made out of pale stones and then continued on the other side.

"You see, I told you I knew what I was doing," Alex said with her head held high.

"Yeah, yeah, yeah," Conner said.

"Honestly, Conner, I'm a little disappointed in your lack of faith," Alex gloated. "If there's one place I should know my way around in, it would have to be—"

"Grrrrrrrrrrr!"

Conner heard his sister's high-pitched scream before he realized what had happened. A large troll had jumped right in front of them on the bridge. He was short and very wide with an enormous head. He was covered in matted fur with large eyes and a snout. His arms and legs were tiny, but his nails and teeth were sharp and long.

"You are on *my* bridge!" the troll shouted. "How dare you!"

"We're so sorry!" said Alex, clutching on to her brother like a monkey to a tree. "We had no idea this bridge belonged to anyone!"

"Maybe you should put up a sign or something," Conner suggested, and then regretted it once it made the troll even angrier.

"What are you doing on *my* bridge?" the troll demanded.

"Trying to cross into the Charming Kingdom," Alex said. "We didn't mean any harm!"

"No one crosses my bridge without answering a riddle!" the troll said.

"A riddle?" Alex asked, letting go of Conner. "Oh! You're a bridge troll!"

"A bridge troll?" Conner asked.

"Yes, just like in 'Three Billy Goats Gruff'!" Alex said happily. She was so excited to be witnessing another fairy-tale occurrence, all her fear faded away.

"If you wish to cross my bridge, you must answer my riddle correctly!" the bridge troll said. "Answer incorrectly, and I'll bite off your head!"

"Excuse me? Bite off our heads?" Conner said. Steam was practically coming from his ears. "What is wrong with everyone in this place? Why does everyone we meet want to eat us? Can someone please explain to me why this keeps happening?"

"Conner, calm down!" Alex insisted. "Let's just solve the riddle, and then we'll be on our way."

"What if we get the riddle wrong?" Conner said. "He'll kill us! Let's just find another way across the stream—"

"Conner, don't be silly! If a simple billy goat can answer a riddle correctly, I'm sure we can, too," Alex reassured him. "Besides, there isn't another bridge for miles."

Conner grunted and crossed his arms.

"How are we so sure that this is actually *his* bridge?" Conner said. "I'd like to see some ownership identification before we continue."

Alex ignored this.

"What's your riddle, Mr. Bridge Troll?" she asked. "May I call you Mr. Bridge Troll?"

The bridge troll eyed the twins and jauntily swayed from side to side as he began the riddle.

"What can be as small as a pea or as large as the sky and is not owned by the person who purchases it?" it asked.

The wheels in Alex's head began turning immediately. She loved riddles.

"That's a tricky one!" Alex said, and pressed her index finger against her lips as she thought. "Do you have any guesses, Conner?"

"Nope, you're on your own," Conner said.

"You have one guess before I bite off your head, so guess wisely!" the bridge troll said, doing a small dance and clapping his hands.

"That's it. I'm out of here!" Conner said. He walked off the bridge and slowly made his way down to the stream.

"Conner, what are you doing?" Alex called out.

"I'm crossing the stream!" Conner yelled back. "No bridge is worth that much trouble!"

He slowly stepped into the stream and began traveling across it. The water was freezing, but his frustration kept him warm enough that it didn't matter. The water rose higher and higher as he traveled farther across it.

"It's not that deep, Alex!" Conner said. "The current isn't even that strong!"

He reached the middle of the stream, and at its deepest the water came to just above his waist.

"You're cheating!" Alex said, and then asked the bridge troll, "Is that even allowed? Can he do that?"

"He isn't the one who asked for the riddle. *You* are!" the bridge troll said.

Conner had crossed the stream by now and was soaking wet. Alex continued thinking about the riddle.

"So, it can be as small as a pea and as large as the sky, so basically you're telling me that it can be any size. And the person who buys it doesn't own it, so that means someone else owns it," she thought out loud.

"Hurry up, Alex!" Conner shouted.

"Oh, hush!" Alex said. "I'm going to say that it must be... *a gift*! A gift can be any size and the receiver is who owns it, not the person who purchases it!"

The bridge troll stopped swaying from side to side and slumped over.

"That is correct," the bridge troll said disappointedly. "You may pass."

Alex clapped her hands together and did a small jump. She extended her hand out to offer the troll a handshake, but he ignored it. Instead, he crawled back below to wherever he had jumped out from.

"See!" Alex said once she'd met up with her brother on the other side of the bridge. "I knew I'd answer it correctly!"

Conner shook his head. "And I'm sure I'll have to hear about it for the rest of our lives," he said. "But let's try to make it to Cinderella's palace by sundown, okay?"

The twins continued their journey into the Charming Kingdom. They were excited to see different scenery as they traveled. The evergreen trees they had seen so much of became scarce and were slowly replaced by large oak trees. There were also vast fields of tall grass and wildflowers everywhere they looked.

"It's so beautiful here!" Alex said.

They had been walking for hours and still saw no sign of anything. Conner was practically dry by now.

"Where is everything?" Conner asked.

"The Charming Kingdom is a very big place," Alex said. "It's going to take a while to get to the palace."

It began to get dark, and the twins became very worried; there was no shelter in sight. Soon, the moon was their only source of light.

They walked a short distance off the path and found a grassy area among a few trees that they assumed (and hoped) was safe, and they decided to spend the night there. Conner tried making a fire by rubbing two sticks together but was unsuccessful.

"Now I really wish I had signed up for Boy Scouts," he said.

It was their first night sleeping outside. Both kept waking up every hour or so to make sure they were still safe, because every sound terrified them.

"What was that?" Alex gasped in the middle of the night.

"That's an owl," Conner said. "Or a very inquisitive dove, but either way I think we're safe."

The next morning, the sunrise woke them. They restlessly got to their feet and returned to the path.

"We're running out of food," Alex said after eating one

of their last apples. "We'll have to stock up as soon as we find a market or something."

"I'm so tired of rolls and apples. I'm starting to think we should have asked Froggy to pack us some flies," Conner said. "Gosh, I would kill for a cheeseburger! Maybe that's why everyone eats each other here; they just haven't discovered fast food yet."

They found a small pond on the side of the path and splashed some water on their faces.

"We look so tired," said Alex, looking at their reflections in the water.

The twins heard a galloping sound coming from behind them on the path. They turned to see a small cart of firewood being pulled by a gray horse. It was steered by a man with a big, floppy, green hat.

"Let's ask him how much farther until the palace!" Alex said, and ran over to the cart. "Excuse me, sir?"

"Whoa," the man said, slowing his horse to a stop. "May I help you?"

"How much farther until we reach Cinderella's palace?" Alex asked.

"Are you traveling by foot?" the man asked.

"Unfortunately," Conner said.

"Then it'll take you days to get there," the man said.

Alex and Conner looked at each other, completely exasperated.

"I'm delivering this firewood near the palace tonight," the man said. "I can give you a ride if you'd like."

Before he could finish his sentence, Conner had climbed aboard the cart.

"Thank you so much!" Alex said. "That is so kind of you!"

The twins traveled with the man for the rest of the day. Conner made himself comfortable on top of the firewood and napped almost the entire trip, waking up every so often whenever they hit a bump in the road. Alex, on the other hand, took full advantage of having an actual human to talk to from the fairy-tale world.

"What's your name?" Alex asked the man.

"Smithers," the man said.

"Where are you from?" she asked.

"I grew up in a small village in the northeastern part of the Charming Kingdom," Smithers said.

"What's it like here?" Alex said dreamily. "My brother and I...um...haven't been around this kingdom very much."

"The Charming Kingdom is a quiet place," Smithers said. "It has many small villages on the outskirts of the kingdom and many wealthy estates in the center, near the palace."

"Have you ever been to the palace before?" Alex asked.

"Oh, yes, I make many deliveries there during the year," he said. "In fact, tonight the king and queen are having a huge ball."

"They are?" Alex's eyes doubled in size. She shook Conner awake. "Conner, did you hear that? Cinderella's having a ball tonight! Isn't that wonderful? What are the chances?"

"What? Oh . . . er . . . that's great," Conner said, and then immediately fell back asleep.

"Why are they having a ball?" Alex asked.

"They've had one every month since their wedding," Smithers said. "It's a celebration of their marriage."

"What's Queen Cinderella like?" she asked.

"Absolutely beautiful, and the best queen our kingdom has ever had," Smithers said with a big grin. "Not too many people were eager to accept her when she first moved into the palace, though. Many of the aristocratic families were upset that Prince Charming hadn't chosen one of their daughters to wed. But she's overcome all that since."

Alex could tell they were getting much closer to the palace. They passed more small villages, which grew in size and population as they went along. She was so excited to be so close to people, actual *people*, who had spent their entire lives in the fairy-tale world. She wished with all her heart she could say she'd grown up in the Charming Kingdom.

"Do you ever find it overwhelming?" Alex asked Smithers. "Does it ever get frightening living here and knowing that at any moment a fairy could fly by and grant you a wish, or an ogre could run up and eat you?"

Smithers looked at her curiously. "Does such a place exist where people can't unexpectedly be helped or hurt?"

Alex couldn't think of any. Maybe this world and the world she was from weren't so different after all.

The cart began passing large estates. Everywhere they looked, they saw another huge, elegant home. They were all so bright and colorful, with pointed roofs that curved on the sides. Some were made from wood, others from brick, and some were covered completely in ivy.

It was something straight out of a storybook, and Alex kept reminding herself that she was in one.

"We're almost at the palace," Smithers said.

The cart began to vibrate as the dirt path beneath them turned into a cobblestone street. Shops and markets started popping up on the sides of the street as they traveled into the city. They shared the road with other carts and carriages. Villagers and townspeople alike walked alongside them and went about their day-to-day routines of shopping and trade.

"Are we there yet?" said Conner, stirring back to life.

The cart rounded a corner onto a very long and wide street. At the end of the street was an enormous palace.

"I'll take *that* as a yes," Conner said.

The palace took Alex's breath away. It was perfectly symmetrical and smooth, as if it were made out of sky-gray porcelain. Three prominent towers in the middle of the palace shared a base with a gigantic clock large enough for the whole kingdom to see. The palace almost seemed fake, it was so majestic, and was grander than they had ever imagined.

"This is where I'll drop you off," said Smithers, pulling his cart and horse over to the side of the street. "Best of luck to both of you youngins. Enjoy the town!"

"Thank you so much!" the twins said together.

They tried to offer him a few gold coins as a thank-you, but Smithers insisted that they save their money, and then went on his way.

The twins walked around the town for a good while. Everyone seemed to be buzzing with anticipation for the ball later that evening.

They found a small market and were able to purchase fresh fruit, vegetables, and breads. Alex kept trying to make small talk with every person she encountered, but most of the townspeople ignored her.

Conner kept rolling his eyes at his sister; *everything* she saw excited her.

"I don't know how I'm going to survive traveling with you if you keep up this constant state of excitement," Conner said. "It's exhausting, and it's really getting on my nerves."

"I'm sorry," Alex said. "We've been around so many trees the last couple of days. I'm just so excited to see all the people and their—ooooh! Look at that doorknob on that building! It's in the shape of a slipper! Isn't that cute?"

After a busy afternoon of sightseeing, they found a quiet hill that overlooked the town, and they sat under the shade of a large tree. The sun was starting to descend, and the twins grew anxious at the thought of another day ending.

"What's our plan?" Conner asked.

"Let's see what the journal suggests," Alex said, and pulled it out from her school bag. She flipped through the pages until she came across the section about the glass slipper.

Cinderella's glass slipper is a very difficult item to retrieve. Her slippers, without doubt, are the most cherished possession of the kingdom.

First, you must find a way into the palace. This is rather difficult, as there is only one entrance. One of Cinderella's first acts as queen was to get rid of all the servant entrances, so that when people come to the palace, they all enter as equals.

Once inside, find a way into Cinderella's royal display room. This will also be difficult, since no one is allowed in the queen's chambers without an invitation from her. The slippers are on display in a glass box on the top of a pillar in the center of the room.

The slippers are not hard to remove from inside the glass box, but the room is under constant watch by two guards at its entrance. Find a way to be alone in the royal display room and remove a slipper quietly and quickly.

Leave as fast as you can, because as soon as they notice something is missing, the guards will close the palace doors, and you'll be trapped and taken to the dungeon to be hung upside down from your toenails. Best of luck!

"How are we going to get into the palace?" Conner asked.

Alex began to think of a plan, but she was distracted by a long line of carriages driving down the main street of the town toward the palace. They were elegant and colorful, and each was of its own design. Each carriage had at least two horses pulling it, a coachman, a footman riding on the back, and a number of passengers inside.

"The ball," Alex said. "We'll have to sneak into the ball!"

"Uh-huh," said Conner, contemplating this information. "And what are we supposed to wear? Look at us! We're not dressed formally enough! And I bet we smell really fresh after walking for three days straight with no showers!"

"I have an idea," Alex said.

She opened their bags and took out their blankets. She grabbed hold of Conner and began wrapping the blanket around him, folding it strategically in certain places so it would stay up. Alex wrapped herself in the other blanket.

"There," Alex said. "Now we look like we're wearing sensible robes!"

"We look ridiculous," Conner said.

"Do you have any other ideas?" Alex asked him.

"Do you think there's a fairy godmother hotline we could call?" Conner asked.

The twins walked down to the main street. They followed the traffic of carriages toward the palace. The closer they came to the palace, the larger it grew and the more real it became.

Many of the coachmen glared at the twins with bewildered and judgmental looks. A few passengers leaned out of their carriage windows to see what the twins were doing.

"Take a picture—it lasts longer!" Conner shouted at them.

"Conner! They don't know what that means!" Alex said.

They reached the palace just as the sun was setting. As each carriage neared the front steps of the palace's entrance, its footman would run around the carriage and gently help the passengers out.

Alex and Conner had never seen such beautiful clothing. All the women wore long ball gowns of various colors, fabrics, and stitching. They wore gloves and diamonds; some wore bows and feathers in their hair. The men all dressed beautifully, too, some in formal armor and some in suits with broad, fringed shoulders and square cuffs.

All the effort and flair that the guests had put into their appearance made the twins feel very insecure about their impromptu robes. They stuck out like sore thumbs. They were the youngest people there, they were the only ones not dressed in lace or satin, and they were the only ones carrying bags. They looked exactly like what they were: a couple of kids sneaking into a ball.

An extensive row of steps led up to the palace's entrance. Alex and Conner began climbing them with the rest of the attendees. It was such a climb, they wondered if they would ever reach the top of it.

"This world has goblins and fairies, but where's an escalator when you need one?" Conner said.

"Conner!" Alex gasped. "Look at this!"

She pointed to a silver star placed in the steps underneath their feet. It said:

THIS MARKS THE VERY PLACE
WHERE CINDERELLA LEFT HER
GLASS SLIPPER BEHIND
ON THE NIGHT SHE MET
PRINCE CHARMING.

"Can you believe that's the very spot Cinderella left her glass slipper?" Alex said with both hands pressed against her heart.

"Absolutely," Conner said. "I wouldn't have climbed these steps again if I had left my shoe, either."

The twins caused quite a scene at the entrance. Everyone was absolutely appalled by their clothing. Alex could feel herself blushing from the way everyone was staring at her; she felt like she was back at school.

One palace guard in particular couldn't stop staring at them—not in a judgmental way, but as if he had seen them somewhere before and couldn't remember where. He was standing just a step inside the palace entrance, and he greeted all the guests as they passed him. He wore more badges on his uniform than any other of the guards, and he had a very thin, dark beard.

Another palace guard was collecting invitations at the doors. The twins began to panic.

"What are we going to do?" Alex whispered to her brother.

"Let me handle this," Conner said. "I saw this in a movie once. Just go with it."

"Invitations, please," the guard said.

"Our parents have our invitations, but they're already inside," Conner said.

"And who are your parents?" asked the guard snootily.

"Who are our parents?" yelled Conner, causing a bigger scene than they had already. "You mean, you don't know who we are?"

All the guards and guests looked among one another.

"Conner, calm down!" Alex said. What was he thinking?

"This man doesn't know who our parents are, Alex!" Conner continued. "I'll have you know that our parents invented wishing wells! How dare you show us any disrespect!"

Alex wanted to slap him. She looked apologetically at the people around them. They all scowled in the twins' direction, except for the guard with the thin beard. He was actually smirking at them with gentleness in his eyes.

"I'm afraid you two have to leave now," said the guard collecting the invitations.

"Leave? You're making the heirs to the wishing-well fortune leave?" Conner exclaimed loudly enough for everyone to hear.

"*Conner. Just. Shut. Up,*" Alex whispered directly into his ear.

"Is there a problem?" the guard with the thin beard asked as he approached the twins.

"Not at all!" Alex said, and began backing up, forcing Conner to move with her.

"They don't have an invitation," the other guard said.

"We were just leaving!" Alex said. "Sorry for the confusion."

"Nonsense," the guard with the thin beard said. "I just saw your parents inside the palace. Why don't I take you to them?"

Alex and Conner froze.

"You did?" Conner said, and then quickly remembered that he had to keep up with his own lie. "I mean, of course you did!" He threw a dirty look to the other guard.

"Come with me, and I'll take you straight to your parents," the guard with the thin beard said.

Before they knew it, Alex and Conner were being escorted into the palace. They were completely in over their heads. Did this guard know they were lying, and was he now escorting them directly to the dungeon? Or perhaps Conner's lie was truer than they thought, and they were about to meet a couple that were definitely not their parents.

"Allow me to introduce myself," the guard said. "I'm Sir Lampton, the head of the queen's Royal Guard. Welcome to the palace!"

"Thank you," Conner said. "I'm Conner *Wishington*, and this is my sister, Alex."

"Where are you from, Mr. and Ms. Wishington?" Lampton asked.

"Upstate Northern Kingdom," Conner said. Even he looked surprised by the words coming out of his mouth. "But our parents have a summer home in the south of the Sleeping Kingdom and a condo in the Fairy Kingdom."

Alex's eyes opened so wide that she had to remind herself to blink.

"Ah...I see," Lampton said with a curious look. "Would you like me to take your bags for you?"

"No, that's quite all right," Alex said. "We'll manage."

Lampton led the twins down a long hallway behind all the other guests. There were many large portraits of past rulers on the walls, and a red carpet ran under their feet. Alex and Conner were all eyes; they had never been inside a royal palace before. There were so many shiny things to look at.

Lampton seemed to be enjoying their excitement. He leaned between them and softly said, "You're sneaking into the palace, aren't you?"

Alex desperately looked to Conner, but he was out of lies for the night.

"Please don't throw us in the dungeon!" Alex pleaded. "We didn't mean any harm."

Conner looked at his sister with a raised eyebrow. Did she mean no harm *besides* breaking into the place and stealing a cherished item?

Lampton chuckled. "I've seen a lot of youngsters try to sneak into a royal ball before, but never have I been so entertained by such an attempt," he said.

"So, you aren't going to throw us in a cell and hang us upside down by our toenails?" Conner asked.

"We stopped doing that ages ago," Lampton said. "On the contrary, it would be my honor to show you two around."

"Really?" Conner said.

"That would be lovely!" Alex said, clasping her hands together. "Thank you!"

At the end of the hall, Lampton led the twins through a pair of golden doors into the ballroom.

At first, the sight was overwhelming. There were so many things to look at, it was impossible to focus on any one thing long enough to comprehend what it was. There was so much movement and color.

The biggest chandelier they had ever seen, with thousands of candles, hung from the ceiling above an enormous dance floor. Hundreds of formally dressed men and women filled the space. Some mingled on the sides while others danced to the music played by a small orchestra in the corner.

Everything from the archways to the accents on the walls was golden. A grand staircase descended in the back of the room just behind two empty thrones.

Conner knew it would only be a few seconds before Alex started crying.

"It's so beautiful!" Alex said, with teary eyes. "Is this where they had the ball where Cinderella and the prince met?"

"Indeed," Lampton said. "I'll never forget it. I was just a simple guard back then. The prince was meeting all the young women in the kingdom in hopes of finding a bride. Cinderella was the last to arrive that night. She entered the room, just as we are now, and everyone stopped to look at her."

"How did she look?" Alex asked.

"Magical," Lampton said with a smile, lost in his own memory. "She wore a long, violet dress that sparkled as she walked. I remember hearing the soft taps of her glass slippers as she walked past. As soon as the prince saw her, it was love at first sight; the whole palace could feel it."

Suddenly, a man blew a trumpet at the foot of the grand staircase.

"Ladies and gentlemen," the man with the trumpet announced. "It is with great honor that I welcome you to the royal ball this evening. Now, please give a warm welcome to Their Royal Majesties King Charming and Queen Cinderella!"

The guests cheered and burst into applause. The royal couple entered the ballroom, slowly making their way down the grand staircase. Alex grabbed on to Conner's arm.

"Conner," Alex gasped. "It's Cinderella! It's Cinderella!"

Although the twins had only seen illustrations of her, Cinderella was more beautiful than they had ever expected.

Her hair was auburn and styled up behind a crystal tiara. She wore white gloves and a long, turquoise gown flowed down around her, accentuating her pregnant belly. Despite all the gold and the glorious chandelier, her eyes and smile were the brightest things in the room.

King Charming was the definition of dashing. He was every bit as handsome as any description ever written about him. He had a mesmerizing smile and thick, wavy hair under a large, golden crown. He could easily have been a movie star back in the twins' world.

The king and queen took their seats on the thrones, and the guard with the trumpet blew the opening notes of another announcement.

"Let the ball begin!" the guard with the trumpet proclaimed, and was greeted with another round of excited applause.

The majority of the guests rushed to the dance floor. The orchestra began playing a fast-paced symphony. All the guests paired up and began waltzing around the room, each looking lovingly into their partner's eyes the entire time.

The king and queen remained seated. You could tell Cinderella wanted to join the dance, but her pregnancy was preventing her from doing so. King Charming only had eyes for his wife; he was enjoying her watching the dance more than the actual dance itself.

At one point, each of the dancing men collected a shoe from their partners and circled them with it before placing it back on their feet—a Cinderellian tribute, no doubt.

Time flew by as the twins watched the ball.

The unborn child Cinderella was carrying must have been kicking from all the excitement. Cinderella appeared to have some discomfort, and had been rubbing her belly and shifting in her seat for some time. She eventually whispered something into King Charming's ear. King Charming took his wife's hand and carefully helped her back up the grand staircase.

The guard blew his trumpet again. "The queen is tired and wishes to rest, but she and the king welcome you to continue this celebration without their presence."

The crowd happily obliged and continued their fun.

"Would you like a tour of the palace?" Lampton asked the twins.

"More than anything!" Alex said.

Lampton escorted the twins out of the ballroom and down a hall similar to the one they had first entered the palace through. It, too, was home to several portraits of past rulers and a long, red carpet.

"This palace was built over five hundred years ago," Lampton told them as he walked. "It's been home to the Charming Dynasty since then. This is a portrait of King Chester Charming, Cinderella's late father-in-law."

He referred to a large painting of an old, bearded man with a crown. He looked exactly like his son, but much older.

"How many King Charmings have there been?" Conner asked.

"We've lost count," Lampton said. "There are three currently. King Chester had four sons: Chance Charming, Chase Charming, Chandler Charming, and Charlie Charming."

Each of the Charming brothers had his own portrait on the wall.

"King Chance Charming is the oldest and is married to Queen Cinderella," Lampton said, and gestured to the portrait of the man they had just seen in the ballroom.

"King Chase Charming is the second oldest and is married to Queen Sleeping Beauty," Lampton continued.

Chase looked exactly like his brother, except he was a bit taller and wore a goatee.

"King Chandler Charming is the third oldest and is married to Queen Snow White," Lampton said.

Chandler looked like his brothers, but had the longest hair of all of them.

The last portrait in the hallway caught the twins' eye the most. It was hung slightly away from the rest and depicted the youngest of the Charming brothers. He was young and had a big smile. A single candle was lit beside the portrait; it appeared to be a memorial of sorts.

"Who is that?" Conner asked Lampton.

Lampton's happy expression faded away. "That's Prince Charlie, the fourth son of King Chester. He's the long-lost Charming prince," Lampton said. "He vanished one night many years ago, and no one ever saw him again."

"That's horrible," Alex said.

"His brothers led massive search parties throughout all the kingdoms, but they never found a trace of him," Lampton said sadly. "Fortunately, some good came out of the search. While on the road, Prince Chandler came across Snow White in her glass coffin, and Prince Chase discovered Sleeping Beauty asleep in her castle, and they both broke the spells put on them and were married."

"That's incredible!" Alex said. "So if Prince Charlie never went missing, Sleeping Beauty and Snow White would still be unconscious!"

"That may be," Lampton said. "And since his brothers took all the eligible princesses, Prince Chance had to put on the ball where he met Cinderella. Everything happens for a reason, I suppose."

Alex and Conner couldn't stop staring at the portrait of Prince Charlie. There was a sad energy in this part of the hallway, and the twins were especially sensitive to it. The long-lost prince couldn't have been much older than them when he'd gone missing.

Lampton clearly appreciated the twins' interest. "Now, follow me, I have something very special I want to show you," Lampton said.

Lampton led the twins down another hallway that led deeper into the palace. This part of the palace was completely vacant, and it made the twins more and more nervous as they walked. They had no idea where Lampton was taking them, and they were too timid to ask.

They rounded a corner, and at the end of another long

hall was a pair of black double doors. There were two guards on either side of the doors and a large stone arch above them with a sign that read QUEEN CINDERELLA'S ROYAL ROOM OF DISPLAY.

Alex and Conner looked to each other with light in their eyes. They had made it!

"Hello, Sir Lampton," one of the guards said.

"Good evening," Lampton said. He pushed opened the doors, and the twins followed him inside. They set their bags down and looked around the room.

The display room was a wide chamber with white pillars and a sky-blue tiled floor. The ceiling was domed and covered in golden stars. The room was illuminated by moonlight coming from a large window in the back and then reflected throughout by a series of hanging mirrors.

Several special objects were on display and placed on the top of short pillars and surrounded by thick glass cases. Brooms, buckets, and old raggedy dresses were all put on show. A family of mice lived in a glass case in a miniature replica of the palace.

In the very center of the room were Cinderella's glass slippers. They were beautiful and petite, made from pure crystal glass and decorated with diamonds.

The twins could feel their hearts sink into the pits of their stomachs as soon as they saw them. They were so close!

"Those are beautiful," Alex said. The slippers had put her in a trance.

"I'm quite partial to them myself," said a soft voice that didn't belong to Alex, Conner, or Lampton.

Sitting on the windowsill in the back of the room was Cinderella herself. They had been so astonished by the display room, they hadn't noticed her.

"Your Majesty," Lampton said. "Please forgive me; I didn't see you there. I was just giving some guests a tour of the palace."

"Quite all right, Sir Lampton," Cinderella said, and walked across the chamber to greet them. "I like to come in here occasionally after long days to clear my head. Who might these two be?"

Alex and Conner couldn't speak. They were completely starstruck.

"This is Alex and Conner," Lampton told her.

"Pleasure to meet you," Cinderella said, and held out her hand.

"We're big fans!" Conner said, and shook her hand a little too hard.

Alex couldn't move. "You're...like, my hero," Alex said to her, and that's all she could manage to say.

"Thank you, sweetheart," Cinderella said. "Welcome to my little room of memories."

"It's...*remarkable!*" Alex squeaked.

"Would you like me to show you around?" Cinderella asked.

Alex still couldn't move her limbs but was able to nod.

Cinderella began a small tour and took them around the room to each of the items on display.

"These are the brooms and buckets I used to clean my stepmother's house every day," Cinderella said. "They were my first dancing partners. I remember, whenever I was home alone, I used to dance with them around the house and pretend I was at a big royal dance. Although, I must say they weren't the best at conversation."

Cinderella and Lampton laughed. Alex and Conner were still in shock that they were in her presence. *They were standing next to* Cinderella! *And she had a sense of humor!*

"Over here are my raggedy old clothes that my Fairy Godmother turned into a beautiful ball gown," Cinderella continued. "They're not much to look at now, but whenever my Fairy Godmother visits us, they turn back into the beautiful ball gown she created for me."

"That's really cool," Conner said.

"These are my mice," Cinderella said, and showed the twins the miniature palace full of mice. She opened a latch and took a mouse out of the case. She gently petted it, and it peacefully nestled in her hand.

"Are they the mice that were transformed into horses and coachmen for your carriage?" Alex asked, finally finding her voice.

"The original mice passed away, but these are their children and their children's children," Cinderella said. "I look after them as a thank-you. They have a horrible reputation, but mice are actually very gentle creatures. You just have to give them a chance."

Cinderella put the mouse back with the others and walked to the center of the room.

"And these, I believe, need no explanation," she said, and brought the twins to the glass slippers. She removed the glass case entirely and took one of the glass slippers in her hand.

"Those couldn't have been comfortable," Conner said.

"They were surprisingly easy to move about in," Cinderella said.

"Did your feet ever get sweaty?" Conner went on. "That couldn't have looked really—*uhh*!" Alex elbowed him in the ribs.

Cinderella snickered.

"Would you like to hold one?" Cinderella asked them.

Alex nodded harder than she had ever nodded before. Cinderella gently lifted one from the pillar and handed it to her. A magical feeling went through Alex. She was holding a piece of fairy-tale history. Perhaps the most famous object of all fantasy time was in her hands. She couldn't help but get a bit emotional.

Conner, on the other hand, kept thinking of ways to steal the slipper. Alex looked up at her brother and knew what he was thinking by the intensity in his eyes. For a moment they shared the same thought. Was it possible to take off with it? Conner was actually thinking if it was possible to outrun Lampton and the two guards outside the door.

"What was it like?" Alex asked Cinderella. "What was it like to go from being a servant to being queen? What was it like to be saved from a horrible situation? Your life is literally . . . well . . . a Cinderella story."

A sadness came to Cinderella's face.

"I never thought my life would change so drastically, so I always made the most of what I had," Cinderella said. "I always laugh at the term *Cinderella story*, because, if you ask me, it doesn't matter what life you're living, life never has a solution. No matter how hard the struggles are that you leave behind, new struggles always take their place.

"People forget that I wasn't liked very much by the people of the Charming Kingdom when I first came to live at the palace," Cinderella said. "Not too many people were thrilled with the idea of a servant girl becoming their queen. Many people called me *the Pumpkin Princess* or *the Mouse Monarch* when they first discovered the details of how I had come to the ball that night. I had to earn the kingdom's respect, and it wasn't easy."

"Being a queen has to have some perks, though, right?" Conner asked. "No more scrubbing floors or dancing with cleaning supplies or talking to mice."

"Meeting the man of my dreams and starting a family is the best thing that will ever happen to me," Cinderella said with a smile, and rubbed her belly. "And that is what makes me the happiest and luckiest woman in the world. However, living a public life is a difficult thing to do, and even now I still find it a bit overwhelming. No matter what you do, you can never please everyone. And that was the hardest lesson to learn. In fact, I'm still learning it."

This was all such a revelation to Alex. Suddenly, the fairy-tale world seemed even more real than it had before. She never thought she could respect Cinderella more than she already did, but she had never thought about the story from *her* point of view.

Alex set the glass slipper back beside the other one. At first Conner shot her a look: *What are you doing? We have to steal that!* But they both knew they couldn't take it; at least not tonight, not after the kindness they had been shown.

"After all the magical things that have happened in my life, this is my most prized possession," Cinderella said, her hands still on her pregnant stomach. "And she's going to be here any day now."

"How do you know it's a girl?" Alex asked.

"Mother's intuition," Cinderella said. "She never sits still when she hears music. So she must have my taste and her father's energy."

One of the guards from the hallway burst into the display room.

"Your Majesty, Sir Lampton, your presence has been requested in the ballroom," the guard said very seriously. Something was wrong.

"What's the matter?" Sir Lampton asked.

"Soldiers from the Northern Kingdom. They've come with a message for the king and queen," he said.

Lampton handed the twins their bags, and before they knew it the twins were following him, Cinderella, and the other guards out of the display room and down the hallway toward the ballroom.

"Now how are we going to get ahold of one of the glass slippers?" Conner whispered to Alex.

"We'll have to collect all the other items first and then come back for it," Alex said. "It should be easier to explain why we need it if we have the other items. We've already established a trusting relationship with them."

"I knew I should have grabbed one when I had the chance," Conner said.

They reentered the ballroom. All the guests were still and the orchestra was dead silent. Cinderella reunited with her husband at the thrones. Dozens of the same soldiers dressed in silver armor whom Alex and Conner had seen on their first day in the Land of Stories were now spread throughout the ballroom.

"Forgive our intrusion, Your Majesty. My name is Sir Grant. I am the head of Queen Snow White's Royal Guard. We have news regarding the Evil Queen," the leader of the soldiers said.

"What is it?" King Charming said.

Everyone in the room could tell it was not good news by his tone. You could have cut the tension and worry in the air with a knife.

"Last night, a magic mirror that belonged to the Evil Queen was stolen from her former chambers," Sir Grant said. "The Evil Queen is still very much at large, and that she has her former mirrors makes her a much greater threat to all of us. We are asking—*pleading*—if anyone in the Charming Kingdom knows anything about where the Evil Queen is hiding, that they please let us know immediately."

Snow White's soldiers filed out of the ballroom. King Charming and Cinderella embraced each other, worried both for themselves and for what the news meant for their kingdom.

"It was lovely to meet you children, but I must go now," Lampton said to them. He patted their shoulders and then headed out after the soldiers.

Many of the guests began leaving as well. Alex and Conner followed them out, down the entrance steps, and away from the palace.

"This whole Evil Queen situation is starting to concern me," Alex said.

"I know, but it's not really our problem," Conner said. "We'll be long gone before anything else happens."

"I suppose so," Alex said.

"Where are we off to now?" Conner asked.

"The Little Red Riding Hood Kingdom is north of here," Alex said. "I say that's the best direction to head. I hope we have better luck getting hold of Red Riding Hood's basket."

"We'd better not chicken out this time," Conner said. "Gosh, we were *so close*!" He clenched a tight fist.

"We just couldn't have taken it, not without permission," Alex said. "It wouldn't have felt right."

"I'm so tired of being a good person," Conner said.

Despite having failed to collect a glass slipper and the abrupt end to their evening, the twins had had a pretty fantastic night. It wasn't every day that they got to have such an intimate conversation with one of the most famous women in history.

Luckily, the twins found a night driver transporting a cart full of pears to a village in the northern part of the Charming Kingdom. They convinced him to let them ride in the back of his carriage in exchange for a few gold coins. It would only be a few miles' walk to the Red Riding Hood Kingdom from there.

Conner fell asleep as soon as they climbed aboard. Alex couldn't sleep, so she decided to read through the journal again. She reached into her bag and was astounded to discover what was inside it.

"Conner!" Alex gasped.

Conner jumped back to consciousness. "What is it?" he asked.

He looked over and saw something very shiny in his sister's hand. His eyes were still a little blurry from sleeping, and he had to let them adjust before realizing what it was.

"A glass slipper!" Conner exclaimed, and Alex gestured for him to keep quiet so the driver wouldn't hear them. "How in the world did we get one? Did you steal it?"

"I thought it was you!" Alex's mouth was so wide, it could have fit a dozen of the pears inside it.

"No, it wasn't me, I swear! Do you think Lampton or Cinderella put it in your bag?" Conner asked. "Do you think one of them knew we needed it?"

"I have no idea," Alex said. She couldn't believe she was actually holding on to one of Cinderella's glass slippers. They both were completely dumbfounded.

"Looks like our trip to the Charming Kingdom wasn't such a waste after all," Conner said.

CHAPTER TEN

THE RED RIDING HOOD KINGDOM

The subtle shakes of the pear cart finally rocked Alex and Conner to sleep. If they hadn't been so exhausted from the previous restless night and eventful day, the shock of discovering the glass slipper in their possession would have kept them up all night.

The next morning, they awoke just as the cart was arriving at the northern village it was destined for. The first thing Alex did when she awoke was to make sure the slipper was still in her tight grip as it had been when she'd fallen asleep. She couldn't let go of it; she was afraid that if it wasn't in her hands at all times, it might disappear just as easily as it appeared.

The mystery of how it had gotten into her bag was still the most prominent thing on their minds.

"Do you think it was magic?" Conner asked Alex. "Maybe the slipper knew we needed it and transported itself into your bag?"

"I've read enough fantasy books to know that that's a possibility," Alex said. "And after everything we've been through, I wouldn't be surprised. But the point is, we have it now. It's one less item we have to collect, so let's focus all our energy into getting ahold of Red Riding Hood's basket."

She wrapped a blanket around the slipper for safekeeping and stored it in her bag. They didn't want any unwanted attention from carrying it around.

"I hope Cinderella or Lampton don't send soldiers after us once they realize it's gone," Conner said.

Alex hadn't thought about that. What if, as they were speaking, Lampton was putting together a band of soldiers to find them and take them into captivity?

"Then we'll tell him the truth and worry about it when it happens," Alex said. "But let's keep moving in the meantime."

There didn't appear to be any roads or paths on the map that went to the Red Riding Hood Kingdom, so the twins were forced to travel straight through a forest of elm trees to get there.

Alex read from the journal as they walked.

As everyone knows, the Red Riding Hood Kingdom is surrounded by a tall wall to keep out the wolves. There are guarded entrances into the kingdom along the perimeter of the wall.

"So we'll find the wall, find an entrance, and be inside the kingdom in no time," Alex said.

"What if they don't let us inside?" Conner asked.

"I can't imagine why they wouldn't let us in," Alex asked. "But if they don't, this time let me do the talking."

An hour or so of walking later, the twins could see the wall surrounding the kingdom in the distance. It was massive. It was thirty feet tall and made from enormous gray bricks. The same warning sign was posted on the wall every few feet or so:

WOLVES BEWARE

BY C.R.A.W.L. DECREE AND APPROVED BY THE

HAPPILY EVER AFTER ASSEMBLY,

WOLVES OF ANY KIND, BREED, OR COLOR

ARE STRICTLY PROHIBITED FROM ENTERING

THE RED RIDING HOOD KINGDOM.

ALL TRESPASSERS WILL BE KILLED

AND TURNED INTO RUGS, COATS, OR DECORATION.

YOU HAVE BEEN WARNED.
NOW BEGONE.

"Wow," Conner said. "The wolves are definitely not getting in there."

They walked beside the wall for another couple of hours but never found an entrance. Alex reread the journal and found a part that she had missed.

> There is a north entrance, a south entrance, an east entrance, and a west entrance. Each has its own path that goes to the center of the kingdom, where the town is. There is only one town in the Red Riding Hood Kingdom; the rest is farmland.

"Oh no," Alex said. "I misread the journal. Apparently there are only four entrances into the kingdom."

"And how close are we to one of them?" Conner asked. Alex looked closely at the map and her eyes widened a bit. Conner could tell it wasn't going to be good news.

"It looks like we're right in between the west entrance and the south entrance, which means—"

"More walking?" Conner said with a furrowed forehead and his hands on his hips.

"Yes..." Alex said, bearing the bad news. "About a day or two's worth."

Conner walked around in a circle, frustrated beyond belief.

"This is so annoying!" Conner yelled. "Why can't anything be easy?"

"Conner, everything's okay. It's just going to take a little longer to—"

"No, Alex, it's not okay!" Conner yelled. "We've been in this world for almost a week! I want to go home! I miss Mom! I miss my friends! I'm even starting to miss *Mrs. Peters*! There, I admitted it!"

Conner was so upset that he kicked a tree, but he ended up just hurting his foot.

"Ouch!" he yelled.

"I miss home, too, but there's nothing I can do about it!" Alex said. "We'll get home *when we get home*, and that's that. But in the meantime, it doesn't do us any good to be angry. We just have to get through it!"

Conner crossed his arms and his shoulders slumped. He was aggravated almost to tears. Alex assumed they were closer to the southern entrance, and led the way toward it. Conner verbalized his frustrations the entire way.

"I miss pavement and sidewalks," Conner ranted. "I miss our crappy rental house. I miss our neighborhood. I miss that dog down the street that barks constantly through the night. I miss homework. I miss getting detention for not doing homework."

"Let it out, Conner," Alex said. "You'll feel better."

"I hate this place," Conner continued. "I hate the dirt paths. I hate the man-eating witches. I hate the mutant-size wolves. I hate sleeping outside. I hate bridge trolls. I hate all the trees . . . wait, *that's it! The trees!*"

Conner searched their surroundings and ran ahead to a big tree next to the kingdom's wall.

"What are you doing?" Alex asked.

"I'm getting inside the kingdom! I'm going to climb this tree and hop over the wall!" Conner yelled back at her. He started climbing it at a very quick and determined pace.

"It's a thirty-foot drop on the other side at least!" Alex shouted at him.

"Come on, Alex!" Conner said and gestured for her to follow him.

"I'm not climbing that tree!" she said.

"You'll climb up Rapunzel's tower but a tree is out of the question?" he asked mockingly.

"And I shouldn't have done that! I agree!" she said, but was ignored.

Conner was almost at the top of the tree. Alex ran over to the tree and climbed a little ways after him.

"Conner, please come down from there! I'd rather travel slowly and safely than quickly and dangerously!" she said.

Conner stood up on the tallest branch of the tree. The top of the wall was just a few feet away.

"I'm gonna jump to the wall and see if I can spot a way down," Conner said.

"Conner! Don't be stupid! Climb down right now! You're going to hurt yourself!" Alex demanded.

"Wish me luck!" Conner said, and prepped himself for the jump. "One...two...*three*!" Conner jumped off the tree branch and soared toward the wall.

"*No!*" Alex yelled.

He had jumped a little too hard. He missed the wall by a few inches and flew over it headfirst.

"Allleeeexxxx!" Conner bellowed as he fell.

She heard a large *thump* from the other side, but she couldn't see anything.

"Conner!" Alex screamed. "Conner, are you all right? Conner, are you alive?" She was hysterical.

Alex clambered up the tree faster than any animal she had ever seen in a documentary.

"Conner, answer me!" she pleaded. "Can you hear me? Are you hurt?"

Alex heard laughter just as she reached the top of the tree. On the other side of the wall, she saw Conner lying safely on a big stack of hay.

"Hi, Alex!" Conner said with a big smile on his face.

"Conner! You scared me to death!" Alex shouted.

"I know! It was so entertaining!" Conner said. "Do you really think I would have jumped if I didn't see something to land on?"

"I'm glad you're alive, so I can kill you myself," Alex said.

"Jump over! It's a soft landing, I promise!" he said.

"Fine!" Alex said. She carefully tossed him her bag before jumping over the fence.

Conner was right: The landing was soft. They were covered in hay, and they brushed it off each other.

"Take a look at this place," Alex said as she and Conner journeyed into the Red Riding Hood Kingdom. They felt as if they had entered another dimension all over again.

There were rolling hills of farmland for as far as they

could see. Cows and sheep were grazing across the fields. Shepherds with curved staffs and shepherdesses in large bonnets attended to the animals with their dogs.

"Everything's so peaceful here!" Alex said. "I feel like I'm in a nursery rhyme."

"They must be bored out of their minds," Conner said.

"I wonder whose land this is?" Alex said.

A few moments later, Alex got her answer. They passed a big, wooden sign stuck into the ground that said:

BO PEEP FAMILY FARMS

The scenery was so pleasant that the time went by fairly fast. After they'd traveled a while longer, the peaked and pointed rooftops of the town came into view. They couldn't see much while looking at it from the outskirts, but once they were in the center of it, the town came to life.

"How adorable!" Alex squealed at first sight of the town.

It was so dainty and picturesque that they felt like they were in a theme park. It was filled with tiny cottage homes and shops made of bricks or stone walls and hay roofs. A bell in the steeple of an old schoolhouse rang. Many staff-carrying men and bonnet-wearing women like the ones they had seen in the fields walked about the town pulling goats and sheep along with them.

Among the many stores and shops were the Henny Penny Bank, Jack Horner's Pie Shop, and the Pat-a-Cake

Bakery. The Shoe Inn, just adjacent to the main town, was a boot of gigantic proportions turned into a working hotel.

In the very center of the town was a grassy park that hosted several memorials and monuments. Alex was doing mental backflips at the sight of each of them.

A small brick wall that stood by itself had a golden plaque on it that said:

SIR HUMPTY DUMPTY'S WALL
YOU WERE A GOOD EGG AND SHALL BE MISSED BY MORE THAN JUST THE KING'S HORSES AND MEN.
REST IN PIECES

Just past Humpty Dumpty's wall was a small hill with a well on top of it. A sign pointing to the hill said:

JACK AND JILL HILL

In the middle of the park was a circular fountain. A statue of a young shepherd boy stood in the center of it and water poured from the mouths of the sheep that were under him. The carved dedication of the fountain read:

IN MEMORY OF THE BOY WHO CRIED WOLF
YOU WERE A LIAR, BUT YOU WERE LOVED.

The twins were so enthralled by everything that they were getting strange looks from the villagers and townspeople.

"This place reminds me of that miniature golf course in town," Conner said. "Not the one by us, but the really legit one across town, where all the rich kids live."

At the edge of town, with the best view of the park, was Red Riding Hood's castle. The castle had four tall towers that could be seen from anywhere in town. It appropriately had red walls with dark red roofs. A moat circled the castle and had its own water mill.

The castle looked massive from far away. However, as the twins moved closer to it, they realized it wasn't very big at all; it was just built to *look* big. The moat around it was so small that one of the twins could have easily stepped over it.

"I bet you Red Riding Hood's basket is in there somewhere," Conner said.

Alex retrieved the journal from out of her bag and began reading the specifics of collecting the basket to Conner.

Unlike every other palace or castle, Red Riding Hood's isn't very difficult to break into. The castle was built so quickly after the C.R.A.W.L. Revolution that the builders forgot to add some basic necessities. The kitchen windows located in the back of the castle have no locks on them.

The Red Riding Hood Kingdom is the safest and smallest of all the kingdoms; therefore, they're short-handed on soldiers and guards. The halls of the castle are only patrolled until midnight, and the guards don't return until dawn. Sneak into the castle between midnight and dawn through the kitchen windows, stay away from the main halls, and you should be fine.

Queen Red Riding Hood has a special room in her chambers devoted to all the baskets she's acquired and been given over the years. Find this room, and you'll find her very first basket, the one she took with her to her grandmother's house all those years ago.

You don't need to collect the whole basket, just a small chunk of the tree bark that surrounds the rim. It should be easy to identify, as there is already a chunk of tree bark missing from when I collected it.

"And I was just hoping we could ring the doorbell and ask for it," Conner said.

Alex looked up at all the towers and windows. She wondered which window belonged to the room they would find the basket in. And as she looked up at the castle, something else entirely caught her eye.

"Look over there!" Alex said, and pointed to the sky.

Conner turned to look in the direction she was pointing. Sticking straight up into the air a hundred feet or so was an enormous beanstalk.

"That must be Jack's beanstalk!" Alex said. "Are you thinking what I'm thinking?"

"No, but I'm sure you want to go see the beanstalk—" Conner said, and before he could finish, Alex had taken off toward it.

The twins ran through the town and had to take a trail leading out of town to get to the beanstalk. They passed a few cottage homes and more farmland as they traveled; it was much farther than they had thought. Eventually, they saw the base of the beanstalk ahead.

It was thick and curly and had huge leaves. It grew right next to an old, decrepit shack that was only large enough to have one room inside of it. A little ways behind the beanstalk and the shack was a large, elegant manor with yellow bricks and enough chimneys and windows to hold a dozen rooms.

"Which one of those is Jack's house?" Conner asked as they approached the beanstalk.

Alex looked at it for a moment until she figured it out.

"That shack must be where Jack lived with his mother when they were poor, and then after he defeated the giant and became rich, they must have built a new home just behind it!" she said happily. "They're both his!"

Conner shrugged. He had no reason to doubt her guess.

"Look how tall it is!" Alex said once they had reached the base of the beanstalk. "It would take a lot of bravery to climb that!"

Just then they heard a door slam, and a man came out of the manor. He was young and tall with short hair and broad shoulders. He was very good-looking, but he wore a subdued expression. He carried an axe and a log.

"Look, Alex!" Conner whispered. "Do you think that's Jack?"

"I don't know," she whispered back. "Let's ask him."

The man set the log on a chopping block in the front yard and began chopping the log into small pieces.

"Hi there!" said Alex, being extra friendly.

"Hello," said the man, never looking up from chopping.

"Are you Jack?" Conner asked him.

"Yup," the man said. "Do you need something?"

"No, we're just traveling around," Alex said. "We saw your beanstalk from all the way in town and wanted to get a closer look."

"Many people do," Jack said. "I have to chop it down once a week because it grows so fast."

His expression barely changed as he chopped the wood. Was he just accustomed to random people approaching his home and beanstalk, and he'd become numb to it?

"You have a lovely home," Alex said.

"Except for that eyesore in the front," Conner said, and nodded toward the shack behind him.

"Conner, be polite!" Alex said.

"I've turned it into a workshop," Jack told them. He finished chopping the wood, collected the pieces in his hands, went into the shack, and slammed the door behind him.

"Well, someone isn't much of a conversationalist," Conner said.

"I wonder what's wrong with him. He seems so different," Alex said.

"Have you met before?" Conner asked. Sometimes he wondered if she had forgotten that they were from another world.

"No, I just mean from the way he's always been described," Alex said. "He was always so energetic and adventurous. I wonder what's troubling him."

"Maybe he doesn't like people coming up to his house," said Conner. "If I were him, I'd get really annoyed, too—"

Conner had another sarcastic comment to add, but he was distracted by a high-pitched sound coming from inside the manor.

"Do you hear that?" Conner asked Alex. "It sounds like *singing.*"

They both turned to face the manor as a set of window shutters were pushed open. The twins wouldn't have believed it if they hadn't been so close, but standing behind the open window was a golden woman.

She happily sang a soprano ballad as loudly as she could. A set of strings played along with her, but the twins couldn't see where the music was coming from.

"Oh, the day is here, and so am I,
To wistfully dream of birds that fly.
If I had legs, I'd see the world and travel away,
But I'm only a harp, and this window is where I
shall stay."

She turned to face the twins as she sang the final note, and they noticed a set of strings connected to her back. The strings played magically along to her voice. She was a magic harp.

"Hello, children! I didn't see you there!" the harp said.

Alex jumped up and down. "Are you the magical harp?" she asked. "The one that Jack saved from the giant?"

"The one and only!" the harp said, and struck a dramatic pose. "And thank God he did, because giants have terrible taste in music! You wouldn't believe the numbers he used to force me to perform for him! All the lyrics were about eating sheep and stepping on villagers! Would you like me to sing for you?"

"No, thanks," Conner said.

The harp took offense to this.

"I remember that day like it was yesterday!" the harp said. "There I was, minding my own business, being a slave for the giant, when suddenly this skinny peasant boy walks by, and I was like, 'Hey there! Why don't you rescue me? I could use some rescuing!' The next thing I know, we're zooming down a beanstalk, being chased by the giant! Jack chopped down the beanstalk and the giant fell to his death! *Splat!* Right on the Bo Peep farms! It was quite a day!"

"How terrifying!" Alex said.

"It was the most excitement I had had in a hundred years! Everything worked out just wonderfully, though. Jack and his mother became rich, I wasn't a slave anymore, and the Bo Peep family said the giant was the best fertilizer their farms had ever used!"

"That's so wrong," Conner said to himself.

"What are you two doing here?" the harp asked them with a big smile.

Alex and Conner looked at each other, both afraid to answer.

"We're just visiting," Alex said. "We've never been to the Red Riding Hood Kingdom before."

"We were in town and saw the beanstalk and wanted to see it up close," Conner said.

"Then, welcome!" the harp said. "Don't you just love it here? I know I do! I've been around the world, and I've never felt more comfortable! It's so safe here! The people are all friendly farmers, and the best part is, no wolves are allowed! Are you two thinking of moving? Wouldn't that be nice? I think you should move here and visit me every day!"

The harp was very chatty, and the twins could tell she was desperate for attention. Spending every day cooped in a house couldn't be easy.

"We're actually on our way home," Conner said. "We just have to make a stop at Red Riding Hood's castle, and then we'll be on our way. We've never been before—"

"You should have Jack take you!" the harp said. "He's headed there this afternoon to meet with Queen Red Riding Hood."

"He is?" Alex asked.

"Oh, yes," the harp said. "He visits her at the end of every week and brings her a handmade basket every time."

The harp looked side to side to make sure no one else was listening, but there was no one in sight.

"Now, you didn't hear this from me," the harp said excitedly, with gossip in her eyes. "Queen Red Riding Hood calls him to the castle every week and proposes to him! Poor thing has been in love with him since they were kids!"

"Really?" Alex said. "Does that mean they're getting married?"

"Oh, heavens no," the harp said. "Jack can't stand her! He turns her down every time."

"Why would he do that? Doesn't he want to be king?" Conner asked.

"His heart belongs to someone else," the harp said sadly, and the strings on her back played a sad chord.

"Who does he love?" Alex asked.

"Let me guess," Conner said. "Little Miss Muffet?"

"Of course not," the harp said. "Miss Muffet married Georgie Porgie but, as everyone knows, he has had countless affairs, but that's another story—"

"Back to Jack," Alex said.

"Oh, right. Well, I'm not sure who he's in love with. I've never seen her," the harp said. "All I know is, he's never been the same since she moved away."

Alex and Conner looked at each other with the same questioning expression. Who could it be? Was that the reason he had seemed so gloomy?

The door of the shack opened, and Jack emerged with a basket made from the pieces of wood he had just chopped.

"Hey, Jack, I have a wonderful idea!" the harp called out. "Why don't you take these two with you to the castle? They've never been inside it before!"

Jack seemed hesitant.

"Please, Mr. Jack!" Alex pleaded. "We won't be any trouble!"

"Come on, Jack! Make their day!" the harp pleaded.

"All right," Jack said.

Jack turned and began traveling toward the town. The twins ran after him.

"Thanks so much," Alex called back to the harp.

"You're welcome!" the harp said. "Come back and visit me ... *please*!"

Jack was a very fast walker. His legs were much longer than the twins', so they found it difficult to keep up with him.

"It's very kind of you to let us tag along," Alex said to Jack, but he never looked up from the ground.

"You're not much of a talker, are you?" Conner said.

"I don't have much to say," Jack said.

Conner nodded at him; he understood completely. As they neared the town, Alex pulled Conner aside.

"How lucky is this?" she said. "If we get inside the castle and get ahold of the basket, we'll be out of this kingdom in no time!"

They traveled into the town and reached the castle. There was a set of large, wooden doors at the castle's entrance. Jack knocked on the door. A moment later, a small window in the middle of the door opened and a set of eyes appeared.

"Who goes there?" said a voice on the other side of the doors.

"It's Jack," Jack said. "Again."

"Who is that behind you?" the voice demanded, and the eyes looked over Jack's shoulder to Alex and Conner. They awkwardly waved.

"Oh...what are your names again?" Jack asked the twins.

"Alex and Conner," Alex told him, and gave him a thumbs-up.

"These are my friends, Alex and Conner. They're accompanying me to the castle today," Jack said.

The doors opened, and the twins followed Jack into the castle.

It felt like a condensed version of Cinderella's palace. The halls weren't quite as long, and the furniture wasn't quite as nice. There were many portraits hung on the walls, but they all were of Queen Red Riding Hood at various ages in different poses, each one more grand than the last.

The twins waited with Jack in a hall outside another set of doors. Jack knocked on the doors and immediately took a seat on a bench outside them.

"This always takes a moment," Jack said.

A series of footsteps and sounds of rushing about came from the other side of the doors.

"Wait, don't open the door. I'm not ready yet!" someone whispered. *"Hand me that cape! No, not that one, the other one, with the hood! Hurry!"*

Jack began to whistle as he waited.

"How do I look? What about my dress, does it seem all right to you?" the whispers continued. *"All right, I'm ready. Let him in! Quickly!"*

Jack stood up just as the doors were opened by a pink-faced and out-of-breath handmaiden. She escorted Jack inside, and the twins followed.

They entered a long room with tall windows on both sides. The walls were covered in more portraits of the queen. Looking up from the floor was a giant wolf head with red eyes and a set of sharp teeth. It looked just like one of the wolves the twins had seen in the Dwarf Forests, and it alarmed them at first, before they discovered it was just a wolf-skin rug spread out on the floor. The twins knew without asking that the rug must have been the Big Bad Wolf himself at one point.

At the very end of the room, perched elegantly—almost *too* elegantly—on a large throne was Queen Red Riding Hood.

"Hello, Jack!" Red Riding Hood said.

Red Riding Hood was a very pretty young woman around the same age as Jack. She had bright blue eyes and blonde hair that was done up glamorously behind her crown. She wore a long, red gown with a matching hooded cape and a pink corset. She wore a necklace with a massive diamond, her shoulders were completely bare, and she wore a pair of long gloves with a dozen sparkly rings on her fingers.

She was showing too much skin, wearing too much makeup, and was dressed too well for the middle of the day.

"Hello, Red," Jack said.

"What a surprise! I wasn't even expecting you!" she said.

"Uh-huh," Jack said.

"And I see you brought . . . *guests*?" Red asked. She was not happy to see that she and Jack were not alone.

"Yes, this is Alex and Conner," Jack said.

"Hello!" Alex said bashfully.

"What's up, Red?" Conner said, and was then elbowed by his sister.

"Helloooo," Red said behind a clenched and very fake smile. "Welcome to my castle. Please have a seat."

Red clapped her hands, and two servants placed a large, cushy chair right next to her throne for Jack to sit on. They brought Alex and Conner each a small stool to sit on some distance away from Red and Jack.

Jack moved the chair back away from the throne a couple feet before sitting on it. He handed Red the basket he had made for her.

"Is this for me?" Red asked him. "Oh, how thoughtful of you! You are just too sweet for words! I'll cherish it!"

"You always do," Jack said.

"So, tell me, what's new with you?" Red asked Jack. She was leaning toward him as far as she possibly could without falling off of her throne.

"Nothing much," Jack said. "Same old, same old." His body language made it obvious that he was ready to leave from the minute he'd sat down. "How's the kingdom?"

"Oh, I never bother myself with all that talk of economy and security and peasant needs and blah blah blah," Red said. "My granny takes care of all that for me. She's much better at it than I would be, anyway."

Red got tired of holding the basket. She snapped her fingers, and her handmaiden collected the basket from her.

"Put it with the others," Red instructed.

The handmaiden collected it from her and headed out of the room. The twins figured this was their chance.

"May we see the others?" Alex asked.

"The others?" Red asked.

"The other baskets," Alex said. Red was looking at her peculiarly. "My brother loves baskets."

Conner nodded, going along with it.

"I do! They're my most favorite thing ever!" Conner said. "You know what they say, life is better with baskets!"

Red was staring at them as if they were the strangest people she had ever met in her life.

"If you wish," she said, and shooed them off.

Alex and Conner jumped up and followed the handmaiden out of the room and down a hall.

"Where does Queen Red Riding Hood keep all of her baskets?" Alex asked the handmaiden, and then winked at Conner. She wasn't very good at playing dumb.

"She has a chamber dedicated entirely to baskets," the handmaiden said.

"So, she has a basket room?" Conner asked.

"Yes, and if you received as many as she did a year, you would, too," the handmaiden said.

"How many are we talking about?" Conner asked.

"You'll see," she said.

The handmaiden opened a door, and the three of them walked inside. The room was twice the size of the room they had just been in and was filled from floor to ceiling with thousands and thousands of baskets.

Some were on shelves, some were stacked neatly, and others were just piled around the room. The handmaiden tossed the basket from Jack in a pile on one side of the room.

"The queen gets them for birthdays, holidays, and any special occasion," the handmaiden said. "Some are from villagers, some from friends, others are from the monarchs of neighboring kingdoms."

Alex and Conner stared around the room with their mouths open. How would they ever find the basket they were looking for in all of this?

"Do you mind if we have a look around?" Alex managed to say through her shock.

"I suppose," the handmaiden said. She looked at the twins curiously and then left them inside the basket room.

The twins could barely breathe. They both felt as if a dumbbell had suddenly been tied to their chests.

"I have never felt so overwhelmed in my life!" Conner declared. "This is like trying to do the whole summer break packet of homework the day before school starts again, but a thousand times worse. How are we going to look through all of these?"

"It's not that bad...." Alex tried convincing him, but she didn't even convince herself. "We just need to start. You take one side, and I'll take the other. Let's do this."

They split and rapidly began looking through the piles and piles of baskets for the one with the bark rim. They knew they didn't have much time and grew more anxious after each second.

They had no idea there could be so many shapes and sizes and designs for baskets. Like snowflakes, each one was different from the next.

Alex was paranoid that she had missed it. Conner kept getting splinters and kept shouting *"Ah!"* every time it happened.

They had been there for almost an hour and still hadn't covered even a fourth of the room. They were making a huge mess. The room was twice as disorganized now as it had been when they'd entered it. Even Alex wasn't hesitating, throwing around baskets that she had already examined.

"This is impossible!" Conner yelled, kicking a pile of baskets.

Just as he kicked the pile, the door swung open and the

handmaiden returned. Alex and Conner froze. She was appalled by the chaos they had caused.

"I don't know what on earth you're doing, but I think it's time for you two to leave," she said.

The handmaiden escorted them back to the throne room. This time, she watched them like a hawk as they sat on their stools.

Queen Red Riding Hood was literally hanging off her throne and grabbing hold of Jack's chair as she talked to him. The twins had never seen Jack look so bored and lifeless. Neither of them had noticed the twins return.

"You know, Jack," Red said, circling his forearm with her finger. "The Red Riding Hood Kingdom isn't much of a *kingdom* without a *king*...."

"Perhaps you should change the name to the Red Riding Hood Queendom," Jack said.

Red laughed much harder than she should have. "You're so funny! But that's not what I meant. What I'm trying to tell you, Jack, is that I've never been more ready to get married. If *someone* asked me for my hand in marriage today, I would say yes! Do you know *anyone* who might be interested in marrying me? In being king? *Anyone?*"

A white dove suddenly flew by one of the windows outside and sat on the window ledge. As soon as Jack saw it, his entire face lit up. His eyes grew wide, and he smiled; for once, he looked happy.

He turned to Red. Clearly she wasn't used to seeing him like this, either. The twins could practically see her heart beating out of her chest as excitement filled her body. Was he going to propose? Was this the moment she had been waiting for for so long?

"Red," Jack said.

"Yes, Jack?" Red said.

"I have to go," Jack said, jumping up and heading out of the throne room. Red almost fell off of her throne.

"Go?" she said. "Go where?"

"Home," Jack called out, not even looking back at her. "I'll see you next week."

Red crossed her arms and pouted. He was the only thing preventing her from having *everything*.

The twins felt it was best to leave with Jack, so they followed him out of the castle.

"It was wonderful meeting you, Alex, Conner," Jack said, and shook their hands.

"Likewise," Alex said. "Thanks again for taking us to the castle."

"My pleasure! I hope to run into you someday soon," Jack said, and then headed in the direction of his home with a new bounce in his step.

It was very strange. Jack was now acting like the person Alex had always thought he would be.

"What is that guy's deal? How does someone go from a zombie to a camp counselor in a matter of seconds?" Conner said.

"I don't know," Alex said, looking after him as he walked away. "He's a very odd man."

"Looks like we'll be sneaking into the castle after all," Conner said, and slumped to a seated position on the ground.

"At least we know what to expect tonight, and we already went through a good portion of the baskets," Alex said. "We just have to wait until midnight."

"And in the meantime, I could really use a nap," Conner said.

The twins traveled up the street and booked a room at the Shoe Inn. Their room had a perfect view of Red Riding Hood's castle. It was somewhere near the shoe's tongue, because a set of laces crossed through one of their walls. The room also had a working bathtub, and they both took turns using it, since they hadn't been able to bathe in so long.

"That was the best bath I think I'll ever have," Conner said.

They both decided to rest for a little bit, and as soon as their bodies touched the bed, they both fell into a deep sleep. They slept for a few hours and woke up shortly before midnight.

"What's our game plan for tonight?" Conner said. "It'll be the first time we'll ever be breaking and entering anywhere, so I'm extra anxious."

"Let's take account of everything we have now," Alex said, and dumped all the contents of their bags onto the bed.

"We have two blankets, a bag of gold coins, a dagger, a

lock of Rapunzel's hair, a glass slipper, a map, a journal, and a satchel of food," Alex listed. "We can use the dagger to cut a chunk of wood out of the basket, but it's going to be dark. We'll need some light."

"Let's take these lanterns," Conner said, and gathered lanterns that were on the bed sides.

"Great," Alex said. "We should plan on leaving the kingdom right after, just in case we run into some trouble. We'll head to the east entrance of the kingdom, and that'll bring us close to the border of the Fairy Kingdom."

Conner lowered his head. "I was so looking forward to coming back to this bed."

At a quarter to midnight, Alex and Conner gathered all their things, lit their lanterns, and left the Shoe Inn. They walked across town to the castle. It was so quiet at night; not even farm animals were up this late.

They hid behind Humpty Dumpty's wall and watched through the castle windows as guards patrolled the halls.

"Just a few more minutes and they'll leave," Alex said.

A few minutes later, they saw fewer and fewer guards walk past the windows.

"Are they gone?" Conner asked.

"They must be!" Alex said. "Let's go."

They ran around to the back of the castle and saw a large kitchen through a set of windows. They hopped across the moat—they knew they'd be able to!—and pulled at the window. Like the journal had said, it didn't have a lock, and it opened easily.

Alex crawled into the kitchen first. She was as quiet as possible; the only sound she made came from the intense beats of her heart. Conner climbed in after and knocked over a stack of pots and pans.

Alex was mortified. "I'm going to kill you!" she mouthed at him.

"Sorry!" he mouthed back at her.

They waited for a moment to see if anyone had heard the disturbance, but no one had.

The twins left the kitchen and found themselves in a hallway with, to no surprise, more portraits of Red Riding Hood.

"That Red Riding Hood sure loves having her portrait painted," Conner said.

"Maybe there are so many paintings of her because she's the first monarch the kingdom has ever had. It doesn't have the history the Charming Kingdom has," Alex said.

"Or she's just a self-obsessed twit," Conner said.

They traveled down the hall, then another one, then up a set of stairs and down another hall.

"Do you know where you're going?" Conner asked.

"I thought I was following you!" Alex said.

"What? Since when do you follow me?" Conner said.

A shadow was creeping toward them from down the hall. As it got closer, they could see it was the silhouette of a guard.

"A guard!" Alex whispered, and pointed at the shadow. They ran down the hall and entered the first room they found.

The room was pitch-black.

"Where are we now?" Conner asked.

"Why are you asking me questions you know I don't have the answers to?" Alex said.

Alex waited by the door and listened for the guard to pass by. Conner moved around the room with his hands stretched out in the darkness so he wouldn't bump into anything.

Their eyes began to adjust to the darkness.

"Alex, I think I can see something—" Conner walked right into what he thought was a doorway and suddenly saw a pale face staring back at him. He fell to the floor with fear. He screamed as quietly as he could.

"Alex! There's someone standing over there in the doorway! He's so creepy and ugly!" Conner said, pointing up.

Alex ran to his side and squinted her eyes to see what he was talking about.

"That's not a doorway; that's a mirror, you idiot!" Alex said.

"Oh," Conner said, and Alex helped him up to his feet.

"Oh my, what big claws you have," said a voice behind Alex and Conner, causing them both to jump five feet into the air.

They turned to see an enormous four-poster bed with silky red sheets and lacy white curtains around it. In the bed, talking in her sleep, was Queen Red Riding Hood.

"We're in the queen's bedroom!" Conner whispered to Alex.

"Oh my, what a big nose you have, Grandma," Red said, still very much asleep.

"Is she having a nightmare?" Conner asked.

"Oh my, what big sharp teeth you have—*Wooolf*!" Red screamed, and sat straight up in her bed, awake. Alex and Conner dropped to the floor, out of her view.

She was out of breath, and beads of sweat appeared on her forehead. She finally caught her breath. "Not again," she said, and then, frustrated, laid back down to sleep.

Alex and Conner were afraid to move.

"Did she go back to sleep yet?" Conner asked.

"How are we supposed to tell?" Alex asked.

"Oh my, what big strong arms you have, Jack," Red said.

"I'm guessing she's asleep," Conner said, and confidently stood.

"Oh my, what soft lips you have, Jack," Red said.

"Let's get out of here before we hear her describe anything else!" Conner said.

They emerged back into the hall and traveled around the castle for a while longer. All the halls looked so familiar, it seemed impossible to find the basket room. Every time they thought they had found the right door, they found themselves in a drawing room or a dining room or a ballroom.

"Let's find the entrance and retrace our steps to the throne room—" Alex began, but Conner interrupted her.

"No need. The baskets are in there," he said, and pointed to a door beside them.

"How do you know?" Alex asked him.

"Because I remember that portrait of Red being next to the basket room," Conner said, and pointed to a portrait where Red Riding Hood was barely clothed, with only a wolf-skin coat to cover her.

Alex gave Conner a really dirty look.

"What?" Conner asked with a smirk. "It's memorable."

They pushed the door open and found the room they had spent the entire afternoon in earlier.

"Let's take it from where we left off," Alex said. She and Conner split up and headed to the areas they had last searched.

It had been hard during the day, but it was even harder at night, since they had only the light from their lanterns to go by. After a few hours of searching, their anxiety levels were as high as Jack's beanstalk.

Suddenly, the twins heard a loud *clank!*

"What was that?" Alex said.

"Alex, look up there!" Conner said, pointing to a window. On the window ledge was a shiny X-shaped object.

"What is that?" Alex asked.

"It's a grappling hook!" Conner said. It jerked slightly in a consistent pattern. "I think someone's climbing up! *Hide!*"

They left their lanterns on the ground and dove behind a pile of baskets.

A moment later, a figure appeared on the window ledge. It took out a sharp knife and cut out a large circle in the window and then quietly crawled into the room. It was a woman who the twins had never seen before. Her clothing was made out of plant leaves sewn together, and her hair was a shade of red so dark it almost seemed purple.

The woman scanned the room and looked cautiously at the two lanterns. Did she know the twins were in there? Like an animal, the woman began sniffing around the room. She searched through the baskets as she sniffed, discarding some by tossing them behind her.

She went around the room, using her nose as her guide, until finally she locked in on one direction. She climbed on top of a pile of baskets to reach the top of a shelf. She reached her hand to the back of the shelf and pulled out a basket. It had a rim made of tree bark.

Alex and Conner looked at each other. *There it is!*

The woman carved a big chunk of bark out of the basket and then tucked it safely into her belt. She put the basket back on the shelf and climbed down the pile of baskets and headed for the window.

She was just about to climb through the window when she heard an *"Ah!"* come from the other side of the room. Conner had given himself another splinter from hiding behind the baskets.

"Conner!" Alex mouthed.

"Sorry!" he mouthed back.

The woman walked toward where they were hiding. She squinted in their direction for a moment. Alex and Conner were both too frightened even to breathe. They knew she knew they were there. What was she going to do to them?

The woman looked to the ground at one of their lanterns, and a coy smile appeared on her face. She kicked it into a pile of baskets and disappeared through the window and back down the rope connected to the grappling hook.

"That was a close one!" Conner said. "Good thing she didn't find us, or we'd be in some—"

"*Conner!* Look!" Alex said. The pile of baskets the woman had kicked the lantern into was on fire.

"Oh boy," Conner said. "We've got to get out of here."

"Not until I get a piece of that basket," Alex said. She reached into her bag and pulled out the dagger. She ran up the pile of baskets to the top of the shelf just as she had seen the woman do. She wasn't as tall as the woman, so she had to reach farther to get it.

"Alex, hurry!" Conner said. The fire was growing and spreading around the room to the different piles and stacks of baskets. He tried blowing the fire out, but it didn't work. These were large flames, not birthday candles.

Alex had to climb up onto the shelf to reach the basket, but she finally wrapped her fingers around it.

"Gotcha!" Alex said, pulling it out. The bark around the rim had two chunks missing, one from whoever had written the journal, and the other from whoever that woman was. Alex sank her dagger into the basket and began cutting out a piece of it.

"Alex! Unless you want to leave this place extra crispy, I suggest you hurry!" Conner yelled. Half of the room was ablaze. It was becoming unbearably hot inside the room. Dark smoke was filling the air, making it hard to breathe.

"I got it," Alex said, and made her way down to Conner. The flames had covered the door they'd entered from.

"How do we get out of here?" Alex yelled.

The sound of running footsteps came from the hall outside the door. Through the flames, the twins could see the faces of several alarmed guards.

"Fire! Fire in the castle!" a guard yelled. *"Get the queen to safety! Get some water!"*

Another guard pointed directly at the twins. *"You two! Stay where you are!"*

"Not likely!" Conner yelled. He picked up a particularly heavy basket and threw it at a window, causing it to shatter. He grabbed his sister's hand and pulled her toward it. They breathed in the fresh air from outside.

"Look, the water mill is right below us!" Conner said, and started climbing out of the window and down toward it. He helped his sister out of the window, and they climbed down the watermill together. Halfway down, flames burst through all the windows in the basket room; the entire room was an inferno.

The water mill began to turn from the twins' weight,

and they fell straight into the moat, which wouldn't have been such a rough landing if the moat had been deeper than three feet.

The twins clambered out of the moat and began running as fast as they could away from the castle. No guards or soldiers were chasing them. They all must have been inside the castle trying to put out the fire.

Alex and Conner ran out of the town and were on their way toward the eastern gate of the Red Riding Hood Kingdom in a matter of minutes. They only looked back once and saw that almost half of the castle was now on fire. A thick trail of smoke filled the sky.

"Was that the fourth or fifth time we've narrowly escaped death this week?" Conner asked.

"Who was that woman?" Alex asked. "And why was she looking for the basket, too?"

"Thank God she found it, otherwise we might never have," Conner said.

The most worrisome thought came to Alex's mind. "Conner, you don't think someone *else* is collecting items for the Wishing Spell, do you?"

He had to think about it, but she could see it was just as troubling for him to consider it as it was for her.

"I doubt it," Conner said. "Think about all the trouble the man who wrote the journal went through to learn about it. I'd be shocked if someone else knew anything about it."

Alex nodded. They both knew it was very unlikely, but the possibility still lingered in their heads.

A few hours later, the twins could see the eastern gate of the Red Riding Hood Kingdom wall in the distance. The guards must have extinguished the fire in the castle, because there was no more smoke filling the air.

The night sky was at its darkest just before dawn. As they reached the gate, they could see something moving near it. Spooked from the events earlier, Alex and Conner dove behind a bush and watched from afar.

It was a man pacing near the gate. He was tall and seemed young. There was something oddly familiar about him.

"Is that Jack?" Alex asked.

Conner took a closer look. "It is! What is he doing all the way out here?"

Suddenly, a hooded figure came into view on the other side of the gate.

"Who is *that*?" Conner asked.

Jack carefully approached the gate. There was so much tension between him and whoever was on the other side of the gate that even the twins could feel it. He had been waiting for whoever it was all night.

"Hello, Jack," said the hooded figure.

"Hello, Goldie," he said.

And then the twins realized who it was: Goldilocks. She was wearing the dark maroon coat they had seen her wear in the Dwarf Forests.

"How do they know each other?" Alex asked.

Conner shook his head. "No idea."

"I saw your dove," Jack said. "I knew you must have sent it."

"I did," Goldilocks said. "I knew you would recognize it. Doves are hard to train these days."

The twins could tell from the way they were standing that Goldilocks and Jack had much to say to each other, but they said very little. Instead, they just stared into each other's eyes with their bodies pressed against the bars between them.

"I hate these bars between us," Jack said.

"It's either the bars of this gate or the bars of a prison cell, I'm afraid," Goldilocks said.

"I worry about you constantly," Jack said.

"I'm a big girl. I can take care of myself," Goldilocks said.

"I wish you would let me come with you," Jack said. "You know I'd pack my things and leave right now if you would let me."

"No sense in ruining two lives," Goldilocks said. "You'll find someone else someday."

"You've been saying that since you left, yet here I am, year after year, meeting you in the shadows," Jack said.

"She's the one he's in love with!" Alex said, putting the pieces together. "She's the reason Jack won't marry Red Riding Hood. She's the girl the harp was telling us about."

"Oh," Conner said. "This is like a soap opera!"

Jack placed his hands over Goldilocks's hands.

"I swear, if I ever find the person who wrote you that letter, I'll kill them," Jack said. "They're the reason for this whole mess."

"What is done is done, and it can never be undone," Goldilocks said. She and Jack were touching foreheads through the bars.

"One day, I'll clear your name," Jack said. "I promise. And then we can be together."

"Clear my name?" Goldilocks said, and backed away from him. "I'm a fugitive, Jack! I steal! I run! I even kill when I have to! No one can clear me of that; it's who I am. It's what I've become."

"It didn't start off as your fault, and you know it," Jack said.

Goldilocks grew silent.

"I love you," Jack said. "And I know you love me. You don't have to say it back. I just know."

"I'm a criminal, and you're a hero," Goldilocks said with teary eyes. "A flame may love a snowflake, but they can never be together without each harming the other."

"Then let me melt," Jack said. He reached through the gate and pulled Goldilocks close to him, and they kissed. It was passionate, pure, and long overdue.

Alex became misty-eyed. Conner scrunched up his face as if he'd smelled something foul.

"Good thing those bars are between them," Conner said.

"Shut up, Conner," Alex said.

Goldilocks pushed herself away from Jack.

"I have to go," she said. "I have to be as far away from this place as I can get by sunrise."

"Let me come with you," Jack begged.

"No," Goldilocks said.

"When will I see you next? A week? A month? A year?" he asked.

Porridge walked up behind Goldilocks. She leaped up onto the horse's back and took hold of the reins.

"Just wait for the dove," she said, and rode off into the night on her cream-colored horse.

Jack watched her until she wasn't visible anymore. Suddenly, all the life in his body faded away, and he once again became the sad man the twins had met earlier. He sadly turned away from the gate and slowly headed home.

"I guess not every fairy-tale character gets a happily-ever-after," Alex said.

Alex and Conner ran up to the gate. It was locked, so they had to climb over it, finally making their way out of the Red Riding Hood Kingdom just as the sun started to rise.

CHAPTER ELEVEN

THE TROLL AND GOBLIN TERRITORY

A lex and Conner were lost.

"We're not lost. I just don't know exactly where we are," Alex told her brother.

"So, in other words, we're *lost*," Conner said.

"All right, Conner, we're lost!" Alex said, and hit him with the map.

They had left the Red Riding Hood Kingdom in such a hurry, they thought they might have taken a wrong path.

Alex kept looking down at the map, trying to see where they had made a wrong turn, and kept walking into bushes and trees.

"We could be in the Fairy Kingdom, or perhaps we're back in the Charming Kingdom," she said. "But the eastern gate of the Red Riding Hood Kingdom is close to so many borders, we could be in the Sleeping Kingdom, for all I know."

"How is anyone supposed to find their way around this place? It's all just a bunch of trees and dirt roads with the occasional castle!" Conner said angrily. "We're never going to get home!"

"It's just a slight setback. We'll be back on track before you know it," Alex said.

"And exactly what track are we on?" Conner asked. "I hate to bring this to your attention, but we've only collected three of the eight Wishing Spell items, and we have no idea what two of them are. And, to be frank, we're not even sure if the Wishing Spell will work when and if we do collect everything."

"Don't be so negative, Conner," Alex said.

"Alex, I'm just being realistic," Conner said. "We still have so many places to go, and so much more ground to cover. And after seeing that weird jungle woman in Red Riding Hood's castle take a chunk of the basket, we may not be the only ones going after this Wishing Spell thing. What if we don't succeed? Have you thought about what we'll do if we get stuck here?"

She hadn't thought about it and didn't want to. She was afraid that thinking about it made it much more possible.

Alex inspected the map further, tracing it with her index finger.

"All right, I think I figured out what we did wrong," Alex said.

"*We?* You've been hogging the map since we got it," Conner said.

"All right, I think I figured out what *I* did wrong," Alex said, her cheeks reddening. "The path we should have taken is just on the other side of the forest next to us. We'll walk through the forest, get on the correct path, and then be on our way into the Fairy Kingdom."

"Great," Conner said.

They walked off the path and into the forest beside them. After walking for a while, they noticed that the forest was very still and eerily quiet—too quiet, especially for Conner. He'd had a bad feeling in the pit of his stomach since they'd entered the forest.

The trees grew taller here, but whenever the twins looked up, there were no birds or bugs or anything to be seen gliding from tree to tree. The whole forest, excluding the trees, seemed lifeless.

"Hey, Alex?" Conner asked.

"Yes, Conner?" Alex said.

"Have you noticed we haven't seen any animals or birds for a while?" he said.

"No, I haven't; I've been a little preoccupied," Alex said, still looking down at the map.

"I'm just saying, don't you think it's kind of strange we're the only—*aaaaah!*"

Without warning, the twins were jerked suddenly upward and suspended in the air. They were dangling above the ground in some sort of roped net. They had walked right into a trap.

"What's going on?" Alex yelled. "What is this?"

"It's some kind of trap!" Conner said.

"Help!" Alex screamed. "Somebody help us!"

Unfortunately for them, their cries were heard by the wrong people. Two figures ran through the forest straight toward them. One was tall and lean, the other was short and round.

"Egghorn, we caught something!" said the low, growly voice of the smaller.

"It's about time!" said the high-pitched, raspy voice of the taller.

They came close, and the twins could make out the frightening faces of a goblin and a troll standing before them. The goblin was gangly and thin with big, yellow eyes and pea-green skin. The troll was fat and frumpy with a huge nose and horns. Both had big, pointy ears that stuck out on the sides of their heads.

"Let us go!" Conner demanded.

"You can't do this!" Alex yelled.

The goblin and troll paid no attention to what Alex and

Conner were saying. They stared at the twins like insects in a jar.

"Ooooh, look how young they are, Bobblewart!" the goblin said.

"Plenty of time to serve!" the troll said.

"What do you mean *serve*?" Conner said. "You'd better not hurt us!"

"Let us out of this net right now, or I'll report you to the local authorities," Alex said, not knowing whom she could be referring to.

"And they'll grow bigger and stronger every day!" the troll said.

"Bobblewart, get the cart!" the goblin instructed. "They're going to make the perfect slaves."

The twins struggled twice as hard against the net when they heard the word *slaves*. They remembered what Froggy had told them over tea. The trolls and goblins had been banished for kidnapping and enslaving innocent people... and now Alex and Conner were living proof that it was still happening. How were they going to escape this?

Bobblewart, the troll, ran off and returned a moment later driving a small cart pulled by a frail donkey. Egghorn, the goblin, cut a rope above the net, and the twins fell hard into the cart. They continued to fight against the restraints of the net, but it was no use.

Egghorn climbed aboard the cart and sat next to Bobblewart. They both took the reins and whipped the donkey belligerently until the cart reached full speed.

They traveled for the rest of the day. All the twins could see through the net were treetops and sky zipping past them.

"Alex, what are we going to do?" Conner asked, still fighting against the ropes of the net.

"I don't know," Alex said. She was trembling like a small dog.

Alex managed to squirm her way to a seated position under the net to see where the troll and goblin were taking them. They were headed straight toward a line of boulders the size of mountains. Alex gasped; she recognized the rock formation from the map.

"What is it? What do you see?" Conner asked her.

"They're taking us into the Troll and Goblin Territory," Alex said, completely white-faced. "I can see the boulders that surround it!"

They remembered Froggy telling them the boulders had been placed around the territory to keep the trolls and goblins inside, but, clearly, as the cart squeezed through a crack between two of the boulders, the inhabitants had found ways around their imprisonment.

The cart went through the boulders and into the kingdom, but there was nothing to see. There were no trees or buildings or life of any kind. For miles around them, the land was only littered with piles of rubble and broken bits of stone.

"I don't understand," Conner said. "Where do they live?"

"This looks like a medieval junkyard," Alex said.

The cart went through a gigantic hole in the ground and traveled down, deep into the earth. It was pitch-black, and the twins could barely see their hands in front of their faces. The smell of mildew and decay was horrible.

"The whole kingdom must be underground!" Alex said.

After descending in the dark for quite a distance, they saw tiny lights ahead of them. They came from lanterns scattered around a group of humans digging tunnels.

"What are people doing down here?" Conner asked, and then saw the trolls and goblins behind them.

"Faster!" the trolls and goblins demanded, whipping the humans.

Alex had to cover her eyes at the sight of it. "They must be slaves! Oh, Conner, this is horrible! This is so horrible!" she said.

Conner hugged his sister, and she cried into his shoulder.

"It's okay, Alex. We'll find a way out of this," Conner said, but even he was scared.

There were hundreds of huts and small homes stacked on top of one another all around them. It was an enormous underground world.

"This place must be like one giant ant colony," Conner said.

The cart moved through a stone arch with large statues, one of a goblin and one of a troll, on either side of it. They were frightening, with harsh features, and they were anything but welcoming. A sign carved into the arch read:

BE TROLL, BE GOBLIN, OR BE AFRAID

"Most people just have welcome mats," Conner said.

Past the arch was a long tunnel constructed of stones. The cart traveled through the arch and a light could be seen at the end of the tunnel. There was much noise coming from the end of the tunnel, a combination of high-pitched laughter, rumbling conversation, and loud clanking.

The twins were soon driven into a massive common room with hundreds of goblins and trolls spread everywhere on numerous levels. Some were even hanging from a chandelier.

Everything was made of stone; they ate and drank from stone plates and goblets and sat on stone chairs at stone tables. They were served by other enslaved men and women. Each troll and goblin behaved in a more vulgar way than the last.

In the center of the chaos, on a platform overlooking the room, were two thrones. The Troll King sat in one and the Goblin King sat in the other. A crown made of rock was on display directly between them, just above their heads, demonstrating that they equally shared power over the kingdom.

They watched over their citizens with crude smirks, enjoying the festivities around them.

As the cart went through the room, many of the trolls and goblins hooted and hollered at the twins; some threw bits of food at them. Alex and Conner held on to each other tighter than ever, both trembling with fear.

The goblins and trolls were all grotesque and dreadful. They had warts and sharp teeth and horrible hygiene. They were the type of monsters Alex and Conner used to have nightmares about when they were younger.

Sitting on the kings' platform was a little troll girl about the twins' age. She had a round face with a small snout, and her hair was worn in pigtails just below tiny horns. She was sitting with her head resting on her hands and seemed bored and lonely; she didn't appear at all interested in the activities around her. She looked up as the twins passed her and gasped when she saw Conner.

This took him by surprise. "What is she looking at?" Conner asked. "Do you think she wants to eat me or something?"

The cart turned a corner and descended down another long tunnel. They were so deep underground that they wondered if they would ever make it back to the surface.

The cart entered a small and dim dungeon with a row of cells in it. Other slaves were imprisoned inside the cells: men, women, children, and elderly alike. They all looked exhausted and were ghostly pale. They were all silent and cowered at the sight of Egghorn and Bobblewart steering the cart into the room.

Egghorn and Bobblewart cut the net around Alex and

Conner, yanked the bags out of their hands, and aggressively forced them inside a cell.

"Get in there!" Egghorn said, and slammed the cell door shut behind them.

"What do we have in here?" Bobblewart said. He took the twins' bags to a table on the side of the room and dumped all their belongings out onto it.

"Stay out of there!" Alex said as she watched helplessly. There for the entire room to see was the glass slipper, the lock of hair, the chunk of basket, the map, the journal, the dagger, their sack of gold coins, and everything else the twins had been carrying.

Thankfully, the troll and goblin only seemed interested in the dagger and the sack of gold coins. They took those with them and dumped everything else in a pile of waste on the side of the table.

"Rest up! You'll have a long day tomorrow!" Bobblewart said, and then shared a laugh with Egghorn and left the room with their cart.

All the other slaves stared at Alex and Conner through their cell bars. They had sympathy in their eyes, so sorry that the twins were about to experience everything they had endured for however long they had been there.

"Does anyone know how to get out of here?" Alex asked, but none of them responded, as if they had been trained not to speak. Even the children were silent.

"How is this happening?" Conner grunted. He violently shook the bars of the cell, but they didn't budge.

"That's no use," said a voice behind the twins. "Those bars are made out of pure stone."

Alex and Conner turned to face the prisoner occupying the cell next to theirs. Crouched over in the darkest corner of his cell was an old man. He was thin and had a long, gray beard and tattered clothing.

"There's got to be some way out of here," Conner said.

"I've heard every man and woman say that when they were first brought here," the old man said. "But sadly, there isn't."

"How long have you been here?" Alex asked him.

"Years," the man said. He leaned forward, and the light fell on his face. His face was as tired and ragged as his clothes. He had a wandering eye, so the twins couldn't tell which one of them he was speaking to.

"Say, don't I know you two from somewhere?" he asked.

The twins knew this wasn't possible, but the man seemed convinced and, for whatever reason, the man seemed oddly familiar to them, too.

"I don't believe so," Alex said. "We're rather new to the area."

"I could swear it," the old man said. "Are you sure I never traded you a magic flute for a chicken? Or perhaps a singing flower for a lamb?"

"No, I'm sorry, we've never traded anything with you before—" Alex said, and then she realized who he was: the wandering eye, the long beard, the raggedy clothing...

could it be? She pulled Conner aside. "Conner, he's the Traveling Tradesman, the one from the journal!"

Conner couldn't believe it. "Are you sure?" he asked.

"Sir," said Alex, kneeling down to him. "Are you by chance known as the Traveling Tradesman?"

The man had to think about it. Obviously the years of enslavement had taken their toll on his mind.

"Yes, I believe that is what they called me," he said. He was happy to be reminded of a time when he wasn't a slave.

The twins were so pleased to hear this. "Ask him if he knows what happened to the man who wrote the journal!" Conner whispered into Alex's ear, and she nodded.

"Mr. Tradesman," Alex said. "Do you remember a man coming to you and asking about the Wishing Spell?"

"The Wishing Spell?" the Tradesman asked. At first, it seemed he had no idea what she was talking about, but then recognition dawned on his face. "Why, yes, I do! He was one of the last customers I did business with before I was brought here. Silly lad, he talked about wanting to travel to another world. And I thought *I* was mad."

"Did he ever make it?" Alex asked. "Did he find all the items of the Wishing Spell?"

"I don't know," the Tradesman said, and the twins slumped. "I never saw him again, so it's possible." He looked up at them curiously. "Why do you ask?"

The twins looked to each other. They didn't know what to tell him.

"Don't tell me you two are chasing after the Wishing Spell, too?" he asked.

They looked at each other guiltily. Conner leaned down next to Alex and began asking questions of his own.

"We're trying, but we don't know everything we're looking for," Conner said.

The Tradesman laughed. "No one does; that's the beauty of it. Some people know the descriptions of the items it requires, but no one knows what they are for sure."

"Like Hagatha," Alex said. "She only knew what the riddles were. The man she told them to had to figure out what they were on his own, but he could have been wrong."

"What if we found Hagatha and asked her for her opinion—?" Conner began.

"Hagatha is dead," the Tradesman said.

"Dead?" Alex gasped. "How did she die?"

"She fell into the Thornbush Pit," the Tradesman said.

"What is the Thornbush Pit?" Alex asked.

"Good heavens, child, are you daft? After the curse was broken on the Sleeping Kingdom, all the thornbush and shrubbery that had grown wild around the kingdom was cleared out and dumped into a large and deep pit," the Tradesman said. "Hagatha was collecting some of the thornbush for her home and fell in."

"That's awful," Alex said.

"She called for help for days, but no one would help her; no one wanted to help an old hag," the Tradesman said. "Just before she died, Hagatha cursed the thornbush so that it would grow onto anything or anyone near it and pull it straight to the bottom, where she was trapped, forever."

"That's intense," Conner said.

"Since then, however, it's been used as a wasteland. People from all over the kingdoms journey there to drop off anything they never want to see again," he said.

"I wonder if there's anyone else we could speak to?" Alex said.

"Whatever journey you were on, I'm afraid it's over," the Tradesman said. "Once you're here, you're here, and there is nothing you can do about it." He turned away from them.

A commotion came from up the tunnel leading into the dungeon. Trolls and goblins led the men and women who had been serving in the tunnels and the common room back into their cells. They all looked as if they could sleep for a year if permitted.

"Time for sleep!" a troll ordered, and then extinguished all the torches in the room with a bucket of water. "And if anyone makes a sound, no one will be fed tomorrow!" The trolls and goblins left the dungeon chuckling.

The room was pitch-black. Alex found Conner in the darkness and they rested beside each other.

"I just don't want Mom to worry," Alex said with big, teary eyes. "The longer we're in here, the longer she's going to be alone."

"I'm sure Grandma is with her," Conner said. "They probably have the entire police department out looking for us. It'll be an interesting conversation once we get home and tell them where we've been all this time."

"Thanks for being positive, Conner," Alex said.

Despite the little comfort her brother gave her, Alex cried herself to sleep.

Conner couldn't sleep. He couldn't stop thinking that, just a week before, he had been safe and sound in his own bed, fearing nothing but schoolwork and Mrs. Peters. And now, here he was, in the dungeons of another dimension, facing a life of slavery. How quickly times had changed. . . .

Conner had just dozed off when he suddenly awoke; he felt like someone was watching him. He opened one eye and saw, standing on the other side of the cell door holding a single candle, the troll girl they had seen in the common room. She had been watching him sleep.

"Can I help you?" asked Conner, very creeped out.

"What's your name?" the troll girl asked him in an airy and engaging voice.

"Why do you want to know?" he asked.

"Because I'd like to know everything about you," she said with a dreamy smile that made Conner feel sick.

"I'm Conner. Who are you?" he asked.

"My name is Trollbella," she said. "I'm a troll princess.

My father is the Troll King. Do you have a girlfriend, Conner?"

Oh no, Conner thought. She had a *crush* on him. He was suddenly so grateful for the bars between them.

"Um . . . can't say that I do," Conner said awkwardly. "It's hard to meet people after having been recently enslaved by trolls and goblins."

"Oh, I know!" Trollbella said, with big flirty eyes. "Trolls and goblins are the worst! I hate living here. I would move away if I could. Everything is so unorganized and everyone is so mean, and don't get me started on troll boys! They don't know how to treat a lady!"

"I'm sorry to hear that," Conner said, hoping a goblin would walk in and take him away to work in a tunnel and save him from this situation.

"I'm just a hopeless romantic myself," Trollbella said, batting her eyelashes and twirling one of her pigtails. "Can I call you Butterboy?"

"Definitely not," Conner said.

"Conner, what's going on?" asked Alex, waking up.

"Who is *she*?" Trollbella asked. Her playful expression fell into a threatened frown.

"Relax, this is just my sister," Conner said.

"Hi?" said Alex, very confused about what was happening.

"I don't like her," Trollbella said, pointing at Alex.

Alex was taken aback. Had she done something wrong?

"She grows on you," Conner said. "And if I had to be enslaved for life with someone, I'm glad it's her."

"Have you enjoyed your stay with us so far?" Trollbella asked.

"Not really," Conner said. Was she kidding or just stupid?

"We'd really like to get out of here if you could help us," Alex said.

"I'm not talking to you!" Trollbella yelled at Alex. She then turned her head slowly and smiled at Conner. "I may be able to give you freedom in exchange for something else."

"What's that?" Conner said. Both the twins would have been on the edge of their seats if they weren't on a dirty dungeon floor.

"A kiss," Trollbella said, staring passionately at Conner.

Conner gulped. "Well, I guess we're going to be slaves forever."

Trollbella frowned. Alex hit Conner upside the head.

"Kiss her, you idiot, and then we'll get out of here!" Alex said.

"Don't hit my Butterboy!" Trollbella said. "And I never said I would let *you* go, I only said I'd let *him* go."

"I think he'd be more inclined if you promised to let both of us go," Alex said.

"No, I wouldn't! Please don't speak on my behalf," Conner chimed in, but neither of them was listening to him.

Trollbella's nostrils flared up. She didn't like negotiating. She turned around and disappeared without saying a word.

"Way to go, Conner!" Alex said. "That may have been our only chance to escape!"

"There's no way I'm kissing *that*!" Conner said. "Freedom or no freedom, you're asking way too much of me!"

The twins both jumped back from the cell door. Trollbella had quickly returned with a key; she was ready to make a deal.

"Pucker up, Butterboy," Trollbella said, and pushed her head up against the bars of the cell door.

"I can't do this. I physically can't do this!" Conner said.

"Do you ever want to see home again?" Alex asked him.

Conner looked as if he were about to vomit and cry at the same time. At a snail's pace he approached Trollbella with his lips extended. He wasn't going fast enough for Alex, so she pushed him toward the cell door and Trollbella grabbed hold of him through the bars. She planted a big, fat, juicy kiss on him.

"Plaaaah!" Conner said, breaking away from her. He was wiping his mouth manically and gasping for air. Trollbella had a huge, satisfied grin on her face.

"That was the worst thing you have ever done to me!" Conner said, pointing at Alex, feeling completely betrayed. "How could you?"

"All right, Trollbella," said Alex, ignoring her brother's dramatics. "A deal is a deal. Let us go."

Trollbella's smile dropped into a scowl. She reluctantly unlocked the cell door and opened it. And as she did, Alex caught sight of the other slaves in the dungeon. The few that were awake had been silently and intently staring at the twins. They had never seen anyone be freed before; they hadn't thought it was possible.

"You're free to go," Trollbella said.

The twins briskly walked out of the cell, but as Alex passed Trollbella, she swiftly grabbed the key and pushed the troll princess into the cell, slamming the door behind her.

"Let me out of here right now!" Trollbella screamed. "This wasn't part of the deal!"

"I can't leave without the others," Alex said. She ran around unlocking the doors on all the cells. "Everyone wake up! We're getting out of here! Come on!"

She ran over to the pile of waste on the side of the room and retrieved all their things.

"Guards!" Trollbella howled. "Guards! The slaves are escaping!"

"Trollbella?" Conner said. "Please be quiet! Would you do that? Please? For your Butterboy?"

Trollbella blushed. "All right, Butterboy. For you, I'll be quiet."

The slaves all stirred to life. It took them a moment to understand what Alex was saying; they had dreamed about this day for so long. Many eagerly jumped up and left their cells, but others hesitated, including the Traveling Tradesman.

"Come on," Alex said. "What are you waiting for?"

"Are you two mad? They'll skin us alive if we try to escape," the Tradesman said. This worried some of the others, especially the children.

"Would you rather die in your cell or die trying to get back the life they stole from you?" Alex said.

Alex's words must have inspired them, because they all gathered around her. Even the Tradesman was willing to take a chance for freedom. He nodded at Alex as he joined the group.

"Does anyone know the best way out of here?" Alex asked.

"We need to get to the tunnels!" a man said.

"Yes, the tunnels!" a woman agreed.

"How do we get there?" Conner asked.

"We'll go up to the common room and past the stone arch. The trolls and goblins have built tunnels leading to every kingdom. That's how they get around," the Tradesman said.

"Do we need to worry about anyone catching us?" Conner asked.

"They're all asleep by now," Trollbella said with a sigh from her cell, "even the guards. That's why no one came when I called."

"All right, let's go," Alex said. "Everyone be as quiet as possible and help the older and younger ones in the group."

Everyone nodded, and Alex led the way out of the dungeon, praying it would be the last time any of them were ever in this room again.

"Until we meet again, Butterboy," Trollbella said, and blew Conner a kiss.

"Whatever," Conner said, and then followed the others out of the dungeon.

Trollbella smiled from horn to horn. This had been the most exciting day of her entire life.

The group of escapees traveled up the tunnel to the common room and snuck past a line of goblin guards. Just as Trollbella had said, they were asleep while standing guard.

They finally reached the common room and covered their mouths in horror at what they saw. All the trolls and goblins that Alex and Conner had seen carousing on the way in were spread across the floor, passed out. How were they going to get to the other side of the room without stepping on one of them?

Some were snoring, others twitched in their sleep. Even the Troll King and the Goblin King were sleeping in their thrones. You could barely see the floor between the unconscious monsters sprawled across the room.

"Quickly and quietly!" Alex whispered to the group. "We can do this; just be as careful as possible."

They began tiptoeing around the sleeping creatures. Carefully they put their feet between the monsters' spread-out limbs, between the broken plates and goblets across the dirt floor, and between the knocked-over chairs and tables.

Every time a troll or a goblin made any noise or movement, everyone froze, their hearts stopped for a moment. If any of the monsters were to wake up and see their slaves walking through the room toward the exit, it would be a disaster.

They were almost at the stone tunnel. Alex stopped in the middle of the room and made sure everyone passed her safely and that no one was left behind. Eventually, everyone had made it except her brother, who remained very still in the back of the room. He was staring at the Troll King and the Goblin King with wide eyes and an open mouth.

"Conner! What are you doing?" Alex asked in her loudest whisper.

"Look!" he mouthed, only a little whisper coming out. "Look at the crown! It's the crown!"

Alex looked up at the stone crown above the Troll King's and Goblin King's heads.

"What about it?" Alex whispered.

"It's the crown for the Wishing Spell!" Conner said. " 'A stony crown that's made to share, found deep within a savage lair'!"

Alex could feel her heart beating in her throat. Conner was right. It fit the description perfectly.

"What are you two doing? We're waiting for you!" the Tradesman said from the stone tunnel.

Alex and Conner looked at each other. They knew they couldn't leave without the crown.

"Go ahead without us!" Alex said.

"Suit yourselves!" the Tradesman said, and then left with the others down the stone tunnel.

"I'm going to get it!" Conner whispered to Alex.

"Be careful!" Alex said.

Conner slowly moved through the room. He accidentally kicked a goblet, and it made a loud *ding*, causing a few of the trolls and goblins to twitch in their sleep.

"Sorry!" Conner mouthed to Alex. He climbed up onto the throne platform. The crown was pretty high up; he would have to climb up onto the thrones to get it.

He climbed onto the armrest of the Troll King's throne. His left leg was so close to the king's face that Conner could feel the king's warm breath through his jeans. Conner swung his right leg onto the armrest of the Goblin King's throne and reached up for the crown. It was still too high. He would have to jump for it.

Alex had to cover her eyes. Her hands were trembling.

Conner jumped and tried to grab the crown, but he was just a few inches too short. He jumped again; the tips of his fingers touched it this time. He jumped once more—this time, the highest jump yet—and grabbed it. Unfortunately, on his way down, he missed the armrests and landed right in the lap of the Goblin King.

"*Ahhhhhh!*" the Goblin King screamed.

Alex took her hands from her face just in time to see her terrified brother sprawled across the Goblin King's lap, with the crown held tightly in his hands. Conner jumped up and ran as fast as he could, grabbing his sister's arm on the way toward the exit.

"After them!" the Goblin King ordered. "Someone grab them!"

The entire room of trolls and goblins began waking up to the Goblin King's yells.

Alex and Conner weren't careful about what or who they stepped on. They ran straight through the common room and down the tunnel of stones. Dozens of trolls and goblins chased after them.

The twins ran past the two horrible statues at the tunnel's entrance. The goblin statue suddenly crashed to the ground just as they passed it, blocking the tunnel. Alex screamed—had they been a second later, it would have fallen on them.

They turned to see the Tradesman, out of breath and holding his heart. He had just knocked over the statue and blocked the tunnel. The trolls and goblins had reached the end of the tunnel and were struggling to get past the fallen statue.

"That should keep them busy for a while," the Tradesman said. "Now run!"

"Where's everyone else?" Alex asked.

"They've fled to the tunnels! They're safe!" he said.

"What about you?" Alex asked.

"I couldn't leave without you," the Tradesman said. "I'm old, children. I'd never outrun them anyway. You two still have a lot of living to do, so run before they get past the statue. Hurry!"

"We're not leaving without you!" Alex said.

"I'm wanted in every kingdom," the Tradesman said between deep breaths. "No matter where I go, I'll end up behind bars. I've done a lot of bad things in my day, children. I've made a lot of trades and deals that I shouldn't have. I deserve this. You don't. Now run!"

Alex's and Conner's feet moved before their minds could decide whether to stay any longer. They ran ahead and found a series of tunnels leading in different directions. Each had a sign above the entrance that said where the tunnel led to.

"Come on," Alex said, and grabbed Conner's arm, pulling him into the tunnel that said FAIRY KINGDOM above it. They tucked the troll and goblin crown safely away in Alex's bag.

"Did we do the right thing?" Alex asked Conner as they ran down the tunnel. "Should we have left him?"

"He wasn't going to come with us; his mind was made up," Conner said. He knew they had done everything they could, but he still felt guilty, too.

"How could a stranger give up so much for us?" Alex said.

"Maybe he thought trading his freedom for ours would be the only honest trade he'd ever make," Conner said.

CHAPTER TWELVE

THE FAIRY KINGDOM

Alex and Conner emerged from underground between a tree and a big rock. They were covered in dirt and cobwebs and were breathing hard and sweating profusely; it had been so stuffy in the tunnel.

"We made it," Alex said. "We're at the surface."

"I never thought I'd be so happy to see the sun and the sky," Conner said.

It was sometime around noon, and the twins had found themselves in a pleasant, grassy field next to a perfectly groomed path.

"Is that the path we should have taken after the Red Riding Hood Kingdom?" Conner asked.

"Yup," Alex said, looking down at the map. "But think of all the fun we would have missed out on."

They shared a laugh. The twins brushed themselves off and headed down the path. They felt very safe in this place. All the trees and fields were perfectly manicured and inviting. Then again, anything would have seemed inviting after narrowly escaping a lifetime of slavery for trolls and goblins.

"Are we positive that we're in the Fairy Kingdom?" Conner said, looking around.

"I'd say it's very possible," Alex said, but she wasn't looking down at the map.

"How do you figure?" Conner asked her.

"Well, *that's* an indication," Alex said, and pointed.

Grazing around a perfect little stream ahead of them, to their amazement, was a herd of unicorns. They were beautiful: white with silver horns, silver hooves, and silver manes.

Conner's forehead wrinkled, and his mouth dropped open. "Oh, jeez," he said. "That is the most obnoxious thing I've ever seen in my life!"

"I want to pet one!" Alex said, and ran toward them.

"Alex, be careful!" Conner said. "They could have rabies!"

"Unicorns don't have rabies, Conner!" Alex said.

"You don't know where those horns have been!" Conner called out.

Alex walked up to the herd, slowing her pace so she

wouldn't spook them. They were so majestic and graceful, she just had to stop and admire them for a moment. One saw her and walked toward her.

Any sane person would have been scared by a wild animal approaching them, but Alex wasn't. For whatever reason, she knew the unicorn wasn't going to harm her. It lowered its head, and she petted its face.

Conner walked up and stood just behind her. All the other unicorns slowly surrounded them.

"Alex," Conner said. "This is making me incredibly nervous."

The unicorns formed a perfect circle around the twins and bowed to them. Alex smiled from ear to ear. Conner raised a suspicious eyebrow.

"This is trippy," he said.

"Maybe they're welcoming us into their kingdom?" Alex said.

The unicorns stood still as if frozen and didn't show any sign of moving. Conner grabbed Alex's hand, and they left the circle and rejoined the path. The stream traveled beside the path as the twins traveled down it.

"Is it just me, or is that water sparkling?" Conner asked. He was right. The farther they walked along the stream, the more it appeared to glow and shimmer.

"That must mean we're getting close!" Alex said happily. "That's Thumbelina Stream. It should take us straight into the Fairy Kingdom."

"I say we grab hold of the first fairy we find and call her

names like 'oversized insect' or 'fish bait' until she cries," Conner said. "That's how we'll get the tears."

"No! We should come up with a really sad story to tell," Alex said, and then a thought occurred to her. "How are we going to collect the tears once they've been shed?"

Conner shrugged. "Maybe we'll have to kidnap a fairy and keep her around until we need her to cry? What does the journal say to do?"

Alex opened the journal and found the section about the Fairy Kingdom.

Acquiring a fairy tear is not an easy task.

"Surprise surprise," Conner said.

Since fairies for the most part are very happy beings, it will be hard to find one so overcome with grief that it is brought to tears. However you manage, hopefully under moral conditions, you can use the vial hidden inside this journal's spine to contain the tear.

Alex turned the book on its side and looked closely through the hole where the pages were connected to the spine. Deep inside the journal's spine was a small glass vial with a cork stopper.

"Look at this!" Alex said, pulling the vial out of the spine. "It says to put the tear in this vial."

"Great. Now all we need is an emotional fairy," Conner said.

Alex stopped walking. "Do you hear that?" she said.

Tiny sniffling sounds came from close by. The twins looked around but couldn't see quite where they were coming from.

"What is that?" Conner asked. He looked down beside him and had to blink a few times to make sure he wasn't imagining what he saw. "No, this can't be real. This is too easy.... *Nothing* has been this easy."

"What are you talking about?" Alex asked him. Conner turned her shoulders to face what he was looking at.

Sitting on a rock on the side of the path was a fairy... and she was *crying.*

She was only a few inches tall and had big, blue wings similar to a butterfly's. She had dark hair and a purple dress made of leaves and shoes made out of flower buds. Her tiny hands were clasped around her big eyes, and tears were running down her face.

The twins just stood there and stared down at her. They were afraid their minds were playing tricks on them, they both wanted to see this so badly.

"What are you looking at?" the fairy said to the twins in a tiny, high-pitched voice.

"We're sorry," Alex said. "Why are you crying?"

Conner jerked his head toward his sister, and she knew he was thinking, *Who cares! Get a tear!*

"That's none of your business!" the fairy said, and sobbed some more.

"Forgive me," Alex said. "I can tell you're upset about something, and I wouldn't be myself if I didn't ask if there's anything I could do to help you."

"That's sweet, thank you," the fairy said, changing her attitude. "I'm just having a very rough day, that's all."

Conner kept trying to grab the vial from his sister's hand, but she wouldn't let him take it.

"What's your name?" Alex asked the fairy.

"Trix," the fairy said.

"Hello, Trix. My name is Alex, and this is my brother, Conner," Alex said. "Would you like to talk about what's troubling you?"

Conner was shocked. She was actually more interested in *helping* this fairy than collecting one of her tears.

"My trial is in a few minutes, and I'm scared," Trix said.

"Your trial?" Conner asked. "Did you kill somebody?"

"Of course not," said Trix. "I used magic on another fairy, and now the Fairy Council may ban me from the Fairy Kingdom."

"I'm so sorry to hear that," Alex said.

"What did you do to the other fairy?" Conner asked.

"I turned his wings into prune leaves," the fairy said, and cried some more. "It was only for a moment! I turned them back! But he was provoking me! He kept teasing me about my size!"

"They're going to ban you from the entire kingdom just

for turning someone's wings into leaves for a couple seconds?" Conner asked.

"They've been very strict ever since that Enchantress put the curse on Sleeping Beauty," Trix said. "The Fairy Council believes that every fairy is a representative of their order and should act as such."

"Those are high expectations," Alex said.

"I can't leave the Fairy Kingdom," Trix cried. "It would be so lonely, and I hate being alone! I don't have many friends to begin with!"

Alex let Trix use the corner of her shirt to dry her tears. Conner turned bright red watching his sister dispose of the tears so carelessly. He had to make the fairy produce more.

"Being banned would really be terrible, though, wouldn't it?" Conner said. "You'd probably have to live in an old bird nest in the Dwarf Forests and be chased by wolves and witches every day, and that's only if an ogre doesn't capture you in a jar and barbeque you first."

Trix started hysterically crying at this.

"Conner, what is wrong with you?" Alex yelled.

Conner snatched the vial from her hand and collected a tear from Trix's face just as it dripped off her chin. Alex gave him a dirty look.

"Would you like us to go with you to your trial?" asked Alex, leaning down to be eye level with Trix. "For emotional support?"

"Yes, I would like that," Trix said. "That's so kind of you!"

"Well, I know what it feels like to think the whole world is against you," Alex said.

"We'd better get going. I don't want to be late!" Trix flew into the air and fluttered down the path. The twins walked after her.

"Alex, are you crazy?" Conner said. "We've got a tear. Let's get out of here!"

"We're the only people in the world who this fairy has," Alex said. "We're going to be good people and help her out."

Conner grunted with frustration. "Helping this fairy isn't going to take away bad memories you have from school, Alex."

Alex ignored him and followed Trix down the path. Conner followed, sulking the entire way.

They traveled deeper into the Fairy Kingdom. Everything in the distance seemed to sparkle. They thought it was a mirage at first, but the closer they got, they saw that the trees, the grass, and the path all shined and shimmered in the sunlight.

"What's up with all the glitter?" Conner asked.

"I don't think it's glitter; I think it's magic," Alex said.

They reached the heart of the kingdom and were completely bewildered by what they saw. It was like they were standing in a gigantic tropical garden with large, colorful flowers of all shapes and species. There were weeping willows over small ponds and vines that grew across the ground and up the trees. There were beautiful bridges over many streams and ponds.

There were fairies everywhere. Many flew around in the air, some just hovered above the ground, and some walked on smaller paths adjacent to the one the twins were on. They were all different shapes and sizes and colors. Some were taller than Alex and Conner, some were as small as Trix, and some didn't seem even to be solid, but rather made from pure light.

There were just as many male fairies as there were female. Some of the fairies wore gowns, others' clothes were made entirely from plant materials, and some wore nothing at all. Many had made miniature homes in the branches of the trees or in mushrooms on the ground, and there were fairies who even lived underwater with colorful fish.

Something about this place made Alex feel as if everything were right in the world. It gave her more hope, excitement, and happiness with every step she took. It was paradise.

"Have you ever seen something so beautiful in your entire life?" Alex asked her brother.

"Not too shabby," Conner said.

"The Fairy Council operates in the Fairy Palace. It's just up ahead," Trix said, and gestured the twins to follow her over a pond. They, of course, took a bridge.

They walked toward a palace made entirely out of golden arches and pillars. It was completely open: There were no more than two walls to line each room, and all the windows were tall with no glass. When you lived in a place as beautiful as this, who would want to keep out the environment?

Trix took the twins to the center of the palace, into a long room with many seats facing the front.

"This would be the perfect place for a wedding!" Alex said.

At the front of the room were seven fairies Alex and Conner's size. They looked like a living rainbow: Each was dressed in a specific color, and they stood behind podiums positioned over an arch.

"That's the Fairy Council," Trix said. "That's Rosette, the red fairy, Tangerina, the orange fairy, Xanthous, the yellow fairy, Emerelda, the green fairy—she's mostly in charge—Skylene, the blue fairy, Violetta, the purple fairy, and Coral, the pink fairy."

Rosette was short and plump and had very rosy cheeks. Tangerina was stylish and wore her orange hair in a large beehive with actual bees flying around it. Xanthous was male; he wore a shiny suit, and parts of him were ablaze. Emerelda was tall and beautiful; she was black, and wore a long, emerald dress that matched her eyes and jewelry. Skylene was very pale and had hair the color of the sky and flowing robes the color of the sea. Violetta was the oldest and had grayish-purple hair. Coral was the youngest, no more than a few years older than the twins in appearance, and wore a simple pink dress and had a pair of pink wings on her back.

There were two empty seats on either side of the podiums.

"Who sits there?" Alex asked Trix.

"The Fairy Godmother sits on the left and Mother Goose sits on the right," Trix said. "They complete the Fairy Council, although they're rarely here. They're always traveling around the kingdoms helping people."

"Is that you, Trix?" Emerelda asked.

"Yes, I'm here," Trix peeped nervously, and flew to the front of the podiums.

"You're late. Please come forward," Emerelda said. She was gracious but authoritative, someone the twins would definitely want in their corner during an altercation. "Trix, do you know why you've been called before the Fairy Council?"

Trix shamefully nodded her head. "Yes, ma'am."

"Being a fairy requires a strong sense of responsibility," Tangerina said. "Responsibility you haven't shown."

Trix nodded some more, her eyes swelling with tears. "I know," she squeaked.

"Unfortunately, we can't let your actions go unpunished," Violetta said.

"We need to make an example of you, to reinforce the number one rule of being a fairy," Rosette said.

"To never, under any circumstance, use your magic harmfully against another person, place, or thing," Xanthous said.

"Unfortunately, there's only one thing for us to do," Skylene said.

"We have to banish you from the Fairy Kingdom," Coral said.

Trix covered her eyes and wept harder than she had all day. "I understand," she said through her sobs.

"Whoa whoa whoa!" Conner yelled from the back. "Hold on! Are you kidding me?"

He promptly walked to the front of the room and stood next to the spot where Trix was hovering.

"Conner!" Alex said, and tried to grab him, but was too late.

"Are you seriously going to ban her for making one little mistake?" Conner asked the council with his hands on his hips.

There was whispering and murmuring among them. They were appalled that someone would so openly question their judgment.

"Please don't try to help me!" Trix whispered to Conner.

"Young man, who do you think you are?" Xanthous said.

"Well, I'm just a kid, but even I can tell you that your ruling is ridiculous," Conner said.

They all gasped except for Emerelda, who kept her calm and imposing demeanor. Alex slapped an open palm against her forehead.

"How dare you!" Tangerina said, and the bees swirling around her hair grew mad and flew faster around her head.

"You are out of line!" Violetta said.

"How disrespectful!" Coral said.

"How rude!" Skylene said.

Emerelda was the only member of the assembly to remain silent. She studied Conner with her emerald eyes.

"Silence," Emerelda ordered. She raised a hand, and all her fellow assembly fairies went quiet. "Let the boy speak. I want to hear what he has to say. Go ahead, young man."

Conner wasn't sure if this was a trick or not, but he didn't hold back.

"Listen, I'm not a fairy—thank God—and I'm not perfect, either. I try to be the best person or the best student possible, but every once in a while I slip up—I forget a homework assignment, or I fall asleep in class. My best effort isn't as good as someone else's might be, and no one should have the right to scold or punish me or publicly humiliate me for it!" Conner said.

"Trix knew what the rules were, and she still committed an offense against one of her peers," Rosette said.

"No one can be perfect," Conner said. "And from what I hear, the guy had it coming! Where is his trial? Why isn't he here? Why do I always get detention for sleeping when it's ancient Mesopotamia that should be punished for being so boring?"

The council continued to be outraged by this outburst. Many members didn't want to tolerate it and tried to leave.

"I hear what the child is saying," Emerelda said.

"But we can't just pardon Trix. We're the Fairy Council; it wouldn't send a good message to the rest of the kingdoms," Tangerina said.

"Look, orange lady," Conner said, "in the last week, my sister and I have almost been eaten by a witch, narrowly missed being attacked by a pack of wolves, were almost killed by a possessive bridge troll, survived a burning castle, and barely escaped a life of enslavement in the Troll and Goblin Territory! If you ask me, you've got bigger problems than a fairy turning a jerk's wings into leaves. Looks to me like you busy yourselves with stupid little things so you feel like you're doing something, when in reality you can't handle what's really going on out there!"

The council went silent and all the members appeared to become very concerned.

"Enslavement?" Skylene asked. "You mean the trolls and goblins are still kidnapping and enslaving people?"

"Yes!" Conner said. "There were dozens of us down there! We really could have used your help, but I guess you were too busy slapping fairies' wrists for playing pranks on one another."

Although they held their stoic expressions, the council was secretly ashamed of themselves. Conner was right. They eyed one another for a moment before Emerelda broke the silence.

"On behalf of this council, I hereby forgive Trix for her crimes," Emerelda said. "Xanthous, Skylene, and Tangerina, I say we pay a visit to the Troll King and the Goblin King immediately. And furthermore, let this be a lesson. To all of us."

Xanthous, Skylene, and Tangerina nodded, and then disappeared into thin air with a *pop!*

"Thank you, Mr. . . . ?" Emerelda said.

"Wishington," Conner said. "Conner Wishington."

Emerelda smiled, and then disappeared with the others.

Trix flew up to Conner's face and gave him a huge hug. "That's the bravest and nicest thing anyone has ever done for me!" Trix said.

Conner looked back at his sister. She was beaming with pride; she was so proud of her brother. It was a look Conner rarely got to see.

"You know, helping a fairy isn't going to take away any unhappy memories from school," Alex told him when she joined Conner and Trix near the podiums.

Conner slyly grinned. "I had to say something. I would have regretted it if I hadn't."

The remaining Fairy Council fairies began to leave. Some simply walked off, and others disappeared into thin air, leaving behind sparks or bubbles as they went. Coral was searching the room for something and patting her lap as she went.

"Here, Fisher! Where are you, Fisher?" Coral said.

A fish with four legs ran past Alex and Conner and jumped up into Coral's arms.

"There you are!" Coral said. "It's just about time for your lunch!"

Alex and Conner looked at each other, confused, each wondering if the other had just seen it, too.

"Is that what I think it is?" Conner asked.

"I think so," Alex said.

Coral was just about to leave when the twins stopped her.

"Excuse me," Alex said. "Where did you get your fish?"

"Oh, Fisher?" Coral said. "I dropped a wand in a lake once and granted him a wish after he swam down and got it for me. He wished for legs, silly thing, so he could play with some boy who lived in a village nearby. The boy ended up dying, sadly, so Fisher came to live with me."

Coral's wings began to flap, and she flew away with her pet fish.

"So that *was* what we thought it was," Conner said.

"Yes," said Alex, her head spinning with questions. "That was the Walking Fish from Dad's story!"

CHAPTER THIRTEEN

A WOLF PACT

There was blood everywhere. White feathers and bits of wood covered the ground. A driver had been transporting a cart full of geese into the Northern Kingdom when the Big Bad Wolf Pack attacked. The only thing that remained in one piece was the green, floppy hat the driver had been wearing.

The wolves were spread out under the trees, chewing on the bones of their victims. Malumclaw jerked his head up and stared into the trees. Someone was coming; he could smell them. Whoever this person was, their scent made him anxious.

"We've got company," Malumclaw growled. All the wolves jumped to their feet, ready to attack again if they had to. But they were no match for who was approaching.

A dark, hooded figure slowly moved through the trees and up to the wolves. It stood fearlessly in front of them for a moment before unveiling itself.

"Hello, Malumclaw," said the Evil Queen.

"Who are you?" Malumclaw barked. The woman before him, less than half his size, was making the hairs on the back of his neck stand up.

"You don't know me, but you know of me," the Evil Queen said. "Everyone does."

"It's the Evil Queen," a wolf snarled.

Malumclaw began shifting his weight on his front paws. He was intimidated, and he didn't like it.

"You have a lot of nerve approaching my pack," he said. "I should have one of my wolves rip your throat out."

"I dare you," the Evil Queen said. There wasn't an ounce of fear in her body. She walked closer to them, and the wolves cowered back, Malumclaw included.

"What do you want from us?" he demanded.

"I've come to make a deal," she said.

"We don't make deals," Malumclaw growled.

"You will once you know what I have to offer," the Evil Queen said.

This intrigued the wolf. "What kind of *deal*?" he asked.

"A trade," the Evil Queen said. "There are two children traveling through the kingdoms, one boy and one girl—twins. I want you to find them and bring them to me unscathed."

"You want *children?*" Malumclaw mocked.

"They have something—several things, actually—that I need," the Evil Queen said. "I would do it myself, but I'm indisposed at the moment."

"And if we bring them to you, what will you give us in return?" he asked.

"*When* you bring them to me, I shall give you the one thing you want more than anything else in the world," the Evil Queen said.

Malumclaw laughed. "Wolves *want* for nothing," he said.

The Evil Queen stared at him as if she were looking into his soul.

"Is that so?" she asked. "Then why do you and your pack crusade around the lands terrorizing everything in your path? What are you trying to prove? Whose revenge are you seeking?"

Malumclaw was silent. He couldn't deny it.

"I will give you the one thing that will avenge your father's death wholly," the Evil Queen said. "I will give you Queen Red Riding Hood in exchange for the twins."

All the wolves, including Malumclaw, growled their doubts, but the idea was intriguing to him.

"And how could you possibly do that?" he said.

The Evil Queen looked at him so sternly that his heart began to race. "Do not question me. I will have the young queen in my possession by the end of the week. Bring me the children, and I will hand her over to you. Do we have a deal or not?"

Malumclaw looked at the frightened members of his pack. They nodded at him; they didn't want to upset the queen.

"Deal," Malumclaw said. "But let me warn you, if you fail to keep your end of the bargain, we'll snap your neck like a twig."

The Evil Queen walked up to the wolf and stood inches from his face, looking him forcefully in the eye.

"Let *me* warn *you*," she said. "Fail to keep your part, and I'll have you all turned into rugs, just as Red Riding Hood did to your father. And if you ever threaten me again, I'll skin you myself."

Malumclaw froze. The Evil Queen knew she had him exactly where she wanted him.

"See you soon," she said. She put her hood back over her head and disappeared into the trees in the direction she had come from.

All the wolves stood still for a moment, afraid to move.

"What are we waiting for?" Malumclaw shouted, his pride bruised. "We have twins to find!"

They charged into the horizon, howling in unison. The sound was deafening.

CHAPTER FOURTEEN

THE SLEEPING KINGDOM

Trix insisted that Alex and Conner stay with her the night after her trial. Of course, that meant the twins slept on the ground underneath her birdhouse-size home hanging from a tree branch, but it was a kind gesture nonetheless.

Alex and Conner couldn't sleep after seeing the Walking Fish in person. They laid under the stars of the Fairy Kingdom—most of which were actually just fairies sleeping in midair—and let their thoughts wander.

"I always thought that the Walking Fish was one of

Dad's stories, one that he made up himself," Alex said. "I wonder how he heard it."

"Probably the same way he heard about all the other stories that come from this place," Conner said.

"But then why wasn't it as well known as Cinderella's or Snow White's stories? Why wasn't it written in *The Land of Stories*?" Alex said, and then asked a question that had been on her mind for a while: "Do you think Dad or Grandma were ever here? Do you think they ever traveled into the Land of Stories and just never told us?"

Conner had to think about it. The idea had crossed his mind once or twice before, considering that *The Land of Stories* had been in their grandma and dad's possession before their grandma had passed it on. Could they just as easily have been transported into this world as Alex and Conner had? And if they had, how had their dad and grandma managed to find a way home?

"I don't think so," Conner ultimately decided. "They loved fairy tales so much. If they ever got here and saw everything we've seen, I doubt they would have left."

The next morning, Trix generously thanked them again and again, and after they shared good-byes the twins started their journey into the next kingdom.

"Sleeping Kingdom, here we come!" Alex said.

"Why do I have a feeling that the spindle is going to be the most difficult item to get?" Conner said.

Alex opened the journal to see if her brother's prediction was true.

The spindle that pricked Sleeping Beauty's finger was the easiest item for me to collect. I had no prior plan of acquiring it and simply pleaded my case to the queen, and she was very sympathetic.

She let me take the spindle on the condition that I would return it to her once I was finished using it. Queen Sleeping Beauty is very wise, especially for someone who had been asleep for a century, and I believe she knew more about what I was after than she was willing to admit.

"Well, that's lucky!" Conner said. "I wonder what sleeping for a hundred years does to you. Every morning when I wake up for school, after about the fourth or fifth time I hit the snooze button, I always think I can sleep for a hundred years. I wonder if you'd wake up super refreshed, or if you'd still be drowsy afterward."

"That's an interesting thought," Alex said. "I wonder if she dreamed about anything. I assume it would have been a very long dream."

The twins had no money left but, claiming to have been separated from their parents, they managed to convince two drivers transporting a cart of goats to let them ride along into the Sleeping Kingdom. The twins didn't mind sitting in the back with the goats, but the goats weren't thrilled about sharing with the twins.

"What are you looking at?" Conner said to one of them after it had stared at him for a good half hour.

The road ran alongside a great sparkling ocean with water that was as blue as the sky. It was like an ocean from their world, except a thousand times more vibrant.

"Look how beautiful the ocean is here!" Alex said. "And look over there, it's Mermaid Bay!"

She was referring to a large bay just ahead that curved into the shoreline.

"It's pretty neat to know that, right now, as we sit in this cart, there are actual mermaids swimming down there," Alex said.

"Yeah," Conner said. "Too bad we didn't bring any snorkel gear."

Alex was flipping through the journal, making a list in her head.

"We have five items collected," she said. "All we need are the spindle, jewels from Snow White's coffin, and the 'saber from the deepest sea.'"

"Whatever that might be," Conner said.

Alex longingly stared out at the water. What could the 'saber from the deepest sea' be? With all her fairy-tale knowledge, she still couldn't figure it out, and it was starting to get to her. She was hoping that at any minute it would just appear in the middle of the ocean.

"We'll figure it out," Conner said. "Or I should say, *you'll* figure it out, and I'll pretend I helped."

After they had been on the road a bit, the twins couldn't help but eavesdrop on the conversation the drivers were having.

"Did you hear about the news from the Charming Kingdom?" one of the drivers asked the other.

"No," he said.

"Both of Queen Cinderella's glass slippers have been stolen!" the driver said.

"Stolen? By who?"

"I don't know, but I reckon there's a reward for anyone with information," he said.

The twins didn't know how to react to this news. If the kingdom was claiming the slippers had been stolen, had Cinderella or Sir Lampton *not* put the slipper in their bag? Was there a warrant out for their arrest? And then, the most troubling question of all: If they had one of the slippers, who had the other one?

"*Both* were stolen?" Alex whispered to her brother.

"It has to be that woman we saw in Red Riding Hood's castle," Conner said. "She must be collecting for the Wishing Spell, too! I knew it!"

"Let's just hope we get to the spindle before she does," Alex said.

The road turned away from the ocean, and the cart headed north into the Sleeping Kingdom.

It was a very hilly place surrounded by towering mountain ranges. It was a surprisingly dismal land, although the twins weren't sure what they had expected. All the fields were dry, and all the trees were bare. Everything seemed like it hadn't been alive for a very long time.

"Why is everything dead?" Conner asked.

"I don't think they're dead," Alex said. "I think they're *sleeping*."

Sleeping Beauty's castle was located in the center of a village called Sleepy Valley, and once the twins arrived there and hopped off the cart, they understood how it had gotten its name. The entire village surrounding the castle looked deserted.

The twins found a man standing behind the open window of a bakery. He was resting his head on his hand and his elbow on the windowsill. He was sleeping standing up.

"Excuse me?" Alex said, not wanting to be rude and wake him up.

"Yes?" the man asked with his eyes still closed.

"Where is everyone?" Alex asked.

"Resting," the man said with a yawn, and then began to snore.

Sure enough, as the twins walked through the village, they could see many other shopkeepers and servants drowsily moving about inside the shops, slowly getting their work done. They all looked as if they were about to fall asleep at any second.

"I thought the curse on the kingdom had been broken," Conner said.

"They don't seem to be sleeping because they *have* to, it looks like they're sleeping because they *want* to," Alex said.

Alex and Conner walked through the sluggish town and found Sleeping Beauty's castle. The castle was a spectacular sight. It was the tallest structure the twins had ever seen.

It was made from peach-colored stones and its many tall towers soared into the sky with the tallest in the very center. When the twins looked closely, they saw the residue left from the vines that had once grown up the castle walls.

There were many vast gardens surrounding the castle, or at least there would have been if anything were alive. Gardeners slept in the garden, still clasping their tools. Every few minutes they would wake up and continue working, but they would fall back asleep almost immediately.

There were guards everywhere, but the twins effortlessly walked past them. Every once in a while a guard would open an eye and consider saying something to them but then decide to go back to sleep instead.

They found the main entrance to the castle and entered. They walked down a long hall with a soaring ceiling that led to the throne room. It had white pillars and a checkered floor. The ceiling was painted the colors of dusk, with vivid pinks and oranges. Guards lined the entire room, and they were all entirely unconscious.

Sitting on the throne ahead of them was a beautiful woman. She was speaking with two men; one was tall and handsome, and the other was short and old with a white beard.

The woman wore a tiara made of silver flowers and had long, flowing, golden hair. She wore a thin gown a shade of pale rose with matching gloves. The twins knew without a doubt that it was Sleeping Beauty.

She was speaking with a royal advisor and her husband,

King Chase. She looked troubled and in a state of deep contemplation. She was tired, too, like the twins' mother looked when there was a lot on her mind.

"Perhaps we should enforce a law: No sleeping permitted during the day," the advisor said.

"Absolutely not," Sleeping Beauty said. "I will not force something so oppressive on my people. Let us not forget that this isn't their fault."

"The curse is over, Your Highness," the advisor said. "It's time for the kingdom to wake up and see that."

"As far as I'm concerned, the curse is upon us until the day this kingdom is in the exact condition it was before the spell was cast," Sleeping Beauty said. "I may be awake, but being asleep for one hundred years has taken a toll on them. They shouldn't be punished or held accountable for any of this."

"Darling, you may have no choice," King Chase said, taking her hand in his. "The kingdom is falling apart. There are no crops being grown or business being done."

"Let me think about this," she said, and let out a long sigh.

"May I make a suggestion?" Conner said, walking toward the trio. He took them by surprise; they didn't know anyone else in the room was conscious. Alex was a little scared. She had no idea what her brother was about to say. She hoped his speech in the Fairy Kingdom hadn't given him a big head.

"Who are you?" the advisor asked.

"I'm Conner, and this is my sister, Alex," he said.

Alex awkwardly waved from behind him. "You have a lovely castle!" she said.

"How did you get in here?" King Chase asked.

"Seriously?" Conner asked him, gesturing to the sleeping guards behind him. "This isn't exactly Fort Knox."

"They don't know what that is, Conner," Alex whispered.

"Young man," the advisor said. "With all due respect, this is a very important matter we're discussing, and—"

"And we've been trying to find a solution for years and still haven't come up with anything that doesn't take away basic human freedoms," Sleeping Beauty said. "So, if this young man thinks he has an answer, I say we let him speak."

The men didn't argue with her. Conner had the floor.

"Have any of you ever heard of coffee before?" Conner asked.

They stared blankly at him.

"Never mind. I've been told it stunts your growth, anyway," he said. "I fall asleep a lot in school. It's not my fault; my brain just turns off when it gets bored. A trick I discovered, when I remember to use it, is to wear a rubber band around my wrist and snap it right when I feel myself drifting off to sleep. The sting keeps me conscious for a good five minutes guaranteed."

They were puzzled by his proposal.

"Look, it isn't a rocket-science solution, but it works," Conner said. "And your people could do it to themselves, so you wouldn't be forcing them into anything. And maybe if they did it enough, they eventually wouldn't need to anymore."

They still needed convincing. Conner turned to Alex for help.

"Alex, do you have any rubber bands on you?" Conner asked.

"I may have some hair ties in my bag," Alex said. She put her bag on the floor and searched through it, accidently knocking the glass slipper out onto the floor. The *clank* echoed through the throne room.

The twins panicked. It was as if time had frozen. Sleeping Beauty, her husband, and the advisor grew very tense.

"How did you get that?" Sleeping Beauty asked.

"It's Queen Cinderella's glass slipper!" the advisor said.

"No, it's not what you think!" Alex said, quickly putting it back into her bag.

"We didn't steal it!" Conner said.

"Guards!" King Chase shouted.

A few guards from behind the twins suddenly awoke and became alert.

"Seize them!" the king shouted.

"Here we go again!" Conner said as the guards sprinted toward them. He grabbed Alex's wrist and pulled her into a run.

"Your Majesty!" Alex pleaded to Sleeping Beauty. "We've come to borrow your spindle! We're collecting objects for the Wishing Spell!"

Sleeping Beauty stood, about to speak, but the twins couldn't wait around to hear what she had to say. They were running around the throne room in circles, barely missing the extended hands of guards trying to grab hold of them.

Alex and Conner ran through a set of open doors leading out of the throne room. They had no idea where they were going, but they knew they had to move. They had been through too much to let guards catch them this time.

"I'm so tired of being chased!" Conner yelled.

They ran down hallway after hallway, making sharp turns whenever they could to throw off the guards. They were moving so fast that the beautiful architecture and artwork of the castle was nothing but a blur.

Suddenly, the hallway they were in came to a dead end.

"Now what are we going to do?" Alex asked.

"Quick! In here!" Conner said, and pulled her through the closest set of open doors. They found a stone staircase on the other side and ran up it. It spiraled higher and higher, and the twins wondered if it would ever end. They were climbing to an impossible height; they must have been headed to the tallest tower in the castle.

They reached the very top of the stairs and found a big, black door. They rushed through it and immediately locked it from the other side.

"Now where are we?" Conner asked, and looked around.

The twins were standing in a large, circular room with tall windows. There were violet drapes and a lavender rug. A balcony wrapped around the entire room outside. Only two pieces of furniture were in the room: an enormous bed and a spinning wheel made from dark wood.

"Conner," Alex said softly. "I think we're in Sleeping Beauty's room. The room she slept in for a hundred years."

Conner walked over to the bed. There was a beautiful engraving on the headboard that said:

FOR ONE HUNDRED YEARS, SHE SLEPT,

THE HEARTS OF HER PEOPLE, SHE KEPT,

SO THEY AWAITED WITH PATIENCE

FOR THE BLISS

OF TRUE LOVE AND TRUE LOVE'S

FIRST KISS.

Alex went to the spinning wheel, but the spindle was gone.

"The spindle isn't here!" Alex said. "I don't understand. The man who wrote the journal promised Sleeping Beauty he would return it after he used it!"

"Is it not here, or did he just not return it because the spell didn't work?" Conner asked.

The lock on the black door began to rattle as someone from the other side unlocked it.

"Hide!" Alex whispered. She and her brother dove underneath the bed.

The black door swung open. The twins expected to see the clunky boots of the guards, but instead they saw a pair of pink heels.

"Is that...?" Alex whispered.

"Is that what—*ouch!*" Conner hit his head hard on the bottom of the bed.

"You can come out from there," Sleeping Beauty said.

The twins couldn't tell if it was a trap.

"I've called off the guards," Sleeping Beauty added. "No one is going to hurt you."

The twins slowly crawled out from under the bed.

"We didn't steal the slipper," Alex said. "It's hard to explain, but I promise we're not thieves."

Sleeping Beauty nodded. "I believe you."

"You do?" Conner asked. He was stunned. "Because if I were you, I'd totally think we were thieves."

Sleeping Beauty smiled at them and took a seat on the bed. "So, you two are after the Wishing Spell?"

The twins nodded self-consciously.

"It's a really long story," Conner said.

"I'm sure," Sleeping Beauty said. "And you've come to ask me permission to borrow the spindle from my spinning wheel, haven't you?"

The twins guiltily nodded again. Sleeping Beauty laughed to herself.

"You know, not too long ago, a man came to my castle and asked me to borrow it," she said. "At first I was completely against the idea, but he convinced me."

"How'd he manage that?" Alex asked.

"He told me all about the Wishing Spell and how he had traveled to another world and fallen in love and was desperate to return. And being somewhat romantic myself,

I let him humor me with the story," she said, and her smile faded back into the contemplative expression they had first seen. "And then he started describing this world to me: a place of machines and technology, a place of enormous structures and lands and people unlike any I had ever seen... and I believed him."

"Why?" Alex asked.

"Because I had dreamed about this place," Sleeping Beauty said. "It's complicated and even I don't understand it, but while I was under that horrible spell, I dreamed about the place he was describing. I dreamed about so many things, I had just assumed it had come from my imagination. I never mentioned a word of it to anyone, so I knew he had to be telling the truth."

"Did he ever return it?" Alex asked, desperate to know. "Did the spell work for him?"

Sleeping Beauty studied the twins' faces.

"You're from there, aren't you?" she asked. "And you're trying to find a way home."

Alex and Conner didn't have to respond; she already knew it was true. She reached under one of the pillows on the bed and withdrew a metal spindle.

The twins felt their spirits soar. There it was! The man had returned it—*the spell must have worked for him!*

"All I'm going to ask in return is that you also return it when you're done," Sleeping Beauty said, and handed it to Alex. "As I'm sure you can imagine, it has sentimental value for me."

The twins were beaming. Now they knew getting home

was a possibility, that they weren't trapped in the Land of Stories forever.

"We're just a couple of strangers," Alex said. "Why are you being so kind to us?"

"There are many things that are out of my control," Sleeping Beauty said, and her smile faded again. "So I like to help as much as I can, when I can."

She stood and walked outside onto the balcony. The twins followed her.

Although the kingdom wasn't in the best condition, the view was spectacular; Alex and Conner could see the entire kingdom and parts of others. The ocean sparkled in the distance, and a beautiful waterfall could be seen in the mountains nearby. It was so beautiful, they forgot how high up they were.

"This used to be the most beautiful of all the kingdoms," Sleeping Beauty said. "The rolling green hills, the wildflowers, the rivers that used to flow...they're all just memories now. Even the natural beauty of the land was put to rest under that awful curse."

"Will things ever get better?" Alex asked.

"I certainly hope so," Sleeping Beauty said. "Can I tell you a secret?" she asked the twins, receiving eager nods. "I haven't slept since Chase awoke me with the kiss."

The twins were shocked.

"Yikes!" Conner said. "You must be exhausted."

"After sleeping for a century, I'll be quite rested for a while," Sleeping Beauty said. "I promised myself and I promised this kingdom that I wouldn't rest until it was restored to its original state. Had my parents just let me die, as the curse originally intended, none of this would have happened. So I'm prepared to spend the rest of my life, the life they ensured, making things right again."

Alex and Conner felt sorry for the young queen. They'd always been so distracted by the thought of a cursed, sleeping kingdom that they'd never thought about the responsibility a monarch would face putting it back on its feet.

"I suppose that's why the Wishing Spell has always intrigued me," Sleeping Beauty said. "It's proof that if someone wants something enough, and they're willing to work for it, they can achieve great things. I keep the spindle as a reminder that even the worst curses cast by the most powerful enchantresses can eventually be overcome."

"The kingdom is very lucky to have a queen like you," Alex said. "A weaker person would have given up."

"Try the rubber band trick," Conner told her. "I promise you won't regret it."

"I will." Sleeping Beauty smiled. "It's probably time you headed out. I may believe you, but convincing my husband and the royal advisor of your innocence won't be easy. Follow me; I know a secret way out of the castle."

The twins left the castle feeling inspired by Sleeping Beauty. The fairy tale had always romanticized the bravery of the young prince and the horror of the curse that had been cast upon the land, but it had failed to mention what a strong and brave woman the sleeping beauty truly was.

CHAPTER FIFTEEN

THE NORTHERN KINGDOM

Alex and Conner traveled into the Northern Kingdom by boat, a first for the twins. They found a fisherman just about to travel up the river into the kingdom and persuaded him to let them come aboard. Alex said they were lost and pretended to cry. She was very convincing, too. Conner, however, was not. He tried to join in on the performance and things just became awkward. Thankfully, the fisherman allowed them to travel with him anyway.

The boat was small and flat and had just enough room

for the three of them. It traveled perfectly along with the river's current, so they didn't even need to row. The twins were enjoying the ride and were able to appreciate the scenery, pointing out every riverside village they saw. It was nice to travel without fear of a wolf or an ogre running up from behind them.

The Northern Kingdom was very misty and cool; the twins could tell it was the type of place that would become freezing in the winter. The kingdom was covered with grassy fields and several bodies of water. An icy, steep mountain range bordered the north.

The boat traveled along the river and poured into *Swan Lake*, which was appropriately inhabited by many swans and other birds. Snow White's palace sat on the edge of Swan Lake. It was short but wide with tan marble walls, dark green domes, and several colorful stained glass windows, including an especially large one shaped as a bright red apple.

"What's up with all the apple tributes?" Conner asked. "Didn't the apple almost kill Snow White? Why does she have it displayed every chance she gets?"

"I suppose it's symbolic for the kingdom, like a cross in a church," Alex said, giving her best educated guess.

There were no towns or villages near the palace. It had been built away from everything else and was an isolated world of its own. It seemed like such a lonely place.

Alex had spent some time with her nose in the journal, re-reading everything she could in case she'd missed something. She put it away and began searching the shore until she finally spotted what she was looking for.

"Excuse me, sir," Alex said to the fisherman. "Can you please drop us off at that riverbank?"

The fisherman steered the boat in that direction, and the twins got off and said good-bye to him.

"Why are we getting off here?" Conner asked. "The palace is that way."

"Conner, I'm tired of explaining everything to you. *Here*," she said, and handed him the journal. He read the pages that she had been looking over during their trip on the boat.

> Snow White's palace overlooks Swan Lake, and part of the lake flows into the moat circling the palace, which works to the advantage of anyone trying to sneak into the palace unnoticed.
>
> There is a hidden gate at the bottom of the palace that the moat runs through. It's right by the dungeon and is used to transport prisoners into and out of the palace by boat. It's easy to swim under the gate and then climb up onto the dock inside.
>
> The glass coffin is in a large storage room that used to be the Evil Queen's private chamber on the third floor. On the second floor you'll find a large portrait of the Evil Queen herself just past the grand staircase off the main entrance. The portrait is actually a secret door that leads up to the chamber.

Travel at night so it's difficult for anyone to spot you in the water. But note that the Swan Lake waters are very deep and can be rough after sundown. Use something as a flotation device, like a log or a piece of wood.

Alex was standing next to a log that had washed ashore on the riverbed, and she gestured down to it.

"See?" Alex said.

"Gotcha," Conner said.

The twins waited for nightfall to travel across the river to the palace. They carefully placed the log into the river and then entered the water themselves. It was unbearably cold. Conner made a high-pitched gasping sound as soon as he was waist deep.

"Wooo! It's so cold, I think we may be twin sisters now," he said through rattling teeth. "I don't think I've ever been this cold in my entire life!"

"Just keep thinking that we only have two more items left to collect and then we'll be home!" Alex said, shivering herself.

"Jewels from Snow White's coffin and the 'saber from the deepest sea,'" Conner repeated to himself. "Jewels from Snow White's coffin and the 'saber from the deepest sea'... Nope, I'm still cold!"

They held on to the log and drifted on the current to the palace. Having the log was a good call, since the water was very choppy, and the twins were getting tired just by holding on to it. They probably would have drowned without it.

The closer they got to the palace the more soldiers they saw marching the grounds.

"There are so many soldiers," Conner said through shivering teeth.

"It's because of the Evil Queen," Alex said. "I doubt there was this much surveillance when the man from the journal came."

The twins submerged themselves completely whenever they thought a soldier might be able to see them. They steered the log into the palace's moat, careful not to make a splash or cause too many ripples. They had to circle the palace twice, but eventually they found the secret gate.

They let go of the log and swam under the gate. It was a much deeper dive than they had thought. Conner came to the surface on the other side and was gasping for air. He treaded water for a moment, waiting for his sister to surface, but she didn't.

"Alex?" Conner asked, looking for her in the water around him. "Alex!"

Conner dove back underwater. He found Alex struggling under the gate; one of the straps on her bag had caught when she'd swum under it. She was stuck, and she desperately needed air. Conner swam down to her and yanked on her bag as hard as he could to set his sister free, but it wouldn't budge. He tugged harder, and the strap finally ripped off.

He helped Alex get to the surface. She was breathing harder than he had ever heard her breathe before. She had been seconds away from drowning.

Conner helped her over to the dock, and they both climbed on top of it. They were both so alarmed that they had forgotten how cold they were.

"Thank you..." Alex said once she had caught her breath. "That was really brave of you."

"I didn't have a choice," Conner said. "You had all the Wishing Spell items in your bag."

Alex playfully hit him, and they quietly laughed.

They were drenched, and their jaws were chattering so hard that the sound of it echoed around them.

The only way out was through a stone doorway. The twins peered inside it and saw a long hallway. At one end was a spiral staircase leading down (to the dungeon, they assumed) and at the other was a spiral staircase leading up. They chose the staircase leading up.

It led straight to another hall with a steamy odor in the air. It was very humid inside this part of the palace, and the twins soon walked by an open door and saw why.

"Look, it's the laundry room!" Alex said.

The room was full of large, steaming tubs of water, and several garments and sheets were hung up to dry around the room. It was past working hours, so the room was empty.

"I have an idea," Alex said, and darted inside the room.

"What are you doing?" Conner asked her. She started

digging through a pile of what Conner hoped were clean clothes and linens.

"If the grounds outside are any indication, I bet the halls of the palace are swarming with soldiers," she said.

"And?" Conner said.

"We're going to seem very suspicious walking around soaked to the bone in our T-shirts and jeans," she explained. She pulled out two dresses and two lacy caps from the basket.

"No way," Conner said, realizing what she intended to do with them. "Absolutely not."

"Conner, put your pride aside and get dressed! We've come way too far to get caught now!" she said, pulling one of the dresses over her head.

"The guys at school can never know about this," Conner said with a very serious face.

"If your friends find out you traveled into the fairy-tale world, I doubt this would be what they were most interested in hearing about," Alex said.

The twins got dressed and looked almost identical in the same outfit. They wrapped their wet clothes and bags in towels and then carried the towels to look busy.

They journeyed higher into the palace, perfectly disguised as two maids working a night shift. The palace had beautiful marble floors and walls on the inside as well. The stained glass windows were even more beautiful with moonlight shining through them.

Alex was right: Every hall and corridor was under constant watch by soldiers. Conner was too embarrassed to look any of them in the eye. He did find a few gold coins in the pocket of his maid's uniform, however, which made him feel better.

Alex and Conner found the grand staircase in the middle of the palace. They climbed it to the second floor and began scanning the halls for a portrait of the Evil Queen. Like Cinderella's palace, there were portraits of past rulers framed on the walls and statues of all seven of the dwarfs that had helped Snow White.

"How do we know what the Evil Queen looks like?" Conner asked. "We've never seen her before."

"We'll just have to guess," Alex said. They walked past a portrait of a woman sitting in a garden. All the plants and flowers were bright around her, but she wore a long, dark gown. The woman was beautiful, but she had a blank, cold expression on her face.

"That's her," Alex said.

There was something about the woman's eyes in the portrait that made Alex sure of it. They were beautiful, but they seemed so empty, as if all the happiness had been drained out of her soul.

Alex waited for two soldiers to leave the hall and then tried pulling on the portrait. It was stuck. She pulled harder, and still it didn't budge.

"Are you sure that's it?" Conner said.

"One hundred percent," Alex said. She gave it another good tug, and the portrait swung away from the wall like an open door. Behind the portrait was a wooden ladder that went up to the third floor.

"Nice one!" Conner said and gave his sister a high five. The twins climbed up the ladder and found the back of another secret door.

The twins entered the storage chamber from behind an exact replica of the portrait they had just gone through on the second floor. The whole room was filled with old furniture covered in white sheets and old trunks and chests. The portrait the twins had climbed through was the only painting hung on the walls; the rest were stacked in piles against the walls around the room.

The room was long and had a set of heavy double doors at one end and a raised platform with a curtain around it at the other. The twins knew without a doubt that this place was where the Evil Queen had kept her magic mirrors.

There was a large counter with tubes, vials, and glass containers. They had all been emptied out, but the twins knew it must have been where the Evil Queen had kept her poisons.

"This room gives me the creeps," Conner said. "It looks like no one has been in here for years."

"I don't see the glass coffin anywhere," Alex said. She started uncovering the furniture trying to find it, but it wasn't in the room.

"The coffin isn't here," she said, feeling a rush of panic come over her. "Let's just look around."

"Look around for what?" Conner asked.

"For anything!" yelled Alex, frustrated and upset. "Try and find anything that says where the glass coffin may have been taken."

The twins searched the room from top to bottom. They looked through all the trunks and cases but found nothing that gave any sign of where it might be. There were so many years of memories packed away in this room, it was impossible to tell what had belonged to the Evil Queen or to Snow White or to the rulers before them.

Alex was going through a stack of parchments. She found interesting handwritten letters among them that she couldn't help but read.

The first letter had masculine handwriting and said:

Dear Evly,

    I love you more than a bird loves the morning sun. Every second I'm away from you is a moment wasted. I am yours forever.

Mira

The next was written by a woman and said:

Dearest Mira,

    You are the last thing I think about before I sleep, and the first thing I think about when I wake, and the time in between is filled with a longing to be in your arms. My heart is yours and yours alone.

Evly

The letters between the two lovers continued; the hand-writing on the next letter seemed rushed.

Evly,

It is the cruelest punishment possible to be kept from you. Not being able to touch your skin or kiss your lips has made my soul hurt. I am hollow without you. I will save you from this wickedness, I swear it.

Mira

Alex could see tiny circles on the paper: teardrops, she figured. The letters were wrinkled from having been held so tight.

Mira,

The thought of being with you again is what keeps my heart beating. Every day is a

day spent searching for a way to be with
you. I live for you. I love you with every
breath I take.

Evly

They were short but so passionate. Alex felt her own heart beating faster after reading them. She looked for more, but found none.

"Alex," Conner said. "Come take a look at this." He was going through the paintings stacked against the wall and had found one that made his heart drop. Conner pulled a large portrait out from the stack. It was of a tall, grizzled man with a bushy, brown beard. He wore a large coat and held a crossbow.

"That must be the Evil Queen's Huntsman," Alex said.

"I bet," Conner said. "But look closer."

Alex took a second look and saw that partially hidden behind the Huntsman in the portrait was a little girl. She had bright green eyes and hair that was so dark red it seemed purple.

"It can't be," Alex said.

The twins felt sick to their stomachs. It was the woman they had seen in Red Riding Hood's castle; her features and hair color were too distinctive for it not to be.

"So . . . is she the Huntsman's daughter?" Conner asked.

"She must be," Alex said.

"I didn't even know he had a daughter," Conner said. "What does she want with the Wishing Spell?"

Alex thought about it. She barely knew anything about the Huntsman; she knew nothing about his daughter. While the wheels spun in her head, coming up with different possibilities, a horrifying thought came to her.

"What if she's not collecting for herself? What if she's collecting for the Evil Queen?" Alex said.

Conner's face went white, and he shook his head.

"No!" he said. "What would she want with the Wishing Spell?"

"It makes sense," Alex said. She couldn't deny the facts. "She escaped from prison for a reason. She has something unfinished, maybe revenge or something *bigger*. Something she can't complete herself."

"What if she needs it for the same reason we do?" Conner asked. "What if she's trying to get into our world?"

The idea hadn't occurred to Alex. She looked back at the portrait of the Evil Queen on the wall. She stared at the painted face and tried to find the answers in her lifeless eyes. What could she be planning?

The twins heard a set of footsteps outside the chamber. The door was unlocked from the outside, and someone started to open it.

"Quick! Hide!" Conner said. He and Alex jumped inside one of the bigger trunks and shut the lid, leaving it open just a crack so they could still see the room.

"Your Majesty," said a booming man's voice from farther down the hall, and whoever was opening the door stopped.

"Yes, what is it?" said a woman's voice just behind the door.

"My men and I have returned," the man said. "We've searched everywhere, and there is still no sign of your stepmother."

The twins recognized his voice. It was Sir Grant, the soldier who had made the announcement about the Evil Queen in the Charming Kingdom during the ball.

"Oh?" said the woman.

"Your Highness, forgive me for asking again, but you were the last person to see her in the palace before she escaped. Are you sure there isn't anything you can tell us about that night? Any detail or clue or something she said that would give us an idea of where she was going?" Sir Grant asked.

"I've told you countless times, I don't remember anything of the sort," the woman said. "I went to simply say a few things that had been on my mind, and once I had done so, I left."

"Your Highness, it's only a matter of time before she strikes, before she poisons a river and kills half a kingdom or something worse," Grant said. "You knew her better than anyone else. For your own safety, please inform us immediately if you remember anything else."

"You will be the first I inform if any memories surface," the woman said. "Now if you'll excuse me, I'd like to be alone."

Sir Grant returned down the hall. The woman slowly turned the handle of the chamber door and opened it. She was a beautiful woman with the darkest hair and the lightest skin the twins had ever seen.

"It's Snow White!" Alex whispered to Conner, and squeezed his arm.

She wore a white nightgown and a matching overcoat. She stood in the doorway for a moment, just looking at the room before she entered it. It seemed hard for her to be in the room where so many attempts on her life had once been planned. The way she surveyed everything around her made the twins assume she hadn't been inside this room in a very long time.

Snow White entered the room and locked the door behind her. She walked around the room and carefully went through all the things, just as the twins had done.

She went to a stack of old books. She went through the pages of one that was black and had a large skull on its cover. Snow White flipped through its pages until she let out a tiny gasp and dropped the book. The twins could see from the open book lying on the ground that she had discovered the page with the recipe for a poisoned apple.

She took a seat on the platform behind her and began crying, burying her face into her hands. The whole situation seemed to have taken a toll on the young queen.

"We should ask her where the coffin is," Alex whispered to Conner.

"Are you sure? She seems like she needs a moment," Conner said.

"Unfortunately, we don't have a moment to spare," Alex said. Alex slowly stood in the trunk and pushed open the lid. "Your Majesty?" she said softly.

Snow White gasped. She was startled and embarrassed to see that she wasn't alone.

"Who are you?" she asked. "How did you get in here?"

"Boy, if we got a nickel every time someone asked us that, we could afford our own palace to sneak into," said Conner, standing up beside his sister.

"We don't mean any harm, Ms. White, we just need to ask you a question, and then we'll be gone," Alex said.

"First, tell me how you got in here," Snow White said.

"The portrait," Conner said. "There's a secret ladder that leads down to the second floor."

"Conner, don't give away all our secrets," Alex said.

"I know that," Snow White said. "I used it when I would sneak into this room as a girl. How did you know about it?"

"We read about it somewhere," said Conner, waving his hands like the subject wasn't a big deal.

"You seem like nice children, but you shouldn't be sneaking into places where you don't belong," Snow White said. "These are very dangerous times we're living in."

"Tell me about it," Conner said with a snort.

"We completely agree and promise never to do it again," Alex said. "We were just wondering where your glass coffin might be?"

Snow White looked at them uneasily; it was such a bizarre question. "It was moved," she said.

"To where?" Conner asked.

"I gave it back to the dwarfs," Snow White said. "It was beautiful, but as you can imagine, it was strange to have that coffin in the palace. They keep it somewhere in their mines."

The twins sighed at the news. The road ahead of them had just become much longer.

"What on earth would you two want with my coffin?" Snow White asked.

They looked at each other, not sure what to tell her and what not to tell her.

"We're on a bit of a scavenger hunt," Alex said. "And we're in a bit of a time crunch, you see, because your step-mother may be after the same things we are."

Snow White looked at them very seriously. "Children, my stepmother is a very dangerous woman. If she is after something and you are in her way, she won't hesitate to kill you. She is *heartless*. If there is any possibility of you cross-ing paths with her, you must stop whatever you're doing immediately."

A loud banging came from the door.

"Your Majesty, are you in here?" a soldier asked. "The king couldn't find you and is concerned."

"Yes, one moment, please," Snow White said, and then turned to the twins. "You two should go."

The twins nodded and climbed up through the portrait.

"Promise you'll think about what I've said," Snow White said to them, just before they shut the portrait door.

"Of course," Alex lied.

Snow White smiled with relief and left the chamber.

The twins decided to exit the palace through the main entrance since they were still disguised as servants.

"The dwarf mines are in the Dwarf Forests, which aren't very far from here," Alex said, looking down at the map. "Remember, Snow White ran there by foot after the Huntsman failed to kill her."

"We're going *back* into the Dwarf Forests?" Conner said. "Do we have a death wish?"

"We don't have a choice," Alex said.

The twins camped out in a safe patch of woods near Snow White's palace and slept for the little night remaining. They hung their wet clothes over a tree branch to dry by the next morning.

They began their return into the Dwarf Forests. Alex's bag had only one strap now, but it worked nonetheless. They walked for a good while before they found a driver willing to give them a ride.

"Are you sure you want to go in there? It's a very dangerous place," the driver said.

"Trust us, we know," Conner said. He gave the driver the coins he had found in his maid's dress the night before to further persuade him.

The cart traveled down the path, past the Ugly Duckling Pond (which Alex found incredibly amusing), and into a forest that had been logged. For miles around there were nothing but tree stumps. It didn't make the twins sad to see all the missing trees; they had seen enough live ones recently to make up the difference.

"I really hope we don't run into the Evil Queen," Conner said during the trip. "That would just suck."

"I just hope she doesn't already have the 'saber from the deepest sea,'" Alex said. "Otherwise we may *have* to cross paths."

"I wonder if she knows about us," Conner said. "If she sent the Huntsman's daughter to find Sleeping Beauty's spindle and the Troll and Goblin kings' crown, and they both were gone, she would realize sooner or later that someone else is collecting objects for the spell."

"I hope she doesn't," Alex said, and then let out a sigh. "It seems like the longer we're here, the worse it gets for us. Something always comes up that makes things more difficult...."

Alex's face went pale, and her mouth dropped open. She looked as if she had just seen a ghost.

"What's wrong?" Conner asked. "You look like you got a B on a pop quiz."

He turned and looked in the direction of her gaze. In the distance, standing in the middle of the field of stumps was a tree that, instead of growing straight out of the ground, was curved and wound in circles like a large vine. It was unmistakably the Curvy Tree, the one their father had told them stories about seeing when he was a kid.

"You're right, Alex," Conner said. "Things always find a way of becoming more complex."

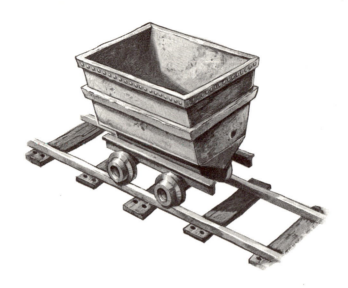

CHAPTER SIXTEEN

THROUGH THE MINES

The twins didn't speak for the rest of the trip into the Dwarf Forests. They couldn't. There was too much to say and not enough words to express what they were feeling. The driver dropped them off a mile or so away from the mines, and the twins walked in silence the rest of the way.

They weren't even alarmed or threatened by the forest around them. Their minds were so full, there was no room to become nervous or timid by the thick and chilling trees around them.

"The mines are just past this hill," Alex said, looking at the map. At least now they were speaking, just not about the subject they needed to address.

The twins reached the top of the hill, and on the other side below were several tunnels leading into the side of a mountain. They were much different from the tunnels they had seen in the Troll and Goblin Territory; they were perfectly rounded and sturdy. Dozens of dwarfs were working in them, transporting wagons of jewels and rocks from one tunnel into the next.

A loud bell rang from somewhere inside the mines, and a dozen more dwarfs emerged, carrying their lanterns and picks with them. It was the end of the day, and they all headed home in single-file lines to different parts of the forest.

The twins waited on the hill for a few moments before going into the mines, making sure no one was lingering behind. They went through the largest of the tunnels and found a row of lanterns hung low on the dirt wall just inside. They each took a lantern and walked deeper into the mountainside.

The mines were huge. The shovels were lined up against the walls and the floor was covered with tracks for the dwarfs' mining carts, and stretched into the mountain for miles. The twins kept walking and walking with their lanterns raised high above them, being on careful lookout for anything that might resemble a glass coffin.

"Are we going to talk about this?" Alex asked her brother as they searched.

"Talk about the mines?" he asked.

"No. You know what I mean," Alex said.

"I don't want to talk about anything but finding the coffin," Conner said.

"Conner, ignoring the situation isn't going to help anything," Alex said.

"Ignoring what situation?" he said, not looking her in the eye. "We saw the Curvy Tree. It was just another story Dad heard and told us when we were younger. Don't make this a bigger deal than it is."

"That's not what this is, and you know it!" Alex said, raising her voice.

"Alex, stop," Conner said.

"Stop denying it!" she said.

"Alex, don't!" he said.

"You've known since the minute we got here! You felt it, too!" Alex said. "I know you did! You may be able to lie to yourself, but you can't lie to me!"

"I'm not lying! You're making things up in your head that you want to be true!" Conner said, trying to hide the tears forming in his eyes.

"All my life I felt like I was missing out on something! Like somewhere in the world there was something going on that I was supposed to be a part of! And now we've found it; it's this place! Part of us belongs here!" she said with tears streaming down her face.

"YOU CAN'T PROVE IT!" Conner said.

"CONNER, FACE IT!" Alex yelled. "DAD IS FROM HERE! HE'S FROM THE LAND OF STORIES!"

"THEN WHY DIDN'T HE TELL US?" Conner shouted, and it echoed through the mines. "WHY DID HE KEEP IT FROM US?" He sat on the ground and quietly sobbed into his hands.

Alex sat on the ground next to her brother and cried with him. It was so much to take on, so much to digest.

"Maybe he felt like he couldn't," Alex said. "He always said he would take us to the places where he grew up when we were older. We're still pretty young. Maybe he thought he would tell us when he thought we were old enough to understand."

"I think 'Hi, kids, did I ever tell you I'm from another dimension?' is pretty shocking no matter what age you are," Conner said.

"It's such a heavy thing to confess," Alex said. "He must have been waiting for the right moment. Unfortunately, the right moment didn't come until it was too late."

"So does that mean Grandma is from here, too?" Conner asked.

"I'm guessing so," Alex said.

"Then how did they get to our world? There must be more than one way besides the Wishing Spell," Conner said.

"There must be," Alex said. "But the Wishing Spell is all we've got so far, so we need to keep looking for the glass coffin if we ever want to see Mom again."

The twins dried their tears and continued their search into the mines.

"You don't think Mom is from here, too, do you?" Conner asked.

"I doubt it," Alex said. "She has photo albums of her childhood. Dad only had stories."

"Do you think she knows?" Conner asked.

"She has to," Alex said. "How could she not? They were married for more than a decade."

"Then maybe she knows where we are," Conner suggested. "Maybe she isn't as worried about us as we thought."

The twins spent another hour just walking through the mines. Conner had seen so many tunnels that he felt like his mind was starting to play tricks on him. He could have sworn he kept seeing things running around in the shadows.

"Did you see that?" he asked, paranoid.

"You're just seeing shadows," Alex said.

"Oh," Conner said. "I could have sworn it was . . . Never mind."

The twins found a long, miniature table with a few dozen miniature chairs around it. It looked like an area where the dwarfs took breaks from working. A large portrait of Snow White hung on the dirt wall behind it, and a glass coffin with rubies and diamonds sat against the wall underneath it.

"Bingo," Conner said. He used a pick that had been left on the table to pry a few of the jewels loose from the coffin and placed them in Alex's bag. He could see where a few had already been taken by others before them.

"That was easy," Conner said.

As soon as he turned around to face his sister, he wished he hadn't just said that.

"Conner?" Alex said, looking at her brother, who was completely petrified.

Through the dim flames of their lanterns, the twins saw a dozen humongous black wolves circling them. They were surrounded by the Big Bad Wolf Pack. The wolves growled at the twins and gritted their teeth.

"Stay back!" Conner said, and swung the pick at them.

This didn't affect them at all. A few of them snickered.

"Are these them?" one wolf said.

"Yes," another wolf said. "We've been tracking their scent for days!"

"Hello, children," said Malumclaw, creeping toward them. "I would say, 'Nice to meet you,' but I can tell from your smell that we have crossed paths before."

"Please don't hurt us!" Alex said. She was shaking with fear and clutching on to Conner.

"Can we eat their limbs at least?" another wolf said. "*She* doesn't need their limbs? Does she?"

"She?" Alex asked. "Who is *she*?"

"We agreed we would bring them to her unharmed," Malumclaw said regretfully, looking toward the twins. "You're coming with us!"

"Conner," Alex whispered to her brother. "What are we going to do?"

"I've got an idea," Conner said. He placed his lantern

on the ground and took a step closer to Malumclaw. *"Bad dog! Very bad dog! Sit!"*

The wolves and Alex all had the same exact expression on their faces. What was he doing?

"I said sit! That's a very bad dog! Go to your basket!" continued Conner, shaking his index finger at Malumclaw. Whatever he thought he was doing was failing miserably, and it was just insulting the wolves.

"I changed my mind," Malumclaw told his pack. "You can eat their limbs."

"Well, I'm out of ideas," Conner said, looking back at his sister.

"I'm not!" Alex said.

In one quick move, Alex kicked the lantern Conner had placed on the ground, and it soared across the tunnel and crashed into one of the wolves, setting him partially ablaze. The wolves rushed to help extinguish their friend. Alex grabbed Conner's hand, and they ran farther down the tunnel, going deeper into the mines.

"After them!" Malumclaw commanded, and the remaining members of the pack chased after them.

The twins ran as fast as they could. They only had one lantern left, so they were practically in the dark. They could hear the wolves stampeding behind them. Their howls were unbearably loud as they echoed down the tunnel. The tunnel began to descend, making it nearly impossible for the twins to run.

"Jump in there!" Conner said, pointing to a mine cart on a track.

"No way!" Alex said, but Conner picked her up and plopped her inside. He jumped inside himself and pulled the brake lever, and the cart began traveling down the tunnel at a rapid speed.

A few of the wolves swiped at them with their claws. The twins ducked down as far as they could in the cart, but not before one of them reached Conner and left a bloody scratch on his forearm. Alex kicked another right in the snout, and it whimpered away. Another wolf barely missed the twins with his claws but knocked the brake lever right off the cart.

The cart gained speed, and soon they were outrunning the wolves.

"We're doing it! We're getting away!" said Conner, holding his hand over his wounded arm.

"I wouldn't celebrate just yet if I were you!" Alex said. She pointed to a sign ahead that said:

DANGER:
USE BRAKE LEVER WHILE GOING
DOWN TUNNEL

"That's not good!" Conner yelled, wishing for the lever to somehow grow back on their cart.

The cart began speeding faster down the tunnel as it

descended at a steeper angle. They were going so fast—*too fast!* They could barely open their eyes with the air rushing by their faces. The track turned and dipped deeper into the mountain. The twins were afraid they were going to fly out of the cart if it didn't fly right off the track first. It was the scariest roller coaster they had ever been on.

"This would be awesome if it weren't for the fear of death!" Conner shouted. He was even tempted to put his hands up, but he knew it wasn't an appropriate time.

The cart zoomed through the mines, showing no sign of slowing down. In a matter of seconds, the twins' greatest fear had gone from being eaten alive by wolves to crashing in a dwarf mine. The track led them through a giant cave with stalactites pointing toward stalagmites and a large pool of water at the very bottom.

To the twins' horror, they passed another sign, which said:

DEAD END

It appeared an avalanche of rocks had fallen on the track many years before, and now the twins were speeding toward the solid wall of rock that had formed there. The twins ducked as low as they could in the mine cart, bracing themselves for the traumatic injuries they were about to receive.

The cart slammed against the rocks. It violently rattled as it broke through the wall. A few rocks fell into the cart and onto the twins. Alex screamed, and Conner covered his head as much as possible with his arm. Just when they thought they were surely about to die, the cart slowly came to a stop.

The twins peeked around from inside the cart. They were outside, somewhere in the Dwarf Forests, on the other side of the mountain.

"I cannot believe we just survived that," Conner said. They were pretty banged-up, but they climbed out of the cart not seriously injured for the most part.

They didn't waste a minute questioning their luck. The twins ran from the cart into the trees.

"We've got to get out of here," Alex said. "It won't be long before the wolves find us again!"

"Who were they talking about? Who were they going to bring us to?" Conner asked.

"I'm afraid to even say it—*Aaaaaahhhh!*" Alex screamed.

They hadn't been in the forest for even a minute when they both felt brutal blows to the backs of their heads. They fell to the ground, slowly losing consciousness.

Right before they passed out completely, the twins saw the faces of Bobblewart the troll and Egghorn the goblin looking down at them, each holding a club in his hand.

The twins woke up with splitting headaches. They were bound together with rope in the back of a very familiar cart.

"Hey, Egghorn, look who's waking up," Bobblewart said.

"The little thieves have arisen," Egghorn said.

The goblin and troll were driving the same exact cart, but it was being pulled by a different donkey; the previous one had most likely been used to death. They kept Alex's bag between them as they traveled down the road. Alex and Conner fought against the ropes, but they were tied with triple knots around their hands and feet.

"Where are we?" Conner asked.

Alex strained her neck looking up out of the cart but managed to recognize some familiar trees.

"We're back where they caught us the first time!" Alex said. "We must have been knocked out for an entire day!"

"Would you like us to make it two days?" asked Egghorn, raising his club.

"This can't be happening again," Conner said. "You can't enslave us again! We told the fairies about you!"

"Oh, yes, we know," Bobblewart said.

"They came and gave us all very long lectures about it," Egghorn said.

"And they shut off all of our tunnels, thanks to you!" Bobblewart said angrily. "Now we have to take the long way into our territory!"

"Then let us go!" Conner said.

"Not this time," Egghorn said. "You stole our kings' crown while in our kingdom. According to the Happily Ever After Assembly's rules, we have every right to bring you back into our kingdom and charge you for your crime."

"It's gonna be one heck of a trial!" Bobblewart said. "Every troll and goblin will be there!"

"And we've already scheduled you for beatings after the trial is over! Everyone in the territory will get a turn!" Egghorn said, and he and the troll howled with laughter.

Conner stayed calm about the matter. He raised his tied hands just over the side of the cart. The scratch on his arm was still healing, and he stretched so a few drops of his blood fell from his wound and onto the ground as they traveled.

"What are you doing?" Alex asked him.

"I'm leaving a trail," Conner said.

She didn't know what to think of this, but she trusted him. Whatever he was doing, he had a plan.

A few hours later, the twins had managed to shift themselves up into a seated position. The troll and the goblin continued entertaining themselves by predicting the horrible things the twins would go through once they got back to the Troll and Goblin Territory.

Conner began seeing dark figures running between the trees in the distance like he had seen in the cave.

"Get ready," Conner said. "They're here."

Alex mentally prepared herself for whatever was about to happen. "That was faster than I expected," she said.

A small howl came from the trees. Egghorn and Bobblewart pulled on their donkey's reins and ordered it to stop. The cart came to a halt.

"Did you hear that?" Egghorn asked.

"Yeah, I did," Bobblewart said.

They both pulled out their clubs and hopped off the cart, circling it for a moment.

"Over there!" Bobblewart said. "I see something!"

The troll and the goblin took off into the trees.

"Help me get to my bag!" Alex said to her brother. They began inching toward the front of the cart. Alex got ahold of her school bag with her teeth and dragged it into the back with them. It landed right by her tied hands, and she managed to open it and pull out Cinderella's glass slipper, almost spraining her wrist in the process.

"What are you doing?" Conner asked her.

"Something that is going to hurt my soul and make me hate myself for the rest of my life," Alex said. She forcefully hit the slipper against the floor of the cart and broke it into three pieces. She used one of the shards to cut her and her brother loose.

"Whoa," Conner said. "Never in a million years did I think you would do that! That was pretty gangster."

"We can glue it back together, right?" Alex said, trying to frantically put the glass slipper back together like a puzzle.

"It'll still work for the Wishing Spell, won't it?" Conner asked.

"The spell never said it had to be in one piece," Alex said.

They put the pieces of the slipper into Alex's bag and

jumped out of the cart. They ran into the forest in the opposite direction than the troll and the goblin had gone. A few moments later, they heard spine-chilling screams and howls as the troll and the goblin were attacked by the Big Bad Wolf Pack.

The horrible sounds made the twins run faster. They knew it would be only a matter of seconds before the wolves picked up on their scents and would be right behind them. They didn't even know where they were going; they just knew they had to get somewhere safe as fast as possible.

Alex was eyeing the forest around them. There was a deep roar coming from close by. Could they be near the ocean?

"We're farther south than I thought!" Alex said. "I think we may be back in the Fairy Kingdom!"

"Then let's find a fairy who can turn these wolves into Chihuahuas!" Conner said. He turned back, and in the distance behind them he could see several wolves running toward them at full speed. A moment later, the twins saw the wolves running slightly ahead of them to both their right and their left, gaining ground and preparing for the attack.

The twins ran through a set of thick trees and then came to a sudden and jarring stop. They were standing on the edge of a very high cliff overlooking the ocean.

"How'd we get to the ocean so fast?" Conner yelled.

"Look," Alex said. "It's Mermaid Bay! We're somewhere between the Fairy Kingdom and the Sleeping Kingdom."

Conner looked behind them. The wolves were only a few feet away from pouncing on them.

"No, it looks like we're somewhere between death and dying!" Conner said. "Alex, I'm really sorry about this!"

"Sorry about wha—*ahhhhhh!*" Alex screamed.

Conner pushed his sister and himself off of the cliff seconds before they would have been tackled by the wolves. They were falling so fast that they couldn't breathe or hear each other's screams. All they could hear was the air rushing past them.

The twins plummeted into the ocean. The wolves stayed on top of the cliff for a few minutes, waiting for them to surface in the water, but they saw nothing. The twins were gone.

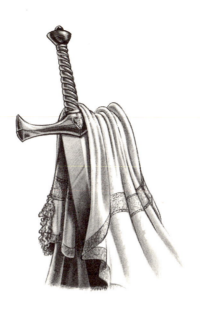

CHAPTER SEVENTEEN

GOLDILOCKS, WANTED DEAD OR ALIVE

It was just before sundown, and soldiers from the Corner Kingdom were hot on Goldilocks's trail. She had been spotted on the outskirts of Baker's Village in the early afternoon, and had been on the run ever since. A group of twenty men were right behind her on their horses, determined to take her into custody by any means necessary. Lucky for her, Goldilocks had the fastest horse in all the kingdoms.

"Come on, Porridge," Goldilocks said to her horse. "You can make it, girl. We're almost to the border."

They passed Rapunzel's tower and crossed into the Dwarf Forests, but the soldiers kept chasing her. In doing so, they were breaking laws that the Happily Ever After Assembly had enacted, but then again, Goldilocks had broken so many laws she had lost count, so she doubted the soldiers would experience any repercussions for it.

Porridge had an advantage over the other horses, since she knew the Dwarf Forests by heart. She and Goldilocks gained a lot of ground from knowing what was behind every tree and which paths led where.

"Split up and find her!" Goldilocks heard one of the soldiers order from behind her.

Goldilocks could feel her horse getting tired. They had been running for hours, and she knew Porridge needed a break soon if they were going to stay on the run any longer.

They came across an abandoned barn that was partially hidden by trees. Goldilocks had often used this place to hide from anyone hot on her trail.

"Porridge, I'm going to hide in here and wait it out," Goldilocks told her loyal horse. "Find someplace safe and rest. Meet me back here tomorrow at sunrise."

Porridge nodded and galloped away. Goldilocks withdrew her sword and approached the barn. The door was off its hinges; it looked like someone or something had forced its way in recently.

The inside of the barn was a disaster. Stacks of hay were knocked over, stables were broken down into nothing but bits of broken wood, and there were bloodstains on the floor and walls. But thankfully, whatever had caused this damage wasn't here anymore.

Goldilocks put away her sword. She wasn't intimidated by the barn in the slightest; she had seen much worse, had been through much worse, and had caused much worse in her days on the run.

She took off her long coat and her sword, and began unlacing her tall boots, getting ready to settle in for the night. Something colorful caught her eye while she was doing so. A bright blue fabric was sticking out from the bottom of a stack of hay.

Goldilocks pulled it out from under the haystack and examined it. It was a beautiful bright blue gown with delicate stitching. It reminded Goldilocks of a dress she had owned when she was a girl. It had been so long since the last time she'd worn a dress.

She discovered a mirror hanging on the barn wall. It was slightly tilted and had cracks on the bottom half, but she could still see her reflection perfectly. She didn't like what she saw. Goldilocks was young, but she had aged so much since the last time she had seen her reflection so clearly. She was a full-grown woman now.

Goldilocks undressed and put on the blue dress. She let her hair down and ruffled it up a bit. She wiped off all the dirt on her face with a handkerchief and looked in the mirror again. She stared at herself, completely awestruck; she had forgotten how beautiful she could be. She only wished Jack could see her looking like this.

"Such beauty, such a waste," said a voice.

In the blink of an eye, Goldilocks had retrieved her sword and extended it in front of her.

"Who's there?" Goldilocks demanded, but she didn't see anyone else in the barn.

"If only the world could see what I see now: Goldilocks, a woman feared throughout all the kingdoms, standing vulnerably in a dress," said the voice.

"Don't be a coward. Show yourself!" Goldilocks said. She turned back to the mirror, but didn't see her reflection. Another woman, with a pale face and in a dark, hooded cloak, was staring back at her.

"Hello, Goldilocks," said the woman in the mirror.

"You!" Goldilocks said. There was only one woman in the world who could possibly have the ability to communicate from mirror to mirror. "I know you. You're the queen everyone is looking for."

"Yes," the Evil Queen said. "We're both women on the run."

"What do you want with me?" Goldilocks said.

"Why do you assume I need something from you?" the Evil Queen said. "I've appeared to you simply to pass along some information I've recently acquired."

"Nice try, but I'm not some ditzy maiden you can con,"

said Goldilocks, getting closer to the mirror. "Try giving *me* a poisoned apple, and I'll shove it down your throat."

"No, of course not," the Evil Queen said in a mocking tone. "You're just poor little Goldilocks, a girl who was tricked into thinking she was going on a date with the boy she loved, and has been running from the law ever since."

Goldilocks stepped away from the mirror. "How do you know that?" she asked with intensity in her eyes.

"I know more about you than anyone," the Evil Queen said. "I know that when you were a young girl, you received a handwritten letter from a young boy you loved named Jack. He asked you to meet him at a house a little way out of town and gave instructions on how to get there. You went to the house and waited and waited for hours, but he never showed up."

"How do you know all this?" Goldilocks asked.

"You became sleepy in that house, didn't you?" the Evil Queen continued. "So you decided to go to sleep in one of the beds and hoped you'd wake to find him. But you didn't wake to him, did you? You woke to find three bears staring down at you, and they almost killed you. You barely escaped the house alive, but the bears pressed charges against you anyway for breaking into their home and, being young and scared, you ran. You ran and have been running ever since.

"For years you wondered how Jack could have done that to you. How could he have framed you like that? And then finally one night you snuck into the Red Riding Hood Kingdom and asked him. But Jack told you he'd grown up poor and illiterate; he hadn't sent you the letter because he never learned to write. Someone *else* did. Someone *else* framed you.

"Jack had been looking for you for years. He was devastated when you disappeared. He even climbed a beanstalk looking for you. You two have been meeting covertly in the shadows for almost a decade now."

"Who told you that?" Goldilocks asked.

"Every driven person comes from a mountain of pain they wish to keep hidden," the Evil Queen said. "I did my research on you, Goldilocks, and you and I aren't so different. Except, I know who wrote you that letter."

Goldilocks shook her head in disbelief. How could she know something Goldilocks had been trying to discover her entire life?

"And who might that be?" she asked.

"Red Riding Hood, of course," the Evil Queen said.

"What?" Goldilocks said. She almost stopped breathing.

"It's true," the Evil Queen said. "The young queen has a large mirror in her bedroom and talks in her sleep. You'd be appalled by the things she confesses in her nightmares."

Goldilocks had to sit down. She didn't even feel human anymore; she felt like an entity made of pure anger.

"Red Riding Hood has always loved Jack, and you were standing in the way," the Evil Queen said. "She was young when she wrote the letter. She had no idea what the consequences would be. She thought you would leave broken-hearted before the bears got home, and then Jack would be hers."

"But she's had years and years' worth of opportunities to make things right," Goldilocks said. Her eyes were staring down at the ground, but she was blind with rage. She stood up, threw off the blue gown, and redressed in her own clothes, sword and all.

"What will you do now that you know the truth?" the Evil Queen asked.

"I'm going to take Red on a trip," Goldilocks said. "And she's not coming back."

"There's only one place where she can disappear forever..." the Evil Queen said, and her reflection faded from the mirror.

Goldilocks burst out of the barn and ran into the night, whistling for her horse. She was about to do exactly what the Evil Queen wanted, but, more important, she was about to get her long-overdue revenge.

CHAPTER EIGHTEEN

THE MERMAID'S MESSAGE

Conner was positive he was dead. The fall into the ocean must have killed him because, wherever he was, he had never been so relaxed. He felt like he was somewhere in the glorious state between being asleep and being awake, a place he knew very well. His eyes were closed, and he was lying down on the softest surface he had ever laid on in his entire life.

The air was cool and refreshing. It smelled a little salty, but he was sure he was only imagining that because the last thing he had seen was the ocean. He opened his eyes a tiny bit and saw his sister lying next to him. She must have died, too, but she seemed so peaceful that he didn't worry about her. He couldn't have worried about anything if he'd tried. He felt so wonderful that, wherever he was, all he could feel was enjoyment. *We must be in heaven*, he thought.

Conner opened his eyes wider. His vision was a little blurry, but he could see so many colorful objects moving in all different directions above him. They looked human the more his eyes adjusted. *They must be angels*, he told himself, and went back to sleep.

Just as he drifted off, a thought occurred to him: Do you sleep when you're dead? Do you feel and smell the air around you? He must have been alive after all to be experiencing all these things. But where was he? He opened his eyes as wide as possible, so they would adjust faster.

He and his sister were lying in a large clamshell at the bottom of the ocean. They were in an underwater cave of sorts, but they were able to breathe in a large air bubble that surrounded them. There were coral pillars in the cave with dark, rocky walls behind them. A sandy floor was underneath them, and they were facing an endless blue ocean.

Swimming around the top of the bubble was a gathering of mermaids. They were gorgeous and colorful. All of them were pale but had long hair that matched their tails in vibrant sea colors; there were blues and greens, purples and pinks. They were friendly and waved at Conner as soon as they noticed he was awake.

Conner looked down at his wounded arm and saw a

seaweed bandage covering his scratch. One of them must have wrapped it.

"Alex!" Conner said. "Alex, wake up!" He tapped her on the shoulder, and she stirred to life.

"Hmm?" asked Alex, who was in an extremely relaxed state of her own.

"Mermaids!" Conner said. "There are mermaids swimming around us!"

This caught Alex's attention, and her eyes fluttered open. It took her a few moments to realize where she was and that it was actually happening.

She sat straight up on the clam. "Conner, why are we at the bottom of the ocean?"

"Beats me," he said. "Check out this bubble around us!" He noticed that the longer they stayed in it, the smaller it became as they breathed in the air.

"The last thing I remember is being chased by wolves and then you—*you jerk!*" she said, remembering being pushed off the cliff. She hit him repeatedly with open hands.

"Hey hey hey, stop it! It was either that or be attacked by wolves! Pick your poison!" Conner said.

"If we survived the fall, how did we get down here?" Alex asked.

"We brought you here," said a mermaid swimming above them. She had long, soft, turquoise hair that matched the shimmering scales on her tail. "The Sea Foam Spirit wants to speak with you."

"The Sea Foam Spirit?" Conner asked.

"She's on her way!" said another mermaid with pink hair and a pink tail.

"I don't think these mermaids get out much," Conner whispered to Alex.

"Here she comes now!" said a mermaid of purple coloring.

Sure enough, a cluster of sea foam drifted through the ocean toward Conner and Alex. It came into their bubble and swirled around before hovering in front of them. It slowly morphed to the shape of a mermaid.

"Hello, children," said an airy voice from inside the sea foam.

"Hello," Alex said, tilting her head like a puppy looking at something peculiar.

"Howdy," said Conner, tensing every muscle in his forehead.

"I hope you are well," the sea foam spirit said. She was frothy, and her foam was constantly rejuvenating itself. "I instructed my mermaids to take very good care of you. You poor things nearly drowned when you fell into the ocean."

Alex gave her brother a really dirty look. "Did we?" she said. "Are you the Sea Foam Spirit?"

"Yes," the spirit said. "But you and your brother may know me best as the Little Mermaid."

Alex's face lit up. This was one person she hadn't thought she would meet in the Land of Stories.

"You're the Little Mermaid?" she asked, completely enthralled.

"Good lord, what happened to you?" Conner asked.

"I thought you died," Alex said.

"Not exactly," the spirit said. "When I was turned into a human by the Sea Witch all those years ago, I had to marry the prince in order for the spell to last. Unfortunately, as everyone knows, the prince married someone else, and my body turned into sea foam. I'm no longer of physical form, but my spirit lives on."

"That's weird," Conner said.

"Oh, that's wonderful!" Alex said. "I was always so sad after reading your story. Not many people know your *real* story; they always assume you had a happily-ever-after."

"There are many who don't," the spirit said. "I believe you two are looking for something that once belonged to me."

"I don't think so," Conner said.

"Wait, do you mean the 'saber from the deepest sea'?" Alex asked anxiously. "Do you know what it is?"

"How do you know we're looking for it?" Conner asked suspiciously.

"I know many things the average entity doesn't," the spirit said. "Especially things said or felt near water."

"Swan Lake!" Alex said. "We were talking about the Wishing Spell items we had left to collect while we were traveling across Swan Lake."

"So, Ms.-Foam-Lady-formerly-known-as-the-Little-Mermaid," Conner said. "What is the 'saber from the deepest sea'? We've been trying to figure it out since we got here."

"As you recall, I traded my ability to speak to the Sea Witch for a pair of legs so I could be with the prince onshore," the spirit said. "After he fell in love with the other woman, my sisters traded their hair for a knife from the Sea Witch. She said that if I killed the prince with it, I could return to the sea as a mermaid, but ultimately I couldn't go through with it and became what I am today."

"The knife!" Alex said eagerly. "The 'saber from the deepest sea' is the knife the Sea Witch gave you! Of course! I was expecting it to be much bigger!"

"Yes," the spirit said.

"Hold up," Conner said. "You went through all that trouble for a *guy*? Were there not any available mermen?"

"Perhaps that is the lesson of my story," the spirit said.

"And where is the knife now?" Alex asked.

"I gave it to a man, not too long ago, who needed it for the same reason you do now," the spirit said. "I gave it to him on one condition: that he destroy it after he finished with it."

"Oh no," Conner said, putting his hands on his head and pulling his hair.

"So, it's gone?" Alex asked, about to cry.

"It is gone, but it isn't destroyed," the spirit said. "The man failed to fulfill his agreement, fearing that he might need it again someday."

"So where did he put it?" Conner asked.

"It's in a place where people put things they never want to see again," the spirit said.

"He flushed it?" Conner asked.

"No, remember that place the Traveling Tradesman was telling us about?" Alex said. "He must have dropped it in the Thornbush Pit!"

"Oh, great!" Conner said sarcastically. "Why did he have to drop it into a cursed pit? Why couldn't he have just dropped it in a gopher hole?"

"We're never going to get it," Alex said. "If we even get close to that place the vines and thornbush will drag us to the bottom of the pit forever."

"Unless you have these," the foam spirit said. She extended both of her hands, and two necklaces, each with a golden shell, appeared in them. "Wear these while you retrieve the knife from the bottom of the Thornbush Pit, and the cursed plants will not harm you."

"Thank you," Alex said.

The twins leaned forward to take the shells out of her foamy hands, but the spirit pulled them away. "I will only give you these if you promise to destroy the knife as soon as you're done with it," the spirit said.

The twins looked at each other and nodded.

"Of course," Alex said.

"No problem," Conner said.

"Very well," the spirit said, and handed them over to the twins. "Be careful, though. The shells are twins, too. If one breaks, the other shell will as well. Remember that."

"Why are you doing this for us?" Alex asked.

"Why do you always ask what someone's motives are when they help you?" the spirit asked.

The question took Alex off guard. "Because people don't really help each other where we come from," Alex said. "They do occasionally, but it's rarely without reason. Good people are hard to find."

"It can't be too difficult. I'm looking at two now," the spirit said. "Which is why I was inclined to help you, and which is why I am also inclined to tell you this: You are not the only ones after the Wishing Spell."

"We know," Conner said. "The Evil Queen is, too."

"She's the one who sent the wolves after us," Alex said, "isn't she?"

"Yes," the spirit said. "She is as determined to find the knife as you are. That is why you must hurry if you are going to beat her to it. Unfortunately, the Wishing Spell can only be used once more."

"What?" Conner said. Both the twins felt like someone had kicked them in the stomach. This definitely complicated matters. "You mean, if she gets to the knife first, that's it, game over?"

"Unfortunately so," the spirit said.

The bubble around the twins was almost gone. It barely covered the clam they sat in. Their time underwater was running out.

"We can't let that happen," Alex said, shaking her head. "We have to get there first! We have to go right now!"

"I'll have my mermaids escort you there as fast as they can, but once you are on land, you must travel the rest of the way on your own," the spirit said. "Stay safe, children."

The Sea Foam Spirit fizzled out and disappeared. The mermaids swam down to the twins and each grabbed hold of the clamshell Alex and Conner sat in. Together they moved the twins through the ocean, on to their next adventure.

CHAPTER NINETEEN

THE THORNBUSH PIT

The mermaids escorted the twins through the ocean and up a river into the northern part of the Sleeping Kingdom. Alex and Conner were only a few miles away from the Thornbush Pit and began their walk to the place where they would find the last Wishing Spell item.

"How do we get the Wishing Spell to work once we find the knife?" Conner asked.

"I think we just put all the items together and let them do the rest," Alex said.

"I suppose," Conner said.

The land was dead and dry around them. The roads were bumpy and covered in stone. It was by far the least attractive area they had been to in all of the Land of Stories.

"I don't know about you, but I am so looking forward to getting out of this place," Conner said.

"I know what you mean," Alex said halfheartedly. "I miss Mom so much."

"I can't wait to get back to air conditioning and television," Conner said. "Boy, have I missed those things. And *food*—don't get me started about food!"

"I bet we have so much homework to catch up on, too," Alex said happily.

Conner grunted. "I didn't think about that." He also wondered if he would have to serve all those detentions when he got home as well. Would being trapped in the fairy-tale world for a week or two get him out of it?

Alex completely sympathized with her brother. She had been so excited to discover the Land of Stories, but they had had so many treacherous experiences that even she was anxious to get home. But now, looking around at the land, even as ugly as this part of the kingdom was, she couldn't help but think how much she was going to miss it.

"We have seen some amazing things," Alex said.

"Very true," Conner said.

"And we have met some extraordinary people," she said.

"Can't deny that," Conner said, shaking his head.

"It's a shame that we can't come and go to this place as we please," Alex said. "You don't think you'll miss it just a tiny bit?"

Conner immediately shook his head, and his mouth positioned into the shape to say, "No," but when he thought about it more, he hesitated. "We've had our moments," Conner said. "We're definitely leaving with memories no one else will have. Think about all the stories we'll be able to tell our kids someday."

"Right," Alex said, but this only made her think about their father.

Without realizing it, being in the Land of Stories had filled the emptiness they were left with when their dad died. Discovering that their dad was from the fairy-tale world had been the most meaningful part of the adventure.

"Mom and Grandma are going to have so much explaining to do," Conner said.

"For sure," Alex agreed. "I wonder where Dad lived."

"We'll find out," Conner said, and smiled. "I wonder if he knew any of the people that we've met or seen? I wonder if we have *family* here!"

Alex stopped walking. Her eyes grew almost as big as her open mouth.

"What if we're related to the Charming or White Dynasties?" Alex proclaimed excitedly.

"Or maybe we're one-sixtieth ogre or elf or something cool!" Conner said.

The idea gave them a new boost in their step.

They finally reached the Thornbush Pit and stopped dead in their tracks—it was a frightening sight. It was extremely wide and incredibly deep and filled to the top with plants, some dead and some alive. The vines and thornbush moved around like thousands of snakes; the pit was alive and hungry. Ruins of an old castle sat on the edge of the pit, consisting of nothing but a few walls and a stony staircase that led to nowhere.

"We're actually going in there?" Conner said.

"Let's put on our shells," Alex said.

They each tied a shell necklace around their necks and slowly walked to the edge of the pit. The vines and thornbush shot straight toward them like a frog's tongue to a fly, but then jolted back, repelled by the magic shells.

"Looks like they work," Conner said.

They began to climb down into the pit. They used the dead thornbush on the side of the pit as a ladder, scratching themselves and drawing blood on different parts of their bodies every few feet. The thornbush and vines that were alive moved away from the twins as they passed. They watched them like hungry serpents, ready to strike at any second.

Alex and Conner climbed as low as they could go. The pit floor was covered in rubbish, like a giant junkyard. The smell was unbearable, and the twins had to cover their noses as they searched.

"Whoa," Conner said. "This is like a massive trash bin.

Can you imagine all the secrets we could discover just by going through this place?"

"Remember what we're here for," Alex said, and then suddenly screamed.

"What is it?" Conner asked.

She had almost stepped on the hand of a skeleton.

"Who is that?" Conner said. "Or should I say who *was* that?"

"I don't want to know," said Alex, shaken up by the discovery. "I've never seen a skeleton before."

It was only the first of dozens. There were skeletons and parts of skeletons everywhere. Each one was harder to look at than the one before; some had been down here longer than others. Alex had to take deep breaths to prevent herself from getting sick.

They found countless knives and daggers and swords scattered across the pit.

"Is this it?" Conner asked, holding up one for his sister to see.

"No, that's wooden," Alex said.

"What about this?" he asked, holding up another.

"No, that's made of steel," Alex said. "Remember, it was made in the ocean."

"Oh," Conner said. "Like *this*!"

He held up a knife that matched his sister's description perfectly. It had a curved handle that was made of coral and bits of shell, and a long blade made of bright sea glass.

"That has to be it!" Alex said gleefully. "Conner, we did it! We found the last Wishing Spell item!"

She gave her brother a huge bear hug and kissed him on the cheek. They were so incredibly happy, tears formed in their eyes. They were going home!

"Let's get out of this pit as fast as possible," Conner said. "It gives me the creeps."

The twins went back to the dead thornbush and began climbing up the side of the pit.

When they were about two thirds of the way up, a branch caught hold of Conner's necklace and ripped it off his neck. As if it were happening in slow motion, Conner saw the shell begin to fall away from him toward the bottom of the pit. He reached for it, but it was too late. It was gone. The shell hit the bottom of the pit floor and shattered.

Alex and Conner looked down at the broken shell and then looked at each other with the same horrified expression.

"Oops," Conner whispered.

The living vines and thornbush vibrated with excitement. The shells were useless now. Vines began shooting toward the twins.

"We've got to get out of here!" Alex yelled, and the twins rushed up the side of the pit faster than they had ever climbed anything before.

Their fingertips were just about to reach the top of the pit when vines wrapped themselves around Alex's and Conner's feet and dragged them downward. Conner stabbed the saber into the ground outside the mouth of the pit, and he and his sister held on to it while they were being pulled, determined not to end up like the other victims of the vines.

More vines wrapped themselves around the twins, increasing the fight. Alex and Conner were nearly completely covered in plants. Alex lost her grip around the knife and began to fall back into the pit, but Conner grabbed hold of her just in time. He couldn't hold on to both for much longer. One by one his fingers began slipping from the knife's handle.

Conner's hand lost its grip on the knife, and he and his sister were both dragged away. But right as his hand slipped away, he felt a cold, clammy hand grab on to his and try to pull him and his sister out of the pit. It was a struggle; the plants weren't giving up. Alex and Conner felt like the rope in a game of tug-of-war.

"Damn you, miserable plants!" said a very proper voice that the twins recognized. "Let them go, you overly advanced shrubbery!"

With one final tug, most of the vines broke, and Alex and Conner were saved. Their momentum piled them on top of whoever had just saved them.

"Froggy!" Alex declared, and gave their old friend a tremendous embrace.

"It's you!" Conner said. Although he had had trouble shaking Froggy's hand when they'd first met him, Conner was now hugging him like he was a long-lost relative.

"Hello, Conner, Alex," Froggy said. He was almost suffocated by their affection.

"You saved our lives!" Alex said.

"How did you know we were here?" Conner asked.

Froggy got to his feet, straightened the tie of his suit, and helped the twins up.

"I've been looking for you two for days!" Froggy said. "The amount of ground you've covered is remarkable! Thank goodness I crossed paths with those mermaids, or I would never have found you!"

"I'm so proud of you," Alex said. "You're out of your house! You're out in the world!"

"What made you come out of your hole in the ground?" Conner said.

"The Fairy Godmother is looking for you two," Froggy said.

The twins were very surprised and confused to hear this.

"What?" Conner said. "What does *she* want with us?"

"Oh no," Alex said. "The glass slipper! She must know I broke it and is furious!"

"Glass slipper?" Froggy said with a raised eyebrow equivalent.

Alex shyly looked around. "Well, yes," she said. "We've been busy collecting." She opened her bag and let Froggy peer into it.

"You've collected all the Wishing Spell items? Already?" Froggy asked. He wasn't sure whether to be proud or shocked.

"Yup," Conner said, pulling the knife out of the ground. "And believe me, it wasn't easy."

"We've got the very last item!" Alex said happily. "We can go home!"

Froggy was speechless. These two children had done something he had only dreamed about doing for years.

"That's extraordinary, children," Froggy said, but his happy expression deflated to a worried one. "But you can't go home yet."

"Why not?" Alex asked.

"Yeah," Conner said. "Why not?"

Froggy was the one who had introduced them to the Wishing Spell in the first place. Why was he saying they couldn't use it now?

"I promised the Fairy Godmother that I would bring you to her," Froggy said. "And in exchange, she said that she would turn me back into my human form. Please, you must let me take you to her."

The twins could tell that he didn't want to ask this of them but was desperately hoping they would agree.

"Froggy, you have no idea what we've been through to get all these items," Alex said.

"We want to go home," Conner added. "Now."

"We want to help," Alex said. "But what if the Fairy Godmother takes away some of the items that we've—how do I say this?—*forcefully borrowed*?"

"Then we'd be stuck here again for who knows how long," Conner said.

Froggy looked ashamed of himself. "I understand, children. Forgive me; I wasn't expecting you to have assembled all the Wishing Spell items so soon." He tried to cover his disappointment with a fake smile. "Can I help you assemble the Wishing Spell, then?"

Alex and Conner each looked to the other, feeling incredible guilty. They wanted to get home more than anything, but how could they tell him no? He had done so much for them.

"I suppose sticking around for another day wouldn't be so bad," Conner said, knowing his sister was thinking the exact same thing.

"It would be a shame to end our journey *here*," Alex said.

"Children, you can't stay for me," Froggy said. "You've got everything you need. Please don't let me stop you!"

"We'd still be lost somewhere in the Dwarf Forests without you, Froggy," Alex said.

"And if the Fairy Godmother tries to take our stuff, we'll just run like crazy away from her," Conner said. "We've gotten so good at it! You've got to see us in action!"

Froggy's big round eyes became more watery than usual. "Children, you are the kindest souls I have ever been fortunate enough to meet."

The twins smiled at him. Doing this for him made them feel better than they had felt in their entire stay in the Land of Stories.

"Where to?" Alex asked him.

Suddenly, a piercing scream sounded across the land. All three of them jerked their heads toward it.

"Let me go!" a woman screamed.

"What's going on?" Alex asked.

Soon they heard a galloping horse approaching and felt the *thump*s of its hooves through the ground. Coming toward them at full speed from the distance was a familiar cream-colored horse.

"It's Porridge!" Conner said. "And Goldilocks!"

Goldilocks and Porridge were charging toward the Thornbush Pit—*and they were dragging Queen Red Riding Hood behind them!*

The twins and Froggy all stood motionless at the sight of it. They thought their eyes were playing tricks on their brains.

"Do you see this, too? Or am I imagining it?" Conner asked.

"I order you to release me at once!" Red Riding Hood said. Her dress was so big and layered that she wasn't harmed from being dragged, but she was extremely aggravated. "Do you have any idea what my soldiers are going to do to you once they catch you?"

"Oh, shut up, you red-hooded harlot!" Goldilocks said.

She and Porridge stopped a short distance from the twins and Froggy. Goldilocks hopped down and then dragged Red Riding Hood past them to the Thornbush Pit. She vaguely recognized the twins.

"I remember you," Goldilocks said.

"Hi there," Alex said.

"Do you need a hand?" Conner asked.

"Nope," Goldilocks said. "Just taking out the trash."

"What are you three doing just standing there?" Red screamed. "Help me!"

"I said *silence*, you basket-carrying bimbo!" Goldilocks said, and dragged her closer to the pit.

"What's going on?" Alex asked, and she, Conner, and Froggy followed them, not sure how or who to help.

"This lunatic broke down one of my kingdom's gates and rode her horse all the way into my throne room, lassoed me, and has dragged me all the way here!" Red said. "And now she's going to kill me!"

"Yes, I am!" Goldilocks said.

"Wait, why are you going to kill Queen Red Riding Hood?" Froggy asked.

"Because she's mental!" said Red.

"She knows why!" Goldilocks said.

They reached the edge of the pit, and the twins grew very nervous that they were about to witness a murder.

"They'll hang you for this!" Red shouted.

"They won't be able to prove anything," Goldilocks said. "They'll never find your body!"

Goldilocks stood Red up on her own two feet. She was still tied up, and Goldilocks began aggressively pushing her toward the pit's edge.

"Please don't do this!" Red pleaded. "It was such a long time ago! We were all just kids."

"We haven't been kids for years," Goldilocks said. "You have had plenty of chances for redemption."

"I love him, too! I was just doing what I thought I had to!" Red said.

"You just couldn't stand that I had something you didn't!" Goldilocks yelled.

Goldilocks went in for the final push, but Red dodged it, and Goldilocks almost fell into the pit herself. Red ran away from her as fast as possible, running along the edge of the pit. The plants below moved with excitement; they knew one of them was bound to fall in.

"Come here!" Goldilocks yelled.

"Get away from me, you fugitive floozy!" Red said.

They did an entire lap around the pit, and Red ran into the castle ruins. Goldilocks took out her sword and began swinging it at her, barely missing her by inches.

"This is awful!" Alex said with her hands covering her cheeks.

"This is awesome!" Conner said. "Five bucks says Goldilocks wins!"

The twins wanted to help, but there was nothing they could do without getting into harm's way.

"We used to be such good friends!" Red said, constantly ducking Goldilocks's sword.

"You don't know what a friend is!" Goldilocks said, her swing coming much closer each time. "You could have cleared my name the day you became queen of that pathetic kingdom!"

"I never even wanted to be queen in the first place! I just wanted to impress him!" Red confessed. "Keeping you an outlaw kept you away from him! It wasn't anything personal!"

"Personal?" Goldilocks said, absolutely infuriated. "Forcing me to live a life of running and committing crimes to survive because you wanted to steal my boyfriend wasn't personal?" She swung her sword hard at Red and knocked a big chunk out of the ruins' stone wall.

Red ran up the decaying staircase; it was the only place left to go. Goldilocks ran up after her, and Red was cornered. The only way to escape was to jump into the pit.

"If you let me go I'll clear you name!" Red begged.

"Liar!" Goldilocks said.

"I'll give you my castle! Half of it is being rebuilt because of a fire! It looks wonderful!" Red said.

"I don't want your castle! I want revenge!" Goldilocks said, and pushed Red off the staircase.

Red screamed and fell down toward the pit. The vines reached toward her, happy to finally be fed. Suddenly, a rope came out of nowhere and lassoed Red around the waist just as she fell into the pit and was swallowed up by the vines and thornbush.

"What the—?" Goldilocks said.

The twins and Froggy turned to see a woman riding a black horse on the other side of the pit holding the other end of the rope.

"It's the Huntsman's daughter!" Conner yelled and pointed at her.

Red screamed as the vines pulled her down toward the

bottom of the pit. The Huntsman's daughter tied the rope to the horse and took off. Red was yanked out of the pit and dragged behind her.

"Not again!" Red screamed. She was dragged off into the horizon, now a captive of the Huntress.

"Son of a witch!" Goldilocks said, watching a stranger ride off with her chance at revenge. She hopped down from the staircase, and Porridge joined her by the ruins.

"What just happened?" Conner asked, completely over-whelmed by all the excitement.

"I don't know," Alex said. "But after seeing the Hunts-man's daughter, I have a bad feeling."

"Who was that woman?" Goldilocks asked.

"The Huntsman's daughter," Conner said. "She's work-ing for the Evil Queen."

"The Evil Queen?" said Goldilocks, growing even angrier.

"We have to get as far away from this place as possible," Alex instructed.

"Oh no," Froggy said softly. He looked more frightened than the twins had ever seen him.

Out of the distance, the Big Bad Wolf Pack crept toward them. The wolves were all growling, more irritated and vicious than ever before. Steam was practically coming out of their nostrils. They surrounded the twins, Froggy, Goldilocks, and Porridge.

Goldilocks stood in front of the twins. Even she was scared. Normally she wouldn't have considered the wolves to be more than she could handle, but the way they stared at their group, hungry and irritated, she knew this wasn't going to be a sporting encounter in the forest.

"After what you've put us through, we ought to claw your hearts out!" Malumclaw growled through gritted teeth at the twins. "And look who's decided to join them! I guess we get Red Riding Hood *and* Goldilocks tonight!"

The rest of the wolves howled their excitement.

"Just to let you know, you *just* missed Red Riding Hood," Conner said.

"Nice try," Malumclaw said.

"What do you want with children and an overgrown frog?" Goldilocks asked.

"We're taking the children to the Evil Queen," Malumclaw said. "We have no interest in the frog.... *Dig in, boys!*"

Froggy's face turned a pale green. The wolves moved toward him, snapping their massive jaws in his direction. Froggy turned to the twins.

"I'm going to get help, children," Froggy whispered to the petrified twins. A wolf leaped toward him, but Froggy jumped twice as high into the air, and the wolf missed him. Froggy landed on the other side of the circle the wolves had formed around them and took off running. A few wolves chased after him as he disappeared into the distance.

"Froggy!" Alex yelled after him. All they could do was pray he would be all right.

"Porridge," Goldilocks said, "I want you to get out of

here, you understand? This is one battle we won't be able to win."

The horse was hesitant to leave her at first, but then nodded. She took off in the same direction Froggy had leaped. A wolf tried to attack the horse as she left, but Porridge kicked the wolf with her hind legs, and the wolf landed in the Thornbush Pit. He whimpered the entire way to the bottom as the vines wrapped themselves around the wolf and dragged him down to the bottom forever.

The rest of the wolves weren't going to allow any more escapes.

"We're going to see the queen," Malumclaw growled. "And if anyone else tries to run off, it'll be the last thing you do."

The twins trembled. Goldilocks put her hands on the twins' shoulders, leaned close to them, and whispered into their ears. "Be brave, children," Goldilocks said. "Courage is one thing that no one can ever take away from you."

CHAPTER TWENTY

HEART OF STONE

The wolves led the twins and Goldilocks across the dead and deserted land. They walked for miles and miles across the rocky ground, never stopping for anything. The wolves kept a close eye on their captives; if the twins so much as breathed too deeply, they would get a threatening growl.

The wolves had confiscated Goldilocks's sword and Alex's bag, so they couldn't get to the Wishing Spell items. Alex closely watched her bag being carried in one of the wolves' mouth; everything she and her brother needed was in there. Their chance at going home was just a few feet away and yet out of reach.

The twins didn't know if they were more angry or scared. Just minutes before they had been positive they were on their way home, and now they didn't even know where they were, where they were going, or if they would even survive what was ahead. Being so afraid gave them an odd sense of courage. They were being taken as prisoners to one of the most infamous villains of all time; they didn't see how things could get much worse.

The area they were traveling through seemed foreign even to Goldilocks, who the twins were certain had seen *every* part of *every* kingdom. Her eyes darted around with as much curiosity as the twins' did. The land looked different from the rest of the Sleeping Kingdom. This land didn't seem to be sleeping like the rest of the kingdom did; this land seemed to have been murdered.

A decrepit castle finally came into view in the distance. It was made of stone but looked so frail that a strong wind could knock it over. Alex and Conner knew without having to be told that this was where the wolves were taking them, and somewhere inside the Evil Queen was waiting.

They reached the front of the castle, and Malumclaw howled. A rickety drawbridge was slowly lowered, and a towering man with a graying beard dressed in several layers of animal skins greeted the wolves.

"She's been expecting them," the Huntsman said.

The wolves guided the twins and Goldilocks over the

drawbridge. As soon as the twins entered the castle they wanted to leave it. All the dust and cobwebs didn't make for a pleasant welcome.

The Huntsman pushed the twins down a stony corridor, through a set of large doors that creaked horribly, and into a long great hall. The great hall was empty except for a few chairs and a small table.

Red Riding Hood was tied to one of the chairs, with a large white scarf tied around her mouth. Her eyes were teary and puffy. She was excited to see the twins at first, happy not to be the only prisoner, but then began to panic under her restraints when she saw Goldilocks and the wolves behind them.

The Huntress stood next to Red, keeping a careful watch over the fidgeting queen.

In the middle of the room, facing two tall mirrors, one gold and one black, was a hooded woman. She was very still and very silent.

"Seat them," the woman said, still with her back toward them. Without any doubt, the twins knew she was the Evil Queen; they could just feel it. They had never been so tense in their lives.

The Huntsman and the Huntress forcefully sat Alex, Conner, and Goldilocks down in the chairs and tied ropes around their torsos, hands, and feet.

"Easy!" Goldilocks said, glaring at the Huntress, who tripled her knots. "Did anyone ever tell you it isn't nice to kidnap other people's hostages?"

Red let out a high-pitched cry and mumbled something along the lines of "This is so unfair." The twins now understood why she'd had a handkerchief in her mouth in the first place.

"We've brought you the twins plus a bonus, Your Majesty." Malumclaw lowered his head in a scornful and mocking bow. There was heavy tension between the two.

"Did anyone escape?" the Evil Queen asked.

"Just an overgrown frog and a horse," Malumclaw growled.

"Then we don't have much time," she said. "Put the items on the table."

The Huntsman seized Alex's bag from the wolf carrying it and placed it on the table next to the twins. The Evil Queen had her own collection of Wishing Spell items on display here: a lock of golden hair, a chunk of Red Riding Hood's basket, and the other glass slipper.

"A deal is a deal!" Malumclaw said. "We've brought you the twins. Now give us Red Riding Hood!"

Red Riding Hood whimpered and said something like "Why is this happening to me?" through the handkerchief.

"You will have her when I am finished with the children," the Evil Queen said. "Now wait outside."

"That was not part of our bargain!" Malumclaw bellowed, and his pack snarled behind him.

"I said wait outside!" the Evil Queen ordered. Her voice was so overpowering that the twins felt tears form in their eyes from the mere sound of it. "You can have Red Riding Hood, Goldilocks, *and* the children when I am satisfied."

The wolves were infuriated, but they left the hall and waited outside the castle.

"Empty the bag," the Evil Queen ordered.

The Huntsman did as he was told. He pulled out all the items the twins had collected, one by one, and placed them on the table surface: the lock of hair, the glass slipper, the chunk of basket, the stone crown, the vial containing the fairy tear, the spindle, the jewels, and the knife.

"We need those!" Conner said, squirming in the ropes. "Why do you need the Wishing Spell anyway? Don't you have powers or something?"

"The only powers I have are the powers of intimidation," the Evil Queen said. She turned away from her mirrors and looked at the twins.

She wasn't the vicious monster they had expected. She was still very much the woman from the portrait in Snow White's palace, but she had been weathered by time and fatigue. Her face was plain, but it was a plainness that had so much potential for beauty had time and circumstance allowed it. Her eyes were dark and bleak; she seemed empty and cold down to her soul.

The Evil Queen walked over to the table and observed all the Wishing Spell items. She picked up the vial that held the fairy tear and stared into it.

"As soon as this tear touches the table, the Wishing Spell will be mine," she said.

Seeing the Evil Queen near all the items they had worked so hard to get ignited a fury inside Conner. He wanted to go home and wasn't about to let her stop them. If they weren't going to get to use the Wishing Spell, then *neither was she.*

Conner struggled against the ropes with all his might. It was painful, but he managed to get one of his feet free. He kicked as hard and as high as he could and knocked the vial out of the Evil Queen's hand.

The vial flew across the room. The Evil Queen's eyes watched it as it soared away from her.

"Catch it!" she demanded.

The Huntsman ran as fast as he could and threw himself on the ground with his hands extended to catch it, but the vial hit the dusty stone floor inches from his fingertips and shattered. The tear sank into the stone and vanished.

The Evil Queen stared at Conner. Her face didn't move or express much, but the slightest movements made Conner very well aware that she was enraged.

"Stupid boy," the Evil Queen said. She struck him hard across the face with the back of her hand. Conner's whole body shifted with the blow.

"Conner!" Alex said.

"I'm fine," Conner said, slowly lifting his head straight to look at the Evil Queen. The whole side of his face began to swell.

"How long will it take to retrieve new fairy tears?" the Evil Queen asked.

"Days, Your Highness," the Huntsman said, getting back to his feet. "The fairy we caught only screamed when we tried to collect tears from her; none were produced. If my daughter left now, she could be back before sunrise two days from now."

"We don't have that kind of time," the Evil Queen said softly to herself. She promptly turned around and faced her mirrors. "Mirror, Mirror, on the wall, how much longer 'til forces invade this hall?" she asked.

The reflection in the black mirror became very cloudy and condensation began to drip down the glass.

"Conner, look. It's the Magic Mirror!" Alex said.

The dark silhouette of a man appeared in the mirror. A low and hoarse voice filled the great hall.

"This castle offered my queen sanctuary for weeks,
But an army now approaches, led by a frog that
speaks.
They move quickly in this direction, ready to attack,
And they've joined forces with a cream-colored
horse and a man named Jack."

"Jack?" Goldilocks said.

"Jack!" Red tried to say.

"Soldiers are coming!" Alex whispered to her brother. "Froggy's alive! He got help!"

"Those are probably my soldiers coming," Red mumbled. "They're coming to rescue me and slaughter all of you—especially *you*," she said, giving Goldilocks a dirty look.

The Evil Queen's eyes drifted from her Magic Mirror to

the Mirror of Truth and watched Alex through the reflection. She stared at her through the mirror absolutely mesmerized; it was the most expressive the twins had seen her since they'd arrived.

"What should we do, Your Majesty?" the Huntsman asked. The Evil Queen ignored him; her attention was fixated on Alex.

"Why is she looking at you like that?" Conner asked.

"I don't know," Alex said with a trembling jaw. Everyone knew the Evil Queen had never cared too much for young girls, and Alex was afraid she would be the next victim to be offered a poisoned apple.

"Your Highness, what are your orders?" the Huntsman pleaded. "If soldiers are coming, we must leave!"

"No," the Evil Queen said. "I'll be finished before they arrive. Now I wish to be alone with the children. Take the others to the dungeon."

The Huntsman was hesitant, but he and the Huntress partially untied Red and Goldilocks and shoved them toward the door.

"Watch it, gramps," Goldilocks said.

"Do we get our own cells?" Red mumbled. "You can't put me in a cell with *her*! You might as well give me to the wolves!"

The doors slammed behind them. The twins were left alone in the great hall with the Evil Queen.

"Alex," Conner whispered to his sister, "I don't want to sound cheesy, but no matter what happens, I just wanted to say that I love you. You're the best sister I could ever have, and these last several days have been the most extraordinary in my entire life."

"Don't do that, Conner," Alex said, holding back tears with all her strength. "You're saying good-bye! Don't say good-bye! We're going to be okay.... Soldiers are on their way. They'll save us...." She didn't know which one of them she was convincing. "They'll save us."

"Unfortunately, no one can save you now," the Evil Queen said.

"So, are you going to kill us, then?" Alex asked.

The Evil Queen was silent. She didn't move a single muscle.

"Why are you doing this to us?" Conner asked. "Why are you so *evil*?"

"Ah," the Evil Queen said. "The age-old question: What makes one become who they are? Let me ask you this, children: What makes you *not* evil?"

The twins didn't understand the question. They were sure she was playing a mental game with them, but they answered with pride and honesty.

"We were raised right," Alex said. "We had two wonderful parents who taught us how to be good people, and we believe good things happen to those who are good at heart."

"So, you were environmentally influenced into being good people? That's precious," the Evil Queen said. "You said you *had* two parents? What happened to them?"

It made the twins sick to hear her ask about something so dear to them.

"Our dad died," Conner said. "Not that it's any of your business!"

"Was he a *good* person? Was he *good* at heart?" the Evil Queen said.

"He was the *best*," Conner said.

"I see," she said. "Then he was wrong, wasn't he? Surely, a good person would never have had such a tragedy happen to him? He must have taught you a lie."

"What are you getting at, lady?" Conner asked.

"I had parents once, too. They taught me a similar lie," she said.

The twins glanced at each other after hearing this, and the queen saw the surprise in their eyes.

"Shocking, isn't it? To know that someone like me had parents, had a life, and had *loved* once . . ." the Evil Queen said, becoming lost in thought.

"So if you had decent parents, who screwed you up?" Conner asked. "Or were you just born miserable?"

The Evil Queen's eyes fell to the floor. "Much like you two, I was environmentally influenced into being who I am today."

She turned her back to the twins and faced her mirrors again.

"I'm going to tell you a story, children, a story that has rarely been told," the Evil Queen said.

"I doubt there's a story we don't know," Alex said.

"You don't know this story," she said. "It's mine."

Alex and Conner looked to each other nervously. Did they want to hear this story?

"Once upon a time, there was an enchantress," the Evil Queen began. "She was unlike all the fairies and witches that had ever lived before her; she lived without consequence and lived on desire and desire alone. She gave herself anything and everything she wanted, never caring how or who she hurt by doing so.

"Many years before I was born, the Enchantress decided she wanted the *world*, and sought it one kingdom at a time. There weren't as many kingdoms to conquer back then, especially after she put Sleeping Beauty's kingdom under the sleeping curse.

"Very late one winter's night, two villagers heard banging on their door and found a young maiden shivering on their doorstep. She was with child and was exhausted from running; she had just escaped from someone or something, but the villagers couldn't ask questions, because she began delivering the child right then and there. The maiden died giving birth to the child that night. Despite the mystery surrounding the maiden, the villagers adopted this child. It was a baby girl, who they named Evly."

"Evly?" Alex asked, and her eyes grew wide. The Evil Queen ignored her and continued the story.

"Evly grew up to be a very beautiful young woman. She was a kind and good-spirited girl, and everyone in her village loved her, especially one young man her age, a boy named Mira.

"He was a poet and used to recite poems to her all day by the edge of a lake a little way away from their village. Evly tried to impress him with her own poems, although they were never very good. She would say to him every day, "Mira, Mira, by the lake, my heart is yours to take." They used to laugh together and hold each other in their arms until dusk every day. The two fell madly in love and were engaged.

"However, on the eve of Evly's wedding, the Enchantress came for her, claiming that she and her birth mother belonged to her.

"The Enchantress killed Evly's adopted parents and took her into the far northeast to this very castle. Evly became just one of many slaves who belonged to the Enchantress. She had very big plans for the newest addition: Evly was groomed to marry Prince White, the future king of the Northern Kingdom, and the Enchantress would control the kingdom through her. But Evly resisted, of course; her heart already belonged to one man.

"Mira looked for Evly for years and eventually found her. They wrote letters to each other and exchanged them through the bars of Evly's cell. The Enchantress ultimately discovered the letters. But the Enchantress was smart; she knew if she killed Mira, Evly would be inconsolable and worthless to her. So instead, she imprisoned Mira inside a magic mirror for eternity. Evly was heartbroken," the Evil Queen said.

"You're Evly!" Alex said.

"The man in your Magic Mirror, he was your *fiancé*?" Conner asked.

"Yes," the Evil Queen said. "I became Evly, the Evil Queen of the Northern Kingdom. It has a nice ring to it, doesn't it? People tend to be creative when they're condemning others."

"So that's how you became queen," Alex said.

"Not exactly," the Evil Queen said, glaring at her. "From the moment Mira was trapped inside the mirror, I refused to continue with the Enchantress's plan. I still pretended to go along with it, gaining her trust and becoming a protégé of sorts. She kept a room full of potions here in the castle. I spent hours of every day in that room, immersing myself with the substances, learning everything about them.

"I concocted a poison so strong and deadly that all the trees and flowers for miles and miles were killed after three drops hit the ground outside my cell window. I was positive it would bring the Enchantress to her end, and it did. The poison weakened the Enchantress to the state of an ailing human. She ran from the castle and died somewhere in the forest nearby, unable to take care of herself without magic.

"I freed her slaves from her castle, including the man who later became my Huntsman. The one person I wasn't able to free, however, was Mira. He was trapped in the mirror, and there was no way to get him out.

"I traveled all over the kingdoms for years, seeking help

from every witch and fairy, but no one knew how to free the man from the mirror; the curse was too strong. Seeing the man I loved every day through a layer of glass, unable to touch him, or kiss him, or hold him was unbearable. I was more than heartbroken. The pain was so deep I could barely breathe. I was sure my heart would eventually stop beating if I didn't do something for it.

"I found an old witch named Hagatha deep in the Dwarf Forests and begged her to help me. She, like everyone else before her, could do nothing about the mirror, but she treated my heartbreak. She cut my heart out of my chest and turned it into stone," the Evil Queen said.

"Gross," Conner muttered.

She walked over to a stool on the side of her mirrors. On top of the stool was a stone that resembled a human heart. Alex gasped when she realized what it was.

"Only when I touch the stone do I feel any heartbreak, pain, or emotion whatsoever," the Evil Queen said.

She picked up the stone and held it tightly in her hand. The Evil Queen's reflection changed in the Mirror of Truth as she held the stone; they saw Evly's reflection instead, the young and beautiful maiden the Evil Queen had once been.

The Evil Queen set the stone back on the stool and her reflection changed back into the cold and hooded woman she was today.

"Then you really are *heartless*," Alex said.

"Why did you become queen, then?" Conner asked.

"I figured being a queen and having a monarch's power

would give me the authority I needed to find a way to free Mira," the Evil Queen said. "Prince White became king and had recently been married. Soon it was announced that his wife was expecting their first child. I decided to strike before the heir was born.

"I used a love potion on the king, and he became enamored with me. That was easy, but getting rid of his pregnant wife was the difficult part. I poisoned her knitting needles and waited until she pricked herself. One cold night, while making a blanket for her future child, her water broke and she pricked herself with one of the needles from the shock of it. She died, but her handmaidens were still able to save the child, and Snow White was born.

"A few months later, I was married to the king, and he was dead a few months after that. I was able to continue my quest to free Mira. Unfortunately, being inside the mirror for so long began to affect Mira. His mind, his memory, and his appearance all started fading away. He began speaking in verse, like his poems when he was younger. He could see things happening in the world that were miles and miles away but couldn't remember his own name. He was no longer a man; he was a reflection. Had my heart not been turned to stone already, watching the man I loved with all my heart slowly forget who I was would have killed me for sure.

"I was getting older, and Mira barely recognized me anymore. I ordered every beautician in the kingdom to my palace and underwent every beauty regimen possible for years and years to preserve the little youth I had left. Word of my new activities got out, and the kingdom criticized me, saying I was vain and obsessed with beauty.

"As I got older, so did Snow White. She became more and more beautiful every day. She longed to find some motherly companionship in me, but I had none to give. She used to sneak into my chambers and watch me undergo preservation treatments for hours.

"One day, Snow White snuck into my chambers while I was away and discovered Mira in the mirror. She looked very similar to myself when I was her age, and Mira believed she was me. For months and months, Snow White was all he could talk about. 'My queen is fair to see, but Snow White is far fairer than thee,' he would say. He had a new face and name to give all the love he felt for me.

"I wanted her dead. I ordered my Huntsman to take her into the woods and kill her. She escaped, but I tried again and again to kill her myself. I was convinced Mira would come back to me once she was dead, but it was too late; Mira was gone. He faded into what he has become today.

"My entire life has been spent trying to recover something that was taken from me so many years ago. However, I'll never be martyred for that life. I'll be forever known as the vain queen who tried to kill the poor, innocent, and helpless Princess Snow White and nothing more," the Evil Queen said. "But who wouldn't have gone to the ends of the earth to be reunited with the person they loved more than life itself? Who wouldn't have ripped their own heart out to stop that kind of pain?"

Alex couldn't stop the tears rolling down her face. There were so many times after the loss of her dad when she'd wished all the pain would go away; she may have turned her own heart into stone if she'd had the option. She couldn't help but see herself in the Evil Queen, and it was unsettling.

"I've done many terrible things in my time, but many terrible things have been done to me over time as well," the Evil Queen said. "So, as far as I'm concerned, the world and I are even."

"But it wasn't you!" Alex said. "You weren't thinking clearly! If you had your heart, you wouldn't have done all those horrible things to all those people. You're still Evly!"

"Think about how differently people would feel about you if they knew this!" Conner said.

"The world will always choose convenience over reality," the Evil Queen said. "It's easier to hate, blame, and fear than it is to understand. No one wants the truth; they want entertainment."

The Evil Queen turned back to the twins and saw the tears running down Alex's face. She walked over to Alex and let one of the tears roll onto her finger. The Evil Queen stared down at the tear, just as she had done to the vial of fairy tears.

"A sentimental story always gets the same reaction out of girls like you," the Evil Queen said.

She flicked Alex's tear onto the table with the Wishing Spell items. Suddenly, all the items began to glow, and a golden light began swirling above them. The Evil Queen had activated the Wishing Spell.

CHAPTER TWENTY-ONE

THE MIRROR

W hat?" Alex said. Her head was throbbing from being so confused. "This doesn't make any sense! It needed a *fairy's* tear!"

"We can't let this happen!" Conner screamed. "We have to stop her! She can't use the Wishing Spell!"

The twins struggled and fought against the ropes, but there was nothing they could do; it was too late. The light rose off the Wishing Spell items and began to circle around the Evil Queen.

"No!" Conner screamed.

"Please, don't!" Alex yelled.

The Evil Queen took a deep breath. "Wishing Spell, I wish to free the man in the mirror," she said.

The light shot toward the mirror like lightning. The whole mirror was consumed in the light for a few moments before it faded. The glass melted away like ice on a warm day. The mirror looked like a doorway into a very dark room.

The twins waited with anticipation. The Evil Queen walked over to the mirror, keeping a cautious distance from it, but nothing happened. She got closer to the mirror, so close that the twins wondered if she was going to climb into it.

"Mira?" the Evil Queen asked.

Suddenly, a man fell out of the mirror and onto the floor. His eyes were closed and he was breathing very heavily. He was pale and seemed paralyzed; it was as if he had just awoken from a coma.

The man was the plainest person the twins had ever seen. He had no distinctive characteristics whatsoever. He had spent so much time reflecting others that he had lost himself completely.

"Where am I?" the man said between deep breaths. He had enough energy to keep one eye open at a time, but not both.

The Evil Queen picked up her heart of stone, and the twins could see the change in her face as her body was reunited with its soul. She was a different person.... She *was* a person.

"Mira, it's me, it's Evly. You're free!" the Evil Queen said. Her voice was different while she held the stone. She spoke softly, with love and affection. Tears poured down her face.

The twins could see the reflection of the Evil Queen and the man in the Mirror of Truth. The reflections weren't those of the pale man and hooded woman who were actually in the room with them. They were of two young people: One was the beautiful girl the Evil Queen had once been, and the other a very handsome young man that Mira must have been before being imprisoned in the mirror.

Evly cradled Mira in her arms and slowly rocked him. "You're free, Mira.... You're free," she repeated softly. "I freed you just like I promised. I'm so sorry it took me as long as it did."

The man opened both his eyes and stared up at her. She had only freed the very little of him that was left. The rest had faded away a long time ago.

"Evly," he said, and a slight smile appeared on his face, recognizing the name. The smile lasted only a moment. His eyes fluttered shut, and he stopped breathing.

"Mira?" the Evil Queen asked. *"Mira!"*

Mira didn't move. He was as lifeless as he looked. His reflection disappeared entirely from the golden mirror.

"No," the Evil Queen said. *"No!"* The tears were running down much faster now. *"Come back! Please, come back!"*

Alex and Conner became emotional at the sight of it. The Evil Queen held the body of the man from her mirror in a tight embrace. She sobbed into him, still holding on to the heart of stone. She had worked her entire life for this, but she was too late.

🍎

The wolves were starting to become impatient outside the castle. Many were pacing back and forth across the drawbridge, others were lying across the entrance corridor, and one was sharpening his teeth with Goldilocks's sword. They had been waiting long enough for the Evil Queen, and they growled and grunted with restlessness.

Suddenly, Malumclaw's ears perked up, and he looked to the horizon. The ground was vibrating, as something large was traveling their way.

"What is that?" he asked.

A cavalcade of soldiers stampeded toward the castle at full speed. The soldiers were dressed in silver-and-green armor and came from the Northern Kingdom. They were led by Froggy and Sir Grant sharing a horse. Jack was riding Porridge beside them.

All the wolves jumped up.

"All right, boys! We're done waiting for the queen," Malumclaw said. "We're going inside to get Red Riding Hood and then we're getting out of here!"

All the wolves obediently howled and they ran into the castle. One of them pulled a lever with his mouth, raising the drawbridge.

The soldiers assembled on the edge of the moat.

"The Evil Queen is in there!" Froggy said to Sir Grant. "The wolves are working for her! They took my friends!"

"Evil Queen!" Sir Grant called out with his booming voice. "This is Sir Grant of Her Majesty Queen Snow White's Royal Guard. You have thirty seconds to surrender, or we will open fire on the castle!"

The soldiers aligned a row of cannons. Jack hopped off Porridge and found Goldilocks's sword on the ground. *She was in there.*

"Prepare the cannons!" Sir Grant ordered, and his soldiers positioned the cannons facing the castle. *"Fire!"*

A cannon blasted the raised drawbridge into pieces. The entire castle rattled from the hit.

"Prepare to fire again!" Sir Grant ordered.

"Hold your fire!" Jack yelled. "There are innocent people in that castle! You mustn't fire until we can safely get them out of there. I have reason to believe Queen Red Riding Hood may be inside!"

Grant looked fearful; he couldn't have the death of an innocent queen on his hands.

"You have ten minutes before we open fire," Grant told Jack. "Get in there and save as many people as you can."

Jack nodded without hesitation. If the woman he loved was in harm's way, nothing would stop him from saving her.

"I'll go with you," Froggy said, secretly alarmed at his own bravery, which had suddenly swept over him. "You may need a hand."

He and Froggy hopped onto Porridge. The horse took a few steps back and then charged toward the castle, jumping over the moat and through the large opening where the drawbridge had been a moment before.

The castle's dungeon was small, but it had a row of several small cells. Goldilocks's and Red Riding Hood's ropes and gags had been removed, but they were each put in their own cell (mostly so Goldilocks wouldn't kill Red before the wolves had their chance). The Huntsman and the Huntress watched over them like father and daughter hawks.

"I just don't understand why my army hasn't rescued me yet! Shouldn't that be their top priority?" Red whined. "If I were Cinderella, none of this crap would be happening!"

"I outran your army because, like most things about you and your kingdom, they're *slow*," Goldilocks said. "Besides, they've probably already elected a new queen by now."

"That's not funny!" Red said. "This has been the worst day of my entire life! I didn't even know it was possible to be kidnapped twice in one day!"

The wolves stormed into the dungeon. Red went white with fear.

"Soldiers are invading the castle," Malumclaw said. "We're not waiting for the Evil Queen any longer! We're taking Red Riding Hood *now*!"

"Get the queen," the Huntsman said to his daughter. The Huntress nodded and ran down to the opposite side of the dungeon and up a small stone staircase. She looked back before climbing it, not sure if leaving her father alone was a good idea.

"No!" Red screamed. "You can't let them take me!" She looked all over the dungeon, unsure who she was talking to. She didn't have any friends in here. "I'm ready for this day to be over!"

"Fine, you can take her!" the Huntsman said to the wolves. He unlocked her cell, and Red jumped up and pushed the door open, knocking the Huntsman back into the wolves. She ran as fast as she could down the other side of the dungeon and up the stone staircase the Huntress had climbed.

"After her!" Malumclaw ordered, and he and his pack ran after the young queen. She managed to get a head start as the wolves had trouble fitting into the staircase.

Moments later, Jack and Froggy emerged into the dungeon. Jack was wielding Goldilocks's sword.

"Stand back!" Jack yelled at the Huntsman, who backed into a corner with his hands up.

"Jack!" Goldilocks said, clutching the bars of her cell. "What are you doing here?"

"Porridge found me!" Jack said. "I knew something must be wrong, because you weren't with her. She led me here, and I met up with Snow White's army on the way."

They stared at each other so lovingly that it made Froggy uncomfortable.

"Splendid. I'll find Queen Red Riding Hood and the twins while you reunite," he said, and hopped back in the direction they'd come from.

The Huntsman pulled a crossbow out from under his fur coat.

"Jack! Watch out!" Goldilocks screamed.

The Huntsman began shooting arrows at Jack. He ducked and dived, barely eluding them. Goldilocks had to dodge the arrows, too; they were ricocheting off the stone walls in every direction. The Huntsman moved like a machine, reloading his crossbow instantaneously each time he fired.

Goldilocks picked up an arrow that had landed near her and began picking the lock of her cell with the arrowhead.

Jack was trying to block the arrows with the sword. It was getting harder; the arrows were coming at him much faster. He hit one perfectly, and it flew behind the Huntsman. The Huntsman grunted and froze. His eyes bulged and he fell flat on his face. The arrow had bounced off the wall behind him and was now sticking out of his back. The Huntsman was dead.

"Jack! Behind you!" Goldilocks yelled.

Jack turned around and the Huntress stabbed him in the arm with her dagger. She had seen the whole thing.

"Ahhh!" Jack screamed.

He dropped the sword and fell to the ground. He crawled across the floor and sat himself up against the wall. He was clutching his arm. Blood was everywhere.

The Huntress walked toward him with her dagger raised. She didn't speak, but she had pure rage in her eyes; as far as she was concerned, Jack had just killed her father. She swooped toward him for a fatal strike.

Goldilocks blocked the dagger with her sword. She had picked the lock of her cell and repossessed her sword just in time to save Jack's life.

"I think it's time you and I had a little girl talk," Goldilocks said, and kicked the Huntress in the stomach. The Huntress rolled to the other side of the room and hopped back to her feet.

Goldilocks and the Huntress circled each other for a moment. They stared each other down, waiting for the other to make the first move. Goldilocks swung her sword at the Huntress and the duel began.

The Huntress only had a dagger half the size of Goldilocks's sword, but she used it well; Goldilocks had finally found her match. They moved all around the dungeon, each shielding offensive strikes from the other.

The Huntress cornered Goldilocks. Goldilocks ran up the wall and flipped over the Huntress, cornering *her* now.

"Where did you learn to do that?" Jack asked.

"I'll tell you later!" Goldilocks said.

The Huntress head-butted Goldilocks and ran out of the dungeon.

"Come back here!" Goldilocks called out, and chased after her.

They continued their fight throughout the castle, climbing higher and higher as they went....

Meanwhile, Red Riding Hood was being chased through the castle by the Big Bad Wolf Pack. She was running for her life, and tears were streaming down her face. She had only been this scared once before, an infamous day when she'd visited her grandmother as a child.

Red wasn't crying from fear alone, though; she was also upset that she was getting one of her favorite dresses ruined. Red also wished she had chosen shoes better equipped for running when she'd dressed herself earlier that day.

She reached one of the highest levels of the castle. Areas of the floor had rotted away and she had to be very careful not to fall through any of the large holes that would drop her several stories below. The wolves behind her were not being so cautious; they had a hard time getting traction on the smooth wooden floor and kept slipping into the holes, howling as they fell to their deaths.

Red ran up a wooden staircase. The upper half of the staircase crumbled away in front of her as she passed the landing.

"That's not good," Red said.

She looked back at the steps behind her and saw Malum-claw. She was trapped. The wolf made his way toward her one step at a time, enjoying the aggravation it caused her.

"I've waited for this moment for over a decade," Malum-claw growled.

"Oh my, what big claws you have," Red said, trembling.

"The better to maul you with, my dear," Malumclaw said.

Red had never expected to die like this. She had always imagined it would be back in her castle with dozens of her and Jack's children by her bedside.

"Oh my, what big teeth you have," Red said.

"The better to bite you with, my dear," Malumclaw said. He was just a few feet away. He arched his back, ready to pounce.

Suddenly, a quiet, whistling sound came from outside the castle. A cannonball crashed through the wall and directly into Malumclaw. The stairs collapsed, and the wolf was knocked into the next room. If he had survived it, he wouldn't be in one piece.

"Oh my..." Red said. She grasped on to the banister of the stair landing as if her life depended on it. The steps on either side of her were gone; she was truly stuck now.

The landing started to teeter. The wood below it was slowly starting to crumble.

"Oh my...oh my...oh my!" Red screamed. The banister collapsed, and Red fell. She screamed the entire way down.

Just a few seconds before Red was about to hit the floor, Froggy jumped into the air and caught the young queen. They both landed safely, courtesy of his strong frog legs.

"You saved my life!" Red said with big, thankful eyes.

"I don't believe we've been formally introduced, Your Majesty," Froggy said. "My name is—"

Froggy never got to finish. Red was repeatedly kissing his cheek. He turned dark green—who knew a frog could blush?

The castle began to shake as more cannons were fired.

"They've started the attack!" Froggy said. "We have to find Conner and Alex and get out of here!"

Alex and Conner didn't know what was going on. All they could hear was the clanking of swords and the whimpering of wolves from outside the great hall, and the muffled announcements of the soldiers outside of the castle. They felt the castle shaking and falling apart around them.

Cannonballs began bursting through the walls of the great hall. Big stone chunks of the ceiling began to fall around them. They knew they had to get out of the castle as fast as possible.

"Your Majesty?" Alex asked the Evil Queen. "We have to get out of here! The castle is falling apart!"

The Evil Queen didn't respond. All she could do was cry over the body of her former lover.

"If we don't get out of here soon, we're going to make Humpty Dumpty's accident look like a scrape on the knee!" Conner said.

The Evil Queen wasn't listening to them. She was so grief-stricken that she couldn't hear. She didn't even seem aware of what was happening to the castle.

"*Evly!* Please! You need to untie us!" Alex pleaded. "Just drop the stone and you won't feel all this sadness!"

The doors into the great hall creaked open, and Froggy ran into the hall. Red watched from the doorway, panicked by all the destruction.

"Froggy!" Conner yelled. "Untie us before we're crushed!"

"I'm coming, children!" Froggy said. He hopped across the room and quickly began untying them as fast as he could. It was difficult, though—the knots were tight. He untied Conner first, and then the two worked together to free Alex.

"Please hurry!" Red called out from the doorway. "My castle's being remodeled, and I'd really like to see it before I die!"

Alex was finally freed. Conner and Froggy ran toward the door, but Alex went to the table and started putting all the Wishing Spell items back into her bag.

"What are you doing?" Conner yelled. "What part of *imploding castle* don't you understand?"

"I'm not leaving without these!" Alex said. "We made promises to return and to destroy them, remember?"

The Wishing Spell was starting to wear off on the Magic Mirror; the glass was starting to *grow back*. A cannonball hit the wall closest to the mirrors. The golden mirror was knocked over by the blast and shattered across the ground. The Magic Mirror started rocking, about to fall at any moment.

"Evly!" Alex yelled. "Please, come with us!" But she was ignored.

The Magic Mirror fell on top of the Evil Queen and Mira and scattered into thousands of pieces on the ground. But the Evil Queen and Mira were nowhere to be found. The mirror had swallowed them just before it shattered.

Alex ran over and started searching for any trace of the Evil Queen or Mira, but there was nothing to find except bits of broken glass. The only thing Alex managed to find was the Evil Queen's heart of stone.

Alex put the heart of stone in her bag. She turned to run toward the door with her brother and Froggy, but something else caught her eye on the floor: It was her reflection in a piece of the golden mirror. It was so bright and colorful, and she saw herself smiling in it—and there was something behind her, something moving like *wings*.

"Come on, Alex!" Conner yelled. "I don't want to be an only child!"

"Coming!" Alex said. She ignored the glass and joined her brother, Froggy, and Red in the doorway of the crumbling great hall.

They found Jack in the corridor outside the great hall, still holding on to his wounded arm. Porridge was impatiently waiting here, too, not wanting to leave without her mistress.

"Jack!" Red said, and went to embrace him. "You came!"

"I didn't come for you!" Jack said, and refused to let her touch him. "Where's Goldilocks?"

Red put a hand on her chest and was short of breath. Pure heartbreak started to consume her like a delayed poison. He really was in love with Goldilocks.

"Let me get everyone to safety, and then I'll go back for her!" Froggy said.

"I'll go with you—*ahhh*!" Jack had begun to speak but screamed when he tried to move his arm.

"No, you won't," Froggy said.

One by one, Froggy took hold of Alex, Conner, Red, and Jack and leaped with them across the moat. Porridge took some convincing, but Jack coaxed her into hopping over the moat with them. They joined the soldiers, many of whom bowed upon seeing Queen Red Riding Hood.

"Forgive my hair, gentlemen," Red said. "It's been a rough day."

"Where is the Evil Queen?" Sir Grant asked.

"She's gone," Alex said softly.

"Gone?" he asked.

"Yes," Alex said sadly. "Trust me, you won't have to worry about seeing her again."

Sir Grant nodded. A huge weight had been lifted off his shoulders and the shoulders of his kingdom.

"Where was Goldilocks when you last saw her?" Froggy asked Jack.

"She was fighting that woman. I don't know where they went," Jack said.

"There she is!" Conner said, pointing upward.

Everyone raised their heads to look. Near the very top of the castle, Goldilocks and the Huntress were still dueling...*on the roof.*

No one could do or say anything. They all just watched the fight with their mouths and eyes wide open. Neither of the women seemed to have an advantage over the other. It was going to be a fight to the finish. The castle was disintegrating around them, but they kept fighting, each determined to kill the other.

Their fight had turned into a battle. They swung their weapons toward each other more violently than ever.

Part of the roof near where they stood caved in, and Goldilocks lost her balance. She dropped her sword while trying to regain her footing. The Huntress saw this as an opportunity to strike; she raised her dagger high above her head. It was aimed for Goldilocks, and there was nothing she could do to defend herself.

"No!" Jack yelled. He ran over to a cannon and lit it. He wrenched it toward the Huntress's direction, and it fired. A cannonball soared toward the women and blasted away the section of roof the Huntress was standing on. She fell the entire height of the castle and into the moat, silently screaming the entire way. There was no way she could have survived the fall.

Goldilocks found her balance and lovingly looked down at Jack. They shared a moment of blissful eye contact before disaster struck again. Dust rose as the castle began to collapse completely underneath Goldilocks.

"Goldilocks!" Jack yelled.

"I can't watch!" Alex said, and buried her face in Conner's shoulder.

It was hard to see anything through the dust. The sound was thunderous; thousands upon thousands of stones were falling on top of one another. Many rolled over into the moat. The dust eventually cleared out once the stones had settled. The castle was now just a massive pile of stone bricks. Goldilocks was nowhere to be found.

"Goldilocks?" Jack hollered, running along the edge of the moat, trying to find any trace of her.

The odds didn't seem in her favor. Froggy jumped across the moat and disappeared into the debris. Everything was silent. The twins thought Jack was going to have a heart attack while waiting. Every second that they didn't hear or see anything felt like an hour.

Slowly but surely, two figures made their way through the wreckage: It was Froggy, and he was helping Goldilocks through the rubble. She was limping, but she was alive.

The twins cheered, and Jack fell to his knees. They had never seen anyone so thankful in their lives. Froggy leaped over the moat with Goldilocks, and she and Jack collided into each other's arms. They shared a kiss so passionate that a few of the soldiers blushed. It was love personified.

Red Riding Hood could feel her entire body ache with heartbreak while watching the scene. This may have been the only time she hadn't gotten what she'd wanted, and Jack had always been what she'd wanted more than anything.

Porridge happily pranced over to Goldilocks, who petted her horse's mane.

"I'm all right, girl," Goldilocks said. "I'm just banged up a little."

"Goldilocks," Sir Grant called out officially. "You're under arrest."

"Wait a second! Hold on!" Jack said, standing in the way of the approaching guards. He turned and gave Red a scornful look. "Do something!"

At first, Red didn't know what to say. She had never really done anything official and queen-like.

"The Red Riding Hood Kingdom would like to pardon Goldilocks for all the crimes she's committed," Red said. "And it's a very long list."

"That may be," Sir Grant said. "But you can't pardon all the crimes she committed in other kingdoms. She's going to spend the rest of her life in prison. *Seize her!*"

CHAPTER TWENTY-TWO

SNOW WHITE'S SECRET

The entire party traveled back to the Northern Kingdom in silence. The pattering of the horses' hooves on the road was the only sound the group made. The whole world seemed to have sighed with relief now that the Evil Queen was gone.

Goldilocks was given permission to ride Porridge back into the kingdom, but her hands and feet were wrapped in chains. An annoyed expression was frozen on her face. Jack faithfully walked by her side the entire trip with his hand on top of the manacles around hers.

Red Riding Hood watched them from afar, looking away only when someone noticed her staring at the couple. She had never experienced so many emotions at once. She remained silent and still, praying that the hurt would go away.

The twins were especially quiet during the journey. After everything that they'd witnessed, it was hard to find words to express what they were thinking and feeling. Their thoughts were filled with the Evil Queen's story. They were haunted by images of her holding the body of the man whom she had loved her entire life, before being consumed by the mirror. And while they were saddened by her tale, they were even more disappointed that the Wishing Spell was gone.

They feared how long it would take for them to discover another way home. What obstacles and dangers would they have to endure when and if they found an alternative? What would they do in the meantime? Where would they live?

"I'm so sorry, children," Froggy said as they went. "I feel completely responsible. Had I just let you use the Wishing Spell instead of persuading you to come with me, none of this would have happened."

"It isn't your fault, Froggy," Alex said. "The wolves would have gotten to us sooner or later."

"Actually, this whole thing *is* your fault," Conner said. "If you hadn't told us about the Wishing Spell none of this would have happened in the first place. We would have never been chased by wolves, kidnapped by trolls, or targeted by the Evil Queen."

Froggy lowered his head. The guilt was heavy and it weighed him down. Alex looked like she was about to punch Conner in the face.

"But," Conner said with a big cheesy smile, "you did save our lives like three times, so I think that makes up for it."

Froggy chuckled. "You are more than welcome to live with me," he said. "I'll help you find another way home. I promise."

The twins nodded and smiled at him. It was comforting to know they had a place to live, even if it was just a hole in the ground.

They traveled for a day and a half before they finally reached Swan Lake and arrived at Snow White's palace. Red Riding Hood seemed intimidated by a palace so regal and large.

"My castle is going to look just like this when it's finished," she told everyone around her, but no one seemed interested.

The soldiers immediately took hold of Goldilocks and escorted her to the dungeon.

"Wait a minute! You can't just throw her into captivity without a trial!" Jack said.

"For her sake, I hope she never gets a trial!" a soldier said.

"Go home, Jack," Goldilocks said. "With good behavior, they should let me out in a few decades."

Jack followed them anyway, protesting the entire time, but even he knew there was nothing he could do.

"Come with me," Sir Grant said to the twins. "We'll find the queen."

The twins, Red, and Froggy followed the soldier into the palace. They went up the staircase to the third floor and down the hall to the door of what must have been the real entrance into the storage chamber.

Grant knocked on the door. "Your Majesty, it's Sir Grant. Are you in there?" he said.

"Yes, please come in," Snow White said from inside.

They all followed Sir Grant inside. The room looked completely different. All the furniture had been uncovered, and the paintings had been placed on the walls. It looked like an actual room again.

"What are you two doing here?" Snow White asked. She was putting the portrait of the Huntsman back on the wall. For the past couple of days, she had been restoring the room by herself.

"Your Majesty," Sir Grant said, lowering his helmet. "We found your stepmother hiding in a castle in the northeast Sleeping Kingdom."

"And?" Snow White asked, bracing herself for the news.

"She's dead," Grant informed her.

Snow White's face became paler, which the twins hadn't thought was possible. She sat down on the platform in the back of the room. She didn't cry, but anyone could tell it was difficult news to process.

"How did it happen?" Snow White asked.

Grant looked down at the twins. "I wasn't there, but they saw it happen," he said.

"She didn't *die*, per se," Alex said, trying to put it delicately. "The castle was falling apart, and her mirror, well, it—"

"It fell on top of her and swallowed her like a bug! *Boom!* And then she disappeared!" Conner said excitedly. "It was crazy! There was nothing left!"

Alex gave her brother a dirty look. "Well, not necessarily," she said.

Alex reached into her bag and pulled out the heart of stone. Snow White gasped upon seeing it. Alex walked across the room and handed Snow White her stepmother's heart.

"This was left behind," Alex said. "I think you should have it."

Snow White looked down at the stone and tears spilled out of her eyes.

"Sir Grant, I'd like to be alone with the children," Snow White said. "Please arrange rooms for the others if they would like to stay," she said, nodding to Red and Froggy.

"Why, thank you, Your Majesty," Froggy said, and bowed.

"That's very nice, thank you," Red said. "Maybe just until my palace is done being rebuilt. I'm putting in a room just like this one—"

Sir Grant ushered them out of the chamber before Red could finish. The twins were left alone with Snow White.

She was very quiet for the first few moments. All she could do was stare down at the stone.

"I guess you didn't listen to my advice, then," Snow White said.

"We listened," Conner said. "We just ignored it."

"Do you know what this is?" Snow White asked them, holding up the heart of stone.

"Yes," Alex told her. "It's her heart. She told us all about it and about her life before she was, well, the Evil Queen."

"It was one heck of a story, too," Conner said. "Did you know that guy in her Magic Mirror was actually her long-lost boyfriend?"

"Yes, I did," Snow White said. "That's why I helped her escape."

Both of the twins gasped and shook their heads in disbelief. They couldn't have heard her correctly.

"What?" Alex asked. "*You* helped her escape?"

"*No way!*" Conner said.

"Yes," Snow White said. She showed no remorse with her confession. "I sat in her cell for hours and listened to her story. It broke my heart. So, in a final attempt to please her, I arranged for her and her mirror to be taken up the river and into the next kingdom so she could continue her work."

The twins couldn't believe it. They wanted to ask so many questions, but only grunts and light stutters came out of their mouths.

"All these years, I wondered why she didn't love me,

and then I finally understood it—it was because she couldn't," Snow White said. "I thought a heart as broken as hers was punishment enough for her crimes against me. Did she free him, then?"

"She did," Alex said. "But unfortunately it was too late. He died in her arms."

Snow White let out a distressed sigh. "I see," she said.

"But they were together," Conner said, "one last time."

"So what happens now?" Alex asked. "Do we clear her name? Do we tell the world the truth about her?"

"I'm afraid that's easier said than done," Snow White said. "I think the best thing we can do now to honor her memory is to live every day with the compassion and understanding no one ever gave her."

The twins looked to each other and exchanged sad smiles.

"I think what I've learned from all of this is that *villains* are mostly just people villainized by circumstance," Alex said.

Snow White nodded, sincerely looking down at the heart. "I agree," Snow White said. "That's the tragic lesson we can learn from the Evil Queen."

The dungeon was a miserable place, as Goldilocks was learning firsthand. Her cell was small and damp. The smell was horrible and the light was scarce. Occasionally a rat would try to run into her cell, and Goldilocks would look down at it meanly and intimidate it into running the other way.

"Don't even think about it," she said multiple times to the rodents.

It was just past midnight and all was quiet in the dungeon. Goldilocks couldn't sleep in her first night of captivity. She knew this day had been bound to come, but as she sat on the hard floor, she couldn't help but feel cheated that it had come so soon.

Suddenly, a pair of footsteps echoed through the dungeon as someone from the palace above made their way down the spiral staircase and past the rows of cells. A young woman in a long hooded cloak slowly made her way to Goldilocks's cell.

"Gross! Eww! Yuck!" the woman said after each step.

Goldilocks recognized the prissy voice.

"Hello," Red Riding Hood whispered awkwardly.

"What are you doing down here?" Goldilocks asked. "Have you come to personally escort me to my execution?"

"Please keep your voice down," Red said. "The guards don't know I'm in here."

"What do you want?" Goldilocks asked her.

"I've come to let you out," Red said.

"What?" Goldilocks said, completely shocked. "Why?"

"Because I've decided to make things right," Red said very haughtily.

"Go ahead, then, let me out," Goldilocks said, almost

daring her. She didn't get her hopes up. She knew there had to be a catch.

"I will, but first, I wrote you a letter," Red said, and pulled out a piece of parchment from inside of her cloak.

"You want me to read your letter first?" Goldilocks said, not even attempting to disguise the annoyance in her voice.

"Of course not. I know you probably can't read," Red said sincerely.

Goldilocks raised her eyebrows. "You're so lucky these bars are between us right now—"

"That was just a joke; lighten up, Goldie. I've been working on this all night and thought it was best if I came down here and read it to you myself," Red said.

"I'm listening," Goldilocks said, and crossed her arms. Red cleared her throat.

"'Dear Goldilocks,'" Red began reading. "'I'm sorry I ruined your life.' Wow, I feel better already after saying that part! 'Looking back on it, I know sending you that letter when we were kids wasn't the right thing to do. I never meant to force you into being a fugitive. I thought the bears would scratch you up or eat one of your arms at most.'"

"Is this letter supposed to make me want to kill you *less*?" Goldilocks asked.

"Let me finish first," Red said. "'I've loved Jack for just as long as you have, but he has chosen to love a less attractive, less intelligent, and less wealthy girl instead. He loves you, not me, and this is the hardest thing I will ever have to realize. I hope that by freeing you from the dungeon tonight you can forgive me. Love, Your friend, Her Majesty the Great Queen Red Riding Hood.'"

Goldilocks had never been so annoyed in her entire life. "It took you all night to write *that*?" she asked.

"Yes, and I meant every word," Red said. "What do you say? Am I forgiven? Are we even?"

"Open the door first," Goldilocks said. She would have rather spent the rest of her life in the cell than spend another five minutes with Red Riding Hood.

Red fussed with a pair of golden keys and eventually found the right one to unlock the cell door. Goldilocks stepped out of her cell, looked Red directly in the eye, and slapped her hard across the face.

"Ouch!" Red yelled.

"There. *Now* we're even," Goldilocks said.

"I know I deserved that," Red said, holding her hand against the side of her face. "Now put this on before we get caught and both end up behind these bars."

Red threw her cloak over Goldilocks, and the two women hurried out of the dungeon.

They crept through the halls of the palace and made their way past the front lawns. They walked through a forest for a little ways and came to Ugly Duckling Pond. Porridge was waiting for Goldilocks by the edge of the pond. At first, Goldilocks could not see, but behind the horse, impatiently waiting, was Jack.

Goldilocks stopped dead in her tracks. "What are you

doing here?" she asked him, although she already knew the answer.

"I did it, Jack! I told you I could!" Red said with a big smile.

"I'm coming with you," Jack said.

"Jack, we've been through this. You can't come with me. Especially now—I'll be wanted more than ever before once they discover I'm missing," Goldilocks said.

"Every day without you is ruined," Jack said. "I won't spend any more of my life wondering if the woman I love is dead or alive or rotting in some prison. I thought I lost you back at the castle, and I refuse to ever feel that way again. I'm coming with you, even if it means that I have to chase you on foot."

Tears filled the eyes of both women for different reasons. Both of their hearts belonged to the same man. Red would have given everything she owned to have heard him say that to her.

"Are you really willing to spend every minute of every day running from the law for the rest of your life just to be with me?" Goldilocks asked.

"I would give up anything to spend every minute of every day with you," Jack said. He hopped onto Porridge's back and reached his hand down to help her up.

Goldilocks's head was filled with reasons and excuses not to let him do this. She wanted to convince him to stay and live his life, but this time her heart wouldn't let her. She took Jack's hand and jumped onto Porridge with him.

Together they took the reins and charged into the night. By sunrise they would be the most wanted fugitives in the world, but, at last, they were in each other's arms.

"You're welcome! No need to thank me! I'll be fine!" Red called out after them as they disappeared into the forest. *"I'll be fine."*

Red fell to her knees and sobbed. Tears poured down her face, and her makeup ran with them. She had never cried this hard in her entire life.

"That was a very noble thing you did," said a voice behind her.

She turned and saw Froggy leaning down by the pond, collecting flies into a large glass jar.

"How much longer until this feeling goes away?" Red asked.

"I'm afraid traces of that feeling may be with you the rest of your life," Froggy said. "But it'll get better over time."

"I thought helping her escape would help the pain, but it only made it worse," Red said.

Froggy leaned down beside her. "It doesn't matter how greatly you've been hurt or how much you're hurting, it's what you do with the pain that counts," he said. "You could cry for years, and rightfully so, or you could choose to learn and grow from it. Take it from me: I spent years hiding in a hole, afraid to come out because of what people would think of me. But one day I decided to leave, and I ended up saving lives!"

Red dried her tears on his coat. He hadn't offered it, but he didn't mind.

"You're very smart for a frog," Red said with a big smile. "Perhaps now, with all of my dreams crushed, I can devote all that empty head space and energy to my kingdom. I am queen, after all."

"That sounds like a wonderful idea," Froggy said. He offered his arm to her and helped the saddened queen to her feet. They escorted each other back to the palace.

"What is your name, by the way?" Red asked him. "I never learned it."

He hesitated. "Froggy," he said. "Just call me Froggy."

CHAPTER TWENTY-THREE

A ROYAL INVITATION

Alex and Conner were both given their own chambers in the palace. It had been the first time since their stay at the Shoe Inn that they had slept in a bed, and it was the first night since they had arrived in the Land of Stories that they had gotten a full night's rest. They were so exhausted that they slept until mid-afternoon the next day.

It was strange for them to sleep apart from each other. Alex and Conner both woke up every hour or so, each looking for the other, and had to remind themselves where they were and that they were finally safe.

The palace servants had taken their T-shirts and jeans to wash, and the twins were given clothes to wear in the meantime. Alex was given a beautiful scarlet dress with fur around the cuffs and neck. Conner, against his will, wore a buttoned-up shirt with a collar far too ruffled for his taste and a pair of bloomers. For the first time in two weeks, they were dressed like they belonged there.

The entire palace had been buzzing with the news of Goldilocks's escape and Jack's disappearance. The twins couldn't help but smile behind the backs of the frantic soldiers they passed in the halls; they knew that, wherever Jack and Goldilocks were, they were together.

The twins offered to go meet the Fairy Godmother with Froggy, but he wouldn't allow it just yet.

"After the journey you've had, I insist you stay a day or two and catch your breath!" Froggy said.

And so they stayed for the next couple of days. They ate every meal with Queen Snow White and King Chandler in the massive dining hall. Snow White told the twins amazing stories as they ate, about growing up in the palace, living with the dwarfs, and the different reactions she'd encountered when people had thought she had come back from the dead.

Snow White invited the seven dwarfs over for dinner one night. The twins had wondered why one half of the table in the dining hall was significantly lower than the other, until the dwarfs marched in and took their places around it. Alex and Conner laughed and laughed until their stomachs hurt at the stories they told. Conner beat all seven of the dwarfs and Froggy in a game of cards and took all their gold coins.

It was the most fun the twins had had since they'd arrived in the fairy-tale world, but things became awkward once Conner asked King Chandler, "Why were you so interested in a dead girl, anyway?"

The twins spent their days in the enormous palace library. Alex scanned through every book on every shelf, looking for anything that could put them on a path to finding a new way home. It took her three days to go through all the books, but she found nothing. Conner watched her from a sofa every day while enjoying dessert after dessert from the kitchen.

"I think it's time we left this place," Alex told Conner.

"You want to leave?" Conner asked. "Why? This place is great!"

"I don't want to overstay our welcome," Alex said. "We're not going to find a way home sitting around a palace. Froggy said he would help us look; the sooner we start, the sooner we'll be home. Besides, despite what she may do to us, we promised Froggy we would let him take us to the Fairy Godmother. Maybe if she isn't too mad at us for breaking the glass slipper, she could give us a tip on how to get home."

"I guess," Conner said, sorrowfully looking down at the

cake he was enjoying. His eyes suddenly lit up. "You know, there's something we haven't tried."

"What's that?" Alex asked.

He stood up, closed his eyes, and began knocking his heels together.

"There's no place like home. There's no place like home," Conner shouted. He opened one eye and was disappointed to see that he was still in the same place. "Just thought I would try it."

The next day, the twins packed up all their things and dressed in their own clothes. They tossed the saber from the deepest sea into the fireplace of Alex's room, destroying it, just as they promised the Sea Foam Spirit. They had just arranged to leave with Froggy after noon that day, when Sir Grant found them with some news.

"We've received a message for you," Sir Grant said.

Curious, the twins quickly followed him to the dining hall, where Snow White, Red Riding Hood, and Froggy stood around excitedly. The queens were each holding bright envelopes. A messenger from another kingdom blew his horn upon seeing the twins and presented them with an identical envelope.

"Cinderella had her baby!" Snow White told the twins. "It's a girl!"

The twins eagerly opened the envelope. It was white and addressed to "Alex and Conner Wishington." A golden wax seal on the back was in the shape of a glass slipper. The invitation said:

His Highness King Chance Charming and
Her Royal Majesty Queen Cinderella
CORDIALLY INVITE YOU TO AN EXCLUSIVE
CELEBRATION OF THE BIRTH OF THEIR CHILD,
THE UNNAMED PRINCESS,
AT THEIR PALACE TOMORROW AFTERNOON.

"How wonderful!" Alex said. "But why are *we* invited?"

"Beats me," Conner said. "Maybe she needs babysitters."

"I wasn't expecting to be invited, either!" Red said. "Elected queens are usually left out."

"So *you're* usually left out?" Conner asked.

Red turned the same shade as her coat and didn't answer.

"Are we going to go?" Conner asked.

"Do you honestly think I'm going to miss this?" Alex asked. "Besides, we should return the glass slipper and the pieces of the other one to Cinderella. It's the right thing to do."

"What about Froggy?" Conner asked.

Froggy made a gesture like he was calming a fire. "Oh, don't worry about me," Froggy said. "I wasn't personally invited, so I don't want to intrude. I've never cared too much for the Charming Kingdom anyway."

"Nonsense!" Red said. "You'll come as my guest, and I won't hear any more of it."

She held her head high. Froggy knew he wasn't getting out of this one.

"We'll go see the baby princess, and then we'll find the

Fairy Godmother with Froggy afterward," Alex decided. "Hopefully she'll still turn you back into a human."

"You mean, you're going to become human?" Red asked with a hand over her chest.

"Yes," Froggy said. "Long story."

"Why didn't you just say so!" Red said. "You have no idea how this changes how I feel about you! Although, I must say I am very proud of myself for being friendly to a...um, well, whatever it is that you are now."

If Froggy had eyebrows, they would both have been raised.

"Come with me right now!" Red said, and linked his arm in hers. "Let's go plan our outfits for tomorrow!"

She led Froggy out of the room. He looked back at the twins, his eyes saying, *Help!* But they were too busy holding in laughs to rescue him.

By that afternoon, the carriages were loaded and the journey into the Charming Kingdom began. Snow White and King Chandler rode in one carriage, and the twins rode in the other with Froggy and Red. They were surrounded by a fleet of soldiers the entire way.

"Now *this* is the way to travel!" Conner said.

The twins kept pointing out familiar land that they had traveled across during their journey. It inspired them to tell Froggy and Red all about the adventures they had had. The frog man and the queen were all ears. Froggy croaked a couple of times during the twins' animated retellings, especially during the part about the trolls and goblins.

Given their audience, they left out the part about

417

sneaking into Red's castle and being partially responsible for the fire. The twins kept stopping each other to say, "We can never tell Mom about that part," when they got to the more dangerous moments of their trip.

The carriages traveled through the night and arrived at Cinderella's palace the following afternoon. Rose petals filled the air and bells rang from afar as the entire kingdom celebrated the birth of their future ruler.

Froggy started acting very strange as soon as they arrived. He was shaky with nerves; the palace made him anxious for some reason. The group climbed the never-ending steps to the front entrance and was escorted down the red-carpeted hall and into the ballroom.

The ballroom was virtually empty and seemed much bigger when not filled with people dancing. Cinderella was sitting on her throne, cradling her newborn daughter. Sitting around her in a big circle, some in chairs and some on the floor, were Sleeping Beauty, Rapunzel, and members of the Fairy Council. Sleeping Beauty's and Rapunzel's husbands congratulated King Chance in the corner of the room.

"What are you going to name her?" Rapunzel asked. She was beautiful, with hair that matched the lock Alex and Conner had collected for the Wishing Spell. She wore it up in the biggest bun the twins had ever seen, and it still ran down her back and trailed behind her.

"I can't decide," Cinderella said.

"You should name her after her aunt Rapunzel," Rapunzel suggested, and everyone laughed.

"I love you, Rapunzel, but I love my daughter too much to ever do that to her," Cinderella said, and everyone laughed even harder.

"Look who's here!" Cinderella said as soon as she looked up to see the group walking toward them.

Everyone was happy to see Snow White and Chandler, but the room grew very tense when they saw Alex and Conner walking in behind them with a giant frog man. Everyone looked at them uncomfortably, as if they were naked.

"Aren't those the twins who stole the glass slipper?" King Chance said, stepping forward from the clump of kings.

"No! We tried telling you, it wasn't us!" said Alex, panicked, afraid history was about to repeat itself and she and her brother would be chased by guards.

"Everyone relax!" Cinderella laughed. "No one stole anything! I invited them here. My Fairy Godmother wanted to have a word with them."

"What does she want with them, dear?" King Chance asked his wife.

"I'm not sure," Cinderella said.

Alex and Conner exchanged looks of dread. This must be even more serious than the broken slipper.

"We may have accidentally broken one of your shoes," Alex said. Conner had never seen her look so ashamed.

"It wasn't really our fault," Conner said. "I mean, it *was*, but it was a really complicated situation and would never have happened unless it absolutely had to—"

"Oh, that's no trouble at all," Cinderella said. "I can't

tell you how many times I've broken them myself. The Fairy Godmother always fixes them when she visits. That's probably all she wants. She'll be here soon."

The twins sighed with such relief that they shrank a few inches. Conner patted his sister on the shoulder, as he knew she had been stressing about it. If there was ever a group of people she wanted to leave a good impression with, it was this one.

Snow White, Red, Alex, and Conner joined the women huddled around the baby. King Chandler dragged Froggy over to where the men were in the corner and introduced them to him. Froggy awkwardly shook their hands; he was the first frog man ever to be inside the palace.

"Look at her!" Snow White said, looking down at the baby princess. "She's beautiful."

"She looks just like you, Cinderella!" Red said. "I was a beautiful baby myself."

The princess was indeed beautiful. She was only a few days old but looked just like her mother, with auburn hair and bright eyes.

"I'm so glad to see you two are all right!" Sleeping Beauty said to the twins. "Did everything work out for you?" She winked at them.

The twins looked down at their feet. "Not so great, unfortunately," Alex said. She reached into her bag and pulled out the spindle. "Thank you for letting us borrow this, though."

"My pleasure," Sleeping Beauty said, and took the spindle from her. "And Conner, I have to thank you for your—what did you call it again? Oh yes, the *rubber band trick*. We've been trying it on a few citizens, and it appears to be helping quite a bit!"

Conner was beaming. "I told you so!" he said, a rare thing for him to say.

"Snow White, I heard they finally found your stepmother," Cinderella said. "Congratulations! That must be such a relief."

The other queens and fairies added their congratulations on the subject. However, Snow White didn't seem happy about it.

"Is everything all right, Snow?" Sleeping Beauty asked.

"Yes, of course," Snow White said. "It's all very bittersweet."

"Bittersweet?" Emerelda asked.

"It's a long story," Snow White said.

"Wonderful! I love stories," Rapunzel said, and made herself more comfortable sitting on the floor.

Snow White looked at the twins. They smiled very supportively at her, encouraging her to tell the others everything they already knew.

Snow White told the queens and fairies all about her stepmother's past. She explained to them about the Enchantress taking her away from her family, how her fiancé was cursed into the mirror, and about the heart of stone. She left out the part about helping her escape, however, because just as the twins had kept details from Red Riding Hood, Snow White knew her audience.

Many of the women looked as if they were on the verge of tears. Some held their hands over their mouths. Others just shook their heads in disbelief.

"I can't believe it!" Rosette said.

"That's the saddest story I've ever heard," said Coral, petting the Walking Fish, who rested peacefully in her lap.

"And even when the whole world hated her, she still never quit trying to free the man she loved," Sleeping Beauty said.

"She never gave up hope," Skylene said.

Cinderella sat straight up in her throne. "*Hope.* That's it," she said, looking down at her daughter. "That's what I'm going to name her. Princess Hope Charming, the future queen."

"It's beautiful!" King Chance said, and kissed his new-born daughter on the forehead.

Everyone *aww*ed and clapped their approval.

"Then I believe it's time we christened Princess Hope with a few gifts," Emerelda said, and gestured to the fairies to get on their feet.

One by one, the fairies each blessed the princess with a christening spell. They gave her gifts of wisdom and health, of compassion and wealth, of pride and discipline, and lastly of beauty, although she already had plenty to spare.

"Would you like to hold her?" Cinderella asked Alex.

"Me?" Alex asked, pointing to herself. "Yes. I would be honored."

Cinderella gently placed her daughter into Alex's arms.

Alex wondered if the baby had any idea where or who it was. Did she know how special she already was just by having been born? Did she know she was a future queen of a kingdom in the Land of Stories? The baby yawned; perhaps she did know and was exhausted just thinking about it.

The doors of the ballroom opened and the twins saw a familiar face coming toward them; it was Sir Lampton, and he had an enormous grin on his face.

"Your Majesty, the Fairy Godmother has arrived," Sir Lampton said.

"Oh, splendid, Lampton," Cinderella said. "Would you let her know where we are?"

"Certainly, Your Highness," Lampton said. "But before she joins you, she would like to have a word with the children. *Alone.*"

All the heads in the room turned to Alex and Conner, who gulped in unison.

"She's waiting in the clock tower," Lampton said.

The twins slowly walked out of the ballroom with Lampton. He guided them through the palace, staircase after staircase, up to the clock tower.

"It's great to see you two again," Lampton told the twins. "The Fairy Godmother has been looking for you two for quite some time now."

"That can't be good," Conner said. "Are we in trouble?"

Lampton didn't answer. The twins grew very worried by his silence. Alex pulled out the map and the journal from her bag along with a piece of the glass slipper.

"If she's upset about something, we'll just explain

ourselves from the very beginning," Alex said. "We haven't done anything wrong. *Have we?*"

"Of course not," Conner said. "Our intentions were always very good with everything we did. *Right?*"

The twins and Lampton ran out of stairs to climb and found a round door that led inside the clock tower. Lampton knocked lightly on the door.

"Come in," said a voice from inside.

"Here we go," Alex said to Conner. "Fingers crossed."

Lampton led the twins inside. The clock tower was gigantic. The twins felt like they were in the inside of an enormous antique clock as there were giant, turning gears and mechanisms everywhere you looked. They could see the entire kingdom through the clock face.

A short woman was standing with her back to the door, looking out over the kingdom. She wore a long, hooded, light blue overcoat that sparkled like the night sky.

"I'll leave you alone now," Lampton said. He promptly shut the door behind him and left the twins alone with the Fairy Godmother.

The twins cautiously tiptoed closer to the woman.

"Excuse me?" Conner asked. "Miss Fairy Godmother? You wanted to see us?"

The Fairy Godmother turned to face the children. She was a beautiful older woman with kind eyes and a radiant smile. Her hair was a light brown and was worn up in a gorgeous hairdo.

The twins froze.

"Grandma?" Alex gasped.

CHAPTER TWENTY-FOUR

A FAIRY'S TALE

I'm so glad you're all right!" their grandmother said, and rushed over to the twins. She gave them the biggest and longest hug they had ever received from her. "Your mother and I have been so worried!"

The twins didn't hug her back; they couldn't. They could barely breathe. They were surprised they were still standing, because neither of them could feel their legs.

"How are you?" their grandma asked. "Are you hurt? Are you hungry? Do you need anything?"

"Grandma?" Alex asked softly. "Is it really you?"

"It's me, sweetheart," she said. "I'm really here."

"*You're* the Fairy Godmother?" Conner asked.

She smiled at them. "I am," she said, with sadness in her voice. "I'm so sorry, I never meant for you to find out this way—"

Their grandmother stopped speaking. Her gaze had landed on the object Alex was holding.

"Good heavens—what on earth are you doing with your father's old journal?" she asked.

Alex and Conner felt like they had swallowed their own hearts.

"This is *Dad's* journal?" Alex asked with big, bewildered eyes.

"We've been following *Dad's* journal this whole time?" Conner asked.

"I think I'm going to faint," Alex said.

Their grandmother pulled out a long crystal wand from inside her overcoat. She waved it, and a sofa magically appeared in the clock tower. She took the twins by the hands and sat them down on the sofa and let them catch their breath.

It took the twins by surprise. Even though she was the Fairy Godmother, Alex and Conner weren't expecting their *grandmother* to be capable of such magic.

Grandma took the journal from Alex and flipped through the pages, amazed that it had somehow found its way into their possession.

"Where did you get this?" she asked.

"It was given to us by our friend Froggy," Alex said. "We've been following it since we got here."

"We've been hunting down all the items for the Wishing Spell," Conner said.

"The Wishing Spell?" their grandma asked anxiously. "No wonder it was impossible to find you!"

"You and Dad are actually from here, then?" Alex asked. "I wasn't making it all up in my head?"

"And Dad wrote that journal?" Conner asked, his mind still stuck on the subject.

"Yes, yes, yes," their grandmother said. "It's all true. I gave this journal to him when he was a boy. I'm glad it was useful."

The twins had gotten used to their heads spinning with questions, but now they were spinning out of control. They didn't know which questions to ask first.

"So Dad wanted the Wishing Spell so he could travel into our world?" Conner asked.

"He wrote that he fell in love with a woman in our world," Alex said. *"Was it... Could it be...?"*

"Your mother, yes," their grandma said.

Alex and Conner exchanged a look, each seeing how the other was processing the information. Neither looked less shocked than the other.

"How long have you been a Fairy Godmother?" Alex asked.

"Why didn't anyone ever tell us any of this?" Conner asked.

"I know you probably have a hundred questions," their grandma said. "But before you worry yourselves too much, let me explain."

"Please," Conner said.

Their grandma took a deep breath. She didn't know where or how to start.

"We always planned on telling you when you were older," she said. "Your father was counting down the days until he could bring you here and show you around. Unfortunately, he never got a chance to. After he passed away, you two were going through so much already, your mother and I didn't want to overwhelm you, so we decided to hold off."

"So Mom knows about this place?" Alex asked.

"She's never been here, but she knows enough," their grandma said. "Your father and I, on the other hand, were both born and raised in this world. Before your father was born, and when I was just a young fairy in training, I accidentally discovered your world."

"So, your cabin in the woods? Your blue car? It was all just for show?" Conner asked.

"Certainly not," Grandma said. "I stay at that cabin during my travels, and I love that blue car. I wish people in this world knew about automobiles."

"So how did you end up in our world to begin with?" Alex asked.

"It happened by total accident," she said. "I had recently just finished a tour of the kingdoms, traveling to those who needed a helping hand, and I was anxious to help more. I waved my wand around me, I closed my eyes, and thought with all my heart, 'I wish to go someplace where people need me the most,' thinking I would just end up in a small village in the Northern Kingdom. When I opened my eyes, I knew I wasn't in the kingdoms anymore.

"I kept it to myself for years before telling any of the other fairies about it. I met a group of children there who showed me around. I was fascinated by their world, but they were even more fascinated with stories about mine. They didn't know anything about magic or fairies before I came along. Their world was so consumed with war and famine and disease . . . it was all they knew. They would sit for hours and listen to my stories about the world I came from. It seemed to take them away from all their troubles.

"I saw how the stories inspired them, how they gave them hope, how they gave them courage and strength, and how they learned lessons from them. It made children without families learn to love and trust a little more than they had before, and it put the sparkle back in the eyes of the children who were ill and had had their childhoods taken from them. I decided from then on that I would do as much as I could to make our stories, our history, as known as possible.

"To date, I am the only one who has had the gift to move between worlds, and I found it to be a great responsibility. I recruited Mother Goose and a few of the fairies to go with me into your world and spread these stories of ours. We found the children who needed to hear them the most, the ones who were down on their luck and needed a little magic, and the term *fairy tales* was born. Your world was moving so fast and growing so large, we couldn't do it by ourselves anymore, so we asked people like the Brothers Grimm and Hans Christian Andersen and a few others to help us over the years."

"So, there *is* a time difference?" Alex said.

"Your world moves so much faster than ours," Grandma said. "I visited once a week, and every time I returned it seemed as if decades and decades had gone by."

"That's why the stories have been in our world for so long!" Conner said.

"Oh no!" Alex exclaimed. "Mom! Does that mean she's grown into an old woman while we've been here?"

"No," their grandmother said. "You see, children, there *was* a time difference. But then something truly magical happened that changed all of that."

"What?" Conner asked.

"You two were born," Grandma said with a smile.

The twins looked at each other, amazed.

"Why are we so special?" Conner asked.

"Because, sometimes magic has a mind of its own," she said.

Grandma looked down at her hands and at her wedding ring.

"Your grandfather loved your world and traveled with me whenever I went. He was the love of my life, but he unfortunately died shortly before your father was born. I raised your father here on my own, but I continued to visit the other world from time to time, although it was painful, because it reminded me of your grandfather.

"Your father was always an adventurous boy. From an early age, he was constantly running off and exploring different lands throughout the kingdoms. He was always very curious about the other world, and I promised to take him one day when he was an adult. Many years later, he came with us to a children's hospital to read stories to the sick children. Your mother had just started nursing there, and I knew from the minute he laid eyes on her that his heart didn't belong to himself anymore.

"Naturally, I forbid him from staying or ever coming back with the fairies and myself again. It was selfish of me, but I was scared he would get lost in the time difference of the worlds and would live the rest of his life without me; I couldn't lose my son after losing your grandfather. But his love for your mother was too strong, and he found his own way back by using the Wishing Spell. I had no choice but to give him my blessing and let him go. It was the hardest thing I ever had to do as a mother.

"However, as soon as you two were born, the most peculiar thing happened: Your world and this world slowly started to move at similar speeds. It's the greatest magic I have seen in my lifetime.

"Being your father's children means that you have part of this world inside of you; you always have. You two are the first children of both worlds; you're the bridge that connects them."

The twins were so relieved to know that their mother would be the same age when they returned.

"You mean," Alex began to ask, but paused because it almost seemed too good to be true, "that Conner and I are *part fairy*?"

"I suppose so, if you put it that way," she said.

Alex placed both of her hands over her heart and tears came to her eyes. Conner rolled his eyes and sighed.

"That's wonderful!" Alex said.

"Oh, great," Conner said sarcastically. "The guys at school can *never* hear about this."

"How else did you think you set off my old storybook?" Grandma said.

Alex sat straight up in her seat. She remembered the night in bed when she was holding *The Land of Stories* and wishing with all her heart to travel inside it, the first night she discovered it wasn't an average book.

"You mean, *I* did that?" she asked. "I made *The Land of Stories* bring us here?"

"Yes," Grandma said. A proud smile filled her face.

Alex couldn't believe it. *She* was magic. *She'd* made it happen.

"It all makes so much sense now!" Alex said. "In the castle the Evil Queen was hiding in, *my* tear activated the Wishing Spell! And I saw my reflection in one of her magic mirrors! I had wings! I thought I was just seeing things!"

"Evil Queen?" their grandma asked. "It sounds like you two have had even more of an adventure here than I thought!"

"You can say that again," Conner said.

"I look forward to hearing all about it," their grandma said. "Your mother has been worried sick! She's had to give your school every excuse known to man as to why you two have been gone. I think it's time I took you home."

Home. She was going to take them *home.* Never had a word sounded so beautiful.

"Can you do that?" Conner said.

"You'd be amazed at the things your grandma can do," she laughed. But her look faded as she sadly looked down at the journal that had belonged to her late son. "Amazing, isn't it? Even in death, your father managed to show you around this place. It had always been his dream."

Alex and Conner had always thought that their father was amazing, but until now, they never knew just how amazing he actually was.

The twins and their grandmother left the clock tower and caught Sir Lampton leaning on the door, closely listening to their conversation. He escorted them back down the stairs to the ballroom.

"I knew your father," Lampton whispered into the twins' ears. "We grew up together. I knew you must have been his children the very second I saw you. That's why I put the glass slipper in your bag."

The twins couldn't even acknowledge it with a smile. Their minds were already overloaded.

They walked into the ballroom, and everyone stood at the sight of the Fairy Godmother.

"Everyone, please have a seat. I've come to bless the baby princess with a gift, and then I'm going to take my grandchildren home," she said, and put her arms around Alex and Conner.

"Grandchildren?" Cinderella asked. "I had no idea! Why, that practically makes us family!" she said, smiling at the twins.

"Did you hear that, Alex?" Conner said, leaning close to his sister. "Cinderella herself just said we're practically her family!"

"I know," Alex peeped. "And I'm trying not to cry."

The Fairy Godmother took the newborn princess into her arms. The twins were excited to see their grandmother in action.

"She's beautiful, dear," she said to Cinderella. "My gift to the princess will be bravery. She may need it in the years to come."

The Fairy Godmother kissed the newborn's cheek. Her lips left a sparkly mark on the infant's face, and it slowly faded away as the gift was absorbed.

"Before I go, I have one more gift to give," the Fairy Godmother said, and took out her long crystal wand. "Will the gentleman known as Froggy please come to the front of the room?"

Froggy, who had been partially hiding behind the

Charming kings, cautiously met the Fairy Godmother in the middle of the room.

"Thank you so much for looking out for my grandchildren," the twins' grandmother said. "I will never be able to thank you enough, but for now, I'd like to take away the curse put upon you."

Froggy's mouth opened extra wide. He kept looking back and forth between the twins and the Fairy Godmother.

"I . . . I . . . I . . ." he started, but couldn't finish.

The Fairy Godmother waved her wand, and the curse cast upon him blew away like dandelion seeds in the wind. Froggy wasn't froggy anymore, he was a *man*. He was a very attractive man, too, with dark hair and eyes that illuminated the entire room. It was shocking for the twins to see him as anything else.

"*Charlie?*" King Chance said. "Is that *you*?"

The Charming brothers all leaned closer to him. They stared at him as if they were looking at a ghost.

"Hello, brother," Froggy said. "It's been a long time."

The Charmings' amazement eventually wore off and turned into celebration. They ran over to their long-lost brother and vigorously embraced him. The room erupted with joy at the long-overdue reunion. Red Riding Hood was quietly blushing to herself. She was looking at Prince Charlie in a completely new way; he wasn't the friendly frog man who'd saved her in the collapsing castle anymore: He was husband material.

"We thought you were dead!" Chandler said, rubbing his brother's head.

"We searched every kingdom for you!" Chase said, patting him on the back.

"Now you know why you couldn't find me," Charlie said, and shrugged.

"Why didn't you tell us?" Chance asked.

"I was ashamed," Charlie said. "I didn't know any better. I thought I had to hide. Please forgive me."

The twins couldn't believe it. Now they knew why he had been acting so strange when they'd arrived.

"So you're a prince?" Alex asked with a gigantic smile on her face. "You forgot to mention that part."

"My apologies," Charlie said. "I could have sworn I mentioned it over lily pad tea."

They laughed together. Charlie ran over to the twins and hugged them almost as tightly as his brothers had just hugged him.

"Thank you," Charlie said, "for inspiring me to come out of that hole in the ground!"

"Thank *you*," Alex said.

"I'm still calling you Froggy," Conner said.

The Fairy Godmother waved her crystal wand one last time, and a door appeared in the middle of the ballroom. She walked over to the twins and placed a hand on both of their shoulders.

"It's time," she said.

The twins recognized the door immediately; it was the front door of their rental house. They had never been so happy to see it. A light was shining through it; they knew their mother was waiting for them on the other side.

All the kings, queens, and fairies in the room looked at Alex and Conner sweetly. Although most of them had had their predicaments with the twins, they were sad to see them go.

"Say good-bye," Grandma told the twins.

Conner couldn't wait any longer and ran straight to the door.

"Bye!" Conner yelled at everyone in the room without looking at them. He ran through the door and disappeared, home at last.

Alex looked up at her grandmother. "Will we ever come back?" she asked, hoping with all her heart for the answer she wanted to hear.

"Someday," her grandma said.

Alex took a step toward the men and women she had grown up reading about her entire life. She could have sworn she had had a dream just like this once. She had been meaning to say something and decided this might be her last chance to say it.

"I know this may not make any sense, but thank you for always being there for me," Alex said. "You're the best friends I've ever had."

They didn't quite understand what she meant, but they were all very touched by her words.

"Come along, dear," her grandma said, and escorted her to the door.

Alex wiped away the tears that had been brought on by saying farewell. She couldn't help but smile as she walked through the door with her grandmother, though, because she knew in her heart it wasn't really *good-bye*.

ACKNOWLEDGMENTS

I'd like to thank my family, Rob Weisbach,
Alvina Ling, Brandon Dorman, the Little, Brown team,
Glenn Rigberg, Meredith Fine, Alla Plotkin, Erica Tarin,
Ashley Fink, Pam Jackson, Jamie Greenberg, the cast
and crew of *Glee*, and last but certainly not least,
Hans Christian Andersen and the Brothers Grimm.